For good

PRAISE FOR
THE HANGING JUDGE

"The protagonist of this novel is a judge, and, improbably enough, so is the author. The result is a marvelous entertainment, a page-turning mystery full of romance and humor, which takes us inside the fraught and rather secretive world of a judge's chambers. In the best way— that is, indirectly—Ponsor informs us about the facts that ought to inform debate on the death penalty. What impressed me most of all was the book's authority; it has the heft of authenticity." —Tracy Kidder, Pulitzer Prize–winning author of *Mountains Beyond Mountains* and *Strength in What Remains*

"That rare gem: a crackling court procedural with authentic characters and beautiful prose." —Anita Schreve, author of *The Pilot's Wife* and *The Weight of Water*

"Novels have shown us what it's like to be a juror, an attorney, even the defendant, but this is the first I've read that puts us up on the bench— a knowing, nuanced portrait of a judge and the often imperfect system he watches over." —Joseph Kanon, author of *The Good German* and *Istanbul Passage*

"A masterful work that took me inside the courtroom, behind the bench, and into the hearts and minds of a cast of unforgettable characters. . . . Thrilling, perfectly paced, beautifully written, witty, so very smart and so satisfying." —Elinor Lipman, author of *Then She Found Me* and *The Family Man*

"A compelling tale, with a cast of vividly drawn characters and a plot that twists and turns—it entertains, as a good novel should, but even better, it also informs, as only the best ones do." —Jonathan Harr, author of *A Civil Action*

"A debut that reads like the work of an accomplished master. A suspenseful page-turner written from the unique perspective not of a lawyer or defendant, but of the judge. I've never before read a book—either fiction or non-fiction—that conveys the dilemma of the death penalty with such a combination of sophistication and humanity." — Joe McGinniss, author of *Fatal Vision* and *The Selling of the President*

"Written with precision and heartfelt passion for the law, this riveting courtroom thriller brings the legal system to life. Filled with memorable characters, infused with a deep understanding of the death penalty and the complex interchange between crime, the police and the justice system, *The Hanging Judge* is an electric story, well told." —John Katzenbach, author of *Just Cause* and *Hart's War*

"Both an ode to the law in all its glory and a reflection on its sometimes tragic limitations, Michael Ponsor's *The Hanging Judge* will appeal to courtroom insiders as well as readers more generally drawn to a taut story well told. Set in western Massachusetts, at the center of the action is a series of trials, historic, present-day, and of the heart. The verdict: this debut author—a federal judge in his other life—is guilty of a tour de force and, we can only hope, the start of a rich new career." —Madeleine Blais, Pulitzer Prize–winning author of *In These Girls, Hope Is a Muscle* and *Uphill Walkers: Portrait of a Family*

THE
HANGING
JUDGE

THE
HANGING
JUDGE

MICHAEL PONSOR

OPEN ROAD

INTEGRATED MEDIA

NEW YORK

Cover design by Biel Parklee

ISBN 978-1-4804-4194-1

Published in 2013 by Open Road Integrated Media, Inc.
345 Hudson Street
New York, NY 10014
www.openroadmedia.com

In memory of
Dominic Daley and James Halligan,
hanged by mistake at Northampton, Massachusetts,
June 5, 1806

And for Nancy, always.

AUTHOR'S NOTE

Because I am a sitting federal judge who has presided over a death penalty trial and could be called upon to do so again, I feel bound to emphasize two points about this narrative.

First, the case of *United States v. Hudson* is entirely invented. I have tried to convey the tone and detail of a federal capital trial, but Judge David Norcross is not me, and *Hudson* bears no factual resemblance to the death penalty case tried in my court. Indeed, with one exception, none of the characters in the story is intended to resemble any human being, living or dead. The exception is Bill Redpath, the fictional defense counsel, who has been drawn in part from my memory of the late William P. Homans Jr., a courageous and skillful defense lawyer. I was privileged to work with Bill during the first years of my legal career.

Second, no one should presume that the opinions expressed or implied in this novel by various fictional characters regarding the American justice system in general, or the death penalty in particular, are necessarily mine.

Finally, the reader should know that Dominic Daley and James Halligan, to whom this book is dedicated, were flesh-and-blood human beings. A monument to the two men stands on the side of Route 66, about one mile west of the center of Northampton, Massachusetts. The portions of the book recounting their story are, to the best of my ability, historically accurate. The quoted passages in these segments are not my invention but have been taken from official records, letters, and other documents of the time.

Michael A. Ponsor, U.S.D.J.
Springfield, Massachusetts
February 14, 2013

THE
HANGING
JUDGE

PROLOGUE

Edgar "Peach" Delgado was down to his last three and a half minutes, though, of course, he didn't know that. He strode out onto the front porch of his girlfriend's house, grinning and pulling along a cluster of red, white, and blue helium balloons. Peals of female laughter and a small boy wearing striped pajama bottoms followed him out the door.

"With three sugars!" a woman's voice called from inside.

The boy danced around, grabbing at the balloons and smiling up at Delgado worshipfully. Delgado bent to hand the trailing strings back to the child. "Go on and get yourself ready for school. I don't care if it is your birthday. I'll kick your butt."

Delgado trotted down the steps and walked up to the corner of Walnut and High Streets. The Flats area of Holyoke, Massachusetts, was a beat-up part of town, but this autumn morning was so pretty even the dented trashcans and peeling storefronts

looked prime. He swung his legs easily, feeling beneath his green
Celtics jersey the .50 caliber Israeli Desert Eagle snug against his
tailbone. He wouldn't feel dressed without it.

Delgado was headed to the Cumberland Farms, where his
cousin Joselito worked, to pick up some free coffee and saltines
for his pregnant girlfriend, Carmella. It was the Tuesday after the
Columbus Day weekend, and above him the October sky contained not a wisp of cloud.

Standing on the corner, Delgado rubbed his eyes and sniffed
hard to clear his head. He'd been up late with connections down
in Hartford, picking up half a brick to cook up into crack. He
recalled with a twinge in his gut how during the negotiations
some punk had stuck a pistol in his ear. People did useless shit
like that all the time now. His own troops, the Walnut Street
Posse, were under siege, and the safe parts of the Flats were getting tighter every day.

For maybe the twentieth time, Delgado decided he'd quit the
street. This spring, he would be setting a grandson on his mother's
lap. He could lose the Eagle, stop hustling, and start acting like
a proper dad. He glanced down the street at the Walnut Street
Clinic, smiling to himself, remembering how crazy he'd gotten
during Carmella's last appointment there, tracing the shadow of
his boy's unit on the ultrasound and laughing like a fool.

Three houses down, Ginger Daley O'Connor, a pediatric
nurse, maneuvered her minivan into a parking spot, uncharac-
teristically late for her volunteer shift at the clinic. As she exited
the car, she tugged at the ends of her short, dark hair. She'd been
rushed, and it was still damp.

Like Delgado, she was cheered by the sunny October morning,

the best time of year in New England. The sawdust and gasoline smell of the Flats reminded her of the crowded apartment where she and her brothers had grown up. For all its grime and problems these days, she still loved to breathe the air of the old neighborhood.

When Ginger pulled open the slider to grab her yellow fleece, an avalanche of sports equipment, tangled helmets and shoulder pads, began tumbling out. She shoved the mess back in with her foot, slammed the door, and crossed the street, scowling. Twice she'd told the boys to get their hockey junk out of her car. Time for another little talk.

As Ginger approached the clinic's entry, a brown-and-white beagle puppy tied to a parking meter wriggled happily toward her. She could not resist bending to give the precious thing a scratch behind the ears while it sniffed at the toes of her green Nikes. When she straightened up, she caught a glimpse of movement in the corner of her eye: an emerald-colored Celtics jersey in a splash of sunlight up by the Cumberland Farms store and a car slowing down.

Peach Delgado was about to step off the curb, then hesitated when he noticed a gray Nissan Stanza crawling through the intersection. A man who looked vaguely familiar threw him the Posse sign from the rear passenger window and called out.

"Yo, Peach, what's up?"

Delgado did not respond right away. He was on the border of WSP territory, and he knew it was a common trick for gang enforcers to flash a rival's sign. He stroked his mustache with his thumb and forefinger, considering. After a pause, he took another look up at the mild blue sky, decided it was too early for this kind of trouble, and halfheartedly flashed back, the three middle fingers of his left hand slapped downward on his thigh—an inverted W standing for the gang's bywords, Loyalty, Duty, and Honor.

The Nissan's rear window blew out in a clatter of gunfire, a smacking sound like a handful of marbles thrown against a chalkboard. Three bullets pierced Delgado: right thigh, stomach, and chest. There was no time even for fear.

Inside the Cumberland Farms, Joe Cárdenas, startled by the shots, stumbled around the counter into the doorway and saw his cousin Peach face-down in what looked like a spreading puddle of dark oil. One of his legs was twisted against the curb, and his right hand was stretched into the crosswalk as though he were grabbing for something. His body squirmed a little then shuddered into stillness. A hard voice inside the Nissan shouted, "*Siempre La Bandera,* motherfucker!" and the car took off, squealing around the corner.

The sound of the sharp cracks and breaking glass also brought the beagle's owner, a neighborhood sixth grader, running to the clinic's entrance. What she saw on the sidewalk was a middle-aged white lady trying to push herself up off the pavement with one hand, while she held on to her throat with the other. The lady's eyes were wide-open, staring.

The girl dashed out to rescue her puppy, who was tangled around the meter and making deep red, clover-shaped paw prints on the concrete. Then she noticed the blood spurting like water from a hose through the lady's fingers, pouring down the front of her yellow fleece and onto the concrete. The girl began screaming. Panicked spectators were crowding the sidewalk. Someone called 911, but it seemed like it was forever before anyone got there.

PART ONE

1

Fifteen miles south, well beyond the sound of the sirens, the Honorable David S. Norcross, U.S. District Judge for the District of Massachusetts, Western Division, looked down from the bench, preparing for his millennium. Today, according to his law clerk, would be his eighty-fourth sentencing. At an average of twelve years per sentence, which was conservative, this meant that in two years on the bench he would have handed down more than one thousand years in prison. He had assumed that by now this would be getting easier. He'd assumed wrong.

Fate had reserved an especially grim task for the judge this morning. The alleged crack dealer he was sentencing was an obese kid in his mid-twenties with a thin ponytail and a spatter of acne across his forehead. Unlike most defendants, however, this one was quite possibly innocent. Certainly, if the case had been tried to him, and not to a jury, Norcross would have found a reasonable doubt and acquitted the man. But the eight women and four men who made up the jury had believed the government's informant, apparently, and Norcross's hands were tied.

The defendant was hunched over the counsel table, bouncing his shoulders and knees as though he were chilly. Was he okay? He seemed to sense the judge's concern and looked up. Their eyes met for a bottomless instant, and the young man squared himself and nodded. He was not going to fall apart.

Norcross, relieved, returned the nod, but as he drew breath to speak, a gulping sob rose from one of the two women seated at the rear of the courtroom. The judge held off, not wanting to seem indifferent, and curious to know which woman the sound came from. The mother or the girlfriend?

It was the defendant's mother, bent forward with both hands over her face. It was almost always the mother. The girlfriend sat with a baby in her lap, her hard eyes staring into the air in front of her.

Norcross never knew what to make of this. The mother might be refusing to believe that her son had gone back to his old street life. The girlfriend might know, or suspect, that he had and might be royally steamed. But maybe these women just had different ways of confronting despair, an emotion Norcross knew well. He took a sip of water and replaced the paper cup at arm's length where it would not soak the presentence report if he knocked it over.

All the applicable procedures had been respected; the defendant had received, technically speaking, his fair trial. The attorneys had made their pitches, and the defendant had exercised his right of allocution—his entitlement to speak before being sentenced, no matter how hopeless the situation might be. In a few minutes now, the sentencing would be over. This evening, the judge would go home, pour himself a Jack Daniel's, and unburden himself in a long soliloquy to his dog.

Norcross shifted his gaze to the right, still hesitating. Through the tall windows behind the jury box a distant bouquet of red and orange was visible and behind that the gold line of a hill under a bright sky. The foliage was at its peak.

A murmur from somewhere in the courtroom brought him back. Time to put the knife in.

"Pursuant to the Sentencing Reform Act of 1984, and having considered the factors enumerated at 18 U.S. Code Section 3553(a), it is the judgment of this court that the defendant be remanded to the custody of the Bureau of Prisons for a term of life without possibility of parole."

The mother's moan—"Oh God!"—set the defendant's knees jiggling again. He rubbed something out of his eye, but he held on. The baby, squeezed too hard perhaps, began whimpering in his mother's arms. Norcross pushed his papers to one side.

"Defendant will remain in the custody of the United States marshal pending designation of the facility where he will be permanently housed. Will there be anything further?"

Defense counsel and the assistant U.S. attorney stood and spoke simultaneously.

"No, Your Honor."

The defense lawyer's eyes were smoldering with disgust, but he could not fairly blame the judge. The term was mandatory. The AUSA, compelled by the statute and, the judge suspected, by her politically ambitious boss to reject all deals and insist on a sentence she must have known was out of whack, looked away and shuffled her papers glumly. *Crack was bad stuff, sure,* Norcross thought *but, even assuming the defendant is guilty, do we really have to lock him up for the next fifty or sixty years?*

"We'll be in recess."

The courtroom deputy called out, "All rise!" Everyone stood, even the mother and the stone-faced girlfriend. The defendant got to his feet, blinked back at the crying infant, and automatically pressed his wrists behind his back. While the judge walked out of the courtroom, he heard the familiar *scritch* of the cuffs going on.

David Norcross was a tall man, and as he loped down the hallway to his chambers, his head bobbed as though he were ducking under a beam every third step. His law clerk Frank Baldwin trotted two steps behind him like a fat squire pursuing a lanky knight.

"Well, that sure sucked," Frank said amiably.

"Go talk to Congress," Norcross said over his shoulder. "Two priors plus fifty grams of crack equals life. No discretion. I'm not a judge. I'm an adding machine for crying out loud."

Frank drew closer. "Some priors! Senior year in high school he sells two baggies of pot. Then he hits some guy with a stick in a fight over his girlfriend."

"It was enough to tie me down." Norcross quickened his step, eager for the comfort of his large desk and the distraction of the next case.

"Do you really think he set up the deal? I mean ..."

Norcross broke in. "The jury thought so, Frank. The buck stops there." He shoved open the door to his chambers suite.

"How about the brain?"

Norcross frowned back at Frank. Then, without saying anything, he turned toward his inner office and the fresh stack of files waiting for him.

2

While Judge Norcross was putting another life sentence behind him, Holyoke patrolman Alex Torricelli was stuck in traffic, late for roll call, and having the worst day of his life. He strained his thick neck to peer over the backed-up cars. What was the problem? Construction again? Some pileup?

Alex had been a police officer for eight years, happily married for the last five. He was crazy about his wife, Janice, but for reasons that were beyond him now he had celebrated the Columbus Day holiday yesterday with a foolhardy tumble at the Motel 6 in Deerfield, the first and only time he had swerved on his wife, and somehow—he couldn't figure how—Janice immediately knew what was up. In thirty sick-making seconds during this morning's breakfast, she'd managed to tip over the entire, well-rehearsed load of bullshit he tried to dump on her.

Groaning, he tried again to see what was causing the traffic. *Forget this,* Alex thought. *Try a shortcut.*

He lunged into the oncoming lane, made a flagrantly illegal U-turn, and gunned it. A half mile through the broken-down Flats and then a left—a roundabout route, but it might save him two days' suspension without pay.

While he drove, scenes from the morning's horror movie replayed in his mind: his wife's furious face as she pegged a jar of grape jelly at him, the crash of the kitchen clock hitting the floor, the looping image of his pathetic self, dodging shoes and crockery, begging her not to go, admitting in two languages that he was the duke of dipshits. Everything he really cared about down the drain, all because of his own unbelievable stupidity.

Now they were going to tear off a piece of his ass for missing roll call, and he couldn't even tell the shift commander the real reason he was late.

It didn't help that his older brother, Tony, would bust a gut laughing about this. A law-school grad with all the family brains and good looks, Tony enjoyed boasting nonstop about the many women he'd shagged behind Cindy's back and the stupendous ejaculations he enjoyed on his junkets to Vegas. He never got caught, the prick.

The traffic thinned out on the back streets, and as Alex pulled through an intersection, his eyes began automatically skimming boarded-up storefronts, checking out groups of guys in low-slung, oversize pants with pockets that were way too bulgy, their gang colors displayed in red-and-white chokers or yellow-and-black wristbands. Down the block, somebody was leaning over, talking to a couple of white guys in a silver Mercedes with New York tags. Might stop and say howdy if he weren't so rushed.

"Whoa! Who's this bozo?" Alex muttered.

Half a block up, a gray Nissan Stanza popped out the wrong way from a one-way side street. Skinny little Puerto Rican driving. A big bite out of the rear window and dirt all over the plate. Somebody in the back? Who might these pinwheels be?

The traffic on his police radio had been so blah Alex had barely listened, but now he sat up straight: reported drive-by, Walnut and High. Male and female subjects down. Suspected vehicle a dark blue or gray sedan, possibly a Jap import, driver and at least one passenger, one or both armed. Shooter may have an automatic weapon, possible AK-47 or M16.

Alex sped up and leaned forward to get a look through the Nissan's chewed-out back window. Definitely something shadowy shifting around back there.

The Nissan slowed, and the backseat passenger jumped out near the Elm Street projects.

"What the fuck?"

Alex registered time and location. Passenger probably Hispanic. Male. Twenties. Medium height or better. Well built, broad shoulders. Black jeans and black or navy hooded sweatshirt. Hood up.

A crumpled brown Vanagon cut in, blocking Alex's view of the Nissan. The Hispanic guy was double-timing down the alley hugging his arms against his chest like he was carrying something under the sweatshirt. No point trying to chase him. The Nissan was taking off.

"Okay, Paco," Alex said. "Let's see where the party is."

He punched the accelerator, squirted around the Vanagon, and nosed in behind the Nissan.

"Let's get up close and personal." He pressed in behind to a quarter car length. The driver sped up. Alex sped up. The driver glanced into the rearview and turned a corner with a squeal. Alex followed, hit the speed dial on his cell for the station, quickly described the situation. As soon as he mentioned the blown-out rear window, the dispatcher cut in and told him to stay with the car, continue to advise location. Back-up on its way. Almost immediately, in the distance, a siren began to moan, then another farther off. Alex reached into the back, retrieved his .357, and placed it on the passenger seat.

"Here's where I get a bullet through my little tiny brain," he whispered. Would Janice miss him? She could pay off the mortgage with the insurance, maybe hook up with a smarter guy.

Three blocks down, the Nissan jumped the curb, knocked over a garbage can, and skidded sideways to a stop in front of a group of sagging three- and four-story apartment houses. The driver leaped out, slipped on a board, and fell—crying out in pain—then took off in a hopping limp toward a fence that barred the gap between two moth-eaten three-deckers. To the north, the chorus of sirens was getting angrier.

Alex got out of his car, shouting, "Police! Stop!"

The kid glanced over his shoulder, black eyebrows over dark, angry eyes, then turned and kept hobbling away, kicking out with his right foot.

"Hey, shit-for-brains! Police! Stop!"

Alex started running, holding his weapon with both hands, barrel pointed up. After twenty yards, Janice's cannolis were catching up with him, and he was puffing hard. His mind scratched away at the details: Hispanic male, probably a juvie; five six, maybe five five; 130 pounds; no beard or mustache; no visible scars or tattoos; no gang insignia.

Now the kid was trying to vault over the chain-link fence. Didn't make it. Small, but not real graceful. Too freaked out, thank God, to notice a gap in the fence ten feet to his left. Out of his usual turf.

Behind Alex, cruisers were skidding in, sirens groaning down, doors slamming, red flashes reflecting off bits of broken window. Heavy footsteps and shouts. Here comes the cavalry. Kid slipped, staggered back up, and glanced over his shoulder again. Just out of junior high and scared shitless.

Son of a bitch, Alex thought as he closed in, *I might just catch this little fucker.*

"Okay, pal. It's over." Then, alarmed and much louder: "Hold it, right there!"

Twelve feet away, close enough for Alex to notice a few gauzy hairs on the kid's upper lip, the boy reached down and picked up a piece of pipe. He swung his arm back uncertainly.

Behind him, Alex heard an urgent voice shout "Gun!"

Alex twisted around. There had to be at least four cruisers, all lit up, and half a dozen cops legging it toward him.

"No, it's just a pipe—just a kid!"

There was a sound like a snapping board, and he felt a sharp sting as a wild shot nipped off a piece of his left ear.

Alex slapped his hand over the wound, then turned back toward his quarry—half expecting to see him on the ground, shot—just in time to have the flying pipe hit him square in the mouth. Alex felt his front teeth snap, tasted the rusty metal.

His bloody hand fumbled onto a pile of construction blocks for support; he leaned over to shake his head clear and spat. The kid had a hold of the top of the fence and was finally working a leg over, heading for greener pastures but still, maybe, within reach.

A black officer ran up. "Al, you okay? You're a mess."

"Hold this." Alex handed the officer his gun.

Unencumbered, Alex dashed through the gap in the fence, intercepted the boy just as he was dropping to the ground on the other side, grabbed him around the waist, and slung him face-first into a brick wall. Then he flipped the kid around, kneed him in the groin, and punched him high in the gut to take the wind out of him. Grunting, Alex followed with a hard left to the side of the boy's face, then held him up by the collar and reached down for a piece of brick. At this point, a baldheaded Holyoke sergeant grabbed his wrist.

"Now, Allie," he drawled, "remember what you learned at the academy." Sergeant DiMasi tossed the brick over the fence, stepped between Alex and the slumping kid. Two officers ran over and yanked the suspect up, not too gently, jerking his arms around for the cuffs.

"First, read the arrestee his rights." DiMasi looked over at where the kid was being dragged toward the gap in the fence. "Then, and only then, proceed to pound the living crap out of him."

The sergeant pointed at the boy's foot, where a scrap of board was dragging along behind him. "Anyway, looks like our munchkin stepped on a nail." He walked off, adjusting his gun belt and tucking his shirt in, then looked back over his shoulder. "Get yourself looked at."

The black officer trotted up, giving Alex his gun and a sick look. Alex recognized him now, Carl somebody, but the world was turning very strange, waltzing around at the edges. It was dawning on Alex that he hurt in several places, that he was having trouble catching his breath, and that soon he was going to need to sit down.

"Man, Allie," Carl was saying. "You need a dentist or something. You look like Dracula's fat-assed little brother."

Alex bent over with his hands on his knees. Drops of blood and sweat were making stains in the dust. The dots of blood were purple; the sweat spots were chocolate brown. Was he going to throw up?

"When you call my wife, do me a favor, will you?"

"What's that?"

"Tell her I might not live."

3

On the evening of what came to be known locally as "the Walnut Street Massacre," Judge Norcross broke off his late commute home to pull into the parking lot of a rural ATM. His gloom at the life sentence he'd imposed that morning still had not lifted and, adding to his distraction, he could almost hear his poor dog pacing on the kitchen tiles, urging him to hurry home and let her out.

Inside the glass kiosk, Norcross set his car keys on the metal shelf and let his eyes drift up into the deepening late-afternoon sky. Would the Bureau of Prisons find a spot for the defendant in Massachusetts or Connecticut, somewhere his family might at least visit once in a while? Texas or California was more likely.

As the machine snapped up his card and began displaying instructions, Norcross heard his cell phone ringing back in his car. He had a monster securities case set for hearing the next morning, but there was a chance the thing might settle, and his courtroom deputy, Ruby Johnson, had promised to get in touch if there was any news. The call might save him from a late night poring over SEC filings.

Norcross decided to abort the ATM transaction and take the call, but even though he pushed all the correct buttons to get his card back, the machine took its time. The phone was already on its fourth ring.

In mounting frustration, Norcross made his fatal mistake. He abruptly shoved the kiosk's door open, scuffed a clump of dirt and gravel underneath the frame to hold it in place, and took three quick steps to retrieve his cell. Just as he plucked it out of the front console—and caught the click of Ruby hanging up—a heavy log truck rumbled by. The vehicle's vibrations loosened the kiosk's door, and it closed just as Norcross, lunging back, grabbed for the handle. He was locked out.

"Oh, for Pete's sake." He tapped his forehead against the kiosk's cool metal frame. When had he become such a total idiot? There was no rush to get the call. Ruby would certainly call him at home later, or he could have phoned her back. Muttering insults at himself, he tried several other credit cards in the door's security slot but got no buzz. Four feet away on the other side of the glass, his card was now sticking out of the ATM like a mocking tongue. The machine beeped derisively. His car keys still lay on the metal shelf.

"Son of a buck!" He looked around to see if anyone was watching, then kicked the doorframe several times. It didn't budge. A couple of cars flew past, but no one stopped to assist or upbraid him.

An old sugar maple was standing at the margin of the crumbling asphalt, waving its yellow and orange leaves against the sky, and the judge lifted his face up to it for consolation. There was a delicious smell of smoke from someone burning leaves nearby, almost certainly in violation of some local regulation. He sighed and was on the point of calling one of his deputy marshals to come fetch him when a lipstick-red Prius pulled up.

The driver was a woman, quite a good-looking woman. Norcross glanced, trying not to be too obvious, at her slim thighs and nicely rounded hips as she unfolded herself from the car. She had on dark glasses, which gave her the blank look of a Secret Service agent or a hit man. She stopped a few steps in front of him and made a sweeping gesture with her left arm; he was blocking the door. She had her ATM card in her right hand.

"Sorry," Norcross said, stepping to one side. "You won't believe what's happened."

The lady ducked her chin and peeped at him over her glasses. "I bet not."

She was wearing a brown leather jacket and a moss green sweater that neither concealed nor overemphasized her pleasing architecture. The sort of woman who knew she was attractive, knew he was noticing, and knew it was no big deal. Probably not a CIA agent after all. A doctor or therapist of some sort, he guessed, or a teacher.

"It's just"—Norcross pointed at the beeping machine—"I've locked my card inside." He paused and looked at her. "Not my brightest moment."

She took off the shades, which made her face less daunting. Her eyes were intelligent and, perhaps, amused. Her light brown hair was pushed back over her ears. Slipping the glasses into her pocket, she said, "So you want me to rescue you." It wasn't a question.

"I'd really appreciate it."

She tilted her head to one side. "I need to think about this." She pointed at him. "Stay." She inserted her card and opened the door.

This was stupid but interesting. Should he shove his way in? He had a good six or eight inches on her. But the doorway was small—he would have had to wrestle her aside—and the judge's good manners made any pushy move of this sort out of the question. He'd wait and see what happened. She went in; the door closed.

Inside, the lady noticed his car keys on the metal shelf and held them up.

"Right. Those are also mine." Norcross sniffed and pulled on the end of his nose. "Been a tough day."

The lady extracted his ATM card from the machine and held it up with another inquiring look.

"Exactly," Norcross said.

While she worked her way through the usual procedure to get her cash, the lady kept jingling his keys in her hand and looking over at him through the glass as though he were someone she might know. This made Norcross uncomfortable. His picture was in the paper a lot. Had he sentenced a friend of hers? Some relative? Her?

She put the cash in her purse and then stood, continuing to look at him.

"Some guy in a suit hanging around the cash machine," she said. "I almost didn't stop."

"Sorry."

At this point, she startled him by sucking on her lower lip and turning up the corners of her mouth in a way that made her face look charmingly goofy. The expression passed quickly.

"Okay," she said. "Here's the deal." She held up his keys in one hand and his card in the other. "I ask you three questions. If you answer them correctly, I give you your stuff back."

"Excuse me?"

He'd heard what she said, but the situation was becoming bewilderingly weird. It had been years since a pretty female had joshed him like this. An odd, fizzing sensation rose in his chest.

She dropped her hands and spoke a little louder. "You answer three questions, and you get your stuff. Easy as pie."

"Is this really necessary?" Norcross asked, trying to sound breezy. "It's just that . . ." He hesitated. "My dog's waiting." He tipped his head to the west. "And it's getting late."

The sky had turned peach and turquoise in the late afternoon, and the bluish light inside the ATM was giving the lady a strange glow. A surge of wind had the sugar maple fluttering.

"This won't take long." She drew in a breath to put her first question, but the judge, on an impulse that startled him, held up his hands.

"Wait. I get to ask you a question for each one you ask me."

"You're not in a very good position to bargain."

Norcross folded his arms. "You're going to have to open that door some time, kiddo."

She did the thing with her lower lip again. It was so nutty the judge had to work hard to keep himself from smiling.

"Okay," she said finally. "But I get to go first."

"Fine, fire away. First one who misses picks up the tab."

She put a finger on her cheek. Clear nail polish, with finger-nails well shaped and not too long.

"What is your name?"

Norcross gave her his name and watched as she confirmed it on the card.

"Okay," he said. "My turn."

"Nope. We agreed I get to ask my questions first."

"You mean you get to ask all your questions before I get to ask any of mine? How fair is that?"

"My answers are 'Yes' and 'Quite.' That's two for you. Back to me."

"What?"

"Rhetorical questions don't count. As I say, my turn. What is your mission?"

Norcross broke off his indignation and blew out a relieved breath. His older brother, Raymond, had force-fed him British comedies all during their boyhood, and he could almost recite the end of *Monty Python and the Holy Grail*.

"What is my name and what is my mission. Right. You're not allowed to ask me the square root of anything."

"Come on, um . . ." She consulted the card. "David. What is your mission?"

"Oh," he rummaged through his mental files for something clever and, as usual, found nothing. "Just, I suppose, to get home before my dog explodes."

She dropped her arms in disappointment. "That's it? Your dog? Oh David, David . . ."

"Okay, and to bring truth and justice to the American way." He paused. "And if at all possible to locate the Holy Grail."

"Derivative, but acceptable. I'll hold my last one. You go."

They'd somehow inched closer during the questions, and there was less than the length of a yardstick between them now. Her green eyes were looking straight into his, and her eyebrows were raised, challenging him to make her laugh. Since he could think of nothing funny, Norcross decided to be crafty.

"What question would you most enjoy having me ask you?"

"Hmm. 'What would you like for breakfast?'"

"Scrambled eggs. Give me the keys."

"Nice try, David! That was my answer, not my question. I still have one more."

" 'What would you like for breakfast?' That's what you'd most enjoy having me ask you?"

"Sorry, you've had your three. Let me think now."

She looked up at the ceiling and weighed the final question, the one that might get him flung, like one of Monty Python's hapless crusaders, into a bottomless crevasse.

"No mathematics now," Norcross said. "Or song swallow questions."

She dropped her eyes and regarded him coolly. "Are you married, or seeing anybody?"

It was not, objectively, a tough question. Still, as the judge struggled to compose an answer with just the right ironical flip, the sound of distant sirens distracted him. He couldn't help wondering, as he always did, what catastrophe was unfolding out there and whether it was going to end up in his courtroom.

4

The next morning, the sun, still in a cloudless sky, dropped a slanting column of apricot light on Frank Baldwin, who was staring at his computer screen.

"Sheeesus!" he groaned. "No one should have to die wearing pea-green tennies!"

Gritty urban tragedies like yesterday's drive-by in the Holyoke Flats still fascinated Frank. He'd spent seven years as a city-desk reporter for *The Hartford Courant* before escaping to law school, badly frayed and in need of a change. Now he was in his second year as one of two full-time law clerks for Judge David S. Norcross.

Frank accepted that he was not conventionally handsome; he had a beer gut and a bad habit of sucking on the end of his scruffy blond mustache. Yet somehow he'd hit the lottery of life; he was a happy man. Pictures of his wife, Trish, and their bug-eyed four-year-old son, Brady, cluttered Frank's desk. Scrawled

crayon drawings of fish, or perhaps horses, decorated his walls
and bookshelves, giving his office the look of a kindergarten art
room.

"What's so awful?"

Frank swiveled to see Eva Meyers, whose office was next door,
poking her head into his doorway. Barely five feet tall, she had
a well-balanced gymnast's posture and a thick topping of curly
brown hair. Her horn-rimmed glasses seemed too large for her
face. This was her first day as Frank's brand-new co-clerk, replac-
ing a man who'd decamped for a corporate law firm in Worcester.
In her right hand, Eva was holding something heavy, like a paper-
weight.

"Another gang banger kisses the pavement in Holyoke. But
this time, they nailed a bystander, too. Take a look."

He tapped the mouse, and a close-up of the hatch of an ambulance appeared with a body being loaded in. Two limp feet with
green Nikes protruded from the end of a sheet.

"Ginger Daley O'Connor, a pediatric nurse volunteering at
the Walnut Street Clinic," he read. "Granddaughter of Martin
Daley, former mayor of Holyoke. Forty-two, three kids. Youngest
eleven. Oh *man*!"

"It was on the news. Terrible." Eva flexed her arm with the
heavy object. "Can I . . . ?"

"Says here she was bending over to pet a puppy when she got
smacked. That's a nifty little journalistic detail." Frank shook
his head and added, more quietly, "At least they didn't shoot
the damn dog. We'd have riots." He closed the screen. "Sorry.
What's up?"

Frank noticed his co-clerk's eyes moving around his office.
Her mouth was open, and she was beginning to smile.

"You have a child, I see. A child who draws pictures."

"If you like those, I have a couple scrapbooks here, just his better stuff." He started to pull out a drawer. "We don't save everything."

"That's okay." Eva removed her glasses and rubbed her right eye in rapid circles. After a few seconds, she continued. "Why is the Bar out here so ratty about our judge?" She replaced her glasses and leaned against the doorframe. "My girlfriend says he's not all that popular."

"A lot of people never wanted him." Frank closed the drawer and twiddled the mouse to open a game of solitaire. "Two years ago, when he was appointed, most locals thought David Norcross was some do-good carpetbagger from Boston." He nodded toward the thing in Eva's hand. "What the heck's that?"

"Mini-barbell," she said, curling it against her side. "I messed up my wrist." Eva pointed with her free hand. "Queen on the king. So how'd our guy get picked?"

"Never hurts to have a cabinet member for a brother." Two aces appeared, and Frank began moving cards briskly. "Now we're cooking. Raymond Norcross, the gazillionaire former governor of Wisconsin, and now our secretary of commerce, happens to be the judge's big brother."

He held up four fingers and waggled them. "So. Western Massachusetts had the following choices: take David Norcross, take nobody, wait to see if the administration changes, or wait until Secretary Norcross screws up and gets fired. In the end, they chose the little piggy that went to market." He paused to examine the screen. "But one or two people are still going 'wee-wee-wee' all the way home."

"So it was rigged?"

"No, no. The ABA gave him its highest rating. But stellar qualifications only get you so far in this game." He made a face at his computer, closed the solitaire screen, and looked up at Eva. "Rumor has it Secretary Norcross got worried after his little brother's wife passed. After the funeral, I guess he was billing, like, eighteen hours a day and sleeping on the foldout in his office. So brother Ray . . ."

The intercom beeped, and Frank picked up. After a pause, he said, "Be right there." He set the phone down. "We're wanted."

Frank led Eva through the library and reception area. They found the judge bent over his computer like a heron studying the surface of a pond. He gestured at them to sit down but did not glance up. The oak credenza behind his desk carried a row of African sculptures.

"What's on for this week?" Frank asked. "Something more cheerful I hope."

Frank enjoyed Norcross's habit of tapping out a fresh quotation for his computer's scrolling screen saver to establish a weekly theme for the chambers. Last week's, in Frank's opinion, had been too leaden—the question to God in Psalm 8: "What is man that Thou art mindful of him?"

" 'Oh spirit of love,' " Norcross quoted. " 'how quick and fresh art thou!' " He scratched his cheek, dropped his eyes from the screen, and checked off something on his yellow pad.

"Much better!" Frank said.

Eva, with a quick glance at Frank, began, "Uh, is it out of line to ask . . ."

Norcross held up a hand and smiled. "Nope. Rule Seventeen."

"Rule Seventeen," Frank said. "No cross-examination about the weekly quote."

"Rule Eighteen," Norcross added. "No cross-examination about why we have Rule Seventeen."

The judge tilted back his chair and blew out a breath. "We're a strange little family here, Eva, but you'll get used to us." He rocked forward. "Anyway, listen. I just got a call from Skip Broadwater. It looks like we may have a doozy coming."

The reference to Delmore "Skip" Broadwater, chief judge of the District of Massachusetts, provoked happy memories in Frank. As a reporter he'd done a profile of Broadwater and had been amused to discover that this powerful Boston Brahmin was actually an elf in half glasses—totally bald, and about five foot three. His penchant for salty phrases made him a journalist's joy. When Frank asked him how he liked his job as chief, he replied that he was "busier than a one-legged man in an ass-kicking contest." Frank was crushed when his editor spiked the quote.

He wrote "Broadwater" on his yellow pad with a smiley face next to it and waited while Norcross pulled on the end of his nose and sniffed, a sure sign something big was up.

Norcross pointed at the two clerks. "I need some banzai research on what constitutes conduct in furtherance of a racketeering enterprise. The word from Boston is that our U.S. attorney will be making moves to shift a gang case, this double homicide yesterday, out of state court into federal court here in Springfield using the RICO statute."

Frank broke in. "So he can . . ."

"Right," Norcross said. "So he can seek the death penalty."

"Oh brother." Eva's shoulders drooped, and she looked up at the ceiling.

"Hogan's been aching to zap somebody for ages," Frank said. "He must have had all the papers ready, just waiting for something like this. The shithead. Excuse me."

"I thought death penalty cases hardly ever happened in federal court," Eva said.

"They don't, but Massachusetts has no DP," Frank replied. "No one's gotten the big jab here in more than fifty years. But in federal court it's allowed, and there's a huge push from Washington to bring federal capital cases in states like Massachusetts. Hogan's happy to . . ."

"Be that as it may, Frank," Norcross interrupted. "We might be toys for the politicians, but the fact is our session will probably have the honor of getting the first of these lollipops. We need to be ready." He sniffed again and shook his head. "Death. My favorite thing."

"It might not happen," Eva said. "They only got the kid who drove the car."

"I don't know," Frank said. "The talk shows are already on fire. The dead nurse, O'Connor? She helped start the Walnut Street Clinic, working for free. Her family even donated the damned building. Now she gets whacked on the sidewalk right outside." He shrugged. "I'm, um, I'm betting the driver caves . . ."

As the end of his sentence trailed off, Frank noticed that the judge was staring out the window, his face blank. After a few seconds, Norcross spoke, and his voice was tired. "This I certainly did not expect." He cleared his throat, turned from his view of the sky, and pointed to the clerks. "So. We'll need to get a jump on this. I want a genius-level summary of the law of continuing criminal enterprises by noon tomorrow. And here's a nice bone for you two to chew on: Can the accidental shooting of a bystander constitute conduct in aid of a racketeering enterprise such as a street gang?"

When the two clerks continued to sit looking at him, he waved them off. "That's it. Go. Work hard. Make me look brilliant."

On the way back to their offices, Frank leaned toward Eva and whispered: "Sorry. Forgot to mention Rule Seventeen." His tongue probed for the tip of his mustache. "Still. Spirit of love? You can't help wondering what's up."

5

By the beginning of November, the bright days of early autumn had passed, and a steady rain was falling on the town of Ludlow. Heavy drops spattered the razor wire surrounding the Hampden County Correctional Center, slapped against the windows, and formed inky puddles on the blacktop sidewalks connecting the towers. At approximately six thirty p.m., in a mustard-yellow, windowless conference room, with the defendant's appointed attorney, Holyoke Police Captain Sean Daley, and an assistant district attorney from Hampden County looking on, Ernesto "Pepe" Rivera, the driver of the stolen Nissan, affixed his wobbly, childish signature to two documents.

The four people in the room were a highly unsociable group. Rivera looked at no one and exuded a sullen wariness just short of outright hostility. His lawyer simply pointed to where his client had to sign. In the lockup after his arrest, the boy had barely condescended to speak to him, asking only if his uncle Carlos had shown up, if his mother knew what happened, and how much rec time he'd get at the jail. The lawyer could hardly believe it when his client phoned him out of the blue two weeks later to say he wanted to meet with the prosecutors.

Captain Sean Daley was Ginger Daley O'Connor's uncle; he looked as though he hadn't slept since her shooting. He glared at Rivera with so much malicious contempt that, without saying a word, he spoke louder than anyone in the room.

The assistant district attorney did little more than make sure the papers were in order, since she suspected, correctly, that Rivera's case would soon migrate from state to federal court. Two FBI agents had already stopped by her office, picking up police reports and getting names. Soon Buddy Hogan, the U.S. attorney for Massachusetts, would be selecting the local assistant who would actually present the evidence to the federal grand jury and, when the indictment came down, try the case. Good luck to him or her. Half of western Massachusetts would want to hang the defendant without bothering with a trial; the other half would hit the roof at the idea of a death penalty case. If this was Hogan's idea of fun, the feds were welcome to it.

The first of the two documents Rivera signed was a plea agreement, which in exchange for the defendant's full and complete cooperation gave him a chance, if the judge went along, at a maximum prison term of no more than twenty years. The second was a three-page statement providing the details of the drive-by and naming the man who shot Edgar "Peach" Delgado and Ginger Daley O'Connor. Rivera initialed each page; then he and his attorney signed both documents at the bottom. Rivera's eyes, as he shoved the papers across to the ADA, returned Captain Daley's icy stare. He said nothing as he rose and limped out of the room, manacled and shackled between two correctional officers.

Later that evening, Alex Torricelli was hunched over a keyboard at the Holyoke Police Headquarters typing out two other documents, both applications directed to the Hampden County Superior Court: the first for a search warrant specifying an address on the outskirts of the Flats in Holyoke, and the second for an arrest warrant naming the man who lived there, Clarence "Moon" Hudson. Hudson was a twice-convicted drug dealer, known to have a grudge against Peach Delgado; he was associated with the street gang La Bandera, and he was the man Rivera had named as the shooter.

As soon as the ADA informed headquarters of the positive identification, Alex phoned the clerk magistrate, Delores Andersen, and made sure she was available to come downtown after hours to swear out the affidavit and sign the paperwork. The clerk was known by law enforcement officers throughout the county, not too affectionately, as Deadly Delores due to her tendency to mess up paperwork, lose documents, and generally get sand in her undies. Given the risks, the police were requesting a "no knock" warrant, permitting entry onto the premises without a prior warning.

Off-duty Holyoke officers were already arriving to beef up the arrest team. Since it was a joint investigation under the auspices of the Western Massachusetts Gang Task Force, city police would be joined by an FBI case agent and two special agents from the Bureau of Alcohol, Tobacco, Firearms, and Explosives. Because of his personal interest, Captain Daley would be joining the group only as an observer. The arrest site was already under surveillance, but the target was not yet on the premises. Moon Hudson was known to be living with his wife or girlfriend and their infant child.

The weeks since Rivera's arrest had not been happy ones for Alex Torricelli. After a bridge, two caps, and many hours in the dentist's chair, his mouth was more or less repaired, but it was still puffy and distorted. Even worse, the work on his left ear had not been entirely successful. Despite the surgeon's best efforts, a gnarled fold protruded. Alex's older brother, Tony, had taken to calling him Mr. Spock, and Alex was still startled and depressed by the face he saw in the bathroom mirror each morning. But his insurance had paid out as much as it was going to, and if he had to spend the rest of his life with a puss that looked like a half-deflated soccer ball, so be it. Alex secretly agreed with his brother that it was no great loss.

After almost three weeks, Janice and the baby finally returned from her parents' home in Billerica, but Alex was still exiled to the spare bedroom.

Alex heard heavy footsteps behind him and felt a hand on his shoulder.

"So, Allie, how's the secretarial work going? Mind if I play with your tits?"

"Don't bug me, Jimmy, and I'll get this done faster."

It was Alex's sergeant, a man with chrome-white hair and a perennial toothpick in his mouth, a famous kidder. Alex didn't bother to look at him. He peered down at a photocopy of Rivera's statement, then resumed typing.

"Some of us were looking at your report from the day of the shooting, Al."

"Uh-huh."

"You said the guy you saw leave the gray Nissan by the projects was probably Hispanic. Could he have been a black guy?"

"Could've been." Alex's typing slowed down.

"Could it have been this joker?"

The sergeant placed a three-by-five color photo of a solemn-faced African-American male on the desk next to the typewriter.

Alex did not look at the picture, but he stopped typing, pushed the photo away, and turned around.

"You're the third guy in the last fucking hour who asked me that question, Jimmy. And guess what? The answer is still the same: It could have been. It could have been him, but I didn't get a decent look at his face so I can't say for sure. Okay? I couldn't say for sure a half hour ago, and I couldn't say for sure fifteen minutes ago. And I won't be able to say for sure ten minutes from now, either. So do me a favor and go direct some traffic while I finish this up."

He returned to the keyboard, but, after a pause, the sergeant continued.

"Hey, Allie, how'd you like to lead the Saint Patrick's Day parade in Holyoke this year?"

"I don't think Italians are eligible, Jimmy. Maybe I'll put in for Columbus Day."

The sergeant picked up the photo. Alex heard the heavy footsteps of one, possibly two, more officers coming up behind him, casting shadows over his work.

"Most guys would love to be in your shoes," the sergeant mused. "All you have to do is say, yep, that's the guy. They'd probably make you the grand marshal. I'd think about it, if I were you, Allie. I really would."

6

While Alex Torricelli labored over the warrant applications, Judge Norcross stood in the drizzle in front of a Tudor-style home near the center of Amherst. As he pressed the doorbell, he wondered whether it was such a good thing that he had ever been born.

Two weeks ago, against his better judgment, he'd accepted a dinner invitation from an oddball classmate from high school, Dixwell Pratt, who'd bobbed up in the Amherst College administration. Then, yesterday, Dix had come up to him in the dog-food aisle at the Stop & Shop, grinning and rubbing his hands together. His wife, he said, had filled out the dinner by organizing a "date" for him with a friend from her book group—a toothsome professor named Claire Lindemann, whom Norcross had apparently met during a hilarious tryst while getting cash—ha, ha, ha. Wasn't it wonderful?

No, it was not wonderful. Despite being deeply smitten, Norcross had not managed to contact Professor Lindemann. He'd thought of Our Lady of the ATM many times, had even Googled her and been impressed to learn that she was a tenured full professor of medieval and Renaissance literature with two well-reviewed books and many articles. She was a baseball fan, too. A humorous piece she'd published in *Sports Illustrated* comparing the Kansas City Royals to the Knights of the Round Table got more enthusiastic hits than any of her academic writings.

Of course, he'd been tempted to call her. At the ATM, he might have even told her he would, for lunch some time. But he kept putting it off. Then, a long wire-fraud trial swamped his evenings, and recurring dreams of his beloved wife, Faye, and the endless gray linoleum in the hospital where she'd died left him lost and empty. Soon it was too late. The lady, he decided, probably wouldn't even remember him.

Now, after all these contortions, here he was, standing on Dixwell's porch, feeling as though it were high school again, and he was on a first date with the captain of the cheerleading squad, going to see *Ghostbusters*. It was ridiculous.

Dixwell's welcome as he threw open the door was like a blow between the eyes.

"Here he is! Here's His Royal Highness!" he hooted. "Here's His Excellency!"

This was the usual guff. It still surprised him, with noodles like Dix and sometimes with fairly intelligent people, too, how uncomfortably his job trailed along with him, causing people to wriggle around and make stupid jokes. It was as bad as being a bishop. Fortunately, after a couple of ducks and bobs, if he stayed good humored, things usually settled down.

Another guest, who had already arrived, looked as though he

might be a problem of a different sort. As Dixwell introduced them over the coffee table, the guy gave Norcross a curt nod, like a boxer touching gloves with his opponent in the middle of the ring.

"Professor Gerald Novotny," Dixwell said. "Gerry's at UMass, in their legal studies department. Likes to peep up under judges' robes and suss out their secrets. Better watch out. I think he's brought his kryptonite!" Dixwell beamed at the two men with his hands on their shoulders, like a referee looking forward to a bout that, with any luck, would include a couple of hard shots below the belt.

Novotny, looked to be around forty—roughly Norcross's age—but his ponytail and a copper ear stud gave him a more youthful air.

"Nice to meet you," Novotny said without smiling. "Interested in this supposed death penalty case we keep hearing about."

"Wait until you hear what Professor Lindemann's been working on," Dixwell said. "An article for the MLA journal entitled, I believe, 'Lesbian Subtexts in Zane Grey.'"

"Don't listen to him, David," came the voice of Dixwell's wife, Anne. "That's just another very dog-eared English department joke."

Anne entered the room now with a striking blonde girl, whom Norcross at first took to be the Pratts' daughter. Anne was laughing, but the young woman looked as though she thought a smile might crack her cool. As they sorted through the introductions, it became clear that the girl, an undergraduate named Brittany, was with Professor Novotny.

The doorbell rang, and Norcross's stomach gave a schoolboy lurch when he heard Claire chatting with Anne in the hall. Their happy, confidential voices confirmed that the two were close friends, and it struck him with a wave of anxious pleasure that they must have spent some time plotting this evening.

After a few seconds, Claire stepped into the archway leading from the entry hall into the living room, hands clasped in front of her. Lord, she was pretty.

"I believe you two have already met," Anne said.

"Uh, yes," Norcross faltered. "Professor Lindemann rescued me from my own, uh, frontal lobe implosion."

Claire tilted her head to one side, taking him in.

"Which was not all that easy," he added.

The professor was dressed simply, in a three-quarter length black skirt and green silk tunic. Her hair was brushed back, revealing small gold earrings with green stones. Her face bore the same appraising half-smile he'd seen back at the ATM.

"Well," she said, "you did answer all my questions. Every good knight deserves favor."

Norcross opened his mouth, but no words came out.

At this point, Anne jabbed Dixwell, who quickly asked what everyone wanted to drink, and the evening unfolded with reasonable civility from there on, through the stuffed mushroom caps and the grilled trout. By the time dessert arrived, Norcross found himself in easy conversation with Claire, at work on his third glass of Chardonnay, and dizzy with benevolence toward the entire universe—with the exception of Gerald Novotny, who kept making arch comments about the American legal system, which he called "the noble protector of the overprotected." Once, he referred to the judge's workplace as "the United Snakes District Court," prompting giggles from his blonde companion.

Norcross did his best to ignore him. He knew at least as well as Novotny how imperfect the legal system was, but he did not appreciate being taunted. He'd played defense on his high school ice hockey team in Wisconsin, and Novotny reminded him of the type of cocky forward he enjoyed elbowing into the boards.

As Anne was pouring the coffee, Claire asked Norcross whether he had any interests outside the law.

Norcross leaned toward her and said in a low voice, "Very few people know this, but I do a terrific Donald Duck imitation."

Her eyes ignited with pleasure. "Fabulous! Show me."

He dropped his voice to a whisper. "I can't do it in front of all these people."

"Course you can. Here, I'll hold up my napkin."

It was a large napkin, and it created a cozy screen. With just the two of them behind it, it felt as though they were under the covers. Norcross drew the moment out. It was warm behind the cloth; Claire's unnameable scent enveloped him.

She cocked her head. "So?"

"What would you like for breakfast?" Norcross asked in a bang-on duck voice.

Claire dropped the napkin. "Amazing!"

But at this moment, Dixwell's voice broke in and grabbed Norcross's attention.

"Our good judge," Dixwell said, leaning back in his chair and leaving his spoon sticking up like a mast in his crème brûlée, "is pointedly ignoring your slings and arrows, Gerry. I'm disappointed, I must say." He peeped over at his wife with a prim, V-shaped smile. "I can't imagine what's been distracting His Lordship."

With some effort, Norcross tried to recall Novotny's latest spitball at the courts, something about the mistreatment of people who couldn't afford lawyers. But those warm seconds behind the napkin with Claire had left his mind in a fog. Who really gave a hoot about the American legal system anyway? Unfortunately, he decided to ask a question.

"What are we doing to annoy you now, Gerry?"

"Can I get anybody more coffee?" Anne inquired, looking with open displeasure at her husband.

"Well, for one thing, you judges like to pretend our justice system is about justice." Novotny reached over and dusted a crumb off Brittany's cheek. "There, perfect." He shone a smile on her before returning to the judge. "When its purpose is actually to maintain a protected environment for a privileged elite."

"Gosh, what a devastating critique," Norcross said. "I'm speechless." He pulled on the end of his nose and sniffed, then picked up his glass and began rocking it, examining the wine as it circulated and caught the light. He knew his response had had too much edge. Worse, his irritation at Novotny and his competitive instincts were threatening to obscure his main focus, which was Claire. At the back of his mind, he could hear his older brother Raymond's voice, careful as ever: *Don't take the bait, Davey. Make a joke.*

"Then there's the delightful racism, of course," Novotny said, grinning around the table.

Norcross envisioned the faces of his Kenyan students from the Peace Corps—so hopeful and open, so different from the faces of the crushed, mostly brown men he sentenced four or five times a week.

"May I ask if you have any suggestions for addressing these problems, Gerry, without creating worse ones? It's a shame, but I'm not an academic. I can't just sit in the stands making sarcastic remarks and sipping my cocoa. I have to get out on the ice and chase the puck."

"Ooh, I like this!" Dixwell said eagerly.

"I'm sorry, I'm sorry," Norcross said with a sinking fear that he'd offended Claire. "That was a cheap shot."

"Two hundred," Novotny said. "More than two hundred men on death row exonerated by DNA evidence. I mean, Jesus! And now I'm hearing that our brave U.S. attorney is hot to bring a capital case out here. I bet you'll love that. It's . . . it's . . ."

Brittany broke in. "It's thickening." This comment completely threw Norcross, until he remembered that the young woman had an adorable, and perhaps genuine, lisp. Had she overheard his duck routine and been offended?

Norcross looked up at the ceiling, addressing the chandelier. "Oh Lord, do I really want to get into this?" He took another long swallow of wine and returned to Claire. "Maybe I'll just say what I think for once, and hope to be forgiven. Is that okay?"

"I'm all ears," she said, then added more quietly, "Well, actually, I'm other things, too."

Norcross noticed again how pleasing he found the shape of Claire's slender fingertips, resting on the white tablecloth. What a treat it would be just to touch one of them.

"Right," Novotny said. "You were going to tell us what you think."

Norcross picked up the crystal salt and pepper shakers.

"Okay. Here goes. Meet Mr. Salt and Ms. Pepper." He held them out, one in each hand, and tapped them together.

"Careful," Dixwell said nervously. "Those are Waterford."

"Ms. Pepper says she saw Mr. Salt stab her boyfriend. There was a lot of confusion, but she's positive it was him. Mr. Salt says he was home at the time, and, uh . . ." He nodded at the table. "Sugar Bowl and Creamer say they were with him, watching *Perry Mason* reruns."

"May I be the gravy boat?" Anne asked.

"Perfect. You, Ms. Gravy Boat, say that Mr. Salt boasted to you that he did stab the guy and even showed you the knife before he chucked it into the Connecticut River. But you're facing drug charges, I'm afraid."

"Oh, wicked me!" Anne said, lifting her glass with a pleased smile.

"So you have a big motive to stroke the prosecutor. It's total pandemonium." He waggled the shakers at each other to simulate a dispute. "*Grrrr!* And the community demands a response." Norcross placed the shakers in front of Novotny and pointed at them. "So, Gerry, who's telling the truth? Ms. Pepper or Mr. Salt?"

"Obviously, I have no idea," Novotny said a little truculently.

"Ta-da! Give that man a paper hat. The point is, we don't know which condiment is right. Sometimes people commit murder, and sometimes they get falsely accused of committing murder. And we don't know who's telling the truth." He raised his voice toward its courtroom volume and leaned toward Novotny. "If we did, we wouldn't need law. We'd only need religion or something."

Norcross caught Brittany staring at him as though he were a species of monkey whose gibbering she was trying to memorize. He was overdoing it.

"Sorry." He broke off and continued more softly, "Our legal system, from where I sit, is just a process for deciding who blew the stoplight, or who killed Cock Robin, in a manner that is as fair and honest as we can possibly make it. It's very human, and it's tricky, so we do make mistakes. The really bad errors are actually pretty rare, considering, but it's not surprising they happen."

"Well, it seems I'm not being clear," Novotny said with maddening deliberateness. "For one thing, if we agree it's a flawed system, then we shouldn't be executing folks, right? But it's not flawed. It's deliberately designed to support power, and it is sheer arrogance ..."

"Oh, arrogance—bah!" Norcross said, waving dismissively.

"Bah yourself," Novotny shot back. "Someone needs to stop …"

But at this point, to everyone's astonishment, Anne burst into an energetic rendition of "The Whiffenpoof Song": "We are poor little sheep, who have lost their way!"

Claire loudly joined her in the chorus, "Baa, baa, baa!"

Novotny managed to absorb Anne's interruption with reasonable grace. He patted his hostess lightly in the arm, saying, "Okay, Anne, point taken. Enough of this."

Norcross shook his head and muttered, "Lord, who invited me up onto the soap box?" There were nineteen standard ways to handle this kind of situation, and his brother, Raymond, would have known all of them. He couldn't think of a single one.

"You know," Claire said, standing up, "I've got a pile of papers to grade tomorrow. I really do have to get going." It dawned on the judge that she had made this announcement once or twice already, somewhere in the conversation. They'd lingered over dessert way too long.

Claire put her hand on his shoulder and said, "Even we professors, sitting up in the bleachers, have to get up early sometimes."

While Norcross tried to recover from this zinger, and absorb the vibrating sensation on his shoulder where Claire had touched him, Novotny resumed poking.

"I'm still curious, Your Honor," he said. "In this fallible process of yours, how would you feel about putting your signature on an execution order?"

"For the nth time, Gerry, I have to pass on that one." He felt sick. Faye would have scorched him to cinders for a spotlight-hogging tirade like that. It was downright un-Midwestern. He'd certainly squandered all the capital his Donald Duck imitation had earned him with Claire. The businesslike way she smiled, shook hands, and headed off for her coat made him deeply, and foolishly, sad. It was only a dinner. It shouldn't bother him. They'd talked, and that was that.

In a kind of dream, he waved as the door closed behind her. Some minutes later, he heard her car's engine harrumph to life and, as he dipped his head to gaze out the window, saw its lights shrinking down the driveway into the darkness.

Conversation around the table resumed, mostly unheard by him for some time. He finished his wine. When his consciousness returned to the present, Norcross noticed Novotny's blonde undergraduate staring at him again with the same intense expression.

"I think Gerry is," she began, glancing nervously sideways. "I mean, I think Professor Novotny is right. If it's wrong, thumb . . ." She hesitated and spoke slowly. "Someone should put a stop to it. I mean, you're the judge, aren't you?"

"I don't make the laws, Tiffany."

"It's Brittany, David," Anne broke in, not unkindly, but with emphasis.

"Brittany. Excuse me. I can't always keep bad things from happening, Brittany. Sometimes my job is just to make them happen in an orderly way."

"Orderly? Is that what you call it?" Novotny asked. His eyes narrowed, and he took on the expression of a boxer moving in to land a knockout punch.

But at that moment, the Pratts' doorbell rang.

Anne looked at her husband. "Jehovah's Witnesses, at this hour?"

"Deus ex machina, at any rate," Dixwell said, glaring at the front hall with the hostility of a man who was being cheated out of something tasty.

Anne went to the door and opened it. Claire had come back.

Although the Norcross clan was Lutheran, and the judge still occasionally attended church services, he had never personally experienced a miracle before. Claire had come back, more beautiful than ever. Norcross, who'd felt rooted in place a minute earlier, now seemed to float up from his chair.

"What happened?" he asked.

She gave him a mildly distraught look, then dropped her eyes to the floor.

"Well," she said, speaking like someone who'd decided to face the guillotine as bravely as possible, "it's slippery as hell out there, and I seem to have dinged your car."

"Really!" A flood of joy almost lifted him onto his toes.

Dixwell, speechless, looked appalled.

"Are you all right?" Anne asked.

"I'm fine," Claire said, "physically." She looked up at Norcross again. "I'm so sorry!"

Norcross and Dixwell bundled on their raincoats and hurried out into the night with Claire. The plunge into the raw, wet elements was shocking at first. Rain was clattering on the brittle leaves, and bursts of wind blew sleet into their faces.

Claire took hold of Norcross's elbow as they worked their way down the slick driveway.

"I was backing up," she said. "And the car just started sliding. I feel terrible."

Even in the darkness, one look told them the impact had produced much more than a ding. The whole right front panel of the judge's car was pushed in, and the tire on that corner was flat. Norcross felt like laughing, clapping his hands, and breaking into a song.

"I could give you a ride home," Claire said. "It's the least I can do."

"Oh, there's no need," Dixwell broke in. "I can take him."

"You cannot!" Anne's voice shot through the wind, clear and

penetrating even at a distance. She was standing on the front porch with her hands on her hips, sheltered from the rain.

"What about the car?" Dixwell said. "We can't . . ."

"We'll deal with it in the morning," Anne responded, even louder.

"But he's way out of Claire's way," Dixwell called back.

"Dixwell, don't make me wake the neighbors," Anne shouted, louder still. Dixwell tucked his chin in, looking alarmed.

"That would be terrific," Norcross said to Claire. "I mean, I'd very much appreciate that."

Dixwell hurriedly said his good-byes and walked up the driveway, bent against the slippery incline. David and Claire waved to Anne, and to Gerry and Brittany, who had joined her in the doorway. Anne swung her arms in an exaggerated fashion, like someone guiding an airplane into a gate.

"Well, finally," Claire said, her eyes shining in the darkness. "Let's go."

7

Sandra Hudson, the wife of Clarence "Moon" Hudson, woke with a leaping heart and a prickle of fear running up the back of her neck. The rain rattled steadily on the roof, and the sleet clicked against the windows. Someone, she was sure, was trying to get into their apartment. She could almost feel the weight of feet on the sagging front porch, hear the soft creak and strain of the door being tested. Was that a muffled voice? A thump?

She reached over and prodded Moon, sleeping deeply, as he always did, on the far edge of their bed. He didn't stir.

Moon's broad back exuded that heavenly, warm yeasty smell that, even in her jangled state, brought Sandra a wave of comfort. They had known each other two years now and had been married just under a year. Their baby, Grace (her grandmother's name), would be six months old next week. Like her daddy, she was a good sleeper.

It was probably nothing, and Sandra knew Moon would tease her again about her suburban nerves, but she needed to see his slow smile and hear his reassuring voice. She'd loved the way he talked right from their first meeting.

Sandra met Moon at the University of Massachusetts while she was working on her master's in library science. She'd seen him in the student union and, like everyone, was intimidated by him at first. His chiseled features were usually expressionless and made him seem reserved and aloof. He was nearly six feet, broad-shouldered, and very dark. A long, pinkish-gray scar drew a ragged furrow on his forearm. People gave him space.

Sandra asked around and learned that Moon was attending UMass part-time through the University Without Walls program. He lived in Holyoke, and the word was he'd spent time on the streets, running with the gangs. Two or three times, in the cafeteria line or buying coffee in the morning, he caught her checking him out. She turned away and brushed her hair back in her most beguiling manner, but his face remained unreadable.

Then one day as she was grabbing a sandwich before class, he slid into the booth across from her and started talking in his deep voice, asking her what she was studying. The delighted smile he gave her when he learned that there was such a thing as library science, and that she was actually taking classes in it, instantly captured Sandra's heart. Moon's tickled expression transformed his face from something brooding and almost scary into the most beautiful thing she had ever seen.

"Library science? They teach that?" He looked at her. Then he tilted his head back and laughed in disbelief. "What do they do—give you lessons on how to shush people?"

Sandra started to reply indignantly, but he just shook his head, continuing to grin. "No disrespect," he said. "I'm learning something new all the time these days."

They never made it to class. Instead, they spent the rest of the afternoon walking from one end of the campus to the other, talking and talking. That day and in the days that followed, Sandra learned the story of Moon's life, which seemed to her to be a kind of social worker's nightmare: a fatherless childhood in the Flats with a mother on and off crack, out of school by fifteen, on his own by sixteen, with more fights and near misses than he could remember. One half-brother was in the grave, killed while in prison in revenge for a busted drug deal, and another was at Cedar Junction doing a twelve-year bid for armed robbery.

There had been a gang phase, too, with La Bandera, dealing heroin, crack, powdered cocaine, and methamphetamine on the street corners and in the dark alleys of Holyoke and Springfield. At one point, he was the chapter's warlord and conducted negotiations with the Latin Kings to form an alliance against another gang, the Walnut Street Posse, that was trying to push into their territory. People on both sides ended up dead; it was not a time he liked to remember. Then, after his second drug conviction, two years followed in the correctional center, where he got his high-school equivalency diploma and finally had time to think about his life.

When he got out, two miracles happened. First, his mother, who had been playing the same two-dollar number each week for years, finally hit. Her win paid more than $15,000, and she gave $7,500 to her recently released son, partly because she'd been playing his birth date and it was only fair, but mostly because she owed it to him after all the shit she'd put him through.

Moon used the cash to get out of the Flats and move into the bottom half of a two-family in a safer neighborhood. For the first time in his life, he had first and last month's rent and a security deposit, with enough money left over to pick up some used furniture and an old Hyundai that was a little squashed but ran okay.

The second miracle was a stubby Pole named Kostecki, who ran a food warehouse in Hatfield and who, even knowing his record, gave Moon a job loading trailers at night. Soon he was driving a forklift from ten p.m. to six a.m., six nights a week. After a couple months, when the crew chief turned up drunk one too many times, Kostecki promoted Moon, who was always on time, never complained, and had an upper body "like George fucking Foreman." Now he was making $16.50 an hour with time and a half for Saturdays, and bringing home more than $500 a week after taxes. He had a credit card and a bank account with free checking, and he paid his bills on time.

"I couldn't believe it," he laughed. "I'm like Columbus, you know? It's 1492, and I just discovered America."

Sandra's protected, upper-middle-class upbringing outside Rochester, New York, where her father had been the first black vice president at Kodak, made her trusting but not stupid, and even as she listened and sometimes cried for Moon, a corner of her mind had the sense to wonder about the stories she was hearing. Her instincts told her that Moon's arsenal of street smarts included the ability to lie convincingly, or at least to hold back the full truth, when the need arose. Once she caught him lying about supposedly not knowing a girl she'd noticed wiggling her eyebrows at him. She got so pissed, she called him an asshole and kicked out the bottom of his screen door. But, even as she recognized the danger, her heart was tumbling.

It impressed her, for one thing, that he didn't try to push her into bed right off. He seemed just to want to talk to her as a friend—the first real friend, he said, that he'd ever had. In fact, for a while she wondered if they would ever move beyond friendship, but when they did, my God! With the Skidmore boys, before grad school, sex was like holding a sparkler on the Fourth of July, very sweet and, most of the time, mildly thrilling. But with Moon, it was like she was inside the fireworks, at the heart of the grand finale, with the shuddering booms and bright colors all around her.

When she'd basically been living at his place for months, unknown to her parents, and accidentally on purpose had gotten pregnant, she'd been terrified he'd take off. But she had no sooner told him, tearfully, than he had folded her into his arms and, to her amazement, asked her to marry him. A month later, at the First Episcopal Church of Springfield, with her parents looking on with that tight look she knew so well, determined to be supportive, her uncle had pronounced them man and wife, and they'd jumped the broom.

In the darkness of their bedroom now, Sandra Hudson was sure she heard something, but this time it was at the back of the house. Somebody walking a dog? It was crazy. Then she was positive, almost positive, she saw a shadow pass the window four feet from her head. What was going on? She lifted herself on one elbow, pulling the sheets up over her breasts. Grace would be ready to nurse soon, and Sandra's nipples were beginning to leak milk.

"Moon," she whispered, and poked at his shoulder with two fingers. He moved but did not wake. Was it their upstairs neighbor, pacing with her grandchild again?

A moment later, as Sandra lay in the dark, she felt Moon finally responding, not to her but to an unmistakable crackling noise on the porch. His whole body tensed, and his head snapped up from the pillow, which scared her more than anything else.

Suddenly, there was a splintering crash, as though a gravel truck had just plowed through the front door and spilled most of its load. A rush of footsteps followed, then a second, smaller crash as something tipped over in the living room—a voice yelling "Go, go! Get to the fucking bedroom!" The baby started to shriek. Everything was happening at once. Someone said, "Son of a bitch!" The lights went on and three huge men—one in a blue uniform, two in orange vests—were standing at the foot of the bed pointing pistols at them, two-handed, just like in the movies. The door to the baby's room made a sickening bang. Lights were going on all over the apartment.

"Freeze! Police! Show me your hands!"

"Get on the ground! On the ground!"

There was another tremendous crash from the back porch. Sandra had already swung her feet to the floor, yanking the sheet around her nightgown, heart pounding, thinking to get to Grace. More people were pouring into the room, coming at her.

"On the fucking ground!"

A large uniformed cop grabbed her shoulder and pushed her roughly toward the floor, his big hands shoving down on the middle of her back. Something—a knee?—was pressing painfully onto her ankles, and a gun near her eye was so close she caught its acrid, oily scent deep in her nostrils and at the back of her throat. Then her arms were being jerked behind her back, and cold metal was snapping around her wrists. The cuffs grabbed so tight they stung.

"The baby," Sandra said, trying to look up.

A deeper voice from the doorway ordered loudly, "I want the canine in the basement. Clear the basement."

"Have you got a weapon in here?" the voice above her asked. "Keep on the ground like I said. Your baby's fine. Stay on the ground!"

"Lie down, babe," she heard Moon's voice from the other side of the bed. "Do like they . . . " There was a sudden splintering crunch as something heavy fell.

"Shit," a voice said.

The deeper voice in the doorway, commanded "Hey, knock it off!" and a mocking, singsong voice over near Moon added, "He got out of bed, and he bumped his head . . ."

Her cheek was flattened on the carpeting. The hand in the middle of her back was still pushing her down. Her breasts, wrists, and ankles hurt fiercely, and she gave a little cry. It was getting difficult to breathe.

The voice of the large man in uniform was in her ear, almost kind, "We're gonna frisk you now, okay? Got any needles on you, lady? Any firearms in the room?"

A new voice, southern, from the doorway: "Basement's clear, not another soul in the joint."

Yet another voice, female, from down near her feet: "Jesus, Alex, where's she going to put any needles?"

And still another from the doorway, commanding and angry: "Get upstairs. Check the neighbor." The order was punctuated with a sneeze, like an exclamation point.

"You do her then. Half these assholes are HIV," the cop named Alex replied.

Sandra realized the shrieking wasn't coming from Grace, after all, but from her neighbor's hyperactive grandchild, Tyler, upstairs. Thank God! But what was happening in Grace's room? Another hard bump reverberated on the wall. She felt the vibration of heavy feet through the floor and heard the mobile over Grace's crib jingling crazily. In the kitchen, cabinet doors were clanging, and something—the juice pitcher?—hit the floor with a sharp crash.

"Can I please get my baby?" Sandra asked the almost-kind

voice. She could see nothing but boots and shoes on the gray-green rug.

"Let her see the baby." Moon's voice.

"Shut the fuck up," said a hard, high-pitched voice from the other side of the bed.

"In a minute." This was the female voice, bending over her now, intimately close to her ear. "We need to know, okay? Is there a firearm anywhere in the room, ma'am? Any kind of weapon? Anyone else in the apartment?"

The high-pitched voice was speaking quickly from Moon's side of the bed.

"You have a right to remain silent. Anything you say can and will be used against you in a court of law. Fuck, I dropped the card. Jimmy, grab that card. It's . . . never mind, give me yours."

"No guns," Sandra said. Every time she inhaled, her breasts hurt.

"Okay, I'm going to pat you down a little," the woman said. "No needles, right?"

"What?"

Sandra was aware of many, many feet tramping through the house, and now, lifting her chin slightly, she noticed blue lights dancing off the walls from several angles. The whole neighborhood would be up. Another hard thump from the baby's room struck her worse than a slap, and the urgency of her desire to get to Grace was nearly unbearable. Soon she would not be able to keep herself from screaming, and then what would happen?

"Let her get the kid," a voice said from somewhere above her.

"Just a sec."

The fast voice resumed from the other side of the bed.

"You have a right to a lawyer. If you can't afford a lawyer, one will be appointed to represent you. If you begin to make a statement, you can stop at any time. Do you understand these rights as I gave them to you?"

"Yes." It was Moon's voice again, but changed—dumb and obedient.

"Having understood these rights, do you now wish to speak with me?"

"No."

"Stand him up. Christ, get some pants on him."

"Hey, Allie, you ever seen this guy before?"

"Shut up, Jimmy," the deep voice in the doorway broke in again. "Go help in the kitchen."

"Okay, ma'am." It was the heavyset cop, Alex, again. But the woman was still there, too, one hand on Sandra's shoulder, tight, the other on the small of her back.

"Sergeant Cramer and I are going to help you up now. We're going to sit you on the bed, okay? Easy does it. Upsy-daisy."

"Díaz, give him his . . . Wait a minute." There was another explosive sneeze. "Give him his rights in Spanish." Someone was blowing his nose.

"I don't think he speaks Spanish, Lieutenant," a voice replied from the closet area. "Hey, buddy, *habla español?*"

"No," Moon said in his new, flat voice.

Sandra was lifted off the floor up into a world that had changed completely. She felt like Dorothy in *The Wizard of Oz*, except that this time the tornado had worked in reverse, taking her happy, brightly colored world and plunging it into grim black and white. She gasped as they dropped her down farther than she expected. The mattress was gone, and she was placed on the hard box spring. Sitting so low, with her hands cuffed tightly behind her back, she felt tiny. What she saw—with her darting eyes, not daring to turn her head—sickened her.

Their small bedroom, their daisy field, was crowded with enormous, jostling, dirty-footed people. The sheets and blankets had been pushed off onto the floor. Two men had the mattress on its end and were running their hands carefully along its underside. A third officer had pulled out the top drawer of their oak bureau, a wedding gift from her parents, and was dumping its contents onto the floor. The bottom two drawers were already leaning against the wall on a pile of underwear. A uniformed Latino cop—Díaz apparently—was at the closet, throwing shirts and pants over his shoulder carelessly. A black officer and a big white guy in uniform were standing next to Moon, who was completely naked with his hands cuffed behind his back. They were helping him step into a pair of jeans. Most horrifying of all, a stream of blood ran down the side of Moon's face and onto his shoulder.

"Moon, you're hurt!"

"It's okay."

The white cop in the doorway pointed. "Hey, if you don't want to talk, shut up!"

All their belongings, their clothing, their sheets and blankets, even their precious framed wedding pictures, already knocked off the bureau and broken, were being stepped on as people passed in and out of the room.

"*Hola!*" Díaz cried jubilantly. He was pulling a shoebox out of Moon's closet, holding the top in one hand. Several officers looked over at him.

"Looks like maybe five, six ounces of pot, bagged for sale, and a shitload of cash here, Lieutenant." He peered into the box and looked up with a happy grin, like a boy with a trick-or-treat bag.

"Don't touch anything, for Christ's sake. Put it back and get the video cam."

"What do they pay you for an ounce of weed these days, Clarence?" the black cop on the other side of the bed asked.

"That's not ours," Sandra exclaimed. "Moon, what is that?"

"Whoa," said the southern voice in the doorway. It was a man in plainclothes with a raid jacket, looking over the lieutenant's shoulder at Sandra with a pleased, lazy smile. "I believe we just heard an excited utterance, admissible in a court of law."

"Baby, hush now," Moon said sharply, and his face made Sandra's stomach plunge. She saw him look quickly over at her and then down at the floor, as if he were ashamed. This was the worst shock yet. Who had she married?

"Somebody might just want to scribble Miz Hudson's remark down somewhere."

Grace did begin to bleat faintly now. The sound expanded in Sandra's mind and pushed its way through everything, one clear, irresistible call in this mass of confusion.

"Get her out of here," the lieutenant said, waving his hand at Sandra. "Let her get the kid. She's okay. What?" He twisted around to speak to someone in the living room, then turned again to look at Sandra in her nightgown and sheet. He seemed frazzled, and he gazed on her with distaste. "Take the cuffs off, Al. She's okay. Seems like King sniffed out more goodies in the basement." He blew his nose into a wrinkled handkerchief.

As Al, or Alex, unlocked the cuffs, Sandra heard the lieutenant mutter to the man in plainclothes, "Holy Mother of Christ, with the kid here and everything." They looked away as she passed. A few seconds later, sleepwalking through the shattered living room, Sandra heard the lieutenant's voice behind her.

"Jimmy, give Mrs. Hudson a copy of the warrant. It must be on the floor there somewhere, by the table. Anybody run across any Tylenol?"

In the baby's room, Grace stopped crying the instant Sandra picked her up. The infant began to smack her lips and peer
around eagerly with her beautiful almond-shaped eyes, watching
the mobile with its dancing figures of Tigger, Kanga, and baby
Roo. She'd be wailing for breakfast soon. Back in their bedroom,
Moon's deep, submissive voice was audible.

"What's all this for? The weed?"

There was a dead silence and then a disgusted snort.

"Sure thing, Clarence," someone said. "Pull that sweatshirt over
him and stick his ass in the cruiser. Grab his sneakers."

"Sean Daley's on the porch," the lieutenant said. "Let him have
a good look."

The female officer, heavyset with short, curly hair, came up to
Sandra in the baby's room, stepping over a strewn pile of Luvs
and crib sheets. She spoke in a hard, automatic voice. "Is there any
place you could take the baby, ma'am? How about your neighbor
upstairs? We're gonna be here awhile."

Ten minutes later, having tossed a few baby supplies into a
grocery bag, Sandra dragged herself up the stairs, bracing Grace
awkwardly against her side. Her neighbor Spanky, an enormous
woman in a fuchsia housedress as big as a tent, stood on the landing reaching out toward Sandra with flabby arms, a dreamlike
figure at the end of a dark tunnel.

8

David and Claire were sitting in the driveway outside David's garage, with rain streaming sideways across the windshield and the car rocking in the gusts of wind. The moment had come, David told himself, either to step off the high-dive or head back down the ladder. The last time he could remember being in this position was with Faye in the back of a school bus, getting up the nerve to hold hands.

He'd been stalling with apologies for his law rant at the dinner table.

"Oh, pooh!" Claire poked his shoulder. "Gerry plays one note—politics—and he always has to be the smartest guy in the room. Your ignoring him for so long was hysterical. I bet he's plotting his revenge at this very moment." A cracking noise made her glance up into the thrashing trees. "Assuming he and his ingenue du jour aren't otherwise occupied."

David began fiddling with the knob on the glove compartment.

"I always end up feeling . . . I don't know . . ."

"Constipated, sure. But there are things you have to tiptoe around, right? Like, obviously, if someone asks your opinion of the death penalty, you go all peculiar and distant."

"Not distant," David said. The glove compartment flopped open, and he reached down between his feet to retrieve a pencil. "Definitely peculiar."

"Okay, not distant." Claire nodded. "Just fencing your garden."

She had beautifully even, very white teeth and a mouth that seemed always about to break into a smile.

"I understand," she continued. "We medievalists have our secrets, too, you know."

"Really? Like what?"

"I can't tell you. That's the point."

"What sort of secrets then?"

"Well . . ." She drew the word out. "One example. After you make full professor, they tell you who murdered the little princes in the Tower of London in 1483."

"Wow! Was it really Richard III? I've always thought he was framed."

"Like I said, I can't tell you."

David shook his head and muttered, "That is so much better than any of my secrets."

The wind died down, and their black leatherette world went very quiet as he looked into Claire's eyes. Just the purr of the idling engine, the thud of the wipers, and the tap of sleet on the glass. Faint scent of vanilla. He felt slightly dizzy, as though the back end of the car were lifting off the ground. This was when he was supposed to do something.

Claire turned to David and put her hand on his shoulder. He had an insane thought that she might reach down, unzip his fly, and propose oral sex. People did that these days, didn't they?

"How about this?" She dropped her voice. "I'll tell you one of my secrets, if you tell me one of yours."

"Uh," David began, but they kissed before he could continue, and his field of consciousness contracted to tongue, lips, and nose, the taste of her mouth, and the need to make spaces to breathe. After a life-transforming interval, they broke, and David said, "I don't know about that."

"I figured."

They resumed kissing, maneuvering as well as they could in the cramped interior. Claire slipped her arms up inside David's jacket, cupping her hands over his shoulder blades and down his long back, pulling him to her. The competence of her touch was as thrilling to David as her tenderness. This was a woman who might be, in the best sense, very easy.

"Okay," Claire whispered, very close, "here's the deal." She kissed him. "I'll tell you one of my secrets for free." She kissed him again, longer this time. "And you can decide if you want to reciprocate."

"I don't . . . I don't know."

Claire's breath played over his face. "You mustn't tell a soul." She put her finger on the tip of his nose and looked into his eyes solemnly. "William the Conqueror had three testicles."

They burst out laughing and fell onto each other with even more appetite. David let his hands slide along the splendid curve of Claire's waist, up over her ribs, brushing up over her breasts and around to the trailing archipelago of her vertebrae. Small things nipped at the edges of his mind—the gearshift and the painful hand brake, the cold nudge of the rearview mirror against his temple, the fact that he badly needed to go to the bathroom—but he was so engulfed in pleasure and amazed at Claire's eagerness that he barely noticed. Even when a sad chill brushed him, the ghost of Faye melting into the back of his mind, he did not pause or, for the moment, even care very much.

On the other side of infinity, they took a break, clinging and breathing contentedly.

"Okay," David said. He laid his nose on the side of Claire's head and breathed in deeply. Distant scent of coconut. "Here's mine. Personally, I don't care much for death."

"Egad. Let me get a pencil."

"Very funny. I mean, for the death penalty. Too much strain on the system."

"The legal system or your system?"

"Everybody's system. The doubts about whether the defendant did it, the pressure to conduct a perfect trial, everything." He sniffed and drew himself up from Claire's head. The air was cool. "Then, to tell the truth, I'm about sick to death of death. We're all going to get there some day. No need to hurry things."

Claire tilted her face up to him, and he kissed her eyelids, then the wings of her nose and her chin. As he put his hands over her breasts again, she moaned softly, cleared her throat, and spoke over his shoulder, slowing things down.

"I've never in my life seen such a tidy garage."

"Rural upbringing. A man's judged more by his barn than his house."

Two sharp woofs came from inside.

"Oh, that's right—you have an exploding dog!" Claire said delightedly.

"Yes." He realized that Marlene had been barking for some time, not in anger but with the mechanical persistence of a car alarm. "Could you, uh, come in for a minute?"

"I think," Claire said carefully, "that might be a little too soon."

"No, no," David said. "I didn't mean that. That would be too much."

" 'Too soon' is what I said."

"I just wanted to rescue my poor dog." He rocked back into his seat, trying discreetly and without success to arrange his erection at a more comfortable angle.

"Uh-huh." She glanced down and looked up at him with her eyes crinkling. "Go release your animal. This will do for now."

As David swung his legs around to get out of the car, he was finally able to reposition himself and stand up with reasonable ease. The blowing rain on his face felt terrific.

"Don't worry about my car," he said, bending down.

"Oh, I won't." She lowered her window. "I did that on purpose, you know." Her voice began to fade into the wind as she drove off. "Just kidding! Maybe. Now call me, you jerk!"

Back in his home, safe out of the weather, David's yellow Lab was waiting; she banged her thick tail against the doorframe and pushed her nose into his knees in greeting.

"Marlene," David said, "we really need to talk."

9

After they took Moon Hudson away, Holyoke Police Captain Sean Daley spent a few minutes checking out the mess inside the apartment. Then he gave Jack O'Connor a call and asked if he could come over and talk to him and the boys. It was late, he said, so he'd only take a minute.

Daley had never married; instead, he'd poured his life into his job. He'd been hospitalized twice for stab wounds and nearly killed when a .38 round struck his "bulletproof" vest. Two civilians and a fellow officer were still alive because of his quick action, and he had four commendations for bravery. On duty, Daley's views on discipline made him as unbendable as a tire iron, but in the supermarket he might easily have been mistaken for a bookkeeper or an introverted shop foreman.

Daley's habit of passing out peppermint balls and telling

hair-raising stories about the criminals he'd caught made him a favorite among his nieces and nephews. He loved to recount the tale of the family's great-great-grandfather Dominic Daley, hanged in Northampton in 1806, supposedly for a murder but, in fact, for the crime of being an Irish Catholic passing through town when a local Protestant turned up with his head bashed in.

Of all the adoring younger generation, his niece Ginger Daley O'Connor had been Captain Daley's secret pet. In fact, when she'd been a nursing student and he'd been in his mid-thirties, he'd had half, and maybe more than half, a crush on her, though of course he never let anyone know. He still remembered how radiant she looked at her graduation from Holyoke Community College, and how jealous he was of that big sap Jack O'Connor. At her wedding, Ginger's were the prettiest brown eyes he'd ever seen and her young spirit the most luminous.

In his decades as a police officer, Daley had looked on death many times, but he had never dreamed that any loss would tear out his heart like this one. It had been Daley who, to spare Jack, had formally identified Ginger's graying body at the morgue for the medical examiner's staff.

Jack was standing on the porch, waiting with his arms crossed, oblivious to the blowing rain as Daley parked his Crown Victoria cruiser. The two men nodded, and Jack pushed the door open for him.

The boys were waiting in the kitchen in their pajamas and bathrobes, looking mussed and sleepy. It was a school night, and already after midnight. Jack Jr., the oldest and handsomest, was at the far end of the kitchen table, sitting like the image of his father with his arms folded. Ed, the middle child, the only one in the family who'd had the poise to speak at his mother's memorial service, was to Jack Jr.'s left with his head resting on his arms, half asleep. Michael, the eleven-year-old, was sitting on the counter next to the flour and sugar canisters. His dark, wide-awake eyes looked scared.

They all said "Hi, Uncle Sean" when he walked in, but there were no smiles these days, and their voices were lifeless.

"Boys," Daley said, standing just inside the kitchen doorway, "you need your sleep, so I'll get right to it. It will be in the papers tomorrow anyway. We just arrested the man we think . . ." He started to say "killed your mother," but he couldn't get the words out, so after clearing his throat he just said, "did the shooting."

"Who is he?" Jack Jr. asked. "Where'd they put him?"

"He's a black drug dealer from Holyoke named Clarence Hudson," Daley said. "They think he's a Flag—that's what they call members of the street gang called La Bandera—or somebody associated with them."

"I wish they'd killed him," Jack Jr. said fiercely, clenching his fists in front of him.

"Well," said Daley, "we'll see what happens."

"How do they know it was him?" Michael asked.

"Now that's a smart question, Mike," Daley responded, nodding at Ginger's youngest boy, the one who reminded him most of her. "Seems like the driver, a kid named Rivera, about Eddie's age, says Hudson did it. He says Hudson was selling drugs up at UMass and got into some kind of beef with Delgado, who was supplying his drugs. Rivera says Hudson told him he was only going to scare Delgado, not shoot him, and that he got a hundred dollars to drive the car."

"That's funny," Michael said. "Why would he just want to scare him?"

Daley scratched his head again and frowned. "Tell you the truth, Mike, it *is* funny. Rivera's uncle Carlos is a big shot in the La Bandera street gang, and he's disappeared. We'll find him, and we'll see what Rivera says in a day or two."

"This Hudson guy," Jack Jr. asked, "will they execute him?"

"God, I hope so!" Eddie burst out, sitting up. "I want to be standing right there when it happens. I want to pull the damn . . ."

The boys' father broke in, "Edward!"

"Sorry." Eddie lowered his head back to the table, staring forward.

"I don't know," Michael said. "It wasn't on purpose, was it? It was, like, a ricochet. If Mom just hadn't stopped and leaned over . . ."

"Right," O'Connor said. "That's all the news for tonight, boys. They got him. We knew they would. Off to bed now. We can talk more tomorrow."

The three boys moved slowly out of the room. Daley brushed a hand through Michael's dark hair as he dragged himself toward the door. The child was thin—the belt of his bathrobe seemed to go around him twice—and he looked as though he were hauling a slab of concrete behind him.

Jack squatted down in front of Michael after his brothers had passed.

"Mikey, listen to me. I'm going to stay home from work tomorrow. We'll talk about this, okay? Just like Dr. Rosen said. And don't forget, I'm not going anywhere."

When he gave the boy a hug, the eyes of both father and son were shining. Daley turned and examined the darkness outside the window over the sink.

After they heard the bedroom doors close, Jack said, "Come in the front room a minute, Sean. You want some coffee?"

Daley shook his head, and they walked down the hall and into a far corner at the front of the house, where their voices would not be heard upstairs. They collapsed into a pair of armchairs.

Daley said, "Sweet Jesus! How do you do this?"

O'Connor threw his head back, put his hands over his face and breathed deeply, then dropped his arms in his lap and leaned forward. Sharp lines were pulling down at the corners of his mouth. His face looked ravaged.

"So what do you think, Sean? What's up?" He looked at Daley. "Can we trust this?"

"Jack, I honestly don't know. This Rivera kid's a born liar, one of these Puerto Rican halfwits. You know me—I don't say this about all of them. We have some fine Puerto Rican officers, but my God, Jack, some of the kids down in the Flats these days are barely human. They grow up with no fathers, their mothers can't cope, they hardly speak English, they can't read or write in any language, and they're peddling drugs by the time they're thirteen."

As he'd been speaking, his voice had increased in intensity, and a flush had spread up his cheeks.

"They're not bad people, most of those poor women," he said, speaking even more quietly, as though talking to himself. "Most of them work like billy-be-damned. What hurts is I couldn't stop this." He paused. "Now she's gone, and she was worth the whole basketful of us."

After a moment, he turned and looked at O'Connor, wiped his hand over his eyes, and continued more briskly.

"I have no idea whether this Rivera kid is telling the truth, Jack. He's got this pipsqueak lawyer, who, I swear, looks like Ronald MacDonald and knows exactly nothing about what he's doing. He couldn't get the pope off. Hudson's another beaut. He prances around that twit factory up in Amherst and pretends to be a student while he sells pot, which he had to be getting from somewhere. Hudson had a dustup with Delgado when they were in Ludlow, I guess. He was a Flag, and Delgado had a deal with some other gang, I forget which, so it seems Delgado and some of his friends gave him a thumping. To me, it doesn't make sense that La Bandera, which is mostly Puerto Ricans, would bring in a black guy, a former member, and pay him to shoot Delgado when they could do it themselves for free. But who knows with these people?"

"Mike's the one I'm worried about," O'Connor said. "He's a special kid, probably the smartest one in the family. You saw how he's taking it." He leaned forward and rubbed his hands together. "I wish they'd stop with all this death penalty stuff, to tell you the truth. It's not helping Mikey one bit."

"I hate it!" Daley said with sudden ferocity. "Some of the people down at the station are all for it, and I keep my trap shut, but I *hate* it, Jack. Sure, I hope Hudson dies soon, and I hope he dies hard, but let God take him when He's ready. Ninety percent of the cops here in Holyoke these days are top drawer. But between you and me, one or two are complete chumps. They screw this up, with all their jabber about lethal injections, and their fancy equipment that doesn't work half the time, and with a decent lawyer Hudson could go scot-free."

Jack nodded. "Why's the case in federal court in the first place?"

"The feds have this RICO statute, and Hogan's using it to go after the gangs. Tell the truth, it's not a bad idea. They can put animals like Hudson away for good." He blew out a breath disgustedly. "But why get everyone's temperature up just to put him out of his misery? I say put the creature in a hole somewhere and let him rot."

"I guess Washington wants to get Massachusetts on board, and Buddy's their guy." Jack said. "They say he's going for governor."

"Well, the Lord knows we could use a sensible Irishman on Beacon Hill, but this is no way to get him there."

He looked at the floor and ran a hand back through his wiry gray hair.

"They're quite capable of making a dog's breakfast of this," Daley said, still looking at the carpet. "That's the thing." He lifted his face with an expression of exhaustion almost as profound as Jack's. "It makes me so sick I can't sleep nights, you know? It's bad enough how Ginger went. But, some day a year from now, you and Mike and me could be stopping off at the 7-Eleven, and there will be Hudson, big as life, buying himself a Slurpee. And we'll all just have to stand there minding our manners. We owe it to Ginger not to let that happen."

10

Judge Norcross and Maria Maldonado observed the same court proceeding, one from the front and one from the back, seeing utterly different things.

Maria entered the courtroom through the public doorway, slipping, with as little stir as possible, into the most distant corner of the gallery and hoping to be invisible.

Judge Norcross strode in through a paneled door at the far end and walked quickly to the bench, accompanied by the booming voice of the court officer, which caused Maria to grab the pew in front of her and jerk her small body upright.

"All rise! All persons having anything to do before the Honorable David S. Norcross, judge of the United States District Court, now holden in Springfield, in and for the District of Massachusetts, shall draw near, give their attendance, and they shall be heard." The volume increased a notch for the finale. "God save the United States of America and this honorable court! The court is now in session. You may be seated."

The judge's elevated perch gave him an easy view of the entire courtroom. To the right sat the assistant U.S. attorney, accompanied by a porky cop with a face as round as a pie plate, probably the government's case agent. To the left, at a separate table, was the defendant whose guilty plea Norcross was about to take, along with his lawyer, an attorney he didn't know.

The judge's courtroom deputy called the case: "United States versus Ernesto Rivera, Criminal Action Number 09-30087-DSN." The court stenographer adjusted her chair slightly and sat with her fingers poised over her machine.

Silence. The aroma of wood polish and carpet cleaner, the formal arrangement of the furniture, the vaulted ceiling with a few drifting dust motes turning gold in the sunlight, the bright colors of the flag against the oak paneling—all these elements were, after almost twenty years as a lawyer and judge, deeply comforting to Norcross. This was home. The judge set his water cup well off to one side and scooted forward to the edge of his chair to make sure he didn't snag the hem of his robe in a caster. Showtime.

From the rear of the courtroom Maria Maldonado, tilting awkwardly to try to catch a glimpse of her son's face, saw only the back of his head. Her English was so-so, and except for "God save the United States of America!" she hadn't completely understood the belligerent words of the white-haired man in the blazer. The judge's frown as he looked down at her boy made her heartsick. Nothing good could happen in a place like this.

Judge Norcross began. "We are here, as I understand it, to take the plea of the defendant Ernesto, aka Pepe, Rivera to a one-count information, charging him with conspiring to participate in a racketeering enterprise." He read from the file. "The overt acts committed in furtherance of this conspiracy, according to the information, include two homicides in which he acted as the driver. Before we get started I'm going to ask counsel to identify themselves for the record and also identify the parties sitting at counsel table. We'll begin with the government."

The AUSA, an elegant Latina woman with luxuriant dark hair and an aura of quiet competence, had appeared before the judge many times. He liked and respected her.

"Judge, for the record, my name is Lydia Gomez-Larsen, and I appear on behalf of the United States. With me at counsel table is Holyoke police officer Alex Torricelli, who was injured apprehending the defendant." Torricelli half stood and nodded, shooting a look toward Gomez-Larsen to be sure he'd acted properly, before lowering himself again. The prosecutor missed this gesture, pivoting to let her eyes sweep the gallery. "I see that Holyoke Police Captain Sean Daley is also present in the courtroom." From his seat in the front row, Daley nodded, keeping his arms folded and shifting his jaw as though he were sucking on a Tic Tac.

Gomez-Larsen sat down, and the attorney to the judge's left fumbled to his feet. "Clyde Goodman for the defendant, Judge. For the record, Mr. Rivera is with me in the courtroom."

Goodman had a long neck, a self-conscious grin, and an oversize blossom of curly red hair. The man's professional qualities seemed doubtful. Judge Norcross would need to take things slowly with him.

Maria didn't know anyone. She had come to court straight from the New Life Pentecostal Church in the Flats, where she and the pastor had been offering prayers for the protection of her son's soul since early that morning. At the moment, her eyes were fastened on the depression just below the hairline at the back of Ernesto's head, a place she had kissed so often. A sob was pressing up into her throat, and she was struggling not to do anything embarrassing.

Ernesto was Maria's only child, and she was his only parent. She remembered how well he'd started life: a robust, affectionate little kid, running around her parents' living room with his stuffed monkey, Jocko, or sitting placidly with a coloring book watching cartoons. Now this.

The judge was talking. "This is a proceeding pursuant to Rule Eleven of the Federal Rules of Criminal Procedure. Our task today is to ensure that, if the defendant does admit his guilt to the charge against him, he does so knowingly, intelligently, and voluntarily. I need to say a few things to you, Mr. Rivera, before we go any further. Please listen to me carefully."

Maria thought, *It's like a movie. It's like sitting in the dark and realizing that the person up on the screen is your son. The judge is treating Pepe the same as any criminal, because to him that's what he is.*

Rivera rubbed his ear, using a slow circling motion with his pointer and middle finger, round and round, as though he were trying to massage away a buzzing noise. This was a trademark gesture of her son's, something he'd done since he was a toddler whenever he was nervous or on the spot somehow, and the familiar sight pushed the sob higher until it was touching the roof of Maria's mouth. It really was him. She must not cry.

Up on the bench, Judge Norcross was encountering the recurring problem of eye contact. The sheer number of plea colloquies he'd conducted, using virtually the same words each time, threatened to reduce the process to a meaningless drone. Specific, individual attention needed to be paid, and looking right into the defendant's face seemed like one way to make sure his words really penetrated.

On the other hand, he'd found that eyeballing a defendant could be misinterpreted as an effort to dominate. Stupid, frightened, overproud, or confused offenders sometimes reacted with a look of defiance, or sulky indifference, which, to Norcross, curdled the whole proceeding.

Directing his gaze toward the defense table, Norcross saw that Rivera would be a defendant of the blank variety. In response to the judge's attempt at eye contact, Rivera left off rubbing his ear and lifted his eyes briefly, showing only a flicker of passive inscrutability before dropping them. The corners of the defendant's mouth turned down, and he ran his tongue along the inside of his upper lip as though he had a sore on his gum. The gesture deformed Rivera's face just enough to make it impossible to read his feelings.

Watching from the shadows, Maria felt the judge closing down, just like the teachers when they complained during meetings that her son couldn't sit still, wouldn't do his work on time, and kept bothering the other kids. She wanted to stand up and explain. Ernesto was not being rude; he was just a little scared. With patience, he would begin to show the sweet side of himself. At the same time, she wanted to march the boy out into the corridor, tell him to sit up properly, pay attention, and behave. He knew how to act.

Judge Norcross cleared his throat and pushed ahead. "Mr. Rivera, I have a number of important warnings to give you and some questions to ask you this afternoon. If during the course of what I say, you do not understand me, or if there is some noise in the courtroom and you do not catch something, please ask me to repeat or explain myself. I will not be bothered or offended by this at all. Do you understand, sir?"

Rivera glanced in his lawyer's direction, but Goodman was

down at the floor, rummaging in his briefcase. The defendant directed his eyes at the judge's forehead and nodded minutely.

Judge Norcross forced himself to keep a neutral tone. He'd have to be content simply to get the mandatory questions and answers into the transcript. Maybe the kid understood, maybe not.

"Good. Let the record reflect that you've nodded to indicate that you understand. I want to tell you how this proceeding will go. In a moment, I am going to ask you to take the witness stand. Here." The judge pointed to a wooden enclosure on his left. "Ms. Johnson will place you under oath. I will then have, as I just said, some warnings for you and some questions. After that I will have five or six questions for Mr. Goodman." Attorney Goodman stiffened and sat up straighter. At least now he'd know what was coming. "Then, Assistant U.S. Attorney Gomez-Larsen will summarize the evidence the government would have offered if your case had gone to trial, and after all that, if I'm satisfied that it's appropriate, we'll take your plea. Do you understand, sir?"

Rivera cast a blank look at his attorney, turned to the bench, and nodded.

"Mr. Rivera, you've been answering me up to now just by nodding. In our everyday lives, of course, this presents no problem. But we have a stenographer here"—Judge Norcross gestured down at his court reporter—"who is making a transcript, and your answers need to be audible. You need to speak. So, I'm going to ask you again, do you understand, sir?"

Rivera sniffed. "I understand."

"Thank you. One aspect of the plea is so important that I want to emphasize it now. I will return to it in more detail shortly."

At that moment, the big public door banged open and the comic bane of Judge Norcross's existence wobbled into the courtroom. It was eighty-six-year-old Florence Abercrombie, bosoming a stack of files in one arm and holding a wicker basket topped with a red-and-white checkered napkin in her free hand. "Oh, thank you *so* much," she said in a stage whisper to the court security officer, causing both Alex Torricelli and Attorney Goodman to twitch and look around. AUSA Gomez-Larsen, recognizing the voice, only sighed and rolled her eyes.

Mrs. Abercrombie was a wacky pro se litigant who had represented herself in a half-dozen lawsuits in the Springfield federal court. The judge found it hard, despite the extra work she made for him, not to admire the harmless old screwball. She'd sued Publisher's Clearinghouse Sweepstakes on a theory of promissory estoppel when she had not received her twenty million dollars, filed a civil rights complaint against her electric company for adding a surcharge to her bill, and, more than once, named the president and the secretary of state as defendants based on allegations that they had snooped into her emails. In careful, polite memoranda, Norcross had dismissed each of her lawsuits.

She had long, white hair pinned up in barrettes over her ears and shiny brown eyes as fanatical and unblinking as a peahen's. On one of her appearances, she'd been inspired to bring a basket of homemade ginger snaps to the clerk's office, and unfortunately someone had taken them, probably as the simplest way to get rid of her. Now she brought cookies every time she came to court. From the center aisle of the gallery, Florence was grinning up at the bench and waving the wicker basket back and forth at Judge Norcross. Despite her lack of success, she appeared to think the world of him.

"Good morning, Mrs. Abercombie," the judge said. "Nice to see you. I'm tied up at the moment, as you can see, so you'll oblige me if you have a seat. Or you might wait outside."

To the Norcross's relief, Mrs. Abercrombie said nothing—merely began easing herself onto a pew—and he turned his attention back to the defense table. "As I said, there is one aspect of the plea agreement . . . excuse me, Mr. Goodman?" The defendant's lawyer was still fascinated by Mrs. Abercrombie, who had dropped one of her files and was busy collecting it. "Are you with us?"

"Yes, Your Honor. Sorry."

"There is one aspect of the plea agreement I want to emphasize. The charge against you carries the penalty of mandatory life imprisonment, without possibility of parole. This means that, ordinarily, a person pleading guilty to this charge would be imprisoned and would never, ever be released. Have you discussed this point with your attorney, Mr. Rivera?"

The defendant looked uncertainly at Attorney Goodman, who nodded encouragingly.

After a pause, Rivera nodded. When the judge raised his eyebrows at him, the defendant added a barely audible response: "Yes."

"Thank you."

In the corner, Maria took a shaky breath and closed her eyes to absorb this news once more. She had always been active in her church, but in the past decade, with so much happening, she had surrendered herself entirely to the will of Providence. There was not a doubt in her mind about the imminence of divine judgment, permanent and unbendable. What would it mean to depart this short life in prison? Could her son expect to find mercy?

The judge kept talking. "The only way under the law by which you can avoid life in prison, Mr. Rivera, is if the government files a motion requesting a lower sentence based upon your substantial assistance in the prosecution of another person. If Ms. Gomez-Larsen does file this motion, which is called a 5K1 motion, I will have the power, if I choose, to impose an agreed sentence of twenty years on you. If the government doesn't find your cooperation adequate, you'll stay in prison until you die. Simple as that."

Judge Norcross reached over to retrieve his cup of water and took a sip, a deliberate pause to allow his words to sink in.

"You are dangling from a cobweb this afternoon, Mr. Rivera. The severity of your punishment, if I allow you to plead, will be mostly in the hands of Ms. Gomez-Larsen and her boss, Mr. Hogan, the United States attorney. I want to assure myself that you know where you stand from the get-go. Do you?"

Goodman was leaning forward with his elbows on the table and his hands clasped at the level of his forehead. The attorney looked over his shoulder and shrugged quickly back at his client. In response, Rivera waited for a beat, then shrugged, too.

"I understand."

"Good. Please come forward and be sworn in."

Right at that moment, for the first time, the defendant revealed something. It happened briefly, like a sparrow flying past a window.

Rivera stood, shorter and much younger than Judge Norcross had realized, turned his head, and looked over his shoulder toward the back of the gallery. With the distance and the distortion of the fluorescent lights, the expression on the face of the small woman seated there was too wavering for the judge to read. But as Pepe's head turned to where she would be able to catch his features, this brown, doll-like woman hugged her elbows together, hard, as though a freezing wind were passing over her. When Rivera turned back, Judge Norcross could see that the moment had transformed the boy. For a count of one, two, three, four seconds, Ernesto, aka Pepe, Rivera dropped his disguise, exposing the face of a wounded child, desolate and dumbfounded. Then the moment passed, and in the light of the courtroom, he congealed into his assumed persona again, screwed his mouth around to suck on his teeth, and walked slowly across the burgundy carpeting to take his place in the witness box.

Watching Pepe grudgingly raise his hand to swear to tell the truth, the whole truth and nothing but the truth, so help him God, Maria felt her heart tighten. From the whispers she'd overheard, she suspected that at least one of Pepe's uncles—including her half brother Carlos—and perhaps others in her neighborhood, knew very well who shot Peach Delgado and that poor nurse, and she was very afraid that they all knew, and Pepe knew, that it was not the black man her son had identified. Her child might be on the point of stepping over a line from which he would not, in all eternity, be able to return.

11

Thanks to Crazy Abercrombie's interruption, and Norcross's ponderous approach to plea colloquies, Assistant U.S. Attorney Gomez-Larsen made it back to her office, two floors below the courtroom, barely in time for a scheduled phone call with her boss, Buddy Hogan.

Everyone in Springfield assumed Lydia Gomez-Larsen was Puerto Rican, except the Puerto Ricans. They knew as soon as she shifted into Spanish that she was Cuban. Nevertheless, despite her Havana-Miami idiom, the western Massachusetts Latino community was proud of the AUSA, followed her victories, and looked forward to her predicted appointment to the next state Superior Court vacancy as an overdue sign of growing Hispanic political clout.

When Lydia went dancing, or dined out with her husband and his doctor friends, she liked to lacquer her nails with some vivid color, break out her bright dresses, and let her dark hair fall over her shoulders. At those times, she stood out in dowdy western Massachusetts like an orchid in a potato patch.

In the courtroom, it was different. She knew the gringo community and was intimately familiar with the conservative juries it produced. In a black or navy suit that muted her curves, and with her hair arranged in a discreet chignon, she presented herself during trials like one of the women on the Weather Channel: modestly attractive, competent, and utterly reliable. In her many years of gang-related drug and firearm prosecutions, she had rarely failed to win a conviction.

As soon as she tossed the Rivera file on her desk and sat down, the phone buzzed.

"Yeah, Bud, what's the word?" She curled a leg up, removed a shoe, and tossed it onto her small sofa.

"I'll cut to the chase, okay? The AG's boys rejected the rec. They're ordering us to go forward with the capital designation."

"Oh, for Christ's sake!"

"I know, I know. You heard how they feel about Massachusetts having no death penalty. They think your boy Hudson is a good way to break the ice."

Gomez-Larsen was holding her second shoe in her hand. She could feel her chest rising and falling. When she didn't speak, Hogan said, "Sorry." Then he cleared his throat. "Ours is not to reason why."

Gomez-Larsen burst out. "Do they have any idea how much tougher this will make everything? It's going to be hard enough to explain to a jury how a local street gang like La Bandera engaged in racketeering activity that supposedly affected interstate commerce. With the death penalty hanging over the case, the jury will be looking for any reason to acquit."

"Lydia, I know you. . . ."

"Do they understand we might have problems charging one of the victims? Killing a rival drug dealer may be an act in aid of racketeering, but killing an innocent bystander? How does that help them? The Supreme Court hasn't given us much guidance on that, you know."

"Lydia, you were there. They listened to all this. They don't give a shit."

"We could convict Hudson, and two years later, the Big Nine could decide the nurse's murder wasn't even a federal crime. Jesus!"

"Hey, look on the bright side! The Supreme Court might not get around to clearing up the law until after we've executed him."

"You're a laugh a minute, Buddy."

"I wasn't kidding."

Gomez-Larsen tossed her other shoe onto the sofa, stretched her leg, and wriggled her toes. She and Hogan had gone down to Washington to try to convince the attorney general's "death committee" to adopt their recommendation only to seek mandatory life for Hudson. The recommendation hadn't flown.

"So, anyway . . ." Hogan hesitated and continued more quietly. "Look. We're a democracy, and I'm just a guy who knew a guy, so now I'm the U.S. attorney. I don't have half your courtroom smarts, and I wouldn't know the first thing about trying a big case like this. It certainly won't be easy with Judge Funky up there. I'm not going to try to blow smoke up your butt. You know you're my best choice for this. But if you want to pass, tell me, and I'll get someone else. No hard feelings. It's your call."

An extended silence from Lydia's end followed. She was leaning over her desk with her eyes closed, pinching the bridge of her nose. Had any of those "death committee" mannequins ever tried a major felony? Did they know what this would mean for her?

"Promise me one thing, Buddy," she said at last.

"I'm a politician, Lydia. I'll promise you any fucking thing you want."

"Promise me if we indict this as a death penalty case, and the defendant agrees later to plead to life, and I recommend it, you'll back me."

"One hundred percent." He paused. "I can't promise they'll buy it, though. Washington is hot for this one. They think it's time Massachusetts got on the choo-choo."

"Okay. Give me a day to talk this over with Greg. He and the kids are going to hate it, and it will mean a ton of nights and weekends."

After she put the phone down, Lydia sat for a long time staring into space, not seeing anything or even hearing the hum of the lights. New U.S. attorneys came and went as administrations changed in Washington. Hogan was the third one she'd worked for, and the one she trusted least. He had a habit of shoving his face into the foreground at the press conferences after her successes, but, if Hudson walked, Buddy would have important business elsewhere. She'd be the one left to explain the disaster to the press and to the victims' families. Just how far out on a limb was he prepared to push her? And how far was she willing to go?

12

The day Attorney William P. Redpath Jr. accepted the appointment to represent Moon Hudson did not get off to a great start. Redpath was sitting in his office in Boston, smoking a Lucky Strike, and editing a lengthy draft memorandum when he noticed flames shooting up from his wastebasket.

"Not again," he said, rising from his stupendously cluttered desk. Redpath was an enormous, bearlike man, and the cigarette and the sheaf of papers he held looked tiny in his paws. The wastebasket problem was urgent, not because the building might burn down with him inside, but because his secretary, Judy, would smell the smoke any second, figure out what happened, and quit again. He'd have to spend the whole rest of the morning persuading her to come back. He didn't have the time for that.

Redpath balanced the half-smoked Lucky on the corner of his

overflowing in-box and hurried around his desk into the middle of the room. He spied an old Burger King milk-shake cup, abandoned weeks back, on the windowsill behind a photograph of himself and his son, years ago, at Fenway Park. Tommy had on the Red Sox cap he'd bought him. Redpath paused for a moment to smile at the photograph before snatching up the milk-shake cup and pouring the fuzz-covered contents—half liquid, half lumps—into the wastebasket. It did the trick.

With a sigh of relief, Redpath lowered his heavy frame back into the chair. He lit another cigarette with his Bic and within a few seconds was absorbed in the memorandum once more. Twin trails of blue smoke, one from the cigarette in his hand and the other from the forgotten cigarette tipping over the lip of the in-box, rose companionably into the air.

Redpath was "death qualified." This meant that after more than forty years defending criminals, and on rare occasions an innocent non-criminal, Redpath's experience as a defense attorney was prodigious. Transcripts of his politely remorseless dismemberment of prosecution witnesses were passed around at law schools all over New England as examples of the art of cross-examination at its finest. More importantly, Redpath was one of a handful of lawyers with offices in Massachusetts who had actually represented defendants facing the death penalty in other states. All this made him technically eligible, under the complex rules governing death penalty cases, to take the appointment from Judge Norcross to represent Clarence Hudson in federal court.

There was another, private reason why Redpath was death qualified. As a teenager, he'd shocked his old-money family by joining the marines, desperate to get to Korea before the armistice brought an end to the fighting. The last months of 1952 and first part of 1953 gave Redpath a protracted intimacy with the horror of deliberate killing, and he hated it. He returned home a passionate opponent of the death penalty and a chain smoker.

As Redpath settled back in his chair, there was a knock, and Judy poked her head around the door.

"Bill, I know you didn't want to be disturbed, but . . ." She paused and sniffed the air, which had a sour aroma of smoke and burned sugar. "You did it again, didn't you?" She flapped her hand disgustedly.

"I deny that," Redpath responded in his deep voice, pretending to be lost in the memorandum.

"Didn't you?" Judy approached his desk holding a slip of paper. "You remember what I told you? Phew, it stinks in here. You remember what I said?"

"I deny everything," Redpath repeated, snuffing out his Lucky Strike in the overflowing ashtray and still refusing to meet her eyes.

"Well, you have a message from the federal court in Springfield." She tossed the slip on his desk. "And, by the way, your in-box is on fire." Then she flounced out, saying, "They ought to hang a freaking sign on you or something."

Two hours later, after smothering the embers in his in-box, making some calls, and humbly requesting that Judy cancel his afternoon appointments, Redpath was on the Mass Pike heading west to Ludlow, where his new client was being held.

When Redpath arrived at the Hampden County Correctional Center, he thought at first that the conversation with his client would follow the same rocky path as the rest of the day. He and Hudson faced each other across a scarred pine conference table in a windowless room. The walls were pale yellow; the air carried the powerful smell of Lysol. Although discussions in this area were supposedly confidential, angry shouts from somewhere close by intruded regularly, and the room's door had a mesh window behind which—every minute or two—a guard's unsmiling face would hover and then float silently away. It was a lousy environment for a tête-à-tête.

Redpath began the conversation casually. "So how'd you get to be called Moon?"

Hudson was wearing an orange jumpsuit, tight across the shoulders and chest. He had a listless, distracted air and kept his eyes mostly on his hands. When he did bother to look at Redpath, it was as though he were gazing from the other side of a one-way mirror, only vaguely interested in what he was seeing. He seemed to be weighing whether to answer his lawyer's irrelevant, and possibly condescending, question.

Redpath waited, keeping his face blank. He was worried but not intimidated. In his many years of experience as an attorney, he had found that indigent clients often treated him suspiciously in the beginning, especially black clients. Considering Hudson's record, his restraint was hardly surprising; the defendant's luck with appointed counsel hadn't been very good. What must he be thinking about this ancient, possibly burned-out lawyer, chosen and paid for by the same government that wanted to assassinate him?

Still, Redpath thought, if Hudson couldn't drop the attitude, there was no way he'd let him take the stand and testify. Right now, he was a perfect picture of someone who'd killed two people and didn't care, and his own brooding face would be a ticket straight to the execution chamber. They'd have to work on that.

After a long pause, Hudson began to speak slowly.

"When I was born, right? I was real dark." He looked down at the tabletop, tracing a long gouge in the wood with the tip of his finger. A private smile, perhaps unintentional, flickered over his mouth and sank quickly back into his impassive face.

"I was so black," Hudson said, looking up at Redpath, "that when my uncle Thad saw me, I guess he started laughing. Said I was like a new moon. Nobody can see me in the dark, right? Like a new moon."

Redpath pursed his lips and nodded. He knew it was not the time to smile, even if Hudson had. The story, true or untrue, might be a test to see if the lawyer would laugh at his new client. Hudson paused for two beats, then leaned back and continued.

"When I started school, in kindergarten, I wanted the other kids to call me Clarence, like the teacher did. But they wouldn't. A lot of stuff goes with moon, right? Like prune and goon. Then, they'd be talking about 'mooning' people, you know, just being kids. So, pretty soon . . ." Hudson paused and shook his head at this accidental rhyme. "Pretty soon, I'm getting into a mess of fights."

"What would you like me to call you?" Redpath asked. "You can call me Bill. Should I call you Moon, or Clarence, or Mr. Hudson, or what?"

"I don't care."

The two big men looked at each other for a few seconds, until finally Redpath reached down and pulled his briefcase onto the table. The guards had removed almost everything from it except a copy of the indictment, a scribbled-over yellow pad, and a couple of pencils, which bounced around inside.

"Okay." There was no time to waste. Redpath had only a few minutes before the urge for a cigarette would begin to sap his patience. They needed to get started.

"I'm going to call you Moon, then, okay? I spoke to your wife on the phone, and that's what she called you, so I hope it's all right."

"Fine."

"I've got some questions for you, Moon, but before I get to them, I want to know if you have any questions for me. Do you?"

Hudson tilted his head back and looked at Redpath through half-closed eyes, took his time, then spoke deliberately.

"You ever kill anybody, Mr. Redpath?"

"What the hell difference does that make?"

Hudson shrugged, said nothing, and waited.

Now it was the lawyer's turn to decide whether to give an answer to the question, and if so whether to answer truthfully. The ironic thing was, of course, that this was pretty much the question Redpath himself was planning, in due course, to put to Hudson.

"Probably," Redpath said. "I'm not sure." Reading Hudson's face, he corrected himself and decided to plunge in. Maybe this would help. "Okay, I am sure. Yes, Moon, as a matter of fact I have killed people."

"How many?"

"I didn't count."

Something may have changed in Hudson's face, a slight alteration in the focus of his dark eyes, sifting an answer he hadn't expected and trying to decide whether he could trust it.

"Just one for me," Hudson said after a pause. "But not Peach, and not that nurse."

Redpath busied himself flipping the pages of his yellow pad, searching for a blank one and purposely not looking at his new client.

Hudson was probably lying. At this point, that didn't matter to Redpath; most of the people he represented were guilty. His job was, if possible, to keep his client alive, and to keep the prosecution honest. If, God forbid, Moon were actually innocent, it would only make his job much harder, since there would be little or no chance of a plea bargain.

Redpath positioned the pad in front of him and jotted the date in the upper right-hand corner. After he and Moon got to know each other better, he'd get to the big questions.

"Uh-huh. Did you know Delgado?" He looked up at Hudson and back down at his pad.

"Oh yeah. Pissant jumped me with two other punks last time I was in here. One of them had a shank." He held up his arm with the scar. "They got me real good." Moon stared off into space, his jaw muscles twitching as he gritted his teeth. "There was a time, you know? Not too long ago. When I would have given a lot just to watch that little motherfucker die, slow and nasty."

"Now?"

"It's just a big waste," Hudson said softly. "Waste of him. Waste of me."

"Any more questions?" Redpath asked. "We've only got a few minutes today, and I want to make some other stops. They need the room."

"How'd somebody like you kill anybody? You mean, like, flying airplanes in Vietnam or some shit?"

"Please," Redpath said with a snort. "Take a look at me, Moon!" Bill got up abruptly and walked over to a table against the wall that held a plastic jug of water and a stack of paper cups. "I'm a little old for Vietnam. Ever hear of Korea?" He was pouring the water, spilling a little.

He took a sip and continued. "I was a teenage corporal in a heavy weapons platoon, toting a .30 caliber machine gun. Can't say I'm proud of myself." He began filling a second cup, more carefully now, and spoke looking down at the table. "Caught them with the sun in their eyes. Most of those Chinamen weren't even shaving yet. They looked like girls." He nodded over at Hudson. "You want some water?"

He returned to his chair, sat down heavily, and pushed a cup across the table toward Hudson. "As Justice Holmes said, no man shot below the rib cage dies a hero's death."

Redpath's voice rose to drown out the background shouting, which had started again louder than ever, accompanied by a metallic clang. The noise stopped abruptly, making his question a little too loud. "Is it all right if we get down to business now?"

Redpath pulled his copy of the indictment out and flipped to the first count, reminding himself of the date of the incident. It would not be a bad place to start. He pressed his liver-spotted hands onto the tabletop to keep them from trembling. Korea. It never left him.

"Okay." He took a deep breath and let it out. "Sandra says you were home with her the morning Delgado was shot. Is that true? Or is she just playing the dutiful wife?"

Hudson ignored the question. "With me, it was April 2008. Skinny little Los Solidos warlord named Breeze in the White Castle parking lot. With my Glock. Old Breeze just looked surprised. Dropped his cheeseburger and sat down in the pricker bushes." Hudson shifted in the metal chair, making it squeak faintly. "Waste of him, waste of me."

"Yes," Redpath said quietly. "A complete waste."

Moon looked at the table and nodded to himself. "Now it comes around."

They each drank their water. Moon finished, crumpled his cup and, in one agile movement, tossed it neatly into the small wastebasket in the corner of the room.

"Moon, we need to get started. Were you and Sandra . . ."

"Let me ask you another question, Bill. Sorry. Why are they bringing this in federal court? What's up with that? Is it just because of the, you know, because of capital punishment?"

"Let's not call it that, okay?" Redpath finished his water,

crumpled the paper cup, and eyed the wastebasket. As Moon watched, he lobbed the ball of paper; it hit the wall and bounced in. Moon raised his eyebrows and nodded slightly. It was a beginning.

" 'Capital punishment' makes it sound like something in a philosophy book. I call it the death penalty, because that's what it is. The government wants to strap you down on a wagon, wheel you into a little room, and have a doctor stick a needle in you to stop your heart. Nothing fancy."

"Okay," Hudson said. His finger moved slowly back and forth along the table's scar.

"So, yeah," Redpath said. "The first reason you're in federal court is our government wants to kill you. God only knows why they picked this case. People say we've got a U.S. attorney, this Hogan character, who wants first prize in the 'Tough Guy' category, which is a laugh since I hear he picked a Puerto Rican assistant to try the case, a woman, to be sure he'll have cover if you get off."

Hudson shook his head. "Shit." Then he lifted his chin at Redpath. "You ever done a case like this before?"

"This is my fourth."

"How've you made out?"

"One not guilty. One guilty but with life imprisonment. One I lost."

"Your guy got stuck?"

"Right. I was there when it happened." Redpath looked down at the backs of his hands. His fingers danced, and he added, "Lost a very fine marriage, too."

"How'd he go down?"

"Let's talk about that later," Redpath said. "The second reason you're in federal court is a little more subtle. Even if they lose on the death penalty, you could still get life on the RICO charge for racketeering."

"Racketeering? Who do they think I am, some Mafia guy?"

"Being in a gang can be enough."

"I'm done with gangs, man. Been done for years now."

"Even if they can prove you did some kind of deal with them, it's probably enough. But, let's say the jury acquits you on the RICO count? They still have you on the drug charges, possession of marijuana and cocaine with intent. In federal court, they can hit you a lot harder for those, no matter what happens with the murders."

"That wasn't even my stuff," Hudson said, shrugging. "Don't even know how it got there."

"Really."

"And besides, four or five halfs, right? That's what they said? And maybe a couple eight balls of coke? How much can I get for that?"

"It would be your third strike. That makes you a career offender. And under the sentencing guidelines, you're looking at a range of something like twenty, thirty years to life just for the drugs."

"That's got to be bullshit," Hudson said, leaning back in the chair and shaking his head. "Got to be. If the jury convicts me for Delgado and that nurse, but they don't decide to, you know. Then I get life, right?"

"Life without possibility of parole. Mandatory."

"But I could get almost the same thing for four, five baggies of pot and a couple tablespoons of blow? Come on. That's got to be a joke."

"It's a joke, all right. But it's not all that funny."

Hudson stared at his lawyer, lips slightly parted, and Redpath saw the light dying behind his eyes. Over Hudson's shoulder, a guard's face appeared. The guard held his wristwatch up, tapped it, and vanished.

Hudson said, "Some old granddad in here told me what you just said, but I didn't believe him. I figured he was stuffing me."

"Believe it."

Hudson turned to the side and began scrubbing his forehead with the tips of his fingers, sucking air in through his nose to absorb the sting.

"So, Sandy," Hudson said to himself. "And Grace. That book is closed."

Redpath decided to give Moon some space and wandered over for a cup of water he didn't need. It wasn't the worst thing in the world that they were kicking him out so soon. This might be plenty for the first day.

He returned with two cups of water, set one in front of Moon and began sipping his.

"The worst thing I could do, Moon, is offer false hope. So I'm not going to kid you. You're so deep in the shadow of the eight ball right now, you have moss growing on your north side. But I want to tell you this, before we break up."

"Okay." Moon had drifted off again, back to where things didn't matter.

"I think they botched the search of your apartment. Seems they had a valid arrest warrant, but not a proper search warrant. If we had a judge with some backbone, we could get the drugs thrown out. But we're stuck with this new guy Norcross, and that could make things a whole lot harder."

"Why's that?"

"He's only been on the bench a couple of years, he never tried a serious criminal case as a lawyer, and the easiest thing for him to do is whatever the government wants."

There was a sharp tap on the window.

"I have to go now. You need to have a little chat with Sandy. I'll call this Attorney Goodman and see if he'll let me talk to his boy Rivera. Goodman's another piece of work."

Hudson nodded, saying nothing.

Before they left, they took turns tossing their crumpled cups at the wastebasket. Hudson let Redpath go first. This time, they both missed.

"Bad sign," Redpath said, and he got a grim smile from his client.

13

"If I had a dinosaur," Frank crooned as he tapped away at his computer, "just think where we could go. All the way to Grandma's house, to play her pee-ann-oh!"

The days were getting shorter. Although it was barely six p.m., it was almost dark outside the federal courthouse. With the trial in *United States v. Hudson* looming, Frank and Eva were working late to keep the session current on all its other cases.

"Frank, for the love of mercy," Eva yelled from her office. "Sing anything else."

Frank stopped typing and stared at the wall for a few seconds. Then his voice resumed, "Baby beluga in the deep blue sea—you swim so wild and you swim so free. Sky above and the sea below, just a little white whale on the . . ."

"Oi!"

Eva stood in Frank's doorway yanking fat bunches of dark curly hair out from both sides of her head.

"I love you, Frank, I love you deeply, but you've been lobotomized by fatherhood."

Frank smiled up at her and took a bite of walnut brownie. "Did I tell you what Brady did last night?" he asked. "He was sitting on the potty . . ."

"I can't take this." Eva disappeared with a groan. Her door closed sharply, and Frank put down the pastry and hauled himself up with a worried expression. He really liked Eva. They'd taken to looking after each other. She bugged him to get exercise and had even begun lending him her hand weights so he could do workouts at his desk. He gave her advice on how to handle Norcross when he was in one of his increasingly frequent stressed-out moods. She and her partner, Bonnie, babysat Brady, whose vocabulary now included *schlep* and *schmuck,* which he delivered with impressive amounts of spit.

"I was kidding," he said in a wheedling tone. "Come on!" Eva's office door opened a crack, and her eyes peeped up at him through her oversize glasses.

"No more Raffi songs during work hours," she said.

"Okay, deal," he said. "And I'll even do the horrible pressure valve memo."

Eva opened the door all the way and pointed at a stack of papers. "I already did it, last weekend. His Honor's instinct was right. The patent applicant deliberately concealed prior art. Plaintiff's toast." The file in this intellectual property litigation comprised four three-foot piles; they'd both been dreading it.

"God, Eva, you must have been here all weekend! The airplane engine industry will never be the same. C is for champ."

"Yeah," she said. "Bonnie was at nonstop meetings." She sighed and looked with dejection at her desk. "Do you have a minute? I've got a big problem." Standing on tiptoes, she put her arm around his shoulder. "I need to talk to my bud."

Frank's eyes widened. "Let's use the big guy's office!"

"Are we allowed in there?"

"Who cares?" Frank hurried back to his desk. "I'll bring the goodies."

They crossed the library and Lucille's reception area, crept down the short hallway past the supply room where the printer and photocopier were murmuring, and peered into Norcross's inner sanctum, with its book-lined walls and leather furniture.

Eva hesitated in the doorway. "This place gives me the heebie-jeebies. It always looks like he just got it back from the cleaners." As they entered, she asked, "Did you see this week's computer quote?"

"Uh-huh."

"Who was Jeremiah?

"Hebrew prophet."

Eva gave Frank a look. "I know that. But why was Jeremiah a bullfrog?"

"It's a line from a Boomer song about feeling happy. You can take the couch." He set his plate of brownies on the coffee table and eased into a wingback. "Watch out for crumbs."

A city bus five floors down noisily shifted gears and whined around the Jersey barriers that now ringed the courthouse and blocked half the street. Security had been stepped up since the Hudson indictment. Some routine pretrial rulings had not been received well by the blogs, and Frank had gotten a scrawled note that read: "FYI: Hudson flies; Norcross dies. Start looking for a new job." The judge said it was like several he'd already turned over to the marshals. Just the usual kooks.

Eva sat on the edge of the sofa and set her elbows on her knees, propping her chin on her hands. She glanced quickly at Frank and looked away, going all fidgety. She took off her glasses and rubbed her eyes.

"What is it?" Frank asked. "You're making me nervous."

"Bonnie thinks I should quit."

"Quit what?" Frank swallowed the last bite of his brownie.

"Quit this job."

"Get out!" Frank jerked himself up, sweeping the plate off the coffee table with his foot and launching a volley of brownies across the burgundy carpeting.

Eva spoke quickly, not looking at Frank.

"She thinks it's wrong to work in a court that might order someone's execution. She doesn't believe in capital punishment. Yesterday . . ." Eva nodded down toward the plaza and sighed. "Yesterday she was out there with the protesters."

"I hope she had a helmet on. One of them got hit by a rock."

Eva's chin bobbed, counting the phrases out as though she had memorized them. "She thinks I should make a statement. She thinks if people who work in the courts refuse to have anything to do with the death penalty, our actions might help bring an end to it."

"God," Frank repeated, shaking his head. "God, God, God."

"I can't sleep. I feel like crap," Eva said miserably.

"I can't do this by myself!" Frank shoved himself out of the chair and began duck walking around the coffee table picking the brownies up off the carpet. "I know I'm being a selfish so-and-so, but I can't do this all alone."

"You'd manage." Eva was staring straight ahead, blinking.

"No, I wouldn't!" Two more brownies slid off the plate; he retrieved them, making a little pyramid, and eased the assemblage back onto the table. "Let's face it, I'd be totally screwed without you." He returned to his chair and leaned back, shaking his head. "They couldn't even get a fourth-rate fill-in for you this time of year. But that's not the point."

"What is the point?"

"The point is, we're a *team*," he pleaded. "We're like Bert and Ernie."

"Oh, fuck off," Eva laughed and pulled out a handkerchief. "You're such a fucking idiot." She blew her nose with an emphatic honk. For a small woman, she sounded like a very large moose.

"Can I make a suggestion?" Frank asked.

"Please." Eva sniffed loudly.

"Don't make a decision now, okay? We don't know what's going to happen. Hudson will probably end up pleading to life, right? If he goes to trial, the jury could acquit him, or convict him and not impose the DP. Who knows?"

Eva didn't speak, so he continued.

"I don't know what I think about the death penalty. If some creep killed Brady or Trish, I doubt I'd think it was punishment enough to tell him he was a very naughty boy and had to go sit in the corner for the rest of his life." He stared into the distance, nodding distractedly. "I doubt I'd kill him, but I sure wouldn't mind if somebody else did."

Eva looked over at him, and he went on, picking at his mustache.

"Tell the truth, I try not to think about it," he said. "I know I can't quit—we need the paycheck—and I know I really, really hope you won't. I don't know what else to say."

They fell into silence; Eva's tense body was perched on the edge of the couch, and Frank lay crumpled back in his chair. The night deepened outside, and the stoplight at the intersection below carried farther through the more intense blackness, reflecting pale green, then yellow, then red off the ceiling.

"Which one's the short one?" Eva asked finally.

"That would be Ernie."

"Okay, Bert," she said. "We'll just wait and see what happens. We'll keep our fingers crossed." She hesitated. "Do Bert and Ernie even have fingers?"

14

Bill Redpath stood in the plaza and gazed up at the glass atrium of the Springfield federal courthouse. Another damned smoke-free building. He sighed and stepped in through the revolving door.

The point of the extra trip out from Boston was to see if this Gomez woman might possibly be interested in a plea, something that might allow Hudson, long after Redpath himself was in his grave, to draw breath for a few years as a free man. It wasn't even clear that his client would plead to anything. But it never hurt to ask; if nothing else, it would give him an idea of how confident the prosecutor was in her case. And if she offered him something halfway decent, he could present it to Moon and find out exactly how sure his client was that he was not guilty.

Redpath had no illusion that after decades as a defense lawyer he could instinctively tell when a client was or wasn't telling him the truth. Moon said he was innocent, but he said it in a way that sounded as though he didn't even believe it himself. Something funny was going on with his client. Presenting a possible plea deal to him would force the issue.

The conference with the prosecutor did not get off to a good start. Lydia Gomez-Larsen, wearing black slacks and a blinding coral blouse, looked up from her computer and nodded as Redpath came in. Her fingernails matched her blouse, and she had on her game face.

"So," she said. "What's up?"

"Mind if I have a cigarette?" Redpath asked, reaching into an inner pocket.

"Yes," Gomez-Larsen replied. "I'd mind very much." As Redpath gave her a wounded look, she added more neutrally, "It's not allowed anywhere in the building." She pulled a fresh yellow pad toward her and jotted the date at the top. "Besides, this doesn't have to take long. What did you want to talk about?"

They eyed each other. She knew what he wanted to talk about.

It was the old poker game. Redpath saw a sharp (maybe too sharp), smartly dressed woman who was doing a good job of looking like she was holding all the aces. Gomez-Larsen saw a rumpled, craggy man with an impressively deep voice and shoes that needed polishing, who was trying to give the impression of being a little off-balance, but whose eyes were probing her for soft spots.

"I was wondering what you all were really looking for, for Clarence Hudson," Redpath said, looking over at her with lowered eyebrows. "The government's case has some obvious weaknesses."

"Really. What weaknesses?"

"Well, I assume you know your driver, that Rivera kid, has some problems."

"None I'm that concerned about." She jotted something quickly on her pad, then tossed the pencil on her blotter. "He's too young to have much of a record yet." She produced a short smile. "Just another poor soul who wants to do the right thing."

"What he wants to do is whatever his uncle Carlos tells him."

"That's not going to be very easy now, is it?"

Redpath lifted his large head with a look of concern. "What's that supposed to mean?"

"You didn't know about Carlos?" She jotted something else on her yellow pad. "They found him last week floating in San Juan Harbor. At least they think it's him. The body is not real pretty." She tapped the bridge of her nose. "Ten gauge, probably sawed off, in the face, from close up. Didn't leave much to identify, especially after a couple weeks in the water." Redpath sat, expressionless. "So Carlos has no worries, and Pepe has nobody to protect."

"He's still lying," Redpath said. "He started out with one crackpot story. Now I take it he's cooked up a new one that probably makes even less sense."

"I think he's finally managed to bring himself around to telling the whole truth. If I didn't, I wouldn't put him on the stand." She reached down into a drawer and pulled out a bundle of stapled pages. "Actually, before I forget, I've got a revised FBI-302 for you here. Pepe's been filling in a few more details about his dear departed uncle Carlos and your guy."

She handed the new witness statement over to Redpath, who took it, folded it lengthwise, and slipped it into his jacket pocket.

"So he's getting his memory refreshed," Redpath said. "I hear you and Captain Daley have been seeing a lot of him. And paying a few visits to his mom, too."

"He's a kid, Bill. He's scared. It's natural."

"Flags wouldn't hire an ex-Flag, especially an African-American, to do their shooting. You know that as well as I do. Hudson's had no involvement with La Bandera since he got out of prison the last time."

Gomez-Larsen broke in, "That's what you say. We know different."

"Even your cop," Redpath continued, "the Italian guy, says the shooter was Hispanic."

"An easy mistake. And he said *possibly* Hispanic." She leaned forward, tapping with the point of her pencil on the desktop. "Let's be honest. It's only my opinion, but I think I could win this case blindfolded, wearing nothing but Mickey Mouse ears and my Maidenform bra, right? I have the driver, I have a reliable third party who saw Clarence running down the alley right afterward with the gun under his sweatshirt, and I have all kinds of folks who will say Clarence had a grudge against Delgado. Plus, I have two people who saw Carlos give your guy drugs two days before the drive-by, and I have Clarence magically in possession of large amounts of pot, coke, and cash right after the shooting. Now maybe I'm wrong, and of course you never know what Norcross might do to us, but I really doubt Clarence's trial will be all that tough." She paused, continuing the *tappity-tap* with her pencil on the desktop. "So. I have a lot of stuff on my plate today, Bill. What do you want from me?"

Redpath's fingers involuntarily strayed toward the inside pocket of his old hound's-tooth jacket, where his treasure of Luckies lay nestled. The whiff of tobacco from the jacket's lining was making him ravenous for a cigarette. He pulled his hand away, brushed his lapel self-consciously, and sighed.

"Oh, go ahead and smoke if you have to," Gomez-Larsen said. "Breathe a little my way. I only quit two years ago. Hold on."

She dug down into a lower drawer and pulled out a smoke eater. Perched on her desk and plugged in, the little chrome machine made a swishing noise like a discreet vacuum cleaner. Redpath immediately lit up and inhaled deliciously.

"Thanks," he grunted in his deep voice. "Now maybe I can think." He cleared his throat and pulled on the sagging flesh under his chin. "I've been trying to come up with a way to ask this question that doesn't seem condescending, or . . ."

A troubled look passed over the folds of Redpath's face.

"Doesn't it seem funny to you that, in five decades, Moon Hudson is the first person in this state to deserve the death penalty, and he also just happens to be a black man who supposedly killed a white woman?"

"He didn't just kill a white woman."

"Okay," Redpath said. "How many black and Puerto Rican males have died in drive-bys in Holyoke and Springfield in the last few years? And how many of their killers faced the death penalty? Do you have an ashtray? I'm worried about your carpet."

"What are you saying?" She pointed at herself. "I'm part of some racist conspiracy?" She pulled out a lavender seashell and pushed it toward Redpath.

"No, but I'm wondering, coming from your background . . ."

"Oh, I see, as a Latina, I'm supposed to feel bad for Clarence?"

"No, I mean, in your own life, as a Puerto Rican woman, you must have experienced . . ."

"Look, I don't want to keep interrupting, but can I tell you a story, Bill? First of all, I'm not Puerto Rican, I'm Cuban, okay? It's a small point, but I do get sick of having to tell people fifty times a day. My parents came over on the boat. After they got here, they had me and my brother, so let's get that out of the way."

Redpath nodded and scratched the back of his neck. "Sorry."

"No problem. I grew up in Miami, okay? And I had a lot of boyfriends, mostly nice Cuban guys. Some not so nice. Now, back in those days, my mother is happy because she thinks I'm not going to have any trouble finding a handsome Cuban husband with major bucks. Then I come home from law school with this Norwegian geek from Iowa named Greg. That's a name with a real hot Latin swing, huh? Greg." She looked down at her desk. "My dad won't talk to me, and my mother starts making noises like she's giving birth to a Volkswagen. My brother, Carlos—same name as the Flag floater—wants to take my fiancé for a walk in mom's herb garden and snip off his kazoo with the hedge trimmer. You think I'm kidding? This was not a joke."

"Just enjoying the kazoo bit," Redpath said, pulling back a smile.

"Then Greg and I graduate and move to Springfield for Greg's residency, where his Anglo friends patronize me because they think it's cute that somebody named Dr. Larsen has this enchilada for a wife. That's okay, but most of the Spanish speakers in town are Puerto Rican, and a lot of them think I am a stuck-up Cuban bitch who talks funny. Now I have this death penalty case and, it's terrific, the whole community has come together at last: They *all* hate me. Greg's Doctors Without Borders friends don't invite us to dinner anymore. Our anti-death-penalty governor is probably never going to touch me for a judicial appointment, which, to be honest, I was sort of hoping for. Plus, my own kids think I'm Dracula. So don't talk to me about wondering how I can do this, okay? I'm starting to wonder myself. Can I bum a cigarette? Even the nuns are giving me looks."

Redpath held out his crumpled pack of Lucky Strikes and shook one toward her. Gomez-Larsen's selection had a twenty-degree bend in the middle, which she pulled straight.

"I need a light."

Redpath handed over his Bic, and they puffed away for some time, while the smoke eater filled the room with its swishing sound. Muffled footsteps came down the hall, paused in front of Gomez-Larsen's door, then returned in the original direction. Redpath stared at the carpet looking like an old bloodhound. Gomez-Larsen tapped her cigarette on the lavender seashell and waited.

"You told me a story," he said finally in his cavernous voice. "Now I'll tell you one." Ash fell on his knees, and he brushed it off. "When I was seventeen, I joined the marines and got sent to Korea. My parents wanted me to go to college, but I wanted an adventure, and I was afraid if I didn't sign up right away I'd miss the war."

Gomez-Larsen turned her head to pick a piece of tobacco out of her mouth.

Redpath continued. "Things were a mess. By the time I arrived, the North Koreans had grabbed practically the whole peninsula. I got to see a lot of fighting."

He inhaled deeply and blew out a stream of pale gray smoke. "I had my adventure but good. Now I can't stand listening to people talk about how we have to kill this person or execute that person, people who've never seen anyone die, or even seen a body outside a funeral home. People who will be sitting home watching TV, eating Cheese Nips when we put the needle in." He mashed out his cigarette in the shell. After one more puff, Gomez-Larsen did the same.

"So here we are," he said.

"Right, and what are you saying we should do?"

"I don't know." He couldn't tell her his real fear, the one that tightened the hole in his stomach: that he could blow this case somehow, stupidly, and end up killing Moon. That with some bad decision he'd lose the chance to save his client and bring one of those dead Chinese boys back to life.

"What do you think of the death penalty, Lydia?"

"None of your business."

The sun had moved around and was now shining right into the prosecutor's window, darkening her silhouette and making her features dim. The voice that emerged from this obscurity was so steady and careful it sounded depersonalized, as if it were coming from a telephone answering machine.

"Bill, listen to me. I'm going to take a chance here. Maybe, just maybe, we can settle it in this room, right now, just you and me. Let's put us both out of our miseries and plead this loser. I'll ask Washington for permission to drop the capital designation. Assuming they agree, Hudson gets life without parole. It's over. We go home."

Redpath just looked at her for a moment. "I don't know if I can do that," he said, in the same almost automatic cadence.

"Why not?"

"The problem is," Redpath said with a sigh, "I'm worried Moon isn't guilty. I don't see how I can plead him to a life sentence without parole for a crime he never committed."

"Oh, give me strength!" Gomez-Larsen exploded. "You *know* he's guilty!" The low orange sunlight was making the air in the small office too warm. She rose and turned her back on Redpath to drop the blinds. The result when she faced him again with the sun blocked out was to return her clothing and body to full Technicolor. Her bright coral blouse, her animated face, and her long, black hair jumped into the foreground like a billboard. She stretched out her arms and looked up at the ceiling.

"That is such *crap!*" she exclaimed. Then more softly, almost to herself, as she turned to sit down again: "*Such* crap. You know he's guilty, and you're pretending! This is a waste of my time."

"Well, it's my worst nightmare." Redpath ran his hands through his hair gloomily. "If I have an innocent client. It's impossible to . . ."

"Oh, pass me a hankie!" Gomez-Larsen had picked up her pencil again and was tapping it furiously. She leaned toward Redpath; her intensity seemed to increase the size of her eyes and mouth.

"Is that what he's told you? And you supposedly believe him? I don't know who's playing games now, you or him. I took a chance; I made the offer. I didn't make you beg. I didn't even make you bring it up. But your guy killed two people, okay? And now he wants to play around here, or maybe you do. If you want to run the string out, fine, but don't expect me to hold back when we get to the penalty phase. To be honest, I'm not all that hot to send him off to his doctor's appointment in Indiana—I've got reasons of my own I don't need to get into, plus I doubt my children would ever speak to me again—but this is my job, Bill. This is my job, and if you and Hudson force me to do it, well, then I'll be like the sneaker ad. I'll just do it."

There was another long silence, with only the sound of the smoke eater and Gomez-Larsen's breathing.

"But just remember, Bill, when the time comes." She looked at him steadily. "It didn't have to be this way. I offered. You passed."

"If he were guilty, Lydia, don't you think I *would* plead him? That's my . . ."

"I don't know if I would plead, if I were him. Frankly? I bet he feels bad about Ginger, but he tells himself that was just bad luck—his, not hers. From his point of view, even if he gets convicted, he probably thinks it's less than fifty-fifty that a western Massachusetts jury will give him the death penalty. So it's life in prison anyway. And if he's got a ten percent chance of beating the charges completely—maybe twenty percent with a really good lawyer like you—why plead and tear up his lottery ticket? He's hoping to walk. Kill two people in cold blood and live to brag about it. Great guy. That's his plan."

"Please, no compliments," Redpath said in his gravelly voice, looking more disconsolate than ever. "This is hard enough."

"So why are we talking?" Gomez-Larsen tossed the pencil on her desk and leaned back. "You want me to recommend proba- tion? This was a long way for you to come to dump a load of confetti on me, Bill." She looked at her watch, which hung from her wrist on a delicate gold bracelet. "I had a meeting ten minutes ago. We better wrap up."

Redpath ignored the last comment and spoke deliberately. "The best I could do, given the situation, is to try to convince him to plead to three hundred and sixty months, or even a longer sentence if it held out any possibility that he might be released eventually, some day before he dies. I honestly don't know if he would take it, but that's what I was thinking. I'd like him to have some hope, that's all."

"No chance, and no way," Gomez-Larsen said. She straight- ened up and ran her fingers back through her hair without looking at him. "Now we both know where we are. Call me if you want to talk seriously."

A few minutes later, Redpath was descending the elevator. It was okay, he told himself; he'd had to try it, and now he knew a little more about the person he'd be facing. Anyway, he wasn't sure Moon Hudson would ever plead to anything. The poor bastard really might be innocent. Horrible.

Meanwhile, upstairs in her office, Gomez-Larsen was reading an email from Washington with explicit instructions: no deal for Hudson under any circumstances. The prosecution was part of the attorney general's initiative to bring the death penalty to states without their own capital punishment laws. It was a definite trial.

15

The man's voice was deliberately casual, but persistent.

"So, you kill that white bitch, or what?"

Four black men sat at the end of a long Formica table in the nearly deserted C-pod dining hall. Powerful fluorescent lights blazed off the linoleum floor and cream-colored cinder-block walls, creating an atmosphere of unnatural brightness and sterility. The smell of overcooked broccoli hung in the damp air. In the corner, a fat white man wearing a do-rag was collecting trays on a pushcart. Occasional shouts and clangs from the unseen kitchen staff reverberated in the distance.

"You talking to me?"

"You know I'm talking to you, nigger. And I'm asking you whether you killed that white bitch like everybody says." The questioner, an undersize man with reddish black hair, folded his arms, changing to a tone of faint mockery. "Or, you going to tell me and my friends here you're just another sad-ass, innocent black boy?"

Moon Hudson set down his plastic knife and fork and rested his fingers on the edge of the table. He pulled his legs up underneath him and let his eyes drift briefly from the wiry little interrogator to the two men seated to his right. One was six seven at least, with a close-cropped gray-and-white beard and glasses. His name was Deshawn Santana, but he was known in the jail as Satan. The other was shorter, but broader across the shoulders with heavy upper arms; he clearly spent a lot of time in the weight room. Moon hadn't been around long enough to learn what he was called.

Both these strangers were finishing their meals, eating slowly and keeping their eyes on their trays. The bigger one wiped his mouth on a paper napkin and looked from Moon to the questioner without changing expression. The broad-shouldered prisoner stabbed a piece of pineapple out of his fruit cup and chewed ruminatively, staring down as though he were deaf.

The room had gotten very quiet. Moon slid his chair back a few inches and glanced up into the reflection in the windows facing him. No one coming up from behind. No corrections officers around. The white guy pushed his squeaking steel cart off into the shadowy kitchen, whistling "Danny Boy" under his breath.

Moon finished his mouthful of boiled chicken and swallowed.

"Why don't you tell me what you want me to say, peckerbutt? That way you'll be sure to like my answer."

The small man leaned forward, putting his face so close Moon could see a strand of spit between his lips.

"Listen up," he began, "I asked you a civil question, and I'd . . ."

But as the man spoke, Moon leaned back and kicked out hard

with his foot under the table against the front of his questioner's chair, so that it shot backward and dumped the man over with a clatter onto the floor. Before he could scramble up, Moon leaped behind his own chair, ready for the other two men.

Neither one moved. As the little man crouched to come at Moon, the bearded prisoner said in an authoritative voice, without looking up from his tray: "Squash it, Pinball. This ain't the time, nor the place, for that."

Pinball, still on his hands and knees, glared at the big man indignantly.

"Goddammit, Satan, you told me to ask him, and I asked him. You said you wanted to know."

"Yeah, and now I know. I know enough." Satan pushed his tray away and gestured at Moon. "Sit down, man."

"Motherfucker punking me down like that." Pinball grumbled, picking up his chair up. Moon noticed that the broad shoulders of the third man were jiggling; short spurts of high-pitched laughter were hissing out of him.

He spoke in spasms. "Man, they got your name right. I haven't," he paused and his shoulders shook. "I haven't seen anybody move so fast since Dingo sat on the hotplate." He put down his fork and wiped a napkin over his face. "Satan and me're going to take you to the North Carolina State Fair. Sign you up for human cannonball."

"Sit down, man," Satan said again, looking up at Moon and pointing at his chair.

But Moon still hesitated, hands at his sides, ready.

The prisoner with the big arms stopped laughing and said to Moon, in a different tone. "Gentleman asked you to sit down, friend. Didn't you hear?"

A tense few seconds ticked by; a dishwasher somewhere

kicked on. Finally, Moon pulled his chair back, placing it a long step away from the table, reversed it and sat straddling the seat, setting his elbows on the back and letting his wrists hang loosely. Pinball started to rejoin the group, but Satan waved him away.

" 'Bout time for volleyball, isn't it?"

Pinball scowled but turned without saying a word, tossing a dark glance over his shoulder at Moon as he disappeared down the hallway leading to the rec yard. The fat white man drifted back in, as though he'd been waiting for the coast to clear.

"Mind if I bus them dishes, Rashid?"

"Go ahead," the broad-shouldered man said, pushing the trays down to the end of the table. "Do your job."

The white prisoner piled the dishes onto one tray and moved off.

Moon's chest rose and fell quickly.

"I'm not looking for any trouble." He held his palms up to the two men, fingers splayed, and spoke in a low voice. "But that's three times today some fool tried to tap me. Once more, and we'll have problems. I got nothing to lose here."

"Hold up," Satan said. "First things first." He reached into his pocket and took out two packs of Pall Malls, shoved them across to Moon.

Moon started to push them back. "Never use those things, man."

"Hey, I know you don't, dammit." His enormous hand slapped down on Moon's, and he looked at him steadily. "But when we get done here, you take these—you hear me?—and you give them to Pinball. He's not big, but you don't want that boy over your shoulder, I can tell you that. You make peace."

"You're a jumpy, jumpy man," Rashid added. "Take them."

After a pause, Moon nodded. "I'm still learning." He put the cigarettes into the pocket of his jumpsuit.

"Don't make enemies, that's your first rule," Rashid said. He interlaced his fingers and cracked his knuckles. "Make friends."

Satan was studying Moon. The big man's weathered face, round wire rims, and beard gave him the look of a scholar. He slowly scratched the stubble under his chin.

"Friend of ours asked around," Satan said slowly. "Told us that woman caught a stray. You weren't fixing to shoot her at all."

"Yeah, that's what they're saying," Moon said.

"Right."

A corner of the rec yard was visible through the steamy windows, just a wedge of cracked asphalt and one end of a tattered net. The ball escaped and came bouncing across the thin grass toward the windows—leaping like a playful, living thing. An inmate trotted over, snatched it up, and tossed it back into a chorus of shouts.

"You ain't a rat, anyway," Rashid said. "Not getting any breaks for giving somebody up. That could've been a big problem for you."

"They don't want to talk to me." Moon shrugged. "Think they already know everything."

Outside, there was a hard smack and then a burst of cheers and laughter.

"Be interested some time to know what really happened that morning," Satan said. He looked at the floor and then up at Moon. "Realize, now, I'm not asking—but I'd be interested to know. Some time. Information is as good as cash money around here."

Rashid nodded. "Good way to make friends, too."

Moon turned toward the window and shook his head.

"Shit," he said, more to himself than to the two men.

For the first time since Pinball spoke to him, he let his arms and shoulders relax. Maybe this was not his time.

"Only three people in this wide world know for sure what happened and what didn't happen that morning." He dropped his chin and looked at Satan.

"Maybe three. Dude named Carlos knew, but they say somebody put him down already. Maybe there's just me and this sad, little shitball Pepe, and nobody's going to believe him whatever he says. Maybe he's lying. Maybe he's telling the truth. Maybe he won't be around too long."

"We know all about Pepe," Rashid said. "And we know where he is."

Moon took his hands off the back of the chair and folded his arms. He ran a tongue over his upper lip. "Supposing I tell you I did it."

"Okay," Satan said slowly.

"Half the people around here be thinking I'm stuffing them anyway. Trying to make myself look like some big, bad Bandera hit man. Other half would be getting on the phone, trying to cut a deal. Testify, put me away, and get their asses out of here."

"It's possible," Rashid said. "That's not us, but it surely happens."

"Or, suppose I tell you I didn't do it?"

"Okay," Satan repeated.

"Then y'all be thinking I am definitely a stuff man, which is what I think right now every time I hear some brother wearing people's ears off about how he's innocent. Out loud, I say, 'Right on, brother. Amen!' but inside I'm thinking, *Uh-huh, right.*"

"We're all innocent in here," Satan said. He was looking down, mopping up the remains of his chicken gravy with a wedge of toast.

Moon continued, "The way I see it, it doesn't matter what I say, or even what really happened anymore. Me doing it or somebody else doing it is not going to bring that girl back, and it won't get me out of here. Truth is, I could have done it. I might have done it. I did other things just as bad."

"That's what counts," Rashid said. "So the preacher says."

"I'm here because of me. I set my own self up from jump. Right now, I got nothing else to say to anybody."

The ventilation unit in the ceiling burst into operation with a buzzing rattle and a gush of warm air, as though underlining Moon's defiance.

"You got a wife, we hear," Satan said. "And a little baby girl."

"Light in the darkness, friend," Rashid said.

"Light's fading," Moon said.

"I hear you," Rashid said.

"You can see in her eyes how scared she is. She's bound to pack. You know what I'm saying?"

"They always do," Rashid said. "They have to."

"I've told her so many lies, her head's upside down and backward." Moon tapped the table lightly with his hand. "One way or another, I'm dead and gone unless my lawyer can kick up some problem with my trial. That's all that matters now. Except for that, I'm just, like, dust in the wind."

A female correctional officer, Hispanic, with a large round face and a brown uniform that fit tightly across her ample breasts and belly, stepped briskly into the room.

"Time to be shoving off, fellas. We're bringing in the D-boys."

"Sure thing, Miss Rosa," Rashid said, getting up slowly. "We're all done."

"All set for now," Satan said to Moon. He rose, wincing slightly. "Don't forget about Pinball. Don't wait even five minutes."

Moon nodded, started to say something, nodded again, and walked off.

Satan and Rashid trailed behind down the hallway, their heads together.

"Make sure folks know," Satan said. "Leave that boy alone for now."

"Breeze's cousin's in here, looking for him." Rashid shook his head with a worried expression.

"I know."

"You think he aced that white girl?" Rashid asked.

"Who knows?" Satan scratched his bristly cheek. "But if he didn't, he might as well have."

16

The newspapers covering Moon Hudson's trial made much of the fact that an ancestor of the murdered nurse Ginger Daley O'Connor was an Irish immigrant by the name of Dominic Daley, who was tried in 1806, along with his friend James Halligan, for a killing that occurred no more than fifteen minutes' drive from the site of the Walnut Street Massacre. The fairness of the Daley/Halligan prosecution and the justice of its outcome have been matters of debate in western Massachusetts for more than two hundred years.

Dominic Daley's fate began to unwind on Saturday, November 9, 1805, when John Bliss of Wilbraham, a suburb today of Springfield, Massachusetts, noticed a strange horse in his pasture. Its saddlebags contained a supply of bread and cheese, as well as letters confirming that the horse was owned by one Marcus Lyon of Woodstock, Connecticut. Puzzled at the sudden appearance of the animal, Bliss tied it up to await the return of its owner.

By the morning of Sunday, November 10, no one had appeared to claim the horse, and residents of the area, fearing that something had happened to Lyon, began a search. At about eight in the evening, Bliss and a party of his neighbors saw something submerged in the shallows of the Chicopee River. Upon further examination, the group discovered it to be the body of a man about six feet tall, pinned face-down by a large rock. On the bank of the river nearby, the searchers also found a broken pistol covered with blood, as well as torn shrubbery suggesting that the corpse had been dragged from the adjacent Post Turnpike into the river. The search party hauled the body out of the stream and brought it to the stage house of Ara Calkins where it proved to be that of the horse's owner, Marcus Lyon.

In recounting the incident, The Hampshire Gazette described Lyon, who was twenty-three and unmarried, as "a young man of peculiar respectability." He had been journeying from Cazenovia, New York, where he was employed as a farm worker, back to his home in Woodstock, Connecticut. He had last been seen riding a handsome horse on November 9 on the Post Turnpike passing through Wilbraham.

The murder of Lyon threw the community into turmoil. On November 17, 1805, the Sunday after the discovery of the young man's body, Pastor Ezra Witter delivered a sermon in Wilbraham, in which he asked: "And hath it come to this! Have things gotten to such a pass, in this infant country, that it is dangerous for a man of decent appearance and equipage, to travel on the highway in midday, through fear of being murdered and robbed for his money?" Ominously, he suggested that "we are doubtless justified in saying that a great portion of the crimes abovementioned . . . are committed by foreigners." As a result of the influx of immigrants, he said, "we have ripened, apace, in all the arts of vice and depravity."

Everyone hearing Pastor Witter's sermon would have known what *he intended with the reference to "foreigners." He meant Catholics. Despite sharp doctrinal differences, the dominant Protestant sects of New England in 1805 were united on one thing: a deep abhorrence of Catholicism. The spiritual leader of the roughly 1,200 Catholics living in New England at this time, Father Jean-Louis Lefebvre de Cheverus of Boston, noted that "the Catholic Church in New England is the object of execration, detested utterly, the name of a priest held in horror."*

As recently as 1801, Justice Theophilus Bradbury of the Massachusetts Supreme Judicial Court, joined by Justice Samuel Sewall, had penned an opinion that expressed the icy magnanimity of the prevailing mood: "Catholics are only tolerated here, and so long as their ministers behave well, we shall not disturb them. But let them expect no more than that."

The Massachusetts Attorney General, James Sullivan—himself the son of a Catholic and bitterly outspoken against his father's faith—had brought charges against Father de Cheverus for the crime of performing an illegal marriage, that is, a Catholic marriage, between two Catholic parishioners. Although the indictment was eventually thrown out, Father de Cheverus had been jailed for a time, and Justice Bradbury, who had presided at the unsuccessful trial, publicly expressed his disappointment at losing the opportunity to consign a priest to the pillory.

Within hours of the discovery of Marcus Lyon's corpse, a Jury of Inquest convened in Northampton, the county's shire town at the time, to determine the cause of death and the possible perpetrators. At the inquest, the coroner stated that he'd found a deep indentation over the body's left eye, the back of the head "smashed to a pulp," and a ball fired from a small pistol lodged in Lyon's ribs.

By far the most important witness at the inquest was a thirteen-year-old boy named Laertes Fuller, who lived a short distance from where the body was discovered. He testified that while picking apples he'd seen two strange men "in sailor garb" leading a horse in the area where the body was found, heading in the direction of Bliss's pasture. One of the men rode off, while the other lingered behind, leaning on a stone wall and eyeing the boy, but saying nothing. After about fifteen minutes, Fuller said, the first man returned without the horse, and the two strangers departed on foot in a westward direction toward New York on the Post Turnpike.

Based on this information, Major General Ebenezer Matoon, the sheriff of Hampshire County at that time, immediately organized a posse to locate and apprehend the two suspects. His Excellency Caleb Strong, the governor of Massachusetts and a Northampton resident, issued a proclamation, noting that "a horrid MURDER was committed on one Marcus Lyon, who was there traveling on the highway and it is presumed that divers valuable articles were then and there feloniously taken from the said Lyon." On behalf of the Commonwealth of Massachusetts, he offered "a reward of Five Hundred Dollars"—a considerable sum at the time—to anyone who apprehended and confined the responsible party or parties "until him or they be convicted of the said murder."

The posse organized to apprehend the murderers set out immediately, following the Post Turnpike toward New York, in the direction that Laertes Fuller had told them the two strangers in sailor suits had taken. On November 12, one of the posse's members, Josiah Bardwell, encountered two men who appeared to be the suspects at Coscob Landing, fifty miles west of New Haven, near the present-day city of Rye, New York. Dominic Daley and James Halligan were waiting at a tavern, on the main Boston-to-New York Post Turnpike, about to board a packet boat to take them down to New York.

Daley was in the barroom shaving, when Bardwell approached and told him that he held a warrant for his arrest on a charge of murder. Neither Daley nor Halligan was wearing nautical clothing, and both men immediately protested their innocence. They admitted that they had passed through Wilbraham on the Post Turnpike, but they insisted that they were merely en route from Boston to New York, where Daley expected to collect a sum of money owed him, and Halligan intended to meet up with a cousin. Despite these denials, the posse immediately clapped the men in chains and returned with them to Springfield.

Dominic Daley was thirty-four years old at the time and had been living in South Boston with his mother; his wife, Ann; and his son, Edward, since his immigration from Ireland in 1803. Halligan, who had been in Massachusetts only six months, was twenty-seven, unmarried and without connections in the country. Both men were Catholics and suspected on that account. No contemporary description of the Irishmen's physical appearance is available, beyond the detail that the faces of both men were pockmarked, evidence that each had survived the smallpox.

Authorities swiftly conveyed Laertes Fuller from Wilbraham to Springfield to confirm whether Daley and Halligan were the suspicious men he'd seen near where Lyon's body had been found. When brought before a hastily assembled lineup, the boy picked out Dominic Daley as the one who'd stood near the fence staring at him. He failed to identify Halligan, however, despite the fact that Halligan and Daley were the only men in the lineup in irons. Even with this omission, Fuller's testimony satisfied the officials that they had the killers. Daley and Halligan were transported to Northampton and locked up in the Hampshire County Jail pending trial before the Massachusetts Supreme Judicial Court that spring. From the date of their incarceration in November 1805, until April 22, 1806, two days prior to the commencement of their trial, the prisoners were held virtually incommunicado, having no contact with any outsider except the specially appointed prosecutor, John Hooker, one of the two attorneys representing the Commonwealth.

Contemporary records make it clear that even their internment did not entirely reassure the local people. Nearly two months after the apprehension of Daley and Halligan, on January 7, 1806, the editor of the Hampshire Federalist *wrote that "the panic excited by this event goes to an extreme. It magnifies every assault to a manslaughter—every sudden or accidental death to a bloody assassination."*

The upcoming trial of the two Irishmen acquired added significance in the turbulence of the prevailing political climate. During the most recent election, Governor Caleb Strong, a Federalist, had narrowly defeated Attorney General James Sullivan, the Democratic-Republican candidate and outspoken anti-Catholic. A rematch between the two was slated for the fall of 1806. Recognizing the importance of the case to his own prospects, Sullivan parried Governor's Strong's offer of a reward of five hundred dollars for the capture of Lyon's murderers with his own promise to come to Northampton and personally assist Hooker in prosecuting Daley and Halligan, to ensure that justice would be done.

PART TWO

17

Not long after their dinner at the Pratts, David did manage to call Claire and invite her to an art exhibit at the Smith College museum. His memory of his undergraduate survey course in art history was dim, but it seemed like a respectable Saturday outing, and he was delighted when Claire agreed. He'd be getting a break from reading pretrial memoranda for a few hours, with all day Sunday still in reserve to prepare for the coming week.

During their drive to the museum, David took the opportunity to impress Claire with more of his amazing Donald Duck imitations. She tested him by making him pronounce tough words like "licorice" and "xylophone," and, best of all, "sexual intercourse," which provoked such an explosion of laughter from both of them that the car careened over the rumble strip.

The afternoon, as far as David could tell, was a reasonable success, with lots of easy conversation and eye contact as they wandered through the museum's galleries. Twice, their hands brushed and, once, magically, she leaned against him as they examined some nineteenth-century landscapes. They managed, in dribs and drabs, to exchange summaries of their former marriages—Faye's death and Claire's awful divorce—without getting into too much gory detail.

As they were heading back to the car afterward, Claire asked casually, "So how are things shaping up with your big trial?"

This topic was off-limits, but David did not want to come across too stuffy, so he muttered, "Fine" and quickly added, "Can I show you something fun that hardly anyone knows about?"

"Fun? Sure."

They drove west from the museum for a few minutes and parked on the broad shoulder of a sloping grade. On the far side of the road was a knoll, steep enough that David used it as an excuse to take Claire's hand and draw her up to the top.

A crude monument stood on the crest, its base awkwardly constructed of mortared stone, square slabs, and pink granite bricks. The bricks formed a boundary around a rectangle of dirt in which an upright rock, five feet tall and vaguely penile in shape, had been fixed.

"It's a monument to a couple of Irishmen," David said. "See the plaque?"

Claire dropped David's hand and bent to read. The brass plate contained the names Dominic Daley and James Halligan. Underneath, it read: "Executed 1806" and, beneath that, "Exonerated 1984."

"This is your idea of something fun?" she asked. "Remind me to invite you to my next funeral."

"You're right, you're right. Not fun exactly, but interesting. Two men were hanged on this very spot two hundred years ago." He raised his hands and looked up at the sky. "They were probably innocent, and eventually Dukakis pardoned them." He gazed around the area. "Sheriff Garvey's crew keeps the lawn mowed, but not that many people come here." He looked up at the sky again. "I sort of feel them looking down on me these days."

Claire paced slowly around the stone. On the far side, she called out, "No offense, David, but this is about the most ungainly effort at a memorial I've ever seen."

"Well, their trial was a mess, too," David said, mostly to himself. The visit wasn't working out very well. What had he been thinking? He spoke more loudly. "The judges were the real villains. Shows what happens when you don't do your job."

"Ah," Claire said, rounding the monument. "I see. A cautionary tale on a forbidden topic."

The return trip was quiet at first, but things eventually picked up with an extended gab about Claire's classes and David's impossible brother, Raymond, and a more than friendly kiss when David dropped Claire off at her house in the center of Amherst.

David half hoped Claire would invite him inside, but she did not. As he watched her walking back, he took a deep breath, buzzed down his window, and asked, in a studiously offhand manner, if he might fix her dinner sometime.

Claire turned and made an uncertain noise that sounded like, "Hmmmrrr." The monument thing had definitely been a mistake.

"I don't know," she said. "You're pretty weird."

"I'm only talking about dinner."

"Uh-huh." Her tone was skeptical. "That's all you have in mind?"

"And I can introduce you to my family."

"Your family?"

"Marlene has heard so much about you."

"Ah." She sucked on her lip for a few seconds. "Let me think about it." But when David called a few days later, she agreed.

"I'll try not to burn the swordfish," he said, floating his idea for an easy entrée.

"Delicious." She paused for a beat. "And how Freudian."

When the day of the dinner arrived, David canceled court and took the afternoon off to shop and vacuum the house, feeling jumpier and more happy than he had been in a long while. Twice, while bustling around the kitchen, he stepped on Marlene's tail. Everything was ready an hour and a half ahead of time.

Claire arrived holding a bottle of wine in each hand, and the bottles butted against his spine as she gave him a hug. Her cheek was cool from the wintry air. They immediately began talking with such eagerness that they were most the way through Claire's first bottle before David even got dinner on the table. Everything they talked about, it seemed to him, was fascinating or funny or both. She praised his dog, his appetizers, and his home, a Victorian farmhouse well back in the trees. He complimented her earrings, her choice of plays for her Shakespeare class, and her theories of grading. She gobbled up his painfully simple meal with many a kind word. Then, as they were finishing dessert, she nodded over at David's plate, where a sliver of strawberry-rhubarb pie from a local farm stand lingered.

"You're not going to finish that? It's very good."

David looked down at the pie as though he'd been caught with a trout out of season. After a moment's hesitation, he swallowed and said, "Faye . . . You know?"

Claire nodded.

"Well, she never ate dessert. At least, she *said* she never ate dessert. Instead, she always had some of mine. It got to be a thing with us." He gestured at his plate, then looked up at Claire. "So I . . . I guess I'm still saving her a bite." He looked down. "Tell the truth, I hadn't noticed I still do that. I usually just chuck a napkin over the plate, and off I go."

"Oh dear," Claire said, blinking. "Wow."

David cleared his throat. "Anyway. Why don't we take our coffee back to the fire?"

At the sound of David's chair being pushed out, Marlene scrambled up from under the table. She walked stiffly toward the front hallway and looked over her shoulder wagging her tail. She approved of the new friend.

Claire hadn't budged. "David, I don't know what to say. That is so sweet."

"Well," he said, standing up, "why don't you go ahead. I'll get us some more coffee."

He slipped off to the kitchen, while Claire and Marlene made their way to the living room. An enormous moment was rolling toward him, and it was hoisting David's innards like a swelling wave. The unplanned comment about Faye had knocked him off balance. As he arranged the creamer and the coffee cups on a tray, he reminded himself that the critical question, really, was where Claire would now choose to sit.

The Norcross living room featured a generous, espresso-brown suede sofa, positioned in front of the fireplace, with plenty of room for two people to sit at a civilized distance and at the same time lots of space for maneuvering, if there was to be any maneuvering. A leather recliner and a wingback chair with a hassock were also arranged around the hearth. In front of this grouping, the fire still glowed and occasionally popped; behind it, dark windows looked out into the night. Shadowy branches groping in the wind, and silver patches of snow back in the woods, were dimly visible beyond the glass. Winter had come early; it was a wet, gusty night.

The delay over the coffee had been designed by David to let Claire lead the way and make her choice about where to sit first. If he went ahead of her, he would either have to take one of the chairs, a pathetic move, or plop down on the sofa and look as though he had expectations. He did have expectations, sort of, but he did not want to look as though he did.

The tray rattled as David stepped through the hallway into the living room and discovered Claire seated on the sofa, with her shoes off and her bare feet up on the coffee table. The ocean swelled up beneath him, lifting his spirits, and his stomach, so forcefully that he felt for a moment lightheaded.

He took a deep breath and joined Claire on the couch, maintaining a distance that was respectful but within range. Claire picked up on the topic of nicknames, which they'd been discussing before the crisis with the pie.

"So Raymond called you Stick . . ."

"Right, because I was so tall and skinny. And your grandfather called you Kukla after the prehistoric TV show . . ."

"Because I was so round-faced and cute." Claire draped her arm on the back of the couch; her fingers were only inches from his neck. "Maybe Ray called you Stick because he was afraid you'd beat him." She stared into the fire thoughtfully, then turned to him. "Have you had any other nicknames, other than Your Honor?"

"My favorite, during my two years in Africa, was Twiga—that's what my Kenyan students called me. It's the Swahili word for giraffe."

"Twee-gah," Claire mouthed. "How sweet. I assume that was because you were even more of a beanpole back in your Peace Corps days?"

"Partly that. I think it was also because I was so dumb and innocent. You know how unworldly giraffes always look in *National
Geographic*, staring around as though they just came out of a coma."
David did his giraffe imitation, gazing from side to side blankly,
and felt a surge of happiness when Claire tipped her head back in a
wide smile. "That was me," he said. "Probably still is."

He lifted his arm onto the back of the couch and placed his
hand on Claire's, trying to make it a companionable gesture rather
than a come-on. She responded by interlacing their fingers. The
fire was warm, and they were getting through their coffee. It
would not be long.

"Twiga." Claire looked at David and shook her head. "Man!
Those Kenyan ladies must have thought you were God on ice
cream. I wonder how they managed to keep their hands off you."

David was remembering that they hadn't, actually, when Marlene, who had been lying in front of the fire, got up and began
staring in their direction, as though something was offending her.
The fur on her neck stood out, and she barked sharply, twice, and
began growling.

"Marlene, good grief! What's the problem?"

"I thought she liked me," Claire said, swinging her feet down
off the coffee table.

"She does. She definitely does. Something cuckoo's going on."

Marlene, David suddenly realized, was not looking directly at
them, but past them at the windows facing onto the darkened
yard at the side of the house. As he turned, he saw something
moving out there, a stealthy figure among the shadows. Claire
saw it, too, and grabbed his arm. A person, holding something,
was creeping toward the window.

"Claire," David said. "Walk to the kitchen, please, and phone
911. Not too fast. I'm going to try to . . ."

But as Claire began slipping to one side, a witchlike face appeared in the middle pane of the window, pressed so close its nose was mashed against the glass. David leaped up from the couch with a short cry. Curled fingers cupped themselves around the eyes to peer inside. The creature's long white hair was whipping around in the wind like scraps of tattered laundry.

Claire, catching sight of the specter, jerked upright. "Shit!"

It was crazy Mrs. Abercrombie, the Ginger Snap lady from the Pepe Rivera plea.

"Son of a beehive!" David exclaimed. "Oh brother, this is just way, *way* too much."

Mrs. Abercombie tapped the glass and called out "Helloooo!" She drew out the second syllable in a kind of cackling yodel.

Claire took a deep breath and shook her head in relief. "Son of a beehive? David, do you ever ..."

But he was already hurrying toward the front door. "Oh man. Oh *man*!" he said. "I can't believe this. She's figured out where I live and everything."

Marlene followed, woofing more softly now that she had everyone's attention.

David threw open the door.

"Mrs. Abercrombie!" he bellowed in the wet night air. "Mrs. Abercrombie! Darn it all! What are you doing here? For cryeye! This is too much."

Claire and Mrs. Abercrombie arrived on opposite sides of the threshold more or less simultaneously. The old woman's hair and clothing were spattered with freezing rain, but she had preserved her indomitable smile.

"I, I just wanted to clarify one thing," she began. "About my case." She pointed to a wad of soggy papers in her hand.

"Mrs. Abercrombie, this is really not a good time."

"I know, Your Honor, it's never the right time, but this . . ."

"David," Claire said. "Ask her inside. It's wet out there."

He hesitated, then said, "You're right, sorry. Of course. Mrs. Abercrombie. Come inside. Just for a minute."

The old woman stepped back to the edge of the darkness. "Oh, I wouldn't want to disturb you. There was only this one point . . ."

"Mrs. Abercrombie, come inside, please." When she still held back, he added sharply, "Ma'am, if you don't come inside immediately, I'm going to call the marshals and have them arrest you. They'll lock you up in a nice dry cell in Ludlow, while I invent some felonies to charge you with. Please come in. Really. Professor Lindemann is getting all wet."

"Oh dear, and you have guests." She tottered forward, glancing up at Claire. The door closed, muffling the wind. Marlene's nails clicked on the hardwood as she sniffed Mrs. Abercrombie's boots and the hem of her faded coat.

"I didn't want to be a bother. It's just a quick question. What a nice dog."

"You practically scared us to death, Mrs. Abercrombie." David glanced over at Claire, whose hand was only half concealing a smile. "Or me anyway. Marlene, knock it off."

He looked at Mrs. Abercrombie, sighed heavily, and wiped his hands over his face.

"You're always so nice to me, Your Honor," Mrs. Abercrombie began. "Nicer than the other judges." She hesitated and looked down at her wet papers. "It's just about . . ."

"Please don't talk about your cases, Mrs. Abercrombie," David interrupted. "Don't say one blessed word about them, okay? Professor Lindemann, would you mind taking Mrs. Abercrombie into the living room while I go find her a towel?" He stalked off in the direction of the downstairs bathroom muttering to himself.

"It's just about the page limit," Mrs. Abercrombie whispered to Claire as they moved into the living room and stood in front of the fire.

"Excuse me?" Claire was pulling back the screen and stirring up the embers with a poker. Mrs. Abercrombie began speaking in a fervent monotone, as much to herself as to Claire.

"The Local Rules for the United States District Court for the District of Massachusetts say that legal memoranda can be no more than twenty pages long." She waved the papers. "Well, I've been working and working on my memo, and it's already more than forty pages long, and there's a lot more to say. A lot more. And since I live just around the corner, I thought I'd look in and see if he was busy, because I'm completely stuck." She squinted down at the fire and shook her head. "I don't know what to do. I just can't say everything I need to say in twenty pages. I've tried and tried for days now, and I can't. They're going to throw my case out again, I just know it."

She was starting to tremble.

"Do you have any children, Mrs. Abercrombie?" Claire asked. "Anyone who could help you?" The fire crackled as she dropped a chunk of split birch on the grate; it began to blaze lustily.

"It's not fair."

"Any brothers or sisters in the area?"

Mrs. Abercrombie looked up at Claire as though she had suddenly noticed her. She ran her fingers through her wet hair.

"I had a son, Charles, who went in the service. He gave me a tiny silver pistol, before he left, for protection." She held up her hands to show the gun's size. "He was a good boy, but he was killed at Khe Sanh." She reached down to pat Marlene absently. "I can't even find the pistol now. It must be somewhere. What a nice fire you've made."

"Here we are!" David bustled into the room with an enormous, butter-colored beach towel. Mrs. Abercrombie obediently took it and began dabbing at her face and throat. The buoyancy seemed to have drained out of her. A wet curtain of white hair fell over one eye.

"Now, did you come in a car?" David asked.

"I left it at the bottom of the drive." She tried to push her hair back over her ears. "I thought I'd just take a quick peek and see if you were busy. I guess I goofed up again."

"Well," David said, raising his voice toward its courtroom level, "you're right that it was a mistake to come here, ma'am, and I'm sure you won't do it again. But we all make mistakes. Done with the towel? Thanks. What we need to do now is get you home."

David retrieved the towel, shook it at the fire, and began folding it into squares. He looked down at Mrs. Abercrombie and said more softly, "You won't come here anymore, will you? Professor Lindemann is pretty cool under fire, but I darn near fainted."

"No, Your Honor, I won't be bothering you like this again," Mrs. Abercrombie said. "But it's just a very technical point, and as long as I'm here, could I ask you? It's just a little thing but very important. I won't sleep."

"Nope," David said brusquely. "All set now?" He held up a finger as she started to protest. "No, now, Mrs. Abercrombie, dog-gone it. If you say one word about your cases, I'm going to recuse myself. You know what that means, right? I'll have to send every-thing to Judge Sowerby in Worcester." He tucked the towel under his arm and added, more quietly, "And won't she be thrilled."

"It's pretty minor, David," Claire began.

"Nope, nope, nope," David repeated, giving Claire a warning look. "Let's get you back to your car before things get any worse."

David maintained an obliteratingly hearty patter as he hustled Mrs. Abercrombie through the kitchen, out to the garage, and into his car. Calling from the driver's side to Claire that he'd just be a minute, he backed briskly out and down the long driveway.

The sight of Mrs. Abercrombie's aged Volvo at the bottom of the hill provided the judge with a new topic, and all through her transfer he rhapsodized about what sturdy cars the Swedes built, how Volvos ran forever, and what wonderful qualities they exhibited on ice and snow. Through all this Mrs. Abercrombie, blinking into the darkness, said not a word. She maintained this silence as she got out, restarted her car, and finally pulled away.

The Volvo's taillights receded nearly to pinpoints before swinging onto a side road.

"Gone," David said aloud. He rested his forehead on the steering wheel. Claire, he was sure, would have her coat on, ready to wrap up the evening, by the time he got back up the hill.

18

"So this new girl we hired is sucking my dick, you know?" Alex Torricelli's brother, Tony, was regaling Alex in a half whisper. "It's only fair, right? I gave her a job, so she gives me one." He squirmed with pleasure at his joke.

It was the final stage of a dinner at the Torricellis, and the two brothers' wives were out of the room. From Alex's point of view, the evening had been a washout. Janice scarcely looked at him, and when she did, her eyes were as hard as lug nuts.

Still, here they were. Tony had been bugging him for some sort of family get-together, and, after Janice and the baby came back, Tony's wife, Cindy, started calling Janice and finally succeeded in setting up the dinner. It was not fun, but nothing too bad had happened, so far.

"Come on, Tony," Alex muttered. "I need these stories like a hole in the head right now. Besides, I don't know how you can be intimate with all these girls and still . . ."

Tony stopped tittering and broke in. "I'm not intimate with them," he said indignantly. "I have sex with them."

Janice entered the dining room at this moment carrying the silver coffee service and their nice cups. Tony's wife, Cindy, followed with the treasure Alex had been looking forward to all day—one of Janice's special-occasion nutmeg cakes. Its aroma filled the house reminding Alex of happier days.

Janice looked over at Tony as she and Cindy approached the table. Alex could see Janice read on Tony's blank face the obvious fact that he had been entertaining Alex with some dirty story. She turned and gave her husband a freezing stare.

She thinks we were talking about the meter maid, Alex thought despairingly. *Or about her.*

"What? What?" Tony was mugging, barely able to repress his grin. It was Tony's favorite brand of sadism to want women to know that he had been naughty and to be helpless to do anything about it. Girls, he'd decided, liked this.

Janice set the tray down with a clatter.

"Excuse me," she said in a voice that sounded like glass cracking and walked out of the room. Her footsteps receded into the silence, and there was the sound of the bathroom door opening and closing—not slamming, Alex thought thankfully, but not closing softly, either.

He looked over at Tony, shook his head, and murmured, "What an asshole."

"What? What? What'd I do now?" Tony looked up at his wife with an expression of earnest inquiry, radiating blamelessness.

"Janice is funny sometimes," Cindy said, carefully setting the cake platter on the edge of the table and pushing it toward the center. "Look at this beautiful cake. It smells delicious." She smiled wanly at Alex. "Want me to slice?"

She had a broad, pleasant face that always looked tired, and she was about two years away from losing her waist completely. Early in their marriage, before the boys arrived—when she still had her curves—Alex could recall times when she had tried standing up to Tony, but he had crushed her so thoroughly, and publicly, that now she mostly moved around him like a zombie, going along, vacant-eyed, with whatever he did or said.

When Janice returned from the toilet, Tony started straight in on the subject he'd obviously been wanting to raise all night: the Hudson trial and Alex's testimony. By moving to a new topic like this, and speaking a little loudly as he did, he was showing loopy Janice that he forgave her for leaving a bruise on the very nice evening they'd all been having.

As she sat down—looking at no one—Tony took a quick sip of coffee and said, "So I got to tell you, Allie, you're missing a big opportunity with this Hudson thing. I was telling Cindy here."

"What opportunity is that?" Alex asked, keeping his voice neutral.

"Well, I know a lot of the Holyoke cops, and from what they tell me you could be looking at a promotion this time next year if your memory was better."

"My memory's just fine, Tone."

"And we have some friends in the South End who don't like Hudson, either. Some very important people in the Italian community, if you know what I mean, including a guy who played hockey with Ginger Daley's brother and had the hots for Ginger."

Alex was looking across the table at Janice. He wanted to smooth something over with her, just using his eyes, to let her know he was on her side. But she was giving all her attention to the plate in front of her, taking one joyless bite after another and occasionally glancing past him into the living room. To Alex, it looked as though she were preparing some explosion, something that would reduce him to ashes. He knew Janice's expression when she'd had enough, and she'd definitely had enough. Something bad was coming.

"So?" Alex asked. He was sick of Tony.

"Look, Dumbo," Tony said, shoveling in another large bite of cake. "This cake's outstanding, Jan." He spoke with his mouth full and leaned across the table holding his hands out palm up, as though he were trying to pull something out of Alex.

"If I have to spell this out for you, I will. What you need to do is think back, okay? Even you can do that. Just think back and remember that the guy you saw getting out of the Nissan that morning was Hudson. It's, you know," he gestured at the plate in the center of the table, "it's a piece of cake." A whistling laugh escaped him, and he resumed. "You were only twenty feet away from him, for Christ's sake. You had to have seen him."

"For the hundredth time, Tony, he was wearing a hoodie and he had his back to me. Plus, I was watching the kid behind the wheel."

Janice broke in now, with the leading edge of her anger. "Who he came this close"—she held her thumb and finger an inch apart—"to getting killed catching. Shot by his own supposed buddies."

Tony threw his hands up and leaned back. He stared disgustedly at Alex, taking his time to chew and swallow. "I don't know why I waste my time with you. You hear what I'm saying? You know what I'm telling you? You're not that dumb are you?"

"No, Tony, I'm not that dumb. I hear what you're telling me, loud and clear. You and a few other guys."

"Everybody knows that fucker killed her!" Tony pointed toward the front door at an invisible Moon Hudson. "You could ice the bastard, and do yourself and your family a big favor at the same time. One nod from you would do it, just three little words: 'That's the guy.' Any jury would believe a big dumb puss like yours. I can't believe you could be so stupid with a cookie like this right in your lap." Tony's face went red and the veins in his temples stood out. "Why can't you wise up for once in your life? Jesus!"

Alex put his fork down and gave an exaggerated shrug. "Sorry. That's just me, I guess."

"Jesus, what's the use?" Tony said. "You've been this way your whole fucking life. This is just you to a T." He scraped the last of the cake into his mouth, wiped a dab of frosting off his lower lip, and shook his head again.

Janice, who'd been looking at Tony with her mouth open, now asked, "What's in this for you, Tony?"

"What are you talking about?"

"Uh-uh," she said. "That won't work on me, *paesano*. My parents were both Sicilians, from Sciacca, and I know the smell of a dead fish even when he's using half a bottle of aftershave. What's in it for you, buddy? Eh? Who's putting you up to this? Your cop pals, or your so-called friends from the South End?"

"Cindy, my love," Tony said, smacking his hands on the table and looking over at his wife. "It's late. This has been great, but we have to get the sitter home." He pushed himself up from the table, digging at his teeth with his forefinger, while Cindy looked dutifully around at her feet for her handbag.

Janice stood up and gestured to Tony. For the first time that evening, she smiled.

"Let's have a little talk," she said. "Just you and me. Come in the kitchen for a sec."

"What do you want to talk about?" Tony asked suspiciously. Cindy was wandering into the living room, still in search of her purse. With a hand on her shoulder, Alex was murmuring something in a kind voice. The wind was picking up again and passed with a rattling brush across the roof and over the windows.

Janice lifted her shoulders in an oversize shrug, imitating Alex, and smiled again, nodding at her husband's back. She held up one finger. "*Un minuto,* that's all. I have an idea that might help us both out. In the kitchen." The last three words were delivered in a whisper, as though she didn't want Alex to hear.

It occurred to Tony that somebody in this family might have half a brain, and he let Janice lead the way. His well-practiced eyes took advantage of the opportunity to examine, and imagine fondling, Janice's sweet butt. Did she always move her hips that way?

When she had the door firmly closed behind them in the kitchen, Janice came toward Tony with a look in her eye almost of flirtatiousness and placed her left hand on the lapel of his jacket. She stroked his well-developed right pectoral. Tony's vanity was so boundless that he assumed for a moment that she wanted him to kiss her—she was coming up so close—and he started to bend down with his most urbane smile. She was not a bad-looking woman.

"Look," he started to say, putting his hand on Janice's shoulder. His crotch started to stir lazily. "I'm really sorry if I was out of line back there." His voice resembled something as close to human as he ever got in the presence of a woman.

Janice's movements were swift and precise. Her left hand took a firm hold on Tony's lapel, and her right hand grabbed his testicles, hard. Then she jerked down and twisted. Tony smothered a scream and felt himself starting to black out. He had never realized that anything that happened so fast could hurt so much.

"Jesus, Janice," he gasped. "What the fuck . . ." He tried to get hold of her wrist, but she only twisted harder. His knees were starting to buckle. Something banged off the counter as his free hand groped for balance.

"Have I got your attention now, Tony? Huh? Let go of my wrist or I'll yank them off." She gave another excruciating twist. "Let go of my wrist, Goddammit!"

Sweat was pouring down Tony's face and his eyes were squeezed shut. Only some pride kept him from screaming. He let go of her wrist, and Janice eased her grip. A muffled gasp squeaked out of him. His sister-in-law's furious whisper seemed to come from inside his head.

"I just realized tonight where my problem was, you big prick. I saw it when I walked in just now, right in front of my nose all the time." She twisted again and got a sharp intake of breath from Tony.

"Janice, Christ, you're fucking . . ." He smothered another cry as she bent her knees for leverage and wrenched again.

"You're not a person, Tony, you know that?" Her words were low and enraged now, right in his face, so close he was catching flecks of her spit on his eyelids. "You're nothing but a big cock with a smiley face on it. The only thing you never faked is an orgasm."

"Okay, Christ, just let me . . ." Another squeal of pain squirted out of him.

"And if I ever hear you calling Alex 'Dumbo' again, or anything like that, or shitting on him because he isn't the sneak you are, I'll feed your chickpeas to my cat."

"Okay, okay, Jesus Christ."

She let go and stepped back. Tony was bent over, holding himself and breathing hard. There was a silence long enough for a truck to rumble by in the distance. Then Janice bent down to pick a soup ladle off the floor.

"Good." She stood up. "Now let's go out and say a nice *buona notte* for the lovely evening we've all had. Always such a pleasure to see you two."

Janice reached toward Tony, only intending to pat his cheek, but his half-crippled body dodged sideways, and he grabbed something off the kitchen counter and waved it at her.

"You k-keep away from me, you harpy!"

Janice stepped back and pointed the ladle at him. "I know, Tone, you've got a cheese grater, and you're not afraid to use it." She tilted her head to one side and smiled. "It's like your mama told me: such a sweet boy, but not too bright—and so spoiled."

19

David returned to his house to find good news and bad news. The good news was that Claire had not put on her coat; the bad news was that she had migrated from the sofa to the wingback and put her shoes on. Marlene had her chin on the hassock, and Claire was scratching the top of her head. The fire had died down, and the room was darker.

"Sorry about that," David said. He was standing in the doorway with no idea where to sit. "That's never happened before."

"Really?" Claire looked up at him. "Students do it all the time, usually the night before a big paper is due. Okay, go lie down." She pointed to Marlene's rug, and the dog shuffled sleepily away. It was past her bedtime. "Of course, they don't usually show up at my house, bang on the window, and scare the crap out of me. Most of the time, they just phone at two a.m. Come. Sit."

She patted the hassock.

"Are you talking to me or the dog?" David asked. They both smiled, and he sat as directed, a little breathless at how close they were and how fresh she smelled. Claire took his hand.

"I know why you shooed her away, David," she said quietly. "You can't have people showing up at all hours. That I under-stand."

She looked into the fire and continued. "What I don't under-stand is why you couldn't at least hear what her question was. It was pretty simple, actually, but you wouldn't even listen. You seemed . . ." She hesitated, then turned to look at him. "It seemed a little excessive, frankly. I'm trying to figure you out."

"Was I excessive?" He leaned forward for the poker and began jabbing at the fire. "I didn't mean to be. But she's suing the darn universe, and I have to decide her cases based only on what comes into court—no sympathy, no inside information. She could blurt out something, and to be fair to both sides, I'd have transfer all her pain-in-the-neck cases to some other judge." He poked at the coals. "If I was too hard on her, I'm sorry, but, believe me, I've done things a lot worse."

He got up and pulled another log out of the copper tub at the side of the fireplace.

Claire pressed her lips together to form the word *but*, intend-ing to follow up on her original question. Instead, she swallowed the sound and exhaled through her nose.

"Well, I certainly don't approve of her showing up here." She paused for a few moments while the fire crackled and the wind blew outside. "But it's a hard world you live in. Bright lines and sharp corners."

David was arranging the fire with his back to her, and she turned to examine him closely, as though he were a name she was trying to remember. He sat back down on the hassock, facing the invigorated blaze. Shadows played over his face.

"Fact is," he said, "I'm crummy company these days." He gave a rueful laugh. "I'm screwed down so tight, I feel like my kidneys might squirt out my ears." The poker fell over with a clatter, and he bent to pick it up. "I've got this ugly trial and a tough anniversary coming up."

"Anniversary?"

"Coming up on five years since I lost Faye. Sorry. I'm so boring I get tired of myself."

"You aren't boring."

"Then, someday, not too long from now, I could find myself, like Gerry said, signing an execution order. That's assuming I even get through the trial. A million things could go wrong."

"Really. Like what?"

"You name it." He began swatting at the fire with the poker, sending up sprays of grainy sparks. "The big one at the moment is the jurors." He stared into the flames as though he were examining the problem. "We start selecting them a week from Monday. Among other things, I have to be sure they don't know about Hudson's prior drug convictions, and then somehow keep them from learning about them once we start. It's incredibly prejudicial information, and it's in the papers nearly every day. The whole case would have to be mistried."

"And that would mean . . . ?"

"We'd have to start all over." He turned and resumed beating at the embers.

"David, you're going to set your rug on fire." Claire flicked an orange coal off the rug with her toe.

"Sorry." He shook his head and put the poker in the copper tub. "I shouldn't be talking about any of this."

"You think I'm going to notify the media?"

"I know. It's silly." He looked down at the fire. "Still."

They were silent for a while. The only the sounds were the crackling fire and the dying wind outside.

"So," David said finally, using his winding-up tone to signal the end of the evening.

Marlene got to her feet and approached the wingback, waving her tail.

"What does she want now?" Claire asked with a glance at the dark window.

"Oh, it's time for her bedtime walk down the drive," David said. "It's the last thing we do every night."

"Can I come?"

He looked at Claire with a tired smile.

"Well, it's usually just the two of us." He scratched Marlene under the chin. "What do you say, girl?"

Marlene had no objection, so they got on their coats while she paced back and forth, banging her tail against the door.

Outside, the drizzle had let up, but the air was still wet and swirling. The sodden darkness had a scent of pine and wood smoke. Claire slipped her arm through David's.

"We just go down to the bottom and back." He pointed to where the driveway curved downhill through the pines. "It's dark, but we know the way."

They walked deliberately, as though they were part of a procession through the creaking trees. After a silence, David returned to a topic they'd started discussing over dinner. "What did you mean when you said that white knights can be worse than dragons?"

"Ah," said Claire. "I was wondering if you'd ask me about that." Bending down to pick up a piece of pine branch, she released David's arm. Claire swished the branch back and forth absentmindedly while she chose her words.

"My husband, Kenneth, was a classic white knight. He scooped me up and carried me away from Missouri and brought me east. In a hundred ways, he helped me become the person I am, which was very, very good."

Marlene noticed the stick and began leaping around in front of Claire. Claire understood and flung the branch into the darkness down the drive. Marlene bounded off after it. Even in the end-of-the-evening fatigue and disappointment, David could not help noticing how simple and fluid Claire's movement had been. Professor Lindemann did not throw like a girl.

"He also turned out to be a confirmed and abusive alcoholic, which was very, very bad. Ken could be unbelievably charming when he was sober, and I loved him deliriously, but our life . . ." She stared out into the dark trees. "Our life got ugly fast. He never hit me, but he did other things just as bad."

Marlene returned, panting, and dropped the stick at Claire's feet. Claire picked it up and side-armed it into the shadows. "Actually, that's not true. He did hit me, once. That was enough."

She took David's arm again. "It's crazy, but for half a second I thought that might be him out there in the trees."

They had been walking steadily downhill, out of the light thrown by the lamppost at the edge of the judge's lawn and into the shadows. Behind the overcast, a three-quarter moon was turning the sky a furry gray. Soon they reached a point where they could see neither their feet nor each other and became only voices and touch.

After a bit, David said as simply as he could, "I don't think I'm the Ken type." He pressed Claire's hand. "Not now, Marlene," he said quietly. The dog dropped her stick and trotted into the darkness ahead of them.

"I know," Claire said. "Ken never shared his desserts."

David stepped in front of Claire and ran his fingers over her cheeks into the hair over her ears and around to the back of her neck. "I am definitely a pill, though, sometimes. I know that."

"True."

They kissed. David had intended it to be a tender kiss, a kiss of understanding and reassurance. It started out according to this plan—tentative, unpresumptuous, and sweet. But it was soon obvious that they were starving for each other, utterly famished, and that their release, at last, from the postponements and distractions was practically lifting them off the ground. David found himself, like an undergraduate at the end of a date, fumbling to untie the belt of Claire's London Fog and unbutton its endless buttons to get his hands inside, up her back and onto her breasts, all without removing his mouth from hers. Before long, they were panting like wrestlers.

Suddenly, Claire threw her head back and gave a short laugh. David's face was down along her neck, devouring the skin behind her ear.

"David," she broke into a cackle, "David, for God's sake!" She took a breath to collect herself. "For God's sake, let's go inside."

20

Go.

Judge Norcross tapped the microphone twice and shoved off.

"Welcome! I'm David Norcross, and you're in the United States District Court for the District of Massachusetts." He paused. "Western Division."

He always underlined these last two words. The men and women in the pews, still struggling to get untangled from their parkas and stamp the January slush off their galoshes, might appreciate knowing they were among friends and neighbors, all conscripted from the same four counties of western Massachusetts.

"Usually, I'd start things off by thanking you for coming, but first let's see if we can get everybody a seat."

The jury pool, enlarged with reporters, family members of the victims, sketch artists, and curious onlookers, had overflowed the public gallery and left several people without seats, leaning against the walls. This was not good. The discomfort of these miserable, fidgety standers would press in on him and prod him to rush.

He pointed to the right of the gallery.

"I hate to ask this, but if you folks could scooch down a little bit, I think we might fit one or two more people in there. Just stick your backpack on the floor there, ma'am, if you would. Thank you. That's terrific. Thanks very much."

Tom Dickinson, Norcross's silver-haired court security officer, bustled around in his blazer, touching shoulders and pointing. Two swarthy men, one with a ponytail, who had planted themselves in the front row nearly every time the *Hudson* case was on, looked resentful and shifted minutely.

"Outstanding," Norcross said. "Think of this as an opportunity to make new friends."

Amid the shuffling, one or two grudging smiles rebounded toward the bench.

Smile back, he told himself, *but not too much. Look unconcerned.* Trial judging was a kinetic art, like dance—a matter of posture and presence, aiming to create a certain pattern or atmosphere. A tug on his shoulder made him realize that he was rolling his chair over the hem of his robe again, and he eased back from the bench to free himself.

The seats in the jury box to his right already contained the sixteen potential jurors whose names, churned by the computer, had bobbed randomly to the top of the list. Later this morning, the process of picking out a group of fifty-six neutral, impartial people would start with them. Each side had twenty peremptory challenges, which would leave sixteen—twelve jurors and four alternates—for the final panel. Given all the publicity, it was going to take weeks to find them.

While the people who'd been standing found seats, and the bumps and apologies subsided, Norcross looked over at the jury box to see if today's group included any pretty women. With Claire in his life now, his interest was academic, but, still, lengthy court proceedings were always more pleasant with one or two cute jurors along for the ride. As far as he knew, every judge felt this way, at least every male judge. The present cohort offered possibilities in seats Four and Eleven. Raven-haired Four had an expression of bored impatience, but Eleven was turning her dreamy, symmetrical face up to him, actually making eye contact. Norcross looked away.

"Okay, terrific. Welcome, and thank you all very much for being here. As I said, I'm Judge David Norcross, and you're in my court."

The brush with Eleven tripped the judge's mind toward Claire, and he suppressed a smile. She'd invited him to her house for dinner that Saturday. When he asked if he could bring anything, she told him just to bring a bottle of Wesson oil.

"As you know, we enjoy many privileges as American citizens, but there are responsibilities, too, and jury service is one of them. Our Constitution gives every litigant the right to a trial by jury, and obviously we could not have jury trials without folks like you being willing to come here and make yourselves available to serve."

Norcross let his eyes drop into the well of the courtroom. Lydia Gomez-Larsen looked, as always, perfectly composed. Accompanying her again at the government's table was the Holyoke patrolman—what the heck was his name?—whom Gomez-Larsen had for some reason chosen as case agent over the usual, far smoother FBI investigator. Norcross could see beads of sweat already shining on the man's forehead. William Redpath, the defense counsel, sat at the lefthand table, matching the prosecutor's expression of watchful aplomb. His deeply lined face looked as though it had been carved out of an old tree stump. On Redpath's right, farthest away from the jury box, Clarence "Moon" Hudson occupied the defendant's chair.

Apart from his stiff posture and expressionless face, Hudson looked like someone who'd just walked in off the street. It was important that none of the potential jurors know he was in custody, that he had only a few minutes earlier changed from a jumpsuit into a jacket, open-necked shirt, and gray slacks, or that the courtroom was tied down inside a tight ring of security. Rumors persisted that La Bandera gang associates or friends of the victims might try to start something, and a beefed-up detail of armed deputies and court officers was sprinkled throughout the gallery and the adjoining hallways. A broad-shouldered man with a marine corps haircut sat near the judge's exit door, his arms folded and his eyes shifting side to side watchfully.

Norcross steered into a new area.

"Having said that jury duty is one of the responsibilities of citizenship, let me quickly add that I understand, and all of us here at the court understand, that being in this room right now may be, for some of you, a bit of a pain."

As he examined the jury pool more closely, a familiar sense of frustration began creeping over the judge. Hudson was one of the very few non-whites in the courtroom. Number Nine in the box, the only man with a tie, was plainly African-American, and Eight was possibly Latino, Portuguese, or dark-skinned Italian. Out in the gallery, no more than ten or twelve brown faces dotted the crowd out of nearly a hundred. The Western Division covered mainly suburban and rural areas whose population was slightly more than 10 percent minorities. In that sense, the proportion in the courtroom was about right, but it still was not good. Hudson's very black, very African face was many white Americans' worst nightmare: baleful, alien, menacing.

Norcross recalled how uncomfortable the high cheekbones and slanted eyes of the Kikuyu men had made him feel when he'd first arrived in Kenya as a volunteer. His jitters had quickly disappeared with real human contact, but unless Redpath worked some magic, the trial would give Hudson precious little opportunity to reveal any of his human side to the jurors. Several of them were already darting anxious looks the defendant's way, and the burly man in Seat Five seemed to be sizing Hudson up for a fistfight.

Norcross pushed on. "You've been pulled away from your jobs and your personal lives to play a part in our constitutional process, our living democracy. My staff and I will do everything we can to make sure your time is not wasted."

As he spoke, part of the judge's mind continued rolling along on its private track. Suppose Gomez-Larsen exercised her peremptory challenges to knock off any minority jurors that made it onto the final panel? Would she stoop to that? He jotted, in caps, a single word, *BATSON*, the controlling Supreme Court decision, to remind himself to get Eva or Frank to swat up a memo on the problem.

"So. Let me move quickly to the thing that's probably foremost on your minds: How long is this business going to take? When am I getting out of here?" The judge leaned forward to deliver the whack. "The bad news is that, for reasons I will get to in a moment, jury selection may be lengthy, perhaps as long as three or even four weeks. And you are only our first pool; there are others behind you if we need them to put together the ultimate panel."

At this, many of the occupants of the gallery began to grow mutinous, shaking their heads, murmuring in disbelief, or turning for sympathy to a neighbor. Number Four tossed her dark hair, sighed dramatically, and fixed her mouth in a spoiled pout.

He hurried on. "The good news, however, is that no individual will need to be here longer than one or two days to learn if he or she is going to be a juror. In many cases, we'll be needing you for less than a day."

This helped, but not much. Norcross gathered his robe over his knees, raising his voice slightly and holding up three fingers.

"Now, today, we're going to proceed in three stages. First, we will be distributing questionnaires for all of you to fill out. We've set aside a half hour for this, while I take a recess and you get to work with your pencils. Next, I will be giving the whole group of you some general instructions covering this portion of the process. After that, we're going to be excusing all of you for the day, except these sixteen lucky folks here to my right in the peanut gallery."

Lucky, ha-ha. Not many cheerful looks from the jury box.

"Those of you who are off the hook for today will be coming back tomorrow, later in the week, or next week, in batches of sixteen, for more detailed instructions."

Up to this point the judge's courtroom deputy, Ruby Johnson, had been placidly sitting at her desk below the bench. Her job involved scheduling the judge's cases, making sure everyone was in position before he stepped onto the bench, and handling routine courtroom tasks, such as swearing in witnesses. Ruby's resonant West Indian voice was perfect for the job, employing a tone that was kindly but brooked no nonsense. Now she turned and gave her boss the fish eye: danger. Ruby always managed to do this without making it obvious that the judge needed rescuing, but Norcross knew he was about to flub something. In fact, he might already have.

The numerous reporters—from all the western Massachusetts papers, of course, but also *The Boston Globe*, *The New York Times*, the Associated Press—sat in the front row with their pads and pens, looking like so many vultures ravenous for a gory catastrophe. So far the first death penalty case in Massachusetts in fifty years had been blessedly dull. They were not bad people, these journalists, but he knew if he fouled things up, they'd grind his bones to bake their bread.

"With luck, then, by around eleven o'clock, all but sixteen of you will be on your way. In just a minute, we'll begin distributing the questionnaires, but before we do, I have one or two additional things to tell you."

Think.

Norcross let his eyes drop to Ruby's face again; she was willing him to remember. Then the crackle of connection jumped between their brains; he often forgot this part of the ritual and needed reminding.

Ruby received the judge's minute nod and turned forward without expression. Norcross moved seamlessly on.

"But before we commence actual jury selection, it is part of our process that the defendant be presented formally to those of you who may be making up his jury. We'll take care of that now. Ms. Johnson, if you please."

Ruby rose from her chair. Her voice during this stage was always queenly perfection.

"Clarence Hudson, please stand."

The defendant stiffened and looked at his attorney. Redpath must have failed to mention this phase of the ceremony. The lawyer nodded, and the two men rose together. Norcross saw with a sense of helplessness that Hudson's tight face probably made him appear beyond hope to many of the strangers looking on— just another who-gives-a-damn, street-gang killer, whose picture appeared two or three times a week in every city newspaper.

The whole room was gaping; people were craning their necks and half rising from the benches to stare. The defendant looked down at his hands resting on the counsel table, swallowed, set his jaw, and lifted his eyes to a spot somewhere over the judge's left shoulder, in the area of the large American flag beside the bench.

Ruby's words were soft, but her accent carried easily over the stilled courtroom.

"Clarence Hudson, you are now set to the bar to be tried. These good people who shall be selected are to pass between you and the United States upon your trial. If you object to any of them, you must do so before they are sworn. You may be seated."

21

Lunch recess. Bill Redpath sat on a wooden chair tipped back against the conference room wall, in a shaft of gray winter light from the room's only window. Over his shoulder, a sign in bold red letters shouted ABSOLUTELY NO SMOKING ANYWHERE IN THIS BUILDING!! The court had given counsel an hour to eat, and, desperate for time, Redpath was spending the break with his thermos of black coffee alone in the quiet room.

His right hand held a questionnaire, which he was reading with ferocious intensity. His left hand was squeezed through a four-inch aperture at the bottom of the casement window. This was the widest Redpath had managed to pry the balky mechanism open.

Grimacing from arthritis, the old attorney pulled his hand back into the room and positioned the cigarette he'd been holding outside between his lips. He then flipped the page of the questionnaire, took a drag on the cigarette, and stuck it back out the window. After reading for a few moments, he pulled his arm in, bent to the side, and blew the smoke out through the opening. The arrangement was not working very well—a faint pall was starting to thicken against the ceiling—but, given time constraints, this was his only choice.

Judge Norcross had allowed Redpath and Gomez-Larsen a paltry sixty minutes to eat lunch and read the questionnaires of the sixteen jurors who would be individually questioned this afternoon. Even sticking to coffee, Redpath had far too little time. Any fair-minded judge, any judge who had ever tried a major criminal case himself, would have allowed them to study the questionnaires overnight and come back in the morning. Redpath was furious at being jammed by this judicial greenhorn. A man's life, a possibly innocent man's life, could be lost for this baloney.

Too much pique at a judge's stupidity or meanness, Redpath knew, would only weaken his focus, but he could not help picking at this scab of injury. All the pressure, the judge had told them blandly, was in the cause of "moving the case along" and "not unduly inconveniencing the jurors." From what Redpath could see from his frantically hasty review of almost two hundred pages of questionnaires, precious few of the jurors would be in jeopardy of any real inconvenience anyway, since most of them would probably be excused (as the phrase went) "for cause." In seven of the thirteen questionnaires he'd read so far, including the one filled out by the panel's only black juror, the writer had claimed utter inability to sit for the four to six weeks this trial would take. It was maddening, but, really, who could blame them?

There was a double rap on the door, and the white-haired

court security officer leaned into the room. Redpath released the cigarette to begin its five-floor plunge to the sidewalk and pulled his hand inside, praying there was nothing flammable below.

"Couple of people to see you," the CSO said. He sniffed and looked up at the ceiling. "You aren't smoking, are you?"

"Smoking?"

Redpath innocently ran his left hand through his hair, feeling something like panic. An interruption right now was a disaster. In just a few minutes, he would need to be back in court, and he hadn't even looked at two of the questionnaires. Every single second was precious.

But the anxious, exhausted face of his client's wife was already visible around the CSO's shoulder; she and her older brother, Lucas, were pressing into the room. The officer backed out of the way, angling another suspicious glance upward, and closed the door behind them.

"I'm really sorry to bother you," Sandra said. "I just needed to know, you know, how things were going."

"So far the day hasn't gone too bad," Redpath said. "Can we talk tonight? You're catching me at a tough moment." He glanced at his watch.

"I tried to tell her," Lucas said, sighing and lobbing Redpath an apologetic look.

Both Sandra and Lucas were well dressed. Sandra wore a maroon suit, tastefully set off with a navy-and-gold scarf. She'd lost a shocking amount of weight since Redpath's first meeting with her, and the suit's tailoring flattered her model-slim body. Lucas, in an expensive charcoal suit, regimental tie, and heavy gold cufflinks, looked the picture of the successful corporate lawyer.

"So. Everything's okay?" Sandra's her whole posture begged for some kind of reassurance.

"Sandy," Lucas said quietly, "come on."

"So far, so good." Redpath made a show of looking at his watch again and smiled up at Sandra distractedly.

For the first time, however, Redpath took a good look at Moon's wife, and he could not help but feel sympathy for her. It was as though her pretty, smooth face had been printed on cloth, and someone had grabbed a fistful of it and twisted. One of her eyes seemed lower than the other, and her nose looked enlarged, almost bulbous. As she bent toward Redpath, her lips were parted; they seemed to be holding themselves in readiness to speak but still waiting for instructions from her brain about what words to use. Sandra looked at him intently for a few seconds, and then, as sudden as a sneeze, a sob leaped up from her chest, and she covered her face with both hands.

"I'm sorry," she said through her fingers. "I'm sorry. But . . . to see him sitting there like that." She shuddered, still hiding her eyes, and a tear began working its way down the outside of her hand onto her wrist. "To see him like that. With all those people staring at him. Like some kind of animal."

"Sandy," Lucas whispered. He put his hand on her arm.

"I knew it would be awful, but I didn't know how awful." She was shaking and taking deep breaths.

Redpath dropped the questionnaire onto a pile on the floor and stood up. Bending over his two visitors, he placed his hands on Sandra's shoulders.

"You know what I need you to do?" Redpath asked in his oil drum voice. "You know what Moon needs you to do? He needs you to take care of yourself, Sandy. You need to eat. You need to sleep. Do you hear me?" He squeezed her shoulders.

"Mmm-hmm." Sandra took her hands away from her face, nodding and wiping the tears.

Redpath looked down, shaking her shoulders gently for emphasis. "If he sees you like this, it will make everything ten times harder for him. Do you hear what I'm saying?"

"Okay." She inhaled deeply and swallowed, then nodded again. Her trembling subsided.

"I know it's awful," Redpath said, patting her shoulders. "Believe me, I know exactly how awful it is. But all we can do is not make it worse." He sat down again and picked up the questionnaire. "Now I badly need the next few minutes, all right? We'll talk tonight."

Sandra nodded without saying anything, and Lucas steered her out of the room. By the time the door clicked, Redpath was already lost in Number Twelve's description of the extent of her exposure to pretrial publicity. It took a few seconds for him to realize that Lucas had remained in the room.

"I'd like a moment of your time. Privately, if I might," he said.

"Okay," Redpath said impatiently. "But not now." He paused and softened his tone. "You must know how it is."

Lucas looked steadily at the old lawyer in his rumpled suit and unshined shoes. He looked up at the ceiling and took in the aroma of stale cigarette smoke.

"Fine," he said. "Tonight then."

As he turned to go, there was another knock.

Redpath slapped the questionnaire onto his knee furiously and exploded, "Christ Almighty!" But this time it was the courtroom deputy, Ruby Johnson.

"Showtime! His Highness is coming back in five minutes. I'm rounding everybody up." She crinkled her nose. "Uh-oh! Here's a warning, Bill, free of charge: If Tom Dickinson catches you polluting his conference room . . ."

"Me?"

"He's a fine, kindhearted gentleman, but let's just say I would not provoke him, you know?"

Redpath sighed and began gathering up the questionnaires. Lucas Cummings hurried out of the room and down the hall to catch up with his little sister, who'd managed to get herself into such a world of trouble.

22

Assistant U.S. Attorney Lydia Gomez-Larsen sat in the paneled courtroom at counsel table offering up an expression of well-practiced calm and waiting for the judge to make his entry. The juror questionnaires sat in a neat pile in front of her, arranged in order, one through sixteen. Next to the pile, and exactly parallel to it, lay her yellow pad, with her notes printed out for each juror. In the middle of the pad, at a forty-five degree angle, was her black Sharpie. Like Redpath, she'd skipped lunch and felt a little sick.

What Gomez-Larsen had learned from skimming the questionnaires had not been good at all, and behind her poised façade, an ulcer of anxiety throbbed. A fear that she might tremble kept her elegant fingers folded in her lap.

She could barely remember the last time she had lost a trial, and she really, *really* did not want to lose *United States v. Hudson.* She'd known that Washington's insistence on the capital designation would make her job harder, but she could now see that the situation was worse than she'd imagined. The questionnaires revealed that a great many of the pro-government jurors she normally relied on would be struck from the pool because of their strong views favoring the death penalty. The thought of having, possibly, to face the O'Connors and the Delgados, and explain the defendant's acquittal—the image of Moon Hudson swaggering down the street with his gangbanger friends slapping him on the back—all because of some bullshit out of Washington, was too much. A deep breath dispelled the shakes.

The chair next to her creaked as Alex Torricelli shifted uncomfortably.

"Jesus, I'm suffocating," he muttered. "Can't believe you do this every day." He dabbed at his forehead with a crumpled Dunkin' Donuts napkin.

Alex's chalk-white face was not going to inspire a whole lot of confidence. Maybe it was a mistake putting him up here, shoving him in front of the jury as the everyday hero. She punched him lightly in the shoulder.

"Relax," she said soothingly. "This is fun. By the time we're done, you'll be ready for law school."

Gomez-Larsen knew perfectly well that her case was not airtight. She had a star witness in Ernesto "Pepe" Rivera, the driver Alex had managed to grab immediately after the shooting. But if Pepe failed to impress the jury, her case would be in big trouble, and during preparations so far he was coming across as a sulky little twerp.

She patted Alex's arm. "Everything's going to be fine. All the women on the jury will be swooning for you."

"Swell," Alex whispered. "Exactly what I need." Then he added more urgently, "Where the hell is His Honor? I need to hit the head again."

"All rise!" the court officer called out.

Gomez-Larsen rose smoothly to her feet and watched as Judge Norcross bustled into the courtroom in that odd way he had, bent forward like a stork on ice skates, with his robe wafting out behind him. He was holding a manila folder, an unusual prop. What could that be?

While Tom Dickinson worked through the opening, the judge set the strange folder to one side and poured himself a cup of water. Then the sixteen potential jurors were led into the courtroom. As promised, the other members of the pool had been excused for the day, making their departure with relieved looks. Sleet was forecast for that afternoon, turning to heavy snow as the temperature dropped overnight.

Gomez-Larsen had to admit that, from his perch on the bench, Judge Norcross presented a credible image: tall, moderately good-looking, with just the beginning of gray at the temples— a picture of decency, good humor, and intelligence. In the time she'd been appearing before him, they'd developed a fair working relationship. Still, some judges could be counted on to rescue a floundering prosecutor, especially if they thought the defendant was guilty. Norcross, she knew, would call it straight; she'd sink or swim on her own.

The judge kept his hands folded in front of him and offered up his words slowly.

"All right. Thank you again. We have basically two things left on our plate this afternoon. First, I'll have a few preliminary remarks and questions for you as a group. Second, after we let you return to the assembly lounge, we'll be bringing each of you in, one at a time, for additional questioning from counsel, up to five minutes for each side."

The jurors had been staring up at the bench with cowlike blankness, but at the mention of individual questioning, Gomez-Larsen noted that Three, Six, and Seven twitched noticeably and glanced from side to side. Timid? Perhaps more inclined to defer to authority? She shot a glance at defense counsel to check his reaction, but he was bent over a questionnaire, tracing the text with a large finger.

The judge went on: "As we go through this process, I will not be referring to you by name, but will be using the number our clerk assigned to you, which will help to avoid any unnecessary invasion of your privacy. Along those lines, you may notice that we have sketch artists here in the courtroom. They have been instructed not to draw the faces of potential jurors in any way that might make them identifiable."

Now Six and Seven, two blocklike women in their sixties, looked even more uncomfortable and teetered toward each other for support. Gomez-Larsen noticed that Redpath had begun staring in their direction and was jotting something on his pad. Good or bad?

"I will now give you a brief overview of the charges against Clarence Hudson. Remember, the charges in this case are just that, only charges. They are not evidence in any way against Mr. Hudson. As I have already told you, Clarence Hudson is presumed innocent."

Both the defense and prosecution watched the jurors carefully during this passage, hoping for a clue to measure the impact of the judge's words. With some juries, these phrases would handicap the government badly; with others, they would be treated as lightly as the small print enclosed with a bottle of aspirin. Unfortunately, the faces of this group gave little away. Even moody Number Four, whom Gomez-Larsen had already decided to toss at all costs, was a blank. Were they zoning out?

The description that followed of the RICO charges—the government's burden to prove the existence of a racketeering enterprise and to demonstrate that the murders had been committed to further its activity—was, to Gomez-Larsen's ears, impressively simple and concise, but she could see from the jurors' half-open mouths and crinkled foreheads that they were struggling to follow. By the time Norcross had trudged through this material, and had moved on to the drug charges and the admonition that they refrain from discussing the case or reading anything about it, it was clear that several of the jurors had pulled the plug and were daydreaming. Number Eleven, then Ten, then Three and Four simultaneously, yawned. The room was warm, and the hum of the ventilators, blending with the faint but continuous murmur and rustle of the spectators, was creating an environment ideally suited for a cozy nap. Then, between two of Norcross's paragraphs, Alex punctuated the text with a soft fart, like a squeaking hinge. As the rankness drifted past her, Gomez-Larsen bent forward, rubbed her temples, and cleared her throat.

"Sorry," Alex whispered. Redpath looked over at them, raised his eyebrows, and sniffed loudly. A stifled chuckle rose from one of the two tough-looking guys perennially in the front row of the gallery. Baldie and Ponytail. No one else appeared to notice.

But now their journey was approaching a dangerous curve.

"The trial of this case," Judge Norcross was saying, "may have one stage, or it may have two. We don't know yet." He paused for a sip of water, set the cup at a distance, and pulled the manila folder over to him. Up to this point, he had been speaking extemporaneously, covering standard material. Now, in the deepening quiet of the courtroom, he was preparing to launch into some new segment of his instructions. The portentous folder, and the judge's change in tone, seemed to bring most of the jurors back to the land of the living.

"The first, and perhaps the only, stage of this trial will concentrate on the question of whether the government can prove Mr. Hudson guilty of the actual charges against him, beyond a reasonable doubt. During this stage, the jury may not consider the defendant's possible punishment in any way. If the jury concludes that the government has failed to prove the RICO charges beyond a reasonable doubt, it will return verdicts of not guilty on these charges, and its work will be at an end. Even if the jury finds Mr. Hudson guilty on the drug charges—and I'm not suggesting you should—his sentencing for them will be my responsibility. The jurors will go home, and there will be no second stage."

Thanks a ton, Gomez-Larsen thought. *Show them the wide, inviting shortcut to the exit door.*

"On the other hand," Judge Norcross continued, "the jury may find that the government has proved beyond a reasonable doubt one or both of the RICO murder charges, and return a verdict, or verdicts, of guilty on that charge or those charges." He paused, lifting his voice slightly. "If this occurs, there will be a second stage to this trial."

A stillness was spreading over the gallery, so that by now the loudest sound in the courtroom was the light scrape of the artists' chalk on their sketch pads. It seemed to Gomez-Larsen that the judge was trying to shape his words one by one, suspend them in the air, and let them hang there before the jurors.

"The second stage of the trial," he said, "if there is one, will focus on whether the defendant should be sentenced to death, or to a term of life imprisonment without possibility of parole. As you've heard, ladies and gentlemen, this is a death penalty case. There are two extremely important points I must make to you concerning this fact right now."

Judge Norcross took a moment for another sip of water and turned to the next page of his notes. The sixteen men and women in the jury box were resolving into a kind of tableau. Even restless Number Four was immobile, her right hand covering her mouth. Number Ten, in the middle of the second row, had tilted his chair back against the courtroom wall as though pressed into it. He was resting the tips of his fingers together on his stomach in a gesture suggesting prayer.

"First, the jury is never required to impose a death sentence upon any defendant under any circumstances. Understand this clearly. Whatever the evidence, no juror will ever be placed in a position where he or she *must* vote for death.

"Second, I am also obliged tell you that, if there is a second stage to this trial, and if the jury at the conclusion of this second stage does unanimously find that the death penalty should be imposed upon Mr. Hudson"—and here Judge Norcross nodded at where the defendant sat looking rigidly at his hands—"I will be required as the judge to sentence him to death. I will have no choice in the matter."

The silence had captured the room entirely.

"In other words," Judge Norcross concluded. "I will have no power to change the jury's decision. In the event that this trial moves to a second stage—what we call the penalty stage—the jury of citizens selected in this case, and not me, will bear the ultimate responsibility for deciding whether Clarence Hudson should be executed."

23

Barbara Cummings, Moon's mother-in-law, heard a car door slam and hurried to the parlor window. There, finally, was her prodigal daughter stepping carefully over the flagstones, balancing Grace against her heart with both hands, and wearing that old dear, guarded look on her puss. Always the same, whether they were trying to convince her, as a third grader, to stay with her violin lessons or, as a sixteen-year-old, to sign up for AP physics. Never bad tempered, always unbendable. Now this.

Peeking around the curtain at her youngest, Professor Cummings felt something crowd into her throat and dam up against the back of her eyes. She loved the child to distraction, and yet she had never been able to do a single thing, no matter how much she worried or how hard she tried, to smooth the girl's path.

With jury selection in Moon's trial taking so long, mother and daughter had talked and, after some negotiations, had decided that Sandra should come spend a weekend in Rochester, to get a little break and to drop off Grace. This would free up Sandra to attend the trial every day once it started, something the lawyer said was essential. By good luck, Barbara was on sabbatical, correcting the galleys of a new book, so her time was flexible. She would love taking care of her granddaughter and, with Grace safe, Sandra's father might finally relax a little. Lucas was coming home tonight, too, to spend some time with his sister.

Barbara watched Sandra pause halfway up the walk, sigh, and cast a look of wary exhaustion at the family homestead. Seeing this, Barbara felt tears begin to gather at the corners of her eyes and threaten to trickle down her cheeks. This would definitely not do. Sandy would hate it. Now her nose was running, for heaven's sake. Barbara hurriedly restored herself with a couple of Kleenex. Brave girl! What must it cost her to come here now?

She thought of getting the door but decided to give Sandra time to collect herself. She sniffed and glanced at her face in the hall mirror. Sandra would probably be able to tell she'd been close to crying. She dabbed at her hair. Maybe not.

The knocker emitted two quick claps; Barbara counted three and went to the door.

"Hello, sweetheart."

"Hi, Mom," Sandra said, her voice cracking.

Barbara saw how thin Sandra's face had gotten, and a tear escaped the corner of her eye, too hasty to blink away. Sandra, noticing it, heaved a sob and began weeping.

"Oh," she gasped and stamped her foot. "Dammit! Here."

She handed Grace to her mother and began searching in her purse for a handkerchief. Barbara bent to nuzzle the flannel-smelling bundle, her own silent tears flowing now so quickly that they dribbled onto the baby's eyelashes and woke her up. Sandra gave up her search, and looked at her mother, trying to smile.

"Well, Mom," she said, swallowing, "here I am again."

"Honey."

As they held each other, Grace began to bleat indignantly, wanting air, and some lunch.

The child's cries helped rally the two women, and a half-hour later the arrival of Sandra's dad provided further distraction. Then, just before dinner, Lucas pulled up in his Audi, and the family was all together. Their conversation that evening touched only lightly on the trial and concentrated on happier family chitchat, until later that night when Sandra was up in her old bedroom, getting Grace ready for bed, and Lucas came to talk.

He stood in the entry leaning against the doorframe, arms folded against his chest. A slim, elegant man, she had to admit, a real catch for somebody. Five years ahead of her in school, her brother had been an outstanding pole-vaulter, first in their region and second in the New York State finals, smack on the front page of the sports section. Then he was off to Yale on fifty-seven varieties of scholarships, just as she was starting eighth grade in her mostly white high school and really could have used a big brother around for advice.

"So," he said. "What are you going to do?"

"Well, Lucas, right now I'm going to change this skunky diaper."

Grace was gurgling sleepily as Sandra wiped her bottom. It was not a yucky one. She glanced back over her shoulder at her brother, trying to size him up and get some idea of why he was there. Their parents had headed off to bed an hour ago.

Yes, he looked real fine. His law firm's health club membership was keeping him trim. He was certainly careful about what he ate, trying to avoid their father's chronic high blood pressure. A South Beach type. And she'd noticed a squash racquet on the backseat of his immaculate car.

"Can I come in?" He nodded at the floor. Growing up, they'd had rules about each other's rooms, laid down mostly by Lucas.

"I don't know. Wait a minute." Taped at the corners, Grace's used Luv made a warm, grapefruit-size package.

"Catch." She tossed him the stinky wad, hoping he might dodge out of the way, but he caught the little bundle easily in one hand.

"Nice throw." He held the balled-up diaper at arm's length, grimacing. "What am I supposed to do with it now?"

"Stick it in your briefcase."

"Right."

"Blue bucket in the bathroom. Next to the clothes hamper."

Sandra watched her brother disappear down the hall, a highly intelligent, well-connected man, with his gold wire rims and neatly trimmed mustache. You'd hire him in a minute and figure he was doing you a favor at $550 an hour. She loved him, but, God, what a pain he was.

Having disposed of the diaper, he returned to the doorway. Grace was already falling asleep, pudgy arms gone limp, as Sandra snapped up the back of her jammies. It was after eleven; she'd be hungry again by four.

Sandra waved Lucas toward the far end of the long room, where a window seat and a frayed easy chair with a half squashed footstool made a den she'd once named Homework Hollow.

By the time they got settled—Lucas on the window seat, sitting upright with his legs crossed and his fingers laced over his knee, and Sandra sunk into the chair—Grace was already purring like a distant Evinrude.

"So," Lucas said awkwardly, "how's my baby sister getting on?"

Sandra breathed deeply and closed her eyes. "I'm pretty tired, Lucas."

"Right," Lucas said. "I guess you'll have your jury one of these days. What are you planning to do?"

"What do you mean 'what am I planning to do?'" She kept her eyes closed, staying calm.

"Are you going to be testifying?"

"I guess so. Moon's lawyer thinks I should."

"Redpath." He paused. "I figured." He uncrossed his legs and braced his hands on the window seat. "About Moon being with you when it happened?"

"Correct."

The silence that followed her answer drew itself out so long that Sandra opened her eyes and was annoyed to catch Lucas with that maddening look of brotherly love he got, as though she were a pigeon with a broken wing.

"What?"

"You need to be really careful this time, Sandy." He slumped back against the window frame. "There's a problem here, and I'm trying to think of a way to talk about it without having you tell me to go eat shit or something."

"Just say what you're worried about, Lucas. I promise not to yell." Sandra stretched out her leg and poked her brother's knee with her toe. "You're still my big brother, no matter how trashy you act."

But Lucas drew out the infuriating look, until she glared back at him and made a face. He looked away and pinched his lower lip.

"Okay. Here's how it is. There's this woman, this person I know. A sort of friend, never mind who, at the U.S. Attorney's

Office." He sighed and shook his head. "Anyway. Here's what she says. The whole office is sure you're going to lie, to protect Moon."

"Oh great." Sandra flopped back into the chair. "Big surprise. Should I tell you how much I wish your sort-of-friend at the U.S. Attorney's Office would go to hell? And all her sort-of-friends with her?"

"I'm not saying you're going to lie, Sandy, but that's what they think. And they also think they can prove you're lying, somehow. And if you do lie, Sandy, and they catch you, this person I know says Hogan is definitely planning to come down on you for perjury. They already have an intern doing the research."

"Does that worry you, Lucas, having a perjurer for a sister? A criminal?"

"Right. Fuck you, too."

"Well, then what are you telling me this for? What's your point?"

He stood up abruptly and bent toward her. His wire rims caught the light and gave him, fleetingly, the face of a blank-orbed alien.

"Because I'm not sure you wouldn't lie, Sandy. In fact, I'm pretty sure you would."

"Hush, hush, hush." She gestured toward the crib. "Sit down, please."

But Lucas only leaned back against the wall, facing her with his arms folded. His voice dropped to a whisper but hissed out of him with an even greater intensity.

"I bet you would lie. I might lie myself in your shoes. And if you do lie, and that troglodyte Hogan indicts you for it—which I don't doubt for one minute he will do, Sandy, I know his type, I have to deal with his kind of puffed-up white boy every single day—what's going to happen to that little girl of yours over there?" He flapped his arm toward the crib.

Sandra just looked at him.

"You think Mom and Dad will take care of her while you do two or three years in Danbury? With Dad's heart?" He tapped his chest and looked down at her fiercely. "You want Mom to quit her job? Is that the plan? Because you know that's what she'll do, and you know what she went through to get where she is. Think about it, and ask yourself whether it's worth it, that's all. You're my sister and I love you, Sandy, but do us all a favor this time, will you? For once in your life, just try taking a damn look before you leap."

24

Moon Hudson was sitting at the end of a table in the C-pod rec area trying to read a copy of a memorandum Redpath had sent him. The original was going to their judge, to try to convince him to throw out the pot and coke the Holyoke cops had turned up at his apartment.

It was hard to concentrate. Two strangers had drifted in and were playing Ping-Pong a few feet away, keeping an eye on him in a way he didn't like. Then, and much worse, three more inmates came through the doorway and headed toward him. These men were well known to him—Walnut Street Posse thugs from South Holyoke, all doing short bids for crack. He immediately recognized one of them as a cousin of Breeze, the man he'd killed. Moon set his papers to one side, sat up straighter, and placed his hands on the table. Stay calm.

He shifted his eyes toward the corrections officer up in his pod. He'd get on his radio first, and then it would be over.

"Don't be looking up there, bro," the biggest one of the trio said. "Old Teeters ain't going to get his hands dirty saving your ass." He looked over his shoulder at the two men behind him. "'Sides, we're just talking."

One of the men snickered, showing a gold front tooth. "That's it, man. For now." Breeze's cousin stood at the back. His face, turned down at Moon, was a mask of hatred.

"You ever seen this boy?" The big one slapped a color photo down on the table, a fresh-faced black kid, grinning in his high-school graduation getup, purple-and-gold gown, cap, and mortar. Sweet Breeze, with all his cares behind him.

There was a long silence, and finally Breeze's cousin leaned forward and said, "I think he wants us to think he don't know him." He reached in, picked up the three-by-five and put it in his pocket. "That's my cousin, little Henry. Knucklehead liked to call himself Breeze. I promised his momma I'd look out for him, and I didn't do my job and now he's ... Don't you know him? We all thought you did."

The one with the gold tooth said, "Oh, he knew him. Put Peach and that white nurse down, too. That's three for him. Nigger's bad news."

"At least three," Breeze's cousin said. "Isn't that right, bro? Hey, you awake?"

Moon, holding himself very still, said. "I'm awake."

Moon's half-brother, Monroe, had been gang-raped in prison, then strangled with a coat hanger. He never got to see his twin boys.

The door at the end of the hall banged open, and a large, heavily muscled man strode in. It was Rashid, Satan's lieutenant, whom Moon had met during the fracas with Pinball. Rashid waved up to the corrections officer, smiled, and pointed to where Moon sat with the three men bending over him. Breeze's cousin glanced back at Rashid and spoke quickly, pointing down at Moon. "We pick the time and place, motherfucker. You be done before you see it coming."

"Everybody playin' nice here?" Rashid said, elbowing in and sitting down across from Moon.

"Just talkin'," one of the men muttered.

"Talkin's good." Rashid smiled and looked around. "Everybody enjoys that."

The three men turned with blank faces and stalked off. The two Ping-Pong players put down their paddles and followed without saying a word.

"Hey, man," Rashid called after them. "Who won?"

As they disappeared, Rashid folded his hands and looked down as though he were giving thanks before a meal. After a while he peeped up, looking at Moon without lifting his head or unclasping his hands. He spoke softly. "Seems to me, friend, it's time to choose up." He cleared his throat. "We're the good guys. Those were the bad guys. Giving you a howdy-doody. Next time . . . I don't know." He opened his hands and held them out to Moon. "Satan and me'd sure like to know what happened with Peach and that nurse."

The room had gone silent, just the sound of Moon taking deep breaths through his nose. He pressed his lips together and stared with narrowed eyes into the shadowy hallway where the five men had left. Then he whispered to Rashid, very low. "Never shot fully automatic before." He looked down at the floor. "Fucking gun jumping all over the place. Blew out the back window." He looked up at Rashid, his face full of disgust. "You got the whole story, okay? You got my stones. Now get my back."

25

Alex Torricelli's marriage was still on the rocks. One Friday, after a short, frosty explanation, Janice took the baby and drove off to her parents' house in Billerica again. She had some things to think about, she said. She'd be back Sunday night.

Janice's departure stung, which was probably what she'd intended. Alex's schedule as a patrolman had him working four days on and two days off, and this particular Saturday had rotated around as one of his free weekend days. They could have lined up a sitter and maybe hit a movie. It was depressing as hell to be all alone like this. Tony was bugging him for a boys-only lunch, but Alex was not that desperate yet.

After sleeping late and mooching around the house all morning, Alex decided to kill some time pretending to be a detective. His duties in the uniformed division did not generally include investigative work, but a crisis was brewing, and it looked like somebody had to do something. The trial of Clarence Hudson, according to Lydia, was threatening to bust through the guardrails and over a cliff. She hated the crop of jurors they were getting, and Deadly Delores, it turned out, had screwed up the search warrant paperwork. Norcross might use this as an excuse to keep all the drugs they had found during the search of Hudson's apartment out of the trial. On top of this, although Alex had had no contact with Pepe—other than punching him in the face a few times at their first meeting—the word was the kid had a snootful of attitude, a lousy memory, and a different story for every day of the week. Their case against Hudson had holes big enough for any defense lawyer to drive his powder-blue Lincoln through.

Alex threw a couple of his dad's old extra-wide ties onto the passenger seat of his car and began retracing the route he'd been following the day of the shootings.

He recalled a tiny store, just a hole in the wall fronting on the alley where he saw the passenger jump out of the Nissan that morning. The shop, called Pins and Needles, apparently belonged to a tailor. Its name, and the fact that ties hung in the window, were about all Alex could remember from his glance in that direction on the fatal morning.

On the door of the shop, a handwritten card, yellow and curling at the edges, read OPEN, and Alex stepped out of the freezing winter air into the musty, overheated space. The front of the shop was crowded with clothing hanging along the walls, so close his stocky frame brushed them as he shouldered his way forward. A few feet past the entry, a desk with some slips of paper and one of those old-fashioned calculators with a crank, blocked his progress. In the shadows at the rear a small figure was hunched over a whirring machine, accompanied by the faint sound of opera. The music sounded Italian, which was maybe a good sign.

"Hello?" Alex called out. He couldn't see if the person was male or female.

"Gimme a second," the person said. The tone was mildly irked, certainly not welcoming. Probably male. The vigorous little machine picked up speed, and the soprano began to sing with heartbreaking passion.

After a full minute, the tailor rose and limped slowly toward the desk, sighing and dragging a foot behind him awkwardly.

"Yeah?"

He was a small man, maybe five five, horribly scarred along the left side of his face. The skin covering that cheek, and spreading over his ear and up toward the crown of his head on the one side, was shiny and stretched, and left him half bald. The tautness of the ravaged area pulled the left corner of his mouth into a permanent half grimace.

"Got some fat ties here that need to lose weight," Alex said, tossing his dad's old neckwear onto the counter.

"Oh yeah?" the tailor said. He didn't look at the ties. His left eyelid drooped, but the eye itself darted alertly, sizing Alex up.

Giving me time to get a good look-see, Alex thought. *I know how he feels.*

"Yep," Alex said. "Fat guys shouldn't wear fat ties."

"That right?"

The tailor balanced on his right leg and picked up the ties to look them over.

"You're not so fat," he said. "What happened to your ear? It's sticking out like a mailbox lid."

"Cop shot a piece of it off." Alex rubbed the old wound, flapping the ear forward self-consciously.

The tailor dropped the ties on the desk, braced himself on both hands, and scrutinized Alex closely.

"Aren't you a cop? You walk like a cop."

"Got nailed by one of my own guys."

"An accident, huh?"

"That's their story."

"Lucky they didn't blow your brains out."

The tailor sniffed and ran the back of his hand over the left side of his face. A brief, lopsided smile faded over the undamaged right side of his face.

He pointed at the scarred area.

"Napalm. They told me that was an accident, too." He sniffed again and held up the ties to examine them closely.

"Nice silk. Nice quality material." He looked up at the clock on the wall. "Six bucks for both. Come back in twenty minutes, maybe ten. Or you can wait."

"I'll wait. Your music's nice."

"You like Joe Green?"

"I'm Italian and a big Verdi fan. It's in the blood."

"I'll turn it up."

The little man limped back into the shadows, and Alex took a seat on a chrome-and-plastic chair over by the wall. He reached into his pocket and relocated the mug shot of Moon Hudson. Probably a wild goose chase, but at least he'd get a couple of decent ties out of the expedition and be a few hours closer to having Janice back. The sound of scissors cut through a soaring baritone, some duke probably, and then the machine was whining again.

When Alex was a kid, his parents played *Rigoletto*, *La Traviata*, *Cavalleria Rusticana*, and all the other great Italian operas pretty constantly, and he used to imagine himself loving someone that hard, so strong his passion would fly up out of his chest into the sky. Of course, he never talked about these fantasies, since in the football game of life feelings like these were for the running backs, and maybe the wide receivers, but not for guys like him, who'd always be playing the line, spitting out pieces of sod. These days, though his feelings didn't soar up into the air like a bird, he knew he loved Janice every bit as much as any opera singer had ever loved anyone, and his despair when he thought they'd never get back to where they'd been was as vast as any duke's.

"So," the little tailor said when he returned with the slimmed-down ties. "I figured you for a wop. Me too. Marco Deluviani."

"Alex Torricelli." They shook hands.

Marco nodded at Alex's pocket and rubbed the side of his face with the back of his hand again. It looked itchy.

"Now you can show me your picture."

"Guess you did this before," Alex said, reaching inside.

"Mmm. Four or five times." Marco shifted his weight and grunted uncomfortably. "Couple of Irish potato heads who got cute about how it's not all over until the fat lady sings. Real music lovers. All their taste was in their mouths."

Alex set the picture of Moon Hudson on the counter.

"Would have been last October, in the morning."

"I know. Your buddies came by the day after."

Marco stared down at the photograph for a few seconds, then picked it up and examined it closely, muttering to himself sotto voce. "And the day after, and the day after. Horses' asses."

He sniffed again and shrugged. "I'll tell you what I told them. I saw *the* guy, but I don't know if I saw *this* guy. You know what I mean? I'd like to help a fellow greaseball, but all I can say is I was here at the desk when I heard the car door slam and saw whoever it was trot by the window, holding something against his chest like this. He was black, meaning he had dark skin. Could have been a black guy or maybe a Puerto Rican. Six, seven inches bigger than me, maybe an inch or two taller than you, but real well built, real broad across the shoulders. I never saw his face, since he had his hood up, the way they do."

He tossed the photograph back on the counter. "I gave them all that, and they stopped bugging me."

Alex slipped the picture back into his pocket and tossed the money for the ties onto the counter.

"Well, I thought I'd take a shot. Thanks anyway." He hesitated as he turned to leave. "Sorry about the napalm."

Marco shrugged. "I got a toupee I wear on dates. Other guys weren't so lucky." He gestured in a circle around his contorted lips. "What happened to your mouth, for Christ's sake?"

"Pipe in the kisser."

"Didn't you ever learn to duck?"

"I'm working on it. See you."

"Wait a sec. Wait a sec." The tailor hobbled around to the side of the desk, rubbing the bald half of his head. "I just thought of something I forgot to tell the potato heads. I'll give it to you as a going-away present."

Alex stood in the doorway and watched the undersized tailor, who was swaying from one foot to the other and screwing his mouth around trying to bring his recollection into focus. It must be lonesome in here. How many people dropped by on a Saturday morning?

"The hoodie must have been small for this guy, or his shoulders were too wide across, okay? Because when he held his arms up against his chest like this, you know?" Marco folded his arms against his chest. "It pulled the sleeve up. And right along here," Marco drew his finger down the back of his forearm. "Right along the back of his wrist, he had a nasty scar showing maybe four or five inches, pinkish, like a puckered seam."

26

"So. You were definitely home together that morning?"

Sandra Hudson nodded. "Home together."

Moon asked, "That was a Monday? Or what?"

After a private chat with the sheriff, an old friend, Redpath had managed to get permission for the three of them—Moon, Sandra, and himself—to use the jail's conference room for a hasty weekend meeting, with Redpath's word that there would be no physical contact, no opportunity to pass off contraband or a weapon.

Redpath and Sandra now sat on one side of the scarred pine table; Moon, wearing leg irons this time, sat on the other. The couple reached across, once, just to touch the tips of their fingers, and there was an immediate sharp clack at the window, a heavy key on thick glass from where a correctional officer's flat face bobbed like a chunk of wood in murky water. Despite the awkward arrangement, and the stress on Moon and Sandra, defense counsel had to be sure their stories matched, and this was the only sure way to do it.

"Monday was a holiday. This was the Tuesday after the Columbus Day weekend," Redpath said. His large head shifted back and forth between the couple, observing them closely. "The Holyoke police log has the call on the Delgado shooting from the Cumberland Farms at eight thirty-five a.m. The call from the clinic came in two minutes later, eight thirty-seven. So that's the time we're working with, okay? Tuesday, starting around eight a.m."

His glance rested on Sandy to his right and then moved to Moon, whose legs irons rattled softly. Something funny was going on. Sandra was gaping at Moon, almost pleadingly, but Moon was avoiding her face, frowning and keeping his eyes on the surface of the gouged table, as though he were reading something on it.

Moon's detention was a rotten deal for the couple, and it didn't help Redpath, either. After a while, a locked-up client like Hudson began to exude a sulfurous prison smell as damning as the word *GUILTY* tattooed on his forehead. The jury's nose would nearly always catch the stink.

"I remember it like yesterday," Sandra was saying. "Moon? Remember? It was about breakfast time?"

"Okay, once more," Redpath said. "What were you doing around eight fifteen a.m.?"

"I can't remember for sure. I don't think I worked the holiday," Moon said, still keeping back from Sandra, looking quickly at his lawyer and down. "Didn't leave for work until Tuesday night."

"No, babe, you were sleeping," Sandra cut in. She leaned forward to pat his hand, then pulled back, remembering. "You left home around eight thirty Monday night and worked right through and didn't get home until around seven Tuesday morning with the overtime. You had a bite with me and Grace, like always, and went to bed until at least two or three that afternoon. I remember it like yesterday, I was feeding Grace and . . ."

"I only worked every other holiday," Moon interrupted. "You're talking about the week before." Hudson held his hands up, splaying his fingers, like a man stopping traffic. "Let me say something."

"No, no, sugar," Sandra said, raising her voice, blinking. "I remember it . . ."

"Let me talk," Moon said, his face hardening. They began talking over each other, getting louder.

"One at a time." Redpath held up his hands and glanced at the door. The floating face was still there. Perhaps it was his imagination, but it seemed to be smirking.

"I remember you coming home, and breakfast, and you going to bed. Then I . . ."

"Let's keep it down."

"Let me say something now. Let me say something." Moon was smacking the table with his pointer and middle finger.

"Easy."

"You need to think back," Sandra said. "You're mixing up the days."

"Listen to me now," Moon's voice turned harsh, and he leaned toward them, with his eyes flashing. "Listen to me a damn minute now, will you?"

The last, furious words, almost shouted, brought silence to the room. Redpath put his pencil down and folded his hands on the table. Sandra sniffed and rubbed away an angry tear.

"Girl, I'm not mixing anything up. They'll get my day sheet at

J and K, right? They're going to know when I worked, and when I didn't work. You hear what I'm saying?" He turned to Redpath. "Call Kostecki. Maybe Sandy's right, but I don't think so."

"I did call him," Redpath said, trying to sound relaxed. "And let's keep our voices down." He nodded toward the window. "That thing's probably not as soundproof as they're telling us. I called Kostecki, and he told me he turned all the records over to the FBI. Said he didn't keep any copies."

"Just ask the man, Bill. How hard is that? Just ask the man. He won't need any records."

"I did ask him, Moon. This is not my first trial, okay?"

"Fine, what did he say?"

"His message was, basically, that he was done talking. Actually, he said a few other things, and then he hung up on me." Redpath picked up his pencil and drew slow circles on the pad. "I called back and let it ring for five minutes. I called again, and somebody picked up the receiver and hung up. After that, the line was busy."

They sat for a minute, without a sound, in their separate bubbles of misery.

Finally, Redpath checked his watch to remind them that they did not have all day. Moon was looking at his hands folded on the table, a man vanishing into the underworld. His wife was gazing over the edge, down at him, willing him back up into the free air. Her eagerness to help would make perjury as easy as breathing; she'd simply believe her own lies.

"Uh-huh." Moon nodded. The words made their way slowly out of his mouth. "Makes sense. For a shipper like J and K, they've got books and books of regs. Heat could be all over Kostecki any time they wanted. Shut him down in five minutes."

"Can't you get the records from this Gomez woman?" Sandra asked, sounding chastened.

"I asked," Redpath said. "She told me she'd try to locate them. Says there's a ton of paper, a lot of different investigators doing a lot of different things." He tossed the pencil onto the pad. "She says she's not a hundred percent certain they even have them. Or, they might have gotten shredded accidentally. She couldn't be sure."

He paused and dropped his voice. "I'll tell you both one thing, though, and I want both of you to listen to me carefully." He tapped the table with his finger. "Just as soon as one of you takes the stand and testifies under oath in a way that is not consistent with those records? Are you listening? As soon as you've stuck yourself right out on the end of that dead limb, and Gomez-Larsen can use those J and K records to chop that branch off? Guess what? Those documents will turn up, right out of the blue. I'll scream my head off, but Norcross will let them in. And no juror will ever believe you made an honest mistake. They'll just decide you're damn liars."

"I know he was home, Bill," Sandra began.

"That's what I wanted to say," Moon broke in. "That's what I was trying to say a minute ago. Let me talk now, Sandy. You know how I'm feeling."

"Moon, please . . ."

Hudson looked over at his attorney. His lips were pressed together, his mouth turned down another notch.

"I can't be taking Sandy down with me. I mean, they're coming at Kostecki, right? They could come after her, too." He paused. "We need to keep her away from court."

Sandra Hudson was shaking her head, hands clasped in front of her.

"Moon . . ." she began.

"Who's going to change the diapers? You tell me! Who's going to put Grace to sleep at night?" Moon's nostrils flared, and he breathed deeply in an effort to keep his composure. "We can't take turns anymore, babe. We can't. And we can't take chances. There's only you now."

"I know, but . . ."

Redpath sat back and shook his head. "You mean, keep Sandra off the stand entirely? I don't see how we can afford to do that."

"What do you mean, 'afford'?"

"Well, tell me this: Under this scheme of yours, will Sandra be coming to court at all? I need her there, Moon. You need her there. The jury has to see you're not just some hamburger wrapper blowing down the street. And if the jury does see her, and she doesn't testify, you're dead. Not having her testify will be the same as having her get on the stand and say you did it." Redpath leaned toward Moon. "Sandra's about the only face card I've got in my hand right now. I need her."

"*You* need her. Is that right?" Hudson eyed Redpath as though he were sizing up a rival gang member. He placed his hands in his lap and tipped his head back. "Tell me just this one thing: Whose trial is this?"

"Oh, that's easy." Redpath glanced at the window and dropped his voice, leaning forward, ready to fight. "It's my trial. It's *my* trial!" He slapped his chest. "It's *my* job to put on your defense. I need her, okay? And you need her, too, if you're going to have any chance at all. And, by the way, I don't need you to be trying to do my job. I'm having a tough enough time doing it on my own."

"I'll testify myself. I'll tell my own story."

"I doubt I'll put you on."

"What do you mean, you doubt you'll put me on? What kind of bullshit is that?"

"You testify, and the jury will hear about your drug record."

"They'll hear about it anyway."

"Only if you testify."

"That doesn't make any damn sense." Moon snorted and shook his head.

"You're right, it's a stupid rule, but that's how it works. That's why Sandy has to go on."

"You're not hearing me, man."

Sandra was looking back and forth at the two men. Her frightened expression suddenly dissolved, and she released her constricted breath like a small engine blowing off pent-up steam. She rocked back in her chair with a disgusted laugh.

"Hey," she said, smacking the table with both hands. "Do either of you boys notice I'm sitting here? I'm having to listen to 'she's going to do this' and 'she's not going to do that' and 'I need her' and 'no, you don't need her,' like I'm not even in the room. Well, here I am, boys!" She poked herself with both hands. "Here I am, in full Technicolor! Right? And I can decide for myself what I'm going to do. Do you hear what I'm saying?

"Now take you"—she looked over at Moon—"You say I'm going to get myself in some kind of big, big trouble. And that won't be good for Grace. Okay, I see what you're saying. And we have to talk about that, and then I have to decide what I'm going to do.

"And you"—she turned to Redpath—"You're in a cold sweat because you're afraid I'll mess up. I'll kill Moon trying to help him. That Gomez bitch might tangle me up. I see that. I see that. So I need to think about that, too. And then I'll decide what I'm going to do."

She stood up and smoothed her skirt.

"And now I'm going to leave, because I've got a baby who's

waiting in the car with her grandma, warming up her pucker muscles. I'm going to think about what you both said, and then we'll have one more talk, and then I'll decide."

She walked briskly around the table toward Moon, continuing.

"And when they get those records, Clarence, aka Moon, Hudson, you're going to have to apologize, because you were in bed just like I said you were." As a clatter of metal on glass rose angrily, she gave the startled defendant a hard kiss on the lips, turned, and walked out of the room.

27

Atkins Fruit Bowl was hopping. The morning doughnut-and-coffee crowd had overlapped with the early-bird shoppers, and the combination was generating well-mannered chaos in the farm stand's parking lot. No fewer than six cars idled in various attitudes of congestion while a blue-haired lady in avid discussion with her daughter inched obliviously over the blacktop, dragging her walker.

Claire, behind the wheel of her red Prius, waited in the queue gnashing her teeth and fighting a desire to get out and give the old sweetheart a smart kick in her bum hip. She had a long list of weekend errands, and she was not, she freely admitted, a terribly patient person in these situations.

A door thumped, and traffic finally began moving. Claire snaked through the cars toward the upper parking lot, where a few empty spots beckoned. As she swung around to enter one of them, she nearly collided with a late-model gray Saab whipping in from the other side. Both drivers were caught in mid-glare as they recognized each other and made hasty facial adjustments. The Saab driver was Gerald Novotny, the pushy professor from the Pratt dinner.

Claire had no intention of giving Novotny an opportunity to be chivalrous. Before he could even get into reverse, she had backed out and swung into another place. Now, she told herself as she applied the parking brake, it was going to be necessary to make conversation. Ugh.

"Sorry," he said as they made their way out of the parking lot. "Didn't see you." His face bore a clouded expression.

"I didn't like that spot anyway," Claire said. She knitted her brows and peered over his shoulder in the direction of his car. "Are you getting that tire fixed?"

Novotny jerked around quickly; Claire put her hand on his shoulder.

"Just kidding. Just kidding." She felt bad when he gave her a wounded look. Apparently, Novotny wasn't the type to be teased. An uncomfortable silence followed during their downhill approach to the fruit stand. Having given the man a dig, Claire now felt obliged to sweeten their interchange somehow.

"I enjoyed our dinner at the Pratts," she said.

"You and your new pal hustled off just when things were getting good," Novotny said. He had been staring at the ground moodily but now turned to look at her. "I suppose he's happy. It's official now; he's got his death penalty case." His ponytail flapped as he shook his head. "Just unbelievable," he muttered.

"He's *not* happy," Claire said sharply. They were approaching the front door, where a man of about fifty, sporting an Atkins-green apron, was vigorously sweeping. "The whole trial's incredibly stressful, and difficult. It's like some enormous ..."

"Circus," Novotnyy broke in. "It's a circus. TV cameras outside the courthouse. Protestors. One guy with a big sign that says 'Fry him!' Did you see that? It's worse than third-century Rome. It's worse than Daley and Halligan."

They passed from the freezing air into a cloud of delicious, fresh-bread fragrance beyond the door. He had not stood aside to let her through first, thank God.

"You want a basket?" Novotny asked in a clipped tone, not looking at her.

Claire watched while he separated a couple of red plastic baskets from the stack inside the door and handed one to her.

"You know, that's such garbage, Gerry," she said, taking a basket from him and trying vainly to make eye contact. "I don't believe in the death penalty, either. But different people think different things."

"Right. I know. Salt and pepper." Novotny was speaking over his shoulder. He had wandered off into the store and was pawing through a pyramid of loaves, not bothering to hide his indifference to any opinion Claire might have. His unspoken message, Claire thought, was that she was an overgroomed English teacher in an Ann Taylor outfit, who was setting her sights on a well-heeled representative of the ruling class. Just another embodiment of the banality of evil. This whole scenario was making her cross.

"Where'd they put the cheddar cheese bread?" Novotny asked absently. "It makes great toast."

One more effort, Claire decided, and she would drop this Czech shithead. How much penance was required for a tweak of the male ego? She wondered in passing whether Professor Novotny's political discussions highlighted the tendency of males to feel entitled to interrupt or withdraw from women when confronted.

"Well, it's not easy," she said more calmly. "A million things can go wrong in a trial like this. Here's your bread." She handed him a plump, heavy loaf.

"Really. What kind of things?" He tossed the bread into his basket and turned from her toward the pastry counter. She could not see his expression. His tone was casual.

Claire thought and spoke quickly. "Well, one example: The jurors could find out about Hudson's prior drug convictions. David's keeping that information out of the trial, trying to make things fairer, but it's been all over the papers. Some juror could find out about that, and it would screw everything up. That's just one thing."

But Novotny, caught up in his muffin order, did not seem to hear. He was bent over the counter alternately pointing and speaking to the pretty girl on the other side of the glass.

"Three morning glory, three cranberry nut. Where'd you get those awesome earrings? Three no-fat blueberry and three, uh, bran, I guess." He straightened and, for the first time, smiled thinly at Claire. He put a hand on the small of his back and arched; evidently, bending over the counter had not been easy. Novotny must be older than Claire had thought. Did he use Grecian Formula on his ponytail?

"I'm sorry. I'm in the dumps today." He turned to Claire while the clerk retrieved his pastries. "It's tough on him, I suppose. But this whole thing—this whole . . ." He ran his hands over a pile of grapefruit, fondling them as he searched for the word. "This whole carnival of pseudo-justice is so degrading, it's hard to talk as though it were just some random topic. I thought your friend Dave was kind of pretentious, frankly, but you've obviously put your hands on his good side." He gave Claire a wry look to make sure she knew what he was implying. "The point is," he continued, "it's a corrupt system, and he's perched right on top of it. He's accountable, and he ought to be held to account."

Novotny got his bag of muffins, with a melting look from the girl behind the counter, and placed it in his red basket.

"Why don't we have coffee sometime when I'm downtown," he said. "I can't talk about heavy stuff like this on the fly." He shrugged. "Maybe it's this endless winter that's getting to me. But the first death penalty case in Massachusetts, and it's out here? In Springfield? I mean, for God's sake."

"The weather has been lousy," Claire agreed. "Give me a call next week. I better run." She produced a compact smile, and they swerved off from each other, swept along on parallel currents of relief and with, of course, no intention on either side of ever having coffee or any other beverage with each other, if at all possible, for the rest of their natural lives.

By the time Claire was paying for the lamb chops she planned to grill for David, Novotny was already getting into his Saab. He retrieved his cell phone from the glove compartment and dialed quickly.

"Brit?" he said when she answered. "Just wanted to make sure everyone will be there." He paused and listened, then said in an annoyed tone, "My place, of course." Another pause. "Right." And finally: "Well, I just had a thought I'd like to run past people, okay?"

28

Bill Redpath used Sandra Hudson's dramatic exit as an excuse to step outside and jack up his nicotine levels. Now he was back, and Moon was shaking his head. His face had softened.

"You see why I can't tear her off?" he asked. "How could anybody not want to be with that woman every second he could?" He shook his head. "What I can't figure is, why's she messing with an empty T-shirt like me?"

"My track record in this area is pretty poor, Moon, but my guess is she loves you." Redpath's mind flickered back to his own marriage, the missed anniversaries and birthdays, and, finally, the divorce. Barbara lived in Santa Cruz now, near their son, Tom. Every Christmas, Barbara sent one of her hand-painted cards and a note with the news. Tom was a federal public defender; they talked every Sunday, mostly about their cases. He'd salvaged that at least.

Moon shifted, and his leg irons clanked, bringing Redpath back.

"Well," Moon said, sighing and running his hands over the table, "there's stuff she doesn't know. And I think she's wrong about me being home asleep that morning."

"We'll see," Redpath said.

Moon's reference to other "stuff" was an opening. Soon they'd need to have the hard talk, now that Moon trusted him a little, about exactly what happened. Right now, though, they had other problems.

"We've only got a few more minutes today," Redpath said, "and I need to go over a couple things with you."

Redpath opened his briefcase and withdrew a letter on the U.S. attorney's stationery. He held the two pages in front of him, then set the document on the table and peered at it closely.

"I got the government's revised witness list yesterday, and there are two names I don't recognize." He passed his thumb down the page and stopped.

"Who's Jesús Santiago? And . . . Wait a minute." His thick finger ran down to the bottom of the page, and then flipped to the next. "And who's Manuel Ortiz?"

Moon frowned and shook his head. "Never heard of them."

"Neither one? You sure?"

"I'm sure."

"Well, they're both on Gomez-Larsen's list, and I'd really like to know who they are. I don't even like surprises on my birthday."

Hudson shook his head.

"They wouldn't be using their real names on the street anyway." He sat up and looked straight ahead as a thought struck him. "Hold up. I think I heard someone call this little Flag I knew—his street name was Spider—but I'm thinking I heard somebody call him Jesús once. Nasty, tall, skinny motherfucker, with all this hair on his arms. Everybody called him Spider. Maybe that was Jesús. Could've been him."

"I don't like this," Redpath said, scratching his head.

"Yeah," Hudson was gazing at the far wall, off in his own memories. "Yeah. Shit, yeah. I bet that was him. Spider always went around with this short chunky Flag, looked like a bowling ball, who never said anything, called Nono. They could stand next to each other and look like a one and zero, the number ten. People'd just say 'X,' like, for ten. Like, 'X is going to be there' for the two of them. What was the other name?"

"Manuel Ortiz."

"Don't know. Could be Nono. They didn't like me, that's for sure."

"Why's that?"

"Oh, we got into a beef once. Nono pulled a burner on me and got himself hurt." Moon looked up at the ceiling, searching back. "Yeah, that would make sense."

"How would it make sense, Moon?"

Hudson wrapped his arms around himself and scratched his shoulders, as though he were in a struggle with something inside. Then he let his arms drop, looked down at the table, closed his eyes, and shook his head.

"How would that make sense?" Redpath pursued. "What do you mean?"

"That's what I have to tell you." Moon opened his eyes and settled himself with a deep breath. His expression, when he finally managed to look at Redpath, gave his lawyer a glimpse of Moon as the big-eyed first grader who was always in fights. Some morning a few short years from now, Redpath could find himself watching through a window as this one-time little boy was strapped to a cart and given the needle. It could happen; he'd seen it happen. And he'd never stop wondering whether another lawyer, another strategy, might have saved Moon Hudson's life.

His client, however, was obviously bothered by something other than this horror, maybe something even worse.

"Like I been telling you, I"—Moon cleared his throat—"I didn't put it on Delgado or that nurse. But I've been holding this one big thing back. I was going to tell you, pretty soon, right? If this Santiago motherfucker is Spider and Ortiz is Nono, then I better tell you now." He paused. "But I want a promise. No bullshit. Sandy doesn't know about this until I tell her. If I ever do tell her."

"Okay. Let's hear," Redpath said. "But keep it low."

"Or anybody in her family."

"Fine. Let's hear it."

Moon tilted his head back, looked at the ceiling with his lips parted, and closed his eyes. Then he opened his eyes, looked at Redpath, and began.

"When I got out of here the last time, I had my GED, right? Then I got my own place and a car, and I got a job. And I said to myself, I am never—not ever—going back to the old life, doesn't matter what happens, even if I starve to death. Couple people called up from my old corner, and I was cool, but I stayed away, and pretty soon, you know, nobody is bothering me. I'm clear. I've got money in my pocket. Not too much, but enough. Like, I won't have to quit my job if the car needs new tires. I may have retreads, but I'm going to get to work.

"Then I get this bright idea to try college. I hear, you know, about UWW, University Without Walls, and I think, that'd be cool. And I start with one class. You know all this, this is not new." Redpath shrugged, and Moon continued.

"And pretty soon I'm taking this one class, but sitting in on that other class, having lunch at the Student Union, doing this and that. I'm learning to talk white, working on my Theo Huxtable imitation, everything's okay. I got my UMass sweatshirt on, and I even make a couple basketball games. Watch my alma mater get her sorry ass kicked.

"Then, one day, I'm talking to these white boys after a game, fraternity brothers or some shit. And they're talking about how they want to get a hold of some wicked weed. That's what they call it. The one guy is fiddling with this big fucking roll of bills, and he's talking about how much they like to get high and get laid, and how their girlfriends like to get high and get laid, and maybe I like to get high and get laid, and they say they're looking for some seriously—'seriously' is a big word for these boys—seriously wicked weed. We've been talking, and they know I live down in Springfield or Holyoke, and I come from the projects, and I'm this scary black motherfucker who doesn't smile too much, so they figure I am an expert, which I am. I am an expert on seriously wicked weed. That's what they think.

"But I don't jump. Right? I don't jump, one, because this smells like old times, and, two, because I'm not that stupid. I'm wondering, is this a setup to jump some dumbass who walked into the wrong neighborhood?

"So I don't do anything," Hudson paused and shook his head. "That's not true." He looked at the ceiling. "I do one thing. I beep this one old Flag I used to hang with, and he tells me, yeah, he's fat. He's real fat, he's got shit to move, and he'd be fine with me helping him move some of it.

"But I'm still waiting, right? But now, I'm also thinking. I check out the white boys, and I find out they're not just for show, they take classes and this and that, play sports, and they're not wired, nobody's making a movie of us. So now I'm really thinking, and I'm getting stupider every minute. And the next time I see them . . ." Hudson stopped again and wiped a hand over his face. "The next time I see them, we set it up—half a pound. Fuck!"

He slapped the table hard. By now he was breathing as though he were running a race. Finally, after opening and closing his mouth twice, he continued almost in a whisper.

"And the whole deal just goes like cookies, Bill. A little phone call, a little ride, and my share is two hundred cash, twenty-five an ounce, smooth as your baby sister's ass. Man!"

His voice rose again. "That's two, three days' work for me, after what they take out at J and K. Right? That's twenty, maybe twenty-five hours of hauling boxes and sweating like a Georgia field hand. And now, with this one itty-bitty deal, I've got a little extra in my pocket, with no trouble and no fear. So now, I've got myself really thinking, and I'm just getting stupider and stupider. I'm thinking, all it takes is a couple deals a week like that, and I could double what I'm bringing home. Maybe more.

"Then I met Sandy. Now I really have myself a good reason to get a hold of some extra. I want some nice clothes. Nice TV. Nice big comfy bed. Pretty soon, I'm moving a few ounces a week, regular, just to people I know, and I make, some weeks, two hundred, some weeks four hundred. I don't have to share it with the governor—no taxes. And it's solving a lot of problems for me, especially after I meet Sandy's family. We're getting married, and they expect us to live decent.

"Okay. Next thing, they're asking for coke. These are still my white boys, so they want the powder, not the hard stuff. Seems like they've discovered getting high and getting laid on blow is even better than on weed. So I call my old friend and get myself a finger of coke, and I cut it with so much shit it couldn't get a parakeet high, and I sell it to them for twelve hundred dollars! About a hundred and fifty worth for twelve hundred!

"Next day, they come running up to me over on University Drive, four of them, big giant motherfuckers, from the football team or something, and I think here's where I get my ass kicked. And I'm just about to jump the fence, when I hear them talking all at the same time about what great shit it was, and how they were so high, and how their girlfriends were so high, and how the pussy was so tight—and how soon can I get them more of that great, serious shit I sold them? They think I'm the candy man. I could sell them lime Jell-O and baby powder, and they'd be throwing the money at me.

"So that's what I did. I'd cut back sometimes. Sometimes I wouldn't sell anything for a month or two. But then we'd be running short, we'd need something, and one of my boys was always wanting to talk to me, just ready to start shoveling out money."

Redpath broke in. "So that explains the marijuana and the cash?"

"Right, and the shit in the basement."

"And Sandy?"

"I just always had money in my pocket for this and that. I'd tell her Kostecki'd give us cash bonuses. Which he did, once in a while, but it was like twenty or thirty. And I'd buy her presents, like the changing table, the living room furniture. I'd tell her I'd been saving up to surprise her."

"Well, it could be worse," Redpath said, suppressing a smile.

Toward the end of Moon's speech, the defense attorney had been experiencing, almost to his embarrassment, a ripple of very inappropriate amusement at the irony of their situation. Because the clerk had bungled the search warrant paperwork, it seemed likely that none of the drugs found in Hudson's apartment would be admitted at trial. As a result, they might well beat the charges for the crimes his client actually did commit, while his client went on to face a lethal injection for a crime that he probably never even thought of. It was a strange upside-down world he'd chosen to work in. Unfortunately, the attorney's buzz was short lived.

"It is worse," Moon said. "You know how Gomez has it in her head that Carlos fixed me up to shoot Peach? Well, guess who I was getting my shit from."

"Don't tell me."

"My old friend from La Bandera, Carlos. Three days before Peach went down, I met Carlos at the White Castle in Holyoke, picking up a couple eighths. Spider and Nono were there, and Carlos's nephew, that little pig's asshole, Pepe. They heard us talking, and they saw Carlos front me the stuff."

29

Buddy Hogan's grating voice on the other end of the line exuded an infectious anxiety that was beginning to make Gomez-Larsen squirm. Plus, she was already ten minutes late for her son's game, and she needed to make a visit to the ladies' room before she took off.

"I hear what you're telling me, Lydia," Hogan was saying in his fingernails-on-chalk voice, "but—honestly?—it looks from here as though you're letting yourself get pushed around by Judge Funky. And all I'm asking is, what can we do to give you some help with this prick?"

"Listen to me, Buddy," Gomez-Larsen began. "Just listen a minute now."

"I mean, we lost the motion to suppress, so the drugs are gone, right? And we lost the motion to get Hudson's criminal record in, right? So now that's gone, too."

"Not quite. The convictions still come in if Hudson testifies."

"Well, he won't testify, so what the fuck good does that do us? I mean, it's fucking meaningless."

"I'm not so sure. Redpath looked pretty banged up about that."

"Really? Hmm. That's good." A pause followed while Gomez-Larsen drew squares and triangles on her yellow pad, trying to stay patient.

"Okay, Buddy, listen to me now," she began again.

"Wait. Let me float this to you. Sorry. Just let me think for a minute here. How about some kind of public statement? See, we're just a teensy bit afraid you're being too nice here, maybe a little too feminine—no offense—letting him shove you around and all."

Gomez-Larsen sat up straighter and tapped briskly with her pencil.

"We're not holding any press conferences, Buddy. I don't try cases that way."

"Oh Jesus, no, no, no! That's not what I mean. What I'm thinking is, let me call Sam Craig at Harvard. He's an old classmate, with friends on the Court of Appeals, and he owes me a big fat one. He can find some way to make a statement that will get picked up by the papers—a speech at the Boston Bar or some goddamn thing—something like how he finds Norcross's rulings puzzling in view of First Circuit authority. Hard to square with precedent, some crap like that. We can have it in the *Globe* by the end of the week. Something subtle and understated, like a karate kick in the balls."

"Not a good idea, Bud."

"Does Norcross want to be on the Court of Appeals? Does he have aspirations?"

"I really don't know." Her need to use the bathroom was becoming a distraction.

"And then this bullshit letter to the editor by his law clerk about gay marriage, and the term paper, or whatever the hell it was, by his niece, Ray Norcross's daughter, for Christ's sake, and . . ."

"Buddy! Zip it, and listen to me a minute, all right?" A clatter erupted on the other end of the line. Something hit the floor.

"Just a second. I knocked the phone over," Hogan said. There was a sound of grunting and mumbling while he rearranged things. "Okay," he said at last. "Call me Frasier Crane. I'm listening."

"Everything is fine, Buddy, just fine." Gomez-Larsen spoke slowly and distinctly, drawing the words out as though she were talking to one of her children. "None of these Norcross rulings was a particular surprise. The problem was the idiot clerk who screwed up the warrant paperwork. If Norcross had let the evidence in, we'd just have to defend a borderline ruling on appeal, and maybe end up giving Hudson a remand and new trial. It's no biggie."

"Okay, maybe," he said. "Maybe I overreact. I get calls from Washington, and they rattle my chain, and then I . . ."

"You need to relax. The defense is asking for some old records to help them jury-rig their testimony and, between you and me, I'm not looking real hard for them at the moment. Got a lot of other things to do."

"Documents get lost all the time, Lydia," Hogan said, suddenly quiet. "It's nobody's fault."

"Right, and they can get found, too. So you just need to let me take care of business here. Do you hear what I'm saying to you?"

"I hear you, and it's helping my ulcer."

"Good." Gomez-Larsen picked up a yellow message slip. "Now my son's hockey game is already into the second period, and if I don't leave now I'm going to be Public Enemy Number One. Promise me you won't do anything without talking to me first."

"Like I always say, Lydia, I'm a politician. Promises are us."

"Bye, Buddy."

"So long, sweetheart. Keep in touch."

As Gomez-Larsen put down the receiver and began looking around for her purse, Judge Norcross, squirming like a boy in the principal's office, was picking up his own phone to take a call from Chief Judge Broadwater. Norcross had just come off the bench from three consecutive sentencings, the average age of the defendants being twenty-two, and the average term of imprisonment, by his quick arithmetic, eighteen years. One African-American, two Puerto Ricans—all repeat offenders sentenced for crack. He still had his robe on, open at the front. He was itchy and tired.

"Hey, Skip, what's up?"

"Big problems, Dave, big problems. Spring has sprung, and the folks at the administrative office are dancing around like peas on a hot shovel. Some House sub-committee is going to cut off all funds for the judiciary, now that the District of Massachusetts has declared heterosexual marriage unconstitutional."

"Oh, for heaven's sake!"

Frank Baldwin, in an ill-conceived tribute to Eva Meyers and her partner, Bonnie, had written a tongue-in-cheek letter to the Springfield *Republican* suggesting that the courts should ban heterosexual marriage, since the divorce rate for straight couples in Massachusetts was proving to be higher than the rate for gays. Someone found out Frank was Norcross's law clerk, and the blogs went ballistic.

"Just kidding. What?" The chief was apparently talking to his secretary. "Take a message.

Anyway, I hope you'll excuse me poking my nostrils in here, Dave. I haven't had a death penalty trial, thank God, but I've had a few big cases in my twenty-six years, and I can tell you what you don't need right now is some kid with a big mouth and his own agenda. Picking this moment to stick himself into the spotlight was dumber than chocolate shorts in August. I'd get rid of him."

"He's a good man who made a mistake, Skip, that's all. He had no idea his letter would make such a splash. He's ready to pull off his own head, he feels so bad."

"I'd can him, Dave. He's embarrassed you once, and he'll do it again. Plenty of good clerks where he came from. Ten cents a bushel."

"I appreciate your advice, but I can't do that."

Norcross had been frozen, holding his robe in his outstretched hand as the tension mounted. Now he threw it onto one of the leather chairs facing his desk.

A chief judge's authority was entirely persuasive, not mandatory. Broadwater lacked the power to order Norcross to do anything. Still, he was a valued colleague, a far more experienced judge, and someone whose administrative responsibilities gave him the ability to make Norcross's life miserable if he wanted to. To Norcross's relief, Broadwater veered off to the side, and onto another topic.

"And what's this about your niece, Lindsay? Secretary Norcross's daughter? Her views on capital punishment have filtered all the way to Washington. Barely fourteen, and they tell me the *Today Show* is after her."

Norcross sighed. "It was a term paper she did for a class at Deerfield Academy. Her teacher leaked it to the Associated Press."

"Called you a Nazi, Dave. That was a little harsh."

"Me and some others. 'Resurgence of Fascism in Twenty-First Century Jurisprudence,' I think was her title. She's a sweet kid, but she takes after her daddy and likes to sound off. Ray's been out of the country pretty much nonstop, but I imagine he'll feed that teacher to the crocodiles when he gets back."

"Mmm, not a bad idea." The conversation melted into an awkward silence while Norcross waited for Broadwater to resume. The poor guy was obviously hating having to make this call.

"Well, I guess that's it," Broadwater continued. His breezy tone changed, and his voice deepened. "I guess I just have one other piece of advice, or observation, if I can call it that. You've got a pistol of a trial. Keeping it under control will be like trying to cram a German shepherd into a cello case. You've only been on the bench, what, three years?"

"Little more than two."

"I'd be very careful about the publicity, Dave. It will make everything ten times harder for you. I've seen it happen. If the papers smell blood? You might find yourself so far up the creek no one will hear your screams. Don't forget O.J. If I can do anything at all . . ."

"I appreciate it, Skip. I think I've got things under control here."

"Good, well . . ." Broadwater was turning distant. "I hope you didn't mind my calling." In the silence that followed, the chief judge was either trying to think of something to say, or deciding not to say something he was thinking—or possibly reading a phone message on his desk and getting distracted. "Good," he said finally. "When do you start jury selection?"

"Should be done by next week. Openings the Monday after."

"Wow! That soon? What?" The indistinct voice broke in again in the background. "Have to run. I'm late already. Call me if you need anything."

As he hung up, Norcross could hear Broadwater saying something under his breath, but he could not tell if it was about him.

30

Sunday morning. David gradually became aware of the soft light, the touch of the sheets, and the ache in his left shoulder. He shifted off to Claire's side, carrying his weight on his wrists and elbows.

It was heaven to lie with her like that, two pieces of a puzzle still snugly connected, both of them dozy and sated with pleasure. The dinner and movie Saturday night had been wonderful, and after a sound sleep their happy date had blossomed again, into a perfectly delicious Sunday morning. Now, for a few short minutes, the two of them were the sanest human beings in the universe, warm as mittens and smelling like Cupid's boiler room.

"Grade A," he heard Claire sigh as she rolled toward the cloudy window. David tucked up behind her, placed his hand on her silky stomach, and buried his nose in the tickling fragrance of her hair. His body relaxed into the warm blankets.

Yes, David thought, *Grade A. Like the richest maple syrup.*
Drowsiness settled over him.

With Claire settling into his life now, David could acknowledge some uncertainty about this area of his life over the years. Was he a good lover? The mechanics had always gone smoothly, and he had always had a fabulous time, but when he looked at himself in the mirror, he sometimes wondered what it was like for the women he'd been with. His long, loose-jointed body seemed ill suited to the gymnasium of love.

In the far-off days of his marriage, Faye had been very sweet about everything, of course. They had been shy early on. Then, when they were more comfortable with each other, they fell into, and stuck with, the two or three reliable formats they'd gotten the hang of. In his half dreamy state, with Claire's sweet warmth beside him, he did not feel guilty exactly, but he wondered if Faye somehow knew what was happening now—this fresh and wonderfully satisfying part of his life. What would she think? Everything had been very nice during his marriage, everything that was supposed to happen happened, but he'd never received any gold stars. No "Grade A."

Claire's compliment stuck in his mind and touched him profoundly. In the shower later that morning, he looked down at himself happily while he rinsed off.

"You are one lucky boy!" he whispered, smiling and nodding down at himself.

In the strain of jury selection, the echo of Claire's remark remained for him a cherished comfort. From time to time, he would murmur to her as they kissed and he headed once more to court: "Grade A!" He barely resisted the temptation to wink.

Claire's face in response to David's comment was always a little bemused. It seemed right to encourage her new boyfriend, but his meaning was elusive to her. The fact was, that particular morning as they lay entwined, she hadn't said "Grade A" at all. When she had turned onto her side toward the milky window, she had noticed the cloud-covered skies behind the trees.

"Gray day," she had murmured, to herself and to him, as she dropped off.

As for the sex, it was lovely. She had no complaints at all.

31

After five weeks, the pool of fifty-six eligible jurors was selected. The attorneys then exercised their forty peremptory challenges, and the twelve men and women who would decide *United States v. Hudson,* along with the four alternates, took their final places in the jury box.

To Bill Redpath, the panel was a defense lawyer's dream. The chosen sixteen included not one, but two Smith College faculty, the administrator of a children's museum, an organic farmer, a sculptor, and a nurse who worked on an AIDS unit. As he waited at counsel table for Judge Norcross to enter, Redpath measured his breathing, slowly in and slowly out, preserving his expression of wary indifference. But he hardly dared to look over at the jury box for fear he might laugh out loud with joy and spook the flock of angels perched inside. Never before in his career, certainly never in any of his capital cases, had fate blessed him so lavishly.

He did not, of course, comment on this incredible luck to Moon or Sandra—optimistic remarks of any sort would be unthinkable—but he knew the defendant's street smarts were picking up the change in the courtroom's atmosphere. The jurors chosen in the final round had dropped into place like the tumblers of a combination lock that might, when the last one clicked, open and set Moon Hudson free. The courtroom's fresher environment was finally permitting Moon enough oxygen to breathe a little, providing a view of the defendant as an ordinary human being. This was very good.

The jury could not be allowed to overlook this nuance, and Redpath put his hand on Moon's shoulder reassuringly. His client, he knew, would be hating this and working hard not to pull away, but Redpath kept his large paw up there anyway, appearing to console his vulnerable-looking client, until he was sure most of the jurors had time to take this tender moment in.

Redpath spoke in a low whisper, pretending to scratch his nose with his free hand, screening his mouth, "During her opening, Gomez-Larsen will probably point at you. When she does, don't look down, don't look at your hands. That's what she wants you to do. It'll make you look guilty. Look sad but don't look down. Just nod your head slowly if you understand me. Please don't say anything." He didn't want to take the chance that Moon's deep, virile voice might carry and put someone off.

Moon nodded, and Redpath patted him twice on the shoulder before turning back to his notes. Where the hell was Norcross? The courtroom was packed and getting warm. Redpath could not help noticing one spectator in particular, a young woman, college-aged, with platinum hair and a pretty, pissed-off face. Arriving early, he had seen her with two friends bickering as they settled into spots in the gallery's front row.

The girl had a lisp and was berating a boy with sideburns. "Gerry told us to thit in the front row!" The group's early arrival had managed to displace the two knuckle-draggers who always sat there; now, with sour looks, they were relocated two rows back. Redpath had wondered more than once what this ugly duo might be up to.

But now, who cared? Never before in a capital case had Redpath felt so freed to concentrate on the question of whether his client actually committed the goddam crime. Always in the past, he had been distracted by the possible trial to come, the brutal second phase where, if the jury did find his client guilty, the prosecution moved in for the kill.

This time around, he was virtually certain that, even if they convicted Moon, this group would never produce a unanimous vote for the death penalty. This time, at least, he would not end up with blood on his hands. Juror Number One, the likely foreperson, was a lifelong Unitarian—a *Unitarian* for heaven's sake!—who'd miraculously slipped onto the jury, promising she really, truly, could vote to impose the death penalty if she felt it was warranted. Gomez-Larsen, having burned all twenty of her peremptory challenges, had fought like a banshee to get Norcross to strike this radiantly liberal bird-watcher for cause, but the judge, God bless him, had kept her on.

Breathe in. Breathe out. He'd just had a record-breaking run of luck, that's all, like a man at a roulette wheel betting on red or black and, with each spin of the wheel, blessed by Fortune. Perhaps, this time, he could bring one of those Chinese boys he'd machine-gunned back to life. Maybe this spring, when the trial was over, he'd take a trip to California and visit his son, Tom. Maybe catch a ball game.

"All rise!"

Judge Norcross strode onto the bench, bobbing his head and fiddling with the top of his robe, looking as usual like the Tin Man with half his bolts loose. Redpath and Moon rose respectfully, putting their hands behind their backs, keeping their faces neutral but softened and respectful. Gomez-Larsen had a pad in her right hand and was tapping lightly on the table with her pointer finger. She appeared to be in a foul mood. Wonderful!

"Please be seated," Norcross said. After the usual rumbling shuffle, the judge leaned forward and began.

"Ladies and gentlemen of the jury, in a moment I am going to direct the clerk to administer the oath to you, and then I will be selecting the foreperson. After that, we will proceed with the first formal step in the actual trial, the openings—first on behalf of the government and then on behalf of Mr. Hudson, the defendant."

Gomez-Larsen was on her feet. She wanted one more toss of the dice, apparently, but what about?

"I'm sorry, Your Honor," she said. "May I be heard at sidebar?"

"Now?" Norcross asked sharply. "What for?"

The prosecutor glanced over at the jury, smiled as winningly as she could, and said, "Well, that's what I need to tell you. At sidebar, Your Honor." She paused. "It's important, of course, or I wouldn't interrupt."

Moon looked at his lawyer. Redpath shrugged and raised his hands palms-up in an exaggerated fashion, letting the jury see that he, at least, had nothing to hide.

When both attorneys had gathered at the far end of the bench, Gomez-Larsen began quickly, in a low voice.

"I know Your Honor's usual custom . . ."

"Wait a minute," Norcross said. "Wait for the stenographer, please. Let's be sure we've got this on the record."

The court reporter, normally positioned in front of the bench, elbowed her way in among the attorneys and planted her machine, then looked up and nodded at the judge.

"Okay. Make it quick," Norcross said.

"I know it's Your Honor's usual custom to select as the foreperson of the jury the person who ends up in Seat Number One." Gomez-Larsen was being especially careful to keep her voice down.

"Right," Norcross said. "I always do that, criminal or civil. That way I'm sure my own biases don't taint the process. It's pure chance."

"Well in this case, Judge, because it's so important, we'd ask that the foreperson be drawn by lot, or that the jurors be allowed to elect their own, as many other judges do."

"Nope," Norcross said.

"I'd object to that," Redpath said, knowing instantly what Gomez-Larsen was up to. God save the Unitarian.

"But in this case, Your Honor . . ." Gomez-Larsen whispered.

"I'd object strongly," Redpath said, slightly louder, not minding if the jury happened to hear.

"Nope, nope, nope," Norcross said. "It's the way I always do it. It's within my discretion. I'm not changing." They were leaning so close, Redpath could smell the Listerine on the judge's breath, catch the scent of the prosecutor's lilac shampoo.

"Very good, Your Honor." Gomez-Larsen had drained any trace of resentment from her voice. Right, Redpath thought. This was no time to piss off Norcross.

"And I very much hope we're not going to be having endless sidebars during this trial. Let's keep things moving. Life is short."

"Yes, Your Honor."

"Absolutely," Redpath said, another notch louder, making sure his voice carried. This was an easy victory, but the jurors might as well know he'd won even if they had no idea what the contest was about.

The attorneys resumed their seats. Gomez-Larsen whispered something to Alex Torricelli, nodded in a pleased way, and folded her hands in front of her. She looked not at all bothered, just the way Redpath would look if he were in her position.

"I was just saying," Norcross continued, turning to the jurors, "that we will be leading off with the openings from each side. Before we do that, however, I am going to have the clerk place you under oath. Please stand and raise your right hand. If you are willing to undertake the oath, please say 'I do.'"

Ruby Johnson rose regally, adjusted the piece of paper in front of her, and read: "Do you and each of you solemnly swear that you shall well and truly try the issues between the United States and the defendant at the bar and render a true verdict according to the evidence and the law given to you?"

There was a fumbling "I do" from the group.

"You may be seated."

This is it, Redpath thought. *We have lift-off.* He inhaled and squeezed down a smile.

From this point on, unless there was a mistrial for good cause, this glorious jury was going to provide the government's one chance to prove beyond a reasonable doubt that Moon Hudson had committed the crimes he was charged with. The constitutional prohibition against placing a defendant in jeopardy twice for the same offense would bar any future trial.

"It is my unvarying custom," Norcross was saying, "to select as the foreperson of the jury the person who happens to end up in Seat Number One. Mrs. Coolidge, you ended up in Seat Number One. Therefore, you will be the foreperson of this jury."

Mrs. Coolidge, dear Mrs. Coolidge, with her intelligent, leathery face, passed a look at the older man sitting next to her. She squared her shoulders and nodded. No one was going to stampede her! The older man patted her on the forearm, a quick reassuring touch. The jury, this assembly of saints, was already beginning to coalesce.

"That does not mean, ma'am, that your vote will be any more important than the votes of your fellow jurors. As I have already told you, whatever verdict the jurors shall reach must be the product of your unanimous agreement." Norcross paused, pulled his notes toward him, and cleared his throat to continue.

Suddenly, a rustle and thumping arose from the gallery, then a stamp of feet, and a small female voice piped out, absurdly high: "Clarence Hudson—convicted drug dealer!" Two other lower voices joined in, halting but clear, "Clarence Hudson—drug dealer!"

Grunts and mumbles rebounded through the courtroom as reporters and spectators in the gallery stretched to see what was going on. Redpath shifted around to observe the unfolding catastrophe: The court officer Tom Dickinson, pink-faced and furious, was moving in from his right, people in the back of the courtroom were beginning to stand up for a better look, and in the front row the three early-bird students were holding a scrap of pale-blue bed sheet between them. The banner, turned to face the jurors, read in neatly stenciled, foot-high black letters HUDSON DEALS DRUGS!!!

One of the protesters, the girl with the spectacular blonde hair, shouted, just as Dickinson grabbed her arm: "They won't tell you!" Her thin voice grew shrill. "Hudson's a convicted drug dealer!"

Dickinson jerked the banner out of her hands. Three or four other officers joined him and began pulling the students toward the door. In response, the young man with the sideburns deliberately slumped to the carpet, dragging an older, overweight officer with him. The kid had a good strong diaphragm and bellowed up from the floor: "They're hiding it from you. Hudson's a drug dealer!" A muffled grunt followed. "They don't want you to ..."

The third student, a girl with curly red hair and a round, pale face, cried out as her arm was jerked behind her back, and she was pushed toward the door. A spectator wearing a clerical collar shouted, "Hey, take it easy there!"

With a crash of the courtroom's double doors, all three protesters were dragged, carried, or simply fell, out into the hallway. Several reporters scrambled after them, and the doors banged shut. No more than a minute had passed since the first outcry, but Redpath, sickened, could already feel his carefully constructed world cracking open and starting to collapse.

Norcross tapped sharply on the microphone with his pen, breaking in with a confident voice that pierced the hubbub: "Well! I do apologize for the unexpected entertainment." The noise level in the courtroom immediately dropped. Norcross swept his gaze over the gallery and down to the jurors. The thumps and outcry in the corridor were receding, and the voices in the courtroom quieted further as people paused to catch what the judge was saying.

"You know, this is a wonderful job," Norcross said, scratching behind his ear, speaking to the jurors. "You never know what fascinating thing will happen next." His voice was calm, mildly amused. Most of the jurors smiled back, reassured, and two even chuckled and shook their heads. Life was funny.

"We'll take a short recess to hand out the Academy Awards. Please don't discuss the case, or any of this foolishness. We'll resume in fifteen minutes or so. Ms. Johnson will escort you to your room."

Norcross waited as the jurors passed silently out of the courtroom, but his look of sweet-tempered calm darkened when the door closed behind them. He said curtly, "The court will be in recess. Counsel will remain in the courtroom. I'll see you in chambers shortly."

32

"How the *fuck* did they know to do that?" Eva was leaning in the doorway to Frank's office. "How the fuck did they know?"

Frank was sitting in his chair with his head in his hands. "Had to be somebody coaching them," he said blindly. "They knew to wait until he'd put the jury under oath." He looked up. "Assholes! Five weeks down the tubes."

"He won't scrub the jury!" Eva said, aghast.

"Oh, I bet he will. I bet he'll have to."

Eva paced in a tight circle and stamped her foot. "Oh, fuck, fuck, fuck!"

"Stop," Frank said. "Please. You sound like a chicken."

The judge's secretary, Lucille, came into the library. She'd picked up on the mood and was looking steely. "Judge wants to see you. Pronto."

Norcross was sitting at his desk with his long torso thrown

back, staring at the ceiling. His face when he turned it to the law clerks was so angry and exhausted it was frightening—the countenance of a man who'd been staggering through the last quarter mile of the Boston Marathon, only to be told that, for technical reasons, the race's length had just doubled. Another twenty-six miles still lay ahead, with another Heartbreak Hill.

"I'm going to ask this once," he said. "Has either of you discussed this case with anyone—anyone—outside these chambers?"

"No."

"No, definitely not."

"Judge," Eva said. "People ask me questions, and I just say I can't talk about it."

"Not your partner? Not Bonnie? Not your wife, Frank?"

"Judge," Frank said. "I'm sorry, but they don't care. They don't even ask."

"So how the heck did those brats know to do that?" Norcross asked. "We've busted our tails to keep Hudson's record out. The trial's one Achilles heel!"

"Most lawyers would know," Eva said. She had, in fact, discussed the case with Bonnie, a little, and was feeling defensive. "Anybody who does criminal work."

"No lawyer set this up."

The phone buzzed, and Norcross made a sour face.

Without picking up the receiver, he shouted, "Lucille, take a message please."

"It's Claire," Lucille called back. "Says she just needs a second."

"Okay," he said with a sigh.

Frank and Eva started to get up, but Norcross waved them down. This would be quick.

"Hi," he said to Claire. "I'm pretty tied up at the moment."

"I know," she said. "You're a busy boy. So, here's my message, in shorthand: Don't come at seven. I won't be there. Come at eight, okay? Was that fast enough? I was afraid I wouldn't reach you."

"Great," Norcross said dully.

"Whoa, you sound terrible. Must be some mess."

"I can't go into details, but you remember our friend Brittany? From the Pratt dinner? Well, she showed up in court today with two pals and a nice little banner informing my jury that Hudson was a drug dealer. It just dawned on me who she was. We're trying to figure out how on earth she and her friends knew to do that."

"Oh dear," said Claire. Then, after a slight pause, "That might have been me."

"You? I really doubt it."

"Well, I bumped into Gerry a while back, and I may have mentioned you were concerned about the jurors knowing about Hudson's past crimes, or something like that."

"Ah."

Another, more extended pause.

"God, I'm feeling stupid, David. Have I done something horrible?"

"You didn't do anything. If anybody . . ." He faltered. He wanted to say, "If anybody's to blame, it's me," but he put on the brakes, with Frank and Eva sitting there. "Anyway, we're straightening it out now."

"Oh, David, I'm so sorry. I'm going to strangle Novotny."

"There's an idea." This was dragging on too long. Frank and Eva were killing time on the other side of the desk, heads bent down whispering, trying to look as though they weren't hearing anything.

"I better go," Norcross said. "Listen, let's take a rain check for tonight, okay? I'm going to be totally shot by evening. I'd be rotten company."

"Damn," Claire said.

"I better go, okay? Let me give you a call."

"Sure. This is a bad time to talk, right?"

"Right."

"You have people there."

"Afraid so."

"Okay," she said. "I'm . . ."

"I'll call you."

Norcross hung up. "This is all my fault," he muttered. "Today of all days." The room was spinning a little. He swallowed and took a careful breath.

"Sorry?" Eva asked.

"It's okay," Norcross said. "I apologize for the third degree. Let me have ten minutes here to collect myself. Then we'll get counsel in and give them the bad news."

33

Bill Redpath stood alone in the plaza outside the courthouse, drawing deeply on a Lucky Strike. It was very cold; mounds of snow were piled high against the planters.

The conference with Judge Norcross could not have gone worse. Redpath had told the judge, with all the passion he could muster, that he would waive any objection to the jurors' exposure to the banner, and to the yowling about Moon's prior record. He'd pointed out that Norcross could simply instruct the jurors to ignore their babble and refrain from speculating about whatever they'd heard or seen.

Gomez-Larsen had objected. If she got a conviction, and particularly if the jury imposed the death penalty, Hudson might get a new lawyer and argue that it was plain error, even with a waiver, to proceed to trial with jurors who'd been exposed to such highly prejudicial, totally inadmissible evidence. The prosecutor's tone of buttery earnestness made Redpath want to grind her face into the carpet. She'd previously argued ardently that this "totally admissible" evidence should come in. It was better for everyone, she argued now, to bring in a fresh batch of jurors and avoid the risk of having to retry the case in a year and a half following an appeal.

Despite all his efforts, Redpath and Moon had been forced to watch as the judge resumed court, declared a mistrial, thanked the jurors and alternates, and dismissed them. Most painful had been Mrs. Coolidge's farewell look over her shoulder as she passed out of the jury box, a generous, handsome woman just about Redpath's age.

All his angels had flown. He'd never, this side of heaven, be so fortunate again.

At least, he thought, his son, Tom, would sympathize. As a public defender, the young man—not so young now, actually—knew the life. He'd set aside extra time to talk Sunday. A spring visit no longer seemed very likely.

Pigeons were patrolling the courtyard in mindless clusters, hurrying here and there officiously, like busy little prosecutors. Redpath suddenly hated them. He wished one of them—say, that whitish one, with the iridescent stripe—would stray close enough so he could kick it into a bus. An indignant voice was emerging from the revolving door behind him.

"That sucks! Can he do that? With no trial or anything?"

It was the pale, red-haired girl, speaking angrily to the long-haired blonde as they came out of the building and toward Redpath. The big boy with the sideburns loped behind the two girls, gawking around with a blissed-out smile, as though he were Adam just arriving in paradise, empty-headed and pure, carrying that inimitable look of the true high-minded, nonsmoking vegan.

"Why don't you chill, Denise? It doesn't matter," he said.

"Oh, sure, like, just deal with it." She caught sight of Redpath. "Hey! I'm asking him."

As they approached, Redpath took the measure of these barbarians. A gaggle of pigeons scattered out of their way, and an empty McDonald's milk-shake cup tumbled in the icy breeze across their path. The same cold wind caught the blonde girl's hair, lifted it, and blew it to one side in a shining mane. She glanced disdainfully at the one called Denise but said nothing.

"Um, excuse me? Sir? Mr. . . . ?" Denise fumbled as they got closer.

"Redpath," the blonde girl muttered without changing expression.

Redpath blew out a lungful of smoke and fought off the impulse to bang the two girls' heads together.

"Mr. Redpath, can we ask you a question?"

"It doesn't matter, Denise," the boy interrupted, sounding irritated.

"It matters to me, Peter."

Redpath looked at them without saying anything. He was suddenly very tired. Was he getting the flu, or something? These were decent kids who'd signed up to fight on the right side. Only problem was, they'd shot up the village. Killed the wrong people.

"Can I ask you a question?"

"Go ahead." He sipped out the last puff on his Lucky Strike, keeping his face impassive.

"Can the judge," she flapped her hand back at the building, "that Norcross geek, can he just put us in jail if he wants to, for as long as he wants, without a trial or anything?"

Redpath patted his pockets and located his cigarettes. He shook one out and began to light it off the end of his old butt. The smoke blowing back into his eyes made him squint as he puffed. He tossed the butt on the ground, drew deeply, and blew out the smoke.

"Yep."

The kid called Peter crushed out the butt with his sneaker, then carefully picked it up and put it in his pocket. He pointed at Redpath.

"I suppose you know you'll wreck your lungs if you don't stop smoking those things."

Redpath took his time and responded slowly, leaning toward the boy. "I suppose you know you'll damage your rectum if you don't pull your head out of your ass one of these days."

"That'th pretty crude," the blonde girl broke in, finally deigning to look at him. She'd been staring up at the top of the flagpole where the stars and stripes were snapping in the icy wind.

"I'm a pretty crude guy at the moment."

"Shut up, Brittany. You mean the judge can just do whatever he wants? How can he do that?" Denise's tone was so indignant, and her voice so loud, that four or five people standing near the corner of the plaza looked over. Most of the protestors were gone; they must have heard what happened.

"I'll make you a deal," Redpath said. "It's Denise, right? I'll make you a deal, Denise. You answer me a question first. Then I'll answer yours. Do you realize that, thanks to you, Moon Hudson probably just lost the best chance he'll ever have to hold his baby daughter again?"

"The outcome is irrelevant as long as the system's corruption is exposed," the young man chanted.

Redpath blew a mouthful of smoke in Peter's direction. "What fortune cookie did you read that in?"

"We shut down the trial," he said in an earnest tone. "That's what matters."

"Shut up, Peter," Denise said. She turned to Redpath. "The answer is, no. Okay? We didn't know that."

"I'd thtill do it anyway," Brittany said.

"Okay, fair enough," Redpath said. "And the answer to your question is, yes. You've committed contempt of court by screwing up my trial."

"Right," Denise said. "He found us in contempt."

"I find him in contempt," Peter said.

"And, after Reverend Safford signed our bond, and we promised to stay away, the judge said he'd wait to sentence us until after the trial was over." She paused. "And we don't get a jury? I thought we had a right to a jury of, you know, our peers."

Redpath shook his head. "Sorry. The conduct was in front of him, so he can do whatever he wants to you."

"Crap. That's bad." Denise's mouth trembled. "What sort of sentence can he give us? He looked wicked pissed when they brought us back in."

"He was bananas," Peter said, grinning happily.

"He'th a moron," Brittany said.

"Oh, give up the lisp, Brittany," Denise said. "You got us into this shit box."

"The usual rule," Redpath said with studied casualness, "is to give the contemnors—that's you—the same sentence that the defendant eventually gets out of the trial they disrupted." He waited with relish for this to sink in. He was lying, of course, but it cheered him up enormously to watch as even Peter looked staggered by the implications of Redpath's remark.

"You mean . . ." Peter began, "we could get the death penalty?"

"Whatever!" Denise said.

"It's possible," Redpath said. Then he added reassuringly: "But of course it's very, very unlikely. It's a flukey rule. In all probability, the most you'll be looking at is life."

He tossed the Lucky at Peter's feet and walked off toward the parking garage, feeling a little better. Maybe the pro-death penalty folks were right, after all. Maybe random sadism was good for the soul.

34

After he finally escaped from court, Judge Norcross sat at his desk for a long time, looking west from his windows as the darkness deepened. Five years exactly since Faye had died. He watched, his mind blank and boiling, while the stars slowly took up their positions over the horizon, silver nicks on a black granite cliff of sky. The years went by so fast.

When Faye was pregnant, after the amnio revealed they were having a girl, they'd picked out a name for their daughter: Jessica. To avoid bad luck, they hadn't told anybody. Jessica Norcross. Faye said it sounded like the heroine in a private eye novel.

The starlight deepened and seemed to throb as Norcross stared at it. With better luck, they would have been celebrating their little girl's fifth birthday in a couple months. He shook off the ghostly vision, pushed himself up from his desk, and walked down the silent corridor to take the elevator to his car. Everyone else had left the courthouse hours ago.

The trip north to Amherst was an empty blur. As he clawed up his slick driveway, lined with mounds of dirty, plowed-up snow, he realized that he had no memory of a single landmark during the entire half-hour journey. The garage door groaned slowly open, sounding like death, and the interior light clicked on.

Claire's presence in his life had changed Norcross's parking practice. Before her, he'd put his car in the center, leaving himself plenty of room on both sides. Now, with Claire staying over more and more often, he'd begun, out of politeness and without being asked, to squeeze over to the left to make room for her Prius.

This evening, he followed the new routine without thinking, bouncing up onto the garage's concrete slab to the far left. His numb preoccupation made him sloppy—everything was making him sloppy—and he eased in more snugly than usual. The car grazed the rakes and shovels hanging from nails on the garage's exposed two-by-fours, making them clang musically.

Norcross turned off the ignition, tipped back against the headrest, and closed his eyes. The cold, damp air fell across his face. How could he have been so stupid? Something like this was bound to happen. Anyone, *anyone*, but him would have seen it coming a mile off.

He imagined the swelling force of tomorrow's newspaper stories, today's Internet reports, the tidal wave of words arching over him. Skip Broadwater would be calling, probably this very evening, full of sympathy and concern, offering to help in any way he could, as though Norcross were an imbecile. Horrible. But the harder problem was how, after all this fresh publicity, he would ever manage to rustle up another sixteen unbiased, death-qualified jurors so he could, once and for all, shove this accursed case off his docket. His brother, Raymond, was right. Davy Norcross was a very nice boy. Just soft. Soft—as Raymond loved to say—as a slipper full of shit.

After several minutes, Norcross roused himself and started to get out of the car, but the door only opened a foot before bumping against something. He worked the door back and forth furiously, until a rake fell with a bang over the hood and gave him another two or three inches, just enough to squeeze his exhausted body through.

As he made his way along the cramped space between the car and the clanging tools, he stepped on something and started to topple sideways. Grabbing backward for support, his left hand smacked against one of the garage's two double-hung windows and punched a grapefruit-size hole clean through the upper pane. His hand, when he snatched it back, sported a nasty red smile all the way from the base of his pointer finger across the palm to his wrist.

Regaining his balance, Norcross examined the wound with pleasure. He could actually see where the flesh split open. Blood was busily spreading down his wrist into his cuff and dripping onto his pants. He licked the wound, enjoying the taste.

"Good."

Pressing backward, knocking over tools as he went, he inched free of the car and out into the mouth of the garage. He stood for a moment stooping and pressing his left hand against his pants, breathing heavily. The wound was beginning to sting fiercely. The sound of whimpering reached him, Marlene scratching against the door.

As Norcross walked to the door to let Marlene out, he noticed the unbroken twin garage window, mocking him with its virginity. Next to the door into the house was a set of black metal shelves with used quart and pint-size cans of paint, turpentine, and thinner.

Impulsively, he grabbed one of the pints with his good right hand.

"Batter up!"

He pitched the can toward the upper half of the window, winding up and firing with all his strength, but his aim was off. The can struck the window frame and rebounded, vomiting green paint back at him onto the floor.

He grabbed another can, a full quart this time, and tossed it lightly up and down, adjusting to its heft.

"David," a voice said, not too loud.

Claire had rolled up unnoticed. She was standing next to her car in a pool of light from the garage.

"Oh, hi there," Norcross said. He took aim at the window. "I won't be a minute."

"David," Claire said again.

He paused. "Hmm?"

"May I have a turn?"

"Well." He let his arm drop and examined Claire without expression. The sound of whimpering and scratching was now very loud.

"I don't know," he mused. He began swinging the arm holding the paint can. "It's a version of solitaire, really." He sniffed and frowned. "Kind of a one-man game."

"You hurt your hand."

"That's true. I did." He held it up to her.

Marlene began barking.

"Well," Norcross said.

"If you need any . . ." Claire began.

"You know," he blurted, very loud. "I could always count." He pivoted and fired the paint can with a crash through the upper section of the window, sending it bouncing across the frozen ground on the other side. "I could always count on Faye not to discuss my work."

Claire looked at him, pale in the light from the garage, her face utterly immobile. Then she turned and with a short cry got into her car and sped off, spraying snow and gravel.

Norcross trotted to the mouth of the garage, thinking to call after her. But her lights swerved down the driveway and quickly disappeared into the trees. In a few seconds, he turned toward the house, pressing his hand against his thigh to slow the bleeding. After he let Marlene out, he paused in the doorway and looked back at where Claire's car had been. He'd done one thing right at least. He had heaved the paint can through the window so hard, because his impulse—his horrible, insane, utterly unfair impulse—had been to throw the can at Claire. It was not very nice, perhaps, but that was the truth. The truth, the whole truth, and nothing but the truth.

35

In the atmosphere of anti-Catholic bigotry in Hampshire County in 1806, the configuration of the court that was to preside at Daley and Halligan's trial was ominous. Capital cases in Massachusetts at that time required two judges, and one of the two selected for the upcoming trial was Samuel Sewall of Boston, the same man who'd joined in Bradbury's frosty opinion about Catholics. Sewall had the distinction of being the direct descendant and namesake of the Judge Samuel Sewall who had presided at the infamous Salem witch trials in 1692. The other judge was Theodore Sedgwick of Stockbridge. Sedgwick's contempt for common farmers and working people was so notorious that during the agrarian uprising in 1787 called Shay's Rebellion, Sedgwick's mansion was one of the first to be burned down.

On Tuesday, April 22, 1806, after five months in custody, Dominic Daley and James Halligan came before Sewall and Sedgwick and formally offered their pleas of not guilty to the charge that they murdered Marcus Lyon.

Employing the traditional phrasing, the court clerk, Joseph Lyman, then inquired of them: "Dominic Daley and James Halligan, how will you be tried?" To this, they replied, "By God and my country." And Lyman rejoined, "God send you a good deliverance!"

After they tendered their pleas, the two defendants formally requested that counsel be assigned to defend them. Recognition of the right to appointed counsel under the federal Constitution was still more than 150 years away, but Sewall and Sedgwick, applying state law, appointed two lawyers for each defendant. For Daley they selected Thomas Gould, a member of the bar for one and a half years, and Edward Upham, with seven years' experience. They gave attorneys Jabez Upham and Francis Blake, with eleven and nine years in practice, respectively, the task of representing Halligan.

Having made these appointments, the court then set April 24, 1806 as the day of trial, giving the defense team two days to prepare. Had the defendants' lawyers wished to take the elementary step of visiting the scene of the alleged murder, the trip on foot or horseback from Northampton to Wilbraham and back would have exhausted nearly the entire interval between their appointment and the commencement of testimony. Because of this, defense counsel never viewed the crime scene before the trial, and they had no opportunity to contact potential witnesses in the area.

Meanwhile, as the day of trial drew near, the excitement among the local population intensified. Attorney General Sullivan—himself a former member of the Massachusetts Supreme Judicial Court—rode into town to conduct the prosecution, accompanied by attorney John Hooker, specially appointed to assist him. To accommodate the enormous crowd gathering to witness the trial, Sewall and Sedgwick transferred the case from the courthouse to the Northampton Town Meetinghouse.

On April 24, 1806, shortly before nine a.m., the sheriff's deputies chained Dominic Daley and James Halligan inside a horse-drawn wagon and drove them the short distance from Prison Lane to court to begin their trial. References in the reports of the case indicate that Daley's wife and mother somehow made the long journey from Boston and were awaiting him at the meetinghouse. Halligan had no such support.

Once the defendants arrived, Justices Sewall and Sedgwick called the court to order and supervised the selection of the twelve men to act as jurors. Jury service by women remained more than a century away. The foreperson of the jury was the ironically named Justus Dwight. The eleven others were: Elijah Arms, John Bannister, Elijah Hubbard, Jabez Nichols, Samuel Patridge III, Thomas Lyman, Roland Blackmar, Elijah Allen, Asa Spalding, John Newton, and Jonathan Peterson.

After the men were seated in the area set aside for the jury, Thomas Hooker rose to present the opening statement on behalf of the Commonwealth. Hooker began by noting that the jury's situation was "one of the most solemn to which men are ever called."

"The fondness with which we all cleave to existence," he told the twelve men, "will on the one hand render you slow to condemn; at the same time it should, on the other, make you determined to protect." The jury's consolation would be that "if you follow the dictates of your own understanding as influenced by the testimony, you will discharge your duty to yourselves and to your country, however afflictive the event may be to others."

Dominic Daley, Hooker said, took the lead in the murder of Marcus Lyon, willingly assisted by James Halligan. After shooting the young man in the ribs and then smashing his skull in with the pistol butt, both defendants dragged the corpse from the Post Turnpike and threw it into the Chicopee River. Hooker noted particularly the increased rate of travel adopted by the alleged killers after their crime: Daley and Halligan "were five days, from Tuesday to Saturday, in coming to Wilbraham from Boston, a distance of eighty miles, but a little more than two in going thence to Cross Cob Landing, a distance of one hundred and thirty miles."

Hooker promised to present evidence during the trial that a witness from Boston, a "Mr. Syms," would identify the defendants as having purchased the pistol that was found near Lyon's body. It later emerged during Syms's actual testimony, however, that all he could say was that he sold the pistol to someone with an Irish accent. He could not identify either of the defendants as the purchaser. Moreover, Hooker promised to confirm through another witness that some unusual banknotes found on Halligan at the time of his arrest had previously been in the possession of the victim. No witness ever offered testimony to this effect, and at the end of the trial the prosecution had to concede that the banknote evidence was worthless. But the seeds had been planted.

When Hooker sat down, the Commonwealth called the first of its twenty-four witnesses. By far the most important of these was the thirteen-year-old boy Laertes Fuller. The defense objected to the admission of Fuller's testimony, arguing that the boy's youth rendered him incompetent to take the stand, but Justice Sedgwick quickly overruled this quibble.

After taking his oath, the boy described how on November 9, 1805 at about one o'clock in the afternoon he had seen two unknown men on the Post Turnpike, heading west. A few minutes after they had passed out of sight, Fuller himself began traveling on the same road and in the same direction the two strangers had taken. The sequence of events now described by the witness was somewhat confused. According to his testimony, shortly after the boy began walking down the Post Turnpike going west, he saw the same two unknown men coming back, now with a horse identified by other witnesses as belonging to Marcus Lyon. From the witness box, the boy pointed out Daley as the man leading the horse that afternoon and carrying a bundle tied up in a blue handkerchief. This bundle, the prosecutor suggested to the jurors, contained the murder weapon, the broken pistol later found by the search party. According to the boy, as Daley approached leading the horse, the second stranger followed behind, driving the animal along in haste.

Fuller told the jury that he then followed the two men onto a side road, but when they came to the top of a hill, one of the men jumped on the horse and rode off. Fuller said that, after this, he went on his way to an orchard nearby to look for fallen apples. Daley, now on his own, approached an adjoining stone wall, leaned on it, and stood looking at the boy for about fifteen minutes without saying anything. After this interval, the second man returned without the horse, and the two men resumed walking west down the turnpike. On cross-examination by Halligan's lawyer, Francis Blake, Laertes Fuller admitted that he never heard the discharge of any pistol that day, and that he could not in any way identify Halligan as the man accompanying Daley.

The presentation of the Commonwealth's two dozen witnesses consumed most of the day. After the testimony, Hooker offered a short summary of the prosecution's evidence, arguing that if both the prisoners participated in murdering Lyon, or if one did the killing while aided and abetted by the other, then "they are both murderers in the view of the law and you are bound by your oath to pronounce them guilty."

When Hooker took his seat, Sewall and Sedgwick turned to defense counsel and inquired whether they had any witnesses to present. With only two days for preparation, it could not have come as a surprise that no testimony would be offered on behalf of the two prisoners. The only potential defense witnesses conceivably available would have been the defendants themselves. But in 1806, and for sixty years thereafter, Massachusetts law barred a criminal defendant from testifying on his own behalf on the ground of inherent bias. Before considering the verdict, the jury would never be permitted to hear either Daley or Halligan speak a word denying the murder.

With no witnesses to offer, Attorney Francis Blake of Worcester stepped forward to present his final argument on behalf of James Halligan. By this time, it was about nine in the evening. Blake began by telling the jury that he "read in your countenances the deep and distressing anxiety" caused by the task before them. But "painful and distressing as your situation," he said, "you will readily imagine that mine cannot be less critical and embarrassing than yours." This was the first time, he told the men, that he had addressed a jury in Hampshire County, and the first time he had "ever spoken in the presence of an audience so numerous and so deeply interested in the event of a trial." Moreover, he was suffering from a severe cold—"an indisposition which almost denies me the power of utterance."

Blake noted two other severe handicaps he faced. First, "the prisoners have been tried, convicted, and condemned, in almost every barroom and barbershop, and in every other place of public resort in the county." And, second, he confronted "the inveterate hostility against the people of that wretched country from which the prisoners have emigrated, for which the people of New England are particularly distinguished."

With these preliminaries aside, Blake proceeded with a fierce denunciation of the evidence against Halligan. First, not a single witness could confirm with any certainty that Marcus Lyon had been killed on November 9, the only day the defendants had been in the area, rather than on the day before, or even earlier. Second, the only opportunity the defendants might have had to kill Lyon, even accepting that the murder occurred on November 9, would have been "in the broad glare of day, on a public turnpike road, where travelers were continually passing, and within a few rods of houses in every direction." It was much more likely, he pointed out, that the attack had occurred "on the evening or night preceding, and by some midnight assassin."

Blake reminded the jurors that the defendants' greater speed after November 9 might have many explanations, including the common experience that men traveling on foot tended to increase their pace after the first few days, as they became more inured to the rigors of travel. Moreover, the testimony of the Commonwealth's chief witness, Laertes Fuller, suffered at least three deficiencies: First, due to the boy's age he was "not entitled to full and unlimited credit"; second, his testimony was "in its nature, vague and uncertain," and, third, Fuller's evidence was "highly improbable and inconsistent in itself." The thirteen-year-old never identified Halligan at all, never heard a pistol shot, could not positively identify the horse they were leading, and never mentioned the incident to anyone until the next day. Moreover, according to the time frame described by the boy, Daley and Halligan would have had to ambush Lyon, murder him, dispose of his body in the Chicopee River under a sixty-five pound boulder, and return with his horse, all in the space of only fifteen minutes.

"Is it in the nature of things," Blake asked, "is it within the scope of human probability, is it credible, is it even possible that this complicated work of robbery and murder could have been thus secretly and silently achieved in the little time allowed for the foul purposes by the testimony of this witness?"

No. The only explanation for a conviction in this case, Blake argued, would be what he termed the "national prejudice," which would lead the jurors "to prejudge the prisoners because they are Irishmen."

"With all our boasted philanthropy," Blake declaimed, "which

embraces every circle on the habitable globe, we have yet no mercy for a wandering and expatriated fugitive from Ireland. The name of an Irishman is, among us, but another name for a robber and assassin. Every man's hand is lifted against him, and when a crime of unexampled atrocity is perpetrated among us, we look around for an Irishman. Because he is an outlaw, with him the benevolent maxim of our law is reversed, and the moment he is accused, he is presumed to be guilty, until his innocence appears!"

When Blake concluded, the judges afforded one of the attorneys for Dominic Daley, Thomas Gould, the opportunity to address the jury. Gould, however, only stood and stated: "The evening having so far elapsed, and the prisoners signifying their assent, I decline to address the jury."

The result of Gould's inexplicable waiver was that the jury heard no testimony from any defense witnesses, and not a single direct comment by any advocate for Daley on the flaws in the testimony of the prosecution's witnesses.

After Gould's retreat, Attorney General Sullivan submitted the prosecution's final argument to the jury. His presentation was workmanlike, but compared with Blake's fiery remarks, somewhat equivocal. If the Commonwealth's witnesses were believed, he said, the jurors must conclude that Lyon "was in fact murdered, and the prisoners were in a situation where they might have committed the deed, and there is no evidence that it was committed by anyone else." After that, the case simply rested on whether the jurors believed Laertes Fuller.

"Our state of existence is imperfect," Sullivan said, "and our intelligence limited; yet when our duty calls upon us to act, we need not tremble for fear of doing wrong; we are candidates for another state of existence, on the introduction to which our fate will not depend upon the enquiry whether we have done right, but whether we have acted with an upright heart, and from pure motives."

After these ambiguous remarks, Sullivan resumed his seat, and Judge Sedgwick immediately gave the jury its charge on the law. His directives steered the jury toward conviction with far more force than anything Sullivan had said. Referring to Laertes Fuller, Sedgwick stated, untruly, that the boy's description of the events had always been consistent. Moreover—despite the fact that Fuller's testimony, even if believed, constituted no more than circumstantial evidence against either defendant, and the fact that the boy never identified Halligan at all—Sedgwick instructed the jury that "if you believe this witness, gentlemen, you must return a verdict of conviction. When it is proved to you that Lyon was murdered, that the prisoners were on the same road, in possession of his property almost upon the very spot where the body was found, rendering no account of themselves whatever during that period, you can hardly have a reasonable doubt but they are guilty of the crime of which they are accused."

At ten in the evening, the jurors retired to deliberate; one hour later, they informed the court officer that they had reached a unanimous decision. As Daley's wife and mother looked on, Justus Dwight, the foreperson, read out the verdict in the silent meetinghouse: "We, the jury, being fully agreed, find Dominic Daley and James Halligan guilty of the murder of the foresaid Marcus Lyon in the indictment."

Judge Sedwick promptly scheduled the sentencing for the next day. The trial had consumed, including breaks, a total of fourteen hours.

PART THREE

36

Assistant U.S. Attorney Lydia Gomez-Larsen stepped around counsel table into the well of the court and placed herself before the empty faces of the newly selected jury. Voir dire, the second time around, had produced a far luckier draw. In place of the Dragon Lady, Seat One held a young man bearing an expression of reasonable receptivity—not a trace, thank heaven, of the Unitarian's overt, deadly skepticism. The season, too, had warmed up, drifted into May, and from the courtroom windows the banks of the Connecticut River were visible, with pale-green willows hanging over the water like horses drinking. There was hope.

As was her custom during openings, the AUSA carried no notes and used no podium. Her outfit was a navy business suit—skirt and jacket, white blouse—and she wore no jewelry except for her gold wedding band. Cradled against her right hip, however, was an ugly-looking automatic rifle pointed toward the courtroom's high ceiling. After a nod from Judge Norcross, Gomez-Larsen's mild but crisply audible voice broke the silence.

"May it please the court, Mister Foreperson, ladies and gentlemen of the jury. On October 22 of last year, at approximately eight thirty a.m., this man, Clarence Hudson . . ." Here, she pointed with her free hand at the defendant and looked at him for a count of three. Moon tried to return her gaze, then shifted, and looked down at his hands. ". . . using an assault rifle just like this one, shot down two people in broad daylight, near the corner of Walnut and High Streets in Holyoke, ten miles north of here. In a carefully planned act of premeditated murder, that man right there, Clarence Hudson, sometimes known as Moon Hudson, shot Edgar Delgado in cold blood, firing a customized version of this Norinco SKS assault rifle through the back window of a stolen Nissan Stanza. Delgado, who used the nickname Peach, was twenty-three years old at the time.

"Hudson fired nine shots. Three hit Peach Delgado, one in the left leg, one in the belly, and a third in the upper chest, right through his heart. Delgado died almost instantly. At the same time, a few doors down the street, a stray bullet, fired by this man right here"—again, she pointed to Hudson—"struck his second victim, Ginger Daley O'Connor. As she was bending over to pet a puppy, a bullet from the assault rifle passed through Ginger O'Connor's neck and tore open her carotid artery. That's the big blood vessel, right along the side of your throat, right here. Mrs. O'Connor was forty-two years old, a lifelong resident of Holyoke, married and the mother of three boys, seventeen, fifteen, and eleven. Shot by this man, Ginger O'Connor bled to death on the sidewalk in front of the neighborhood clinic where she volunteered."

Gomez-Larsen now took three steps from her position in

front of the jury over to the government's table. She passed the assault rifle to Alex Torricelli, murmuring, "Thanks, Al." Alex propped the weapon, which had a safety strip of thick orange plastic through the magazine and barrel, against the wooden partition behind him, following Lydia's instructions to keep it in full view.

Gomez-Larsen retraced her steps to the jury box, put her hands behind her, and gazed down at the carpet, giving the jurors plenty of time to return their attention to her. Since she used no notes, her body seemed exposed and defenseless. Her posture told the jurors that here was a woman who neither could, nor would, engage in any sort of deception. After the pause, she lifted her face and continued, in a lowered tone.

"Good morning. As you heard earlier, my name is Lydia Gomez-Larsen, and it is my privilege and honor to represent the United States of America in the case against Clarence Hudson, also known as Moon Hudson. As His Honor told you, this is the government's opportunity to present its opening, a summary of the evidence it will offer—evidence that will convince you beyond any reasonable doubt that the defendant, Clarence 'Moon' Hudson, committed the four crimes he is charged with: the two murders I described, plus possession with intent to distribute marijuana, and possession with intent to distribute cocaine."

Gomez-Larsen proceeded to serve up the government's evidence in simple, easily digestible slices. First, that past fall, Moon Hudson had been selling drugs up at the university. A student would testify to buying substantial quantities of marijuana and high-quality, so-called "fish-scale" cocaine from him. Second, the defendant was an associate of the street gang La Bandera. Two gang members, called Flags, would confirm this. They would also testify that Hudson got his retail supply from a drug wholesaler, Carlos Arcera, the La Bandera warlord. Third, around Columbus Day, Hudson and Arcera were both having problems.

Some jurors leaned forward; others sat with their heads cocked to one side, taking it all in. The judge jotted on his yellow pad. Redpath rocked back in his chair with his arms folded against his chest. Occasionally, he whispered something to Moon and shook his head.

To illustrate her third point, the AUSA stepped over to the table, picked up a stiff square of paper, and returned to the jury, holding the object behind her back. The jurors looked intrigued. "Arcera's problem was that people were invading La Bandera turf in Holyoke, cutting into their drug business." She held up an eight-by-ten photograph.

"One of Arcera's competitors was this man, Edgar Delgado, a drug dealer like Clarence Hudson, who used the street name Peach. Hudson's problem was that his business couldn't keep up with demand. He needed more drugs, but he had no money to pay for them. By coincidence, Hudson also had a grudge against Delgado, who'd beat him up a few years back and put him in the hospital with, among other things, a deep gash in his forearm that left a scar."

Gomez-Larsen paused for a moment here to check off one danger avoided. After a sharp argument, Norcross had allowed her to mention the fight between Hudson and Delgado, but barred her from revealing that it had occurred while the two were in jail. The ruling still rankled, but she had cleared this pothole with no forbidden hint to the jury.

She replaced Delgado's photo on counsel table, picked up a second document, and resumed.

"Three witnesses, Jesús Santiago, Manuel Ortiz, and most

importantly Ernesto 'Pepe' Rivera, Arcera's nephew"—she displayed his photograph—"will testify to being present when Arcera made his agreement with Hudson: five thousand dollars up front, plus a half kilo of cocaine to take down Delgado. With this deal, Arcera would remove an obnoxious competitor. Hudson would have his revenge on an old enemy, and he would get the money and product he needed."

In the minutes that followed, Gomez-Larsen detailed the dramatic eyewitness testimony Pepe would be offering about Moon's ambush; in the corner of her eye, she saw the figure of the judge bent over his pad, jotting rapidly. Several jurors were glancing up at him, clearly noticing Norcross's interest in this portion of the evidence, underlining its importance. Excellent!

When Gomez-Larsen had exhausted this topic and was ready to move on, she paused, cleared her throat, and stepped over to the government's table to pour herself a cup of water. She could have filled a cup ahead of time and left it on the edge of the table, but the pouring gave her a longer break. She managed the operation coolly, drank the entire cup, and returned to her spot in front of the jury.

"I've been going on for some time. I only need a few more minutes to finish up, so I hope you'll be patient with me just a little longer. What I've told you so far is a sad, sad comment on what one particularly vicious human being, Clarence Hudson, was capable of. But the evidence in this case will show heroism as well. Because almost as soon as those shots were fired, things began to fall apart for the two men in that Nissan Stanza: Pepe Rivera and Moon Hudson.

"Rivera will tell you he drove immediately after the shooting from Holyoke toward Springfield to ditch the car. He will tell you he was very, very frightened. Near the Elm Street projects, he dropped Hudson off. Hudson ran down an alley, holding the Norinco under his sweatshirt, up against his chest like this. We will present another witness to you, a tailor named Marco Deluviani, who had a shop adjoining the alley, and who saw that man, Clarence Hudson, running down that alley, holding an object, what we now know was the assault rifle, against his chest.

"Now, here is where the heroics start. After Hudson got out of the car, Rivera looked into his rearview mirror and who did he see? He saw that man."

She pointed to Alex Torricelli and paused. As the two of them had practiced, Alex looked at the prosecutor and then slowly turned to face the jury. The effect was heightened, as Gomez-Larsen knew it would be, by Alex's self-conscious half smile.

"Officer Torricelli noticed the Nissan and something didn't seem right. The rear window was broken out, and the license plate was partially covered with mud. He will testify that he saw Hudson leave the Nissan at the Elm Street projects and trot down the alley carrying the assault rifle, right where Mr. Deluviani will say he saw him. Officer Torricelli began to follow the Nissan.

"Now you'll get this story from two sides. Because when Rivera realized that Torricelli was following him, he panicked. That's the only way to put it. You could say he lost it."

Gomez-Larsen noted an amused nod from the foreperson. Good. He was enjoying the story. The other jurors stayed right with her, too, as she described the apprehension of Rivera and the wounds Alex received.

"Of course, as you now know, two blocks away from where Delgado lay dead in the street, Moon Hudson's cold-blooded crime took on a new dimension." She selected another photograph from counsel table. "This woman, Ginger Daley O'Connor—coming to work at the clinic she had helped to found, coming to give her services for free, and bending to pet a little puppy who happened to be tied to a parking meter—Ginger O'Connor, the mother of the three young boys you see with her in this picture, was struck in the neck by a bullet deliberately fired by this man, Clarence, aka Moon, Hudson. The wound ripped her throat open, ladies and gentlemen. Ripped her throat open."

Gomez-Larsen stopped, allowing the jury to see that she was struggling to control her disgust. Her voice resumed after a few seconds in a more matter-of-fact tone.

"There's another piece of the puzzle I want to mention before I sit down. Remember, the type of cocaine sold by Hudson up at the university, fish-scale cocaine? Agent Swann will tell you that this type of cocaine is rare and gets its name from its shiny, scaly appearance, like the scales of a fish. It is extremely high quality, often more than ninety percent pure, and a seller has to mix in something to dilute it before sale. When the officers arrested Moon Hudson at the apartment he was sharing with his girlfriend they found, in plain sight, a large quantity of inositol, a common cocaine dilutant."

Gomez-Larsen took another drink of water and exhaled a long breath to steady herself. A pang of disappointment rippled through her as she thought of the powerful evidence Judge Norcross had suppressed: the bagged marijuana and the cash, found right in Hudson's closet, and the fish-scale cocaine discovered in the basement—all unavailable to her now because of the defective warrant. But she forced the thought out of her mind and concluded softly.

"Ladies and gentlemen of the jury, at the close of this case, I will have another chance to address you. I submit that, when that time comes, all the pieces of the puzzle will fit. At that time, you

will have no reasonable doubt about Clarence Hudson's responsibility for these terrible crimes. I will be asking you to return
verdicts of guilty on all four charges: guilty of possession with
intent to distribute marijuana, guilty of possession with intent
to distribute cocaine—the drugs Bobby Thompson will tell us
Moon Hudson sold him up at the university—and, much more
importantly, guilty of murder in aid of racketeering in the killing
of Edgar Delgado, and guilty of the same offense in the killing of
Ginger Daley O'Connor. Thank you."

37

"I don't know," Tony Torricelli said, popping a French fry into his mouth, "sometimes I feel like there's not one single thing in this lousy world that means diddly to me anymore."

"Uh-huh," Alex responded.

Tony's my-life-as-tragedy horse manure was ancient and boring, but Alex was content to let the conversation drift down this familiar channel. In maybe fifteen minutes now, he'd be able to beg off and make a run for it. Lydia and Redpath had been at sidebar for so long after Lydia's opening that Norcross had put Redpath's opening over to the afternoon. Even Tony, who'd set up this fucking lunch, would realize his brother couldn't be late getting back to court.

"There were so many things that I used to believe in, Allie, but they just don't have the same buzz anymore."

"Really?" Despite himself, Alex was curious. "What in the world did you ever believe in, Tone?"

At least the restaurant was nice—a popular Springfield institution called The Fort, two blocks from the courthouse. It featured excellent German food and an outstanding selection of international beer. Tony swallowed a forkful of Weiner schnitzel and sighed; his tongue wriggled out to swipe a dab of ketchup from the corner of his mouth.

"Well. Take big boobs, for example."

"Oh, for Christ's sake."

"No, it's just an example." Tony lifted his hands as though Alex were arresting him. "They're like life. You start out, when you first get married, and everything's bouncing around like pink grapefruit. Every day is Christmas, and every night you unbutton your presents and you get exactly what you asked Santa for. You know what I mean?"

"Sort of."

"But then a few years go by, you have a couple of kids and, jeez, all of a sudden, they're like . . ." Tony dropped his voice. "They're like empty water balloons. She's sitting on the edge of the bed, rummaging around in them trying to find her belly button."

"Come on," Alex broke in. "The years let some air out of all of us—even you." He forced himself to look into his brother's face. "She's a nice, nice lady, Tone. And let's face it, neither of us is winning any blue ribbons in the husband department. She's a great mom, she's . . ."

"Allie," Tony interrupted, "I got to tell you something." He set his elbows on the table, put his hands over his face, and sucked in air as though he was taking an ice pick in the gut. It took him three deep breaths before he dropped his arms on the tablecloth, revealing a face that was flushed and, worst of all, apparently on the verge of tears. If this was an act, he was doing a terrific job.

"Jesus, Tone, what's wrong? Did Cindy find out about . . . anything?"

"No, no. It's not that. I could handle that easy."

"So what's the problem this time? I mean, if I can help at all, you know I'll . . ."

"You won't help! That's my problem." Tony snorted. "The sewage is up to my chin, and the joke is you're all I've got for a life preserver." He sniffed up juicily, swallowed, and shook his head. "I've been sitting here for half an hour now, yakking away like a dickhead, trying to think of some way to bring this up, but there isn't any easy way."

"I'm not following you."

"It's your fucking trial." Tony addressed his brother as though he were six years old. "Think hard now. Remember the trial, Allie? Well, Janice was right on the button, as usual. I've got my own reasons . . ."

Alex cut in. "Tony, we're not talking about the trial, period. Especially not out in public like this."

He glanced around. No one seemed to be within listening range, but he couldn't be sure of the table directly behind him without turning around, and he didn't want to make himself conspicuous. A paranoid thought flew through his mind that Tony might be wearing a wire. Backed into a corner, his brother was capable of anything.

"I'm sorry, Allie, but I don't have any choice here," Tony was saying. His voice was turning acid. "I have to talk about it, or . . ."

"Well, we're not talking about it, and that's it! We just got the damned thing started. Jesus Christ! Lydia finds out I'm talking, she'll cut off my nuts with a rusty putty knife." Tony opened his mouth to protest, but Alex leaned forward and banged his forefinger on the table. "I mean it. Don't push me on this, Tone. I'll get up and leave right now." He tossed his napkin onto his plate.

This was exactly what Alex had been dreading about this lunch, but fortunately he was prepared. He just wasn't going to talk about it, that's all. Still, sticking to his guns wasn't turning out to be as easy as it had been when he'd practiced the "rusty putty knife" routine on the way over. His heart was hopping around like a jackrabbit.

The two brothers stared at each other. Tony was clenching and unclenching his softball-size fists. He was capable, Alex knew, of reaching across the table and grabbing him by the shirt collar. The room was full of lawyers who regularly ate here, maybe even a judge or two. Not good.

After ten buzzing seconds, Tony dropped his shoulders and waved in surrender. "Okay, fine, you win. We won't talk about the fucking trial." He folded his hands and put them in his lap. "We'll just talk about me."

"Right. Everybody's favorite topic."

"*Grazie tante,* little brother," Tony said, but he broke off again and ran his hands back through his hair. "Okay, one more touchdown for you. I admit, I deserved that."

Tony wiped his mouth with his napkin and dabbed at the corners of his eyes. Alex looked on warily. Part of this performance was an act, no question, but how much?

Tony stared off into space for a few seconds and shook his head. "I'm trying to think of a way to make this sound funny and cute, but I can't do it. It sucks too much. Fact is, I've got our South End pals down on my neck again."

"Tony, for crying out loud."

For the past ten years, Alex's brother had been through one idiotic jam after another with his addiction to illegal sports gambling. He played using betting cards, or he placed wagers over the telephone with bookies linked to Springfield's local crime syndicate. Various rumors swirled around about the group, including a claim that it was controlled by a branch of the Mafia headquartered in Providence. Whatever the truth might be, Alex knew these were not guys you jerked around.

"It's bad this time."

"Tony, when are you going to . . . ?"

"I know, I know. I'm an asshole." He paused, then burst out, "but, Jesus, who ever thought UConn would get knocked out so early? They were supposed to take the whole thing, and then . . . Fuck." He shook his head angrily.

"How much?"

"I could have wiped out the entire tab if they'd won just two more rounds. I was that close. Two fucking rounds."

"How much this time?"

"Sixty. Sixty-five grand."

"Fucking hell, Tony! They let you get in that deep? They didn't cut you off?"

"I yanked them around a little." Tony chuckled. "Using different names, betting with different guys once one guy snipped me." He took in Alex's horrified expression. "Hey! That's how it works! Sometimes the only way you get out of a hole is to dig deeper." He glared up at the beer steins displayed along the walls. "UConn! Those pussies!" He sighed and scratched his forehead. "Actually, I think it's over seventy with the juice. Things are getting pretty ugly."

"No kidding!"

"I mean, it's worse than you think. This time, somebody paid a visit to Mom and Dad."

"Who? Who did?"

"I'm not even going to tell you. You might do something silly."

"I might do something silly. That's hilarious, Tony. The sons of bitches!"

"Calm down. It was just the usual bullshit. Everything nicey-nice. No threats. They were doing it out of friendship. I owed money to some bad people who might, you know, do something to me. I was too embarrassed to talk about it, they were only coming forward out of respect for the family, yada, yada, yada—you know the drill. Now Mom's in hysterics, and Dad's talking to the bank about"—Tony put his hands over his face again and breathed carefully—"about taking out a mortgage on the house again. Jesus, I feel like such a piece of garbage!"

Alex remembered the six-course dinner his mother had laid out two years ago for the whole family, when she and his dad had finally made the last payment on their little three-bedroom place in Agawam. Unchained, after thirty years, with nothing but the taxes to cover in retirement, and with a small piece of this earth to pass on to their sons free and clear! What a celebration. Then he imagined going to Janice, in her current mood, and trying to explain the grimy corner Tony had boxed himself into this time. If they maxed out all their credit cards and took a second mortgage on the house, they might just about come up with it. His brother, he knew, had zip.

And Alex did know the drill: They'd catch Tony in some parking lot at night and beat him up until he pissed in his pants, making sure there were a few nasty cuts and bruises for him to explain to everyone later, maybe a tooth missing or a broken bone. One dose would do the trick. The family would come up with the cash somehow.

"It was a few weeks ago," Tony was saying. "I told Dad it was just a misunderstanding, everything was fine, and I think he believed me. Course, somebody could drop by again anytime."

Tony plunged on, and Alex, too sickened by what he was hearing, did not stop him.

"Anyway, remember I was talking the other night about our friends from the South End? Turns out one of the guys who calls the shots now played hockey in high school with Bobbie Daley, Ginger O'Connor's brother, and he's still real close to the family. I guess he thought a lot of Ginger."

A puff of memory caused Tony's mind to shift. He broke off and stared into the middle distance dreamily.

"Last year, I paid a couple visits to Bobbie's old girlfriend, Candace. Funny how porking the same girl gives you the fuzzies about a guy, kind of like being frat brothers."

"Stick to the point, okay?"

"Right. Anyway Bobbie's friend heard the scuttlebutt about problems with your trial, and he says if I do him a favor he might talk to my friends about knocking the tab down. Give me time to work something out."

"Uh-huh. What's the favor?"

"He thinks I can deliver you."

"Deliver me? What am I, a baby?"

"I was drunk! We're at the White Horse, watching the girls, and I start bragging about my famous little brother, and how I could make sure that spook Hudson gets what he deserves. I know, Allie, this makes three times now, I'm an asshole. But, all of a sudden, these guys are all smiles. The one in charge has his arm around my shoulder, and I'm everybody's best friend. So we made our bargain: You put the seal on Hudson, who everybody knows is guilty anyway, and there's no more visits to Mom and Dad."

Alex said nothing.

"For Christ's sake," Tony said. "It's not as though I'm asking for much. It's such a little thing. Jesus! It's nothing."

38

Unlike Lydia Gomez-Larsen, Bill Redpath used the court's portable lectern as he addressed the jury; it served as a place to rest his yellow pad. Now, he stood next to it with his hands folded in front of him, looking at the floor. Redpath's big, shambling body, draped in a slightly wrinkled charcoal suit, presented a dramatic contrast with Gomez-Larsen's well-brushed composure. His broad chest rose and fell. Then he began, in a voice that seemed so low, at first, that three of the jurors leaned forward to catch it. Yet, at the same time, the big man's resonant tones carried easily to the farthest corners of the packed courtroom.

"It's so easy to point a finger," he said, shaking his head.

"It's so easy to point at a man, when he can't answer back, and make him look bad. Imagine how that must feel! Imagine your-self, or anyone you know, having to sit here in this room, while someone stood there and kept pointing and pointing at you like that, and you couldn't say a word."

Redpath shifted and stared over at Gomez-Larsen for the same three-count she had used. Gomez-Larsen returned his stare coolly, and Redpath turned back to the jury.

"Let me tell you something, ladies and gentlemen, that finger-pointing is nothing but an old prosecutor's trick, used to put someone on the spot. If we had an angel in this courtroom, or an innocent child, or any one of you, and someone pointed and began making accusations, then that angel, that child, or even any one of you, would find it hard not to squirm. It's just human nature. The prosecutor knows that, which is why she did it."

He held up his hands. "I have fingers. I could point, if I wanted to, I suppose. If I were going to point, I would point at Ms. Gomez-Larsen right now, and say, 'There she sits, the prosecutor, representing the full power of the United States of America, brought down against this one man.' And if I were to do that, maybe I could make even a very clever prosecutor like Ms. Gomez-Larsen squirm a little. Just the same way she tried to make Moon Hudson look bad by pointing her finger at him again and again this morning."

He stepped behind the lectern, adjusted the yellow pad, and leaned toward the jury.

"I'm Bill Redpath, and I'm also very proud—very proud and very honored to be here representing Moon Hudson this morn-ing. I'm going to call him Moon, because that's what his wife, his family, and his friends have always called him. We heard that 'aka' business a lot from the prosecutor, as though it's some scary thing. But Moon has been called Moon since he was a little baby, an infant just about the same age his own little girl, his daughter, Grace, is now. There's nothing scary about it.

"Before I get too far there's something I need to spell out in big capital letters. You probably remember it, because His Honor went over it so carefully, but I need to be sure." He nodded toward counsel table. "Please stand up, Moon."

Moon Hudson rose slowly to his feet, a broad-shouldered, handsome, very dark man in a blazer and open-collared pale-blue shirt. He looked at the jury and then at Redpath.

"This man is presumed innocent. As he stands there, this man—now, I'm pointing, too, for heaven's sake. See how easy it is?"

Several of the jurors thawed out to various degrees; some even smiled and looked a little more relaxed. Moon did not smile, which was good, but his face softened, and he gazed tolerantly at his attorney.

"Sorry, Moon. Have a seat." Redpath drew out the moment, looking down at his notes and scratching his ear. Then he continued, dropping his voice again.

"Moon Hudson is as innocent as anyone in this courtroom. He is as innocent as any of you, as me, as the prosecutor, and even, with all due respect, as innocent as Judge Norcross himself sitting up there on the bench. He can only be found guilty if the evidence—believable, trustworthy evidence, not finger-pointing and 'aka' malarkey—convinces you beyond a reasonable doubt that he is guilty.

"I'm going to review with you, in just a moment, the evidence that the government says it will offer in its case, piece by piece. Before I do that, though, I want to point out two places, two examples of places, where the prosecutor misspoke. That's a polite way of saying that she said something that's just plain false.

"First, she said, toward the end there, sort of in passing, that Moon was living with his girlfriend." He turned and nodded to the front row of the gallery. "Would you stand please, Sandy? I promise not to point." Sandra Hudson stood, slim and serious, nodded and quickly sat down. "That is Sandra Hudson, Moon's wife and the woman he was living with. Sandy Hudson, who is a graduate student at the University of Massachusetts, and Moon were married two years ago in an Episcopal ceremony right here in Springfield, married by Sandy's uncle, who happens to be the chaplain at Syracuse University over in upstate New York. Moon Hudson is a married man, with a full-time job, a wife, and a daughter. He's not living with any girlfriend."

In his peripheral vision, Redpath could see Judge Norcross turn his head and cast a serious, hopefully disapproving, look toward the government's table. He drew this "gotcha" moment out before continuing.

"Sandra will testify that her husband was home with her at the time these despicable crimes were committed. I submit to you that her testimony will be entirely credible and persuasive, but if you conclude that what she says even *might* be true, this case becomes very easy. You must acquit Moon Hudson." He looked up at the ceiling and scratched at the loose skin under his chin.

"The second false, flatly false statement made by the prosecutor was much, much more serious. She said, if I heard her correctly, that Alex Torricelli, the officer sitting with her over there, will testify that he saw Moon Hudson leave the Nissan Stanza that Pepe Rivera was driving that October morning, and run down an alley immediately after the shooting, carrying some version of that assault rifle she kept waving in front of you, hugged up against his chest, like this."

After a pause, Redpath unfolded his arms, stepped from around the lectern, and took half a step toward the jury box.

"Ladies and gentlemen, I will make a promise to you right now. And I ask you to hold me to this promise."

He held up his finger and increased his volume.

"Alex Torricelli will *never* say that! Never. He will testify that he saw *someone*, someone *probably Hispanic*, run down that alley, carrying something, an object that I agree was almost certainly the weapon used by the killer to commit these terrible murders. Moon Hudson is not Hispanic. The man who ran down that alley was *not* Moon. That man was the real murderer, a Hispanic man who was a member of the gang La Bandera. I submit to you that the evidence will show that the man running down that alley was almost certainly Carlos Arcera himself, Pepe Rivera's uncle, who you heard so much about from the prosecutor. Based on Officer Torricelli's own testimony, the man he saw running down that alley could *not* have been Moon Hudson. For the government to make that suggestion is outrageous. It is absolutely false and reveals just what a bag of broken bottles its whole case against Moon really is."

For the next five minutes, Redpath described Moon's background, how he got the nickname Moon from his uncle Thad while he was still in the cradle, his meeting with Sandy at the university, and his job as a warehouse foreman. Redpath returned once more to Grace, lingering to make Moon show some emotion and was pleased to notice two of the jurors glancing his client's way with expressions approaching sympathy. It was a good moment for another dart at the prosecutor.

"And before I leave the topic of the Hudson family, I ought to mention one thing Ms. Gomez-Larsen tried to put such a sinister spin on—this terrible inositol, this so-called drug dilutant." Redpath paused to suppress a smile and shake his head. "The prosecutor gave you the fancy name, inositol, but she never mentioned what it really is, to ordinary folks. It's baby formula, ladies and gentlemen. They mix it with water to make up a bottle for the baby, so Moon can feed Grace on the nights when Sandra needs a little extra sleep. So much for that."

Redpath returned to the podium and flipped a page of his notes to let this sink in.

"The mistake—assuming it was a mistake—about Moon's supposed girlfriend, who was really his wife, the outright falsehood about the police officer seeing Moon when he didn't and won't say he did, the half-truth about the inositol—that's all typical of what you will find is the government's case. Distortion, innuendo, and spin. Let's turn now to what they say their real evidence is."

Redpath counted off the government's proposed witnesses contemptuously. Bobbie Thompson, the recently expelled UMass student, was a joke, completely untrustworthy. Santiago and Ortiz, facing felony drug charges with multi-decade potential sentences would say anything; their stories did not even jibe with each other.

"The very nice man, Mr. Deluviani, who the prosecutor says will testify that he saw my client running down the alley? That's another myth. I should have mentioned it right at the beginning, just like Officer Torricelli. Marco Deluviani will say that he saw *somebody*. He won't be able to identify Moon Hudson, and he won't even be able to tell you whether this somebody was Hispanic or African-American. That's it. His testimony amounts to nothing."

Redpath turned to the side, looked up at the ceiling, and placed his hands together.

"Okay," he said quietly. He looked tired. "Okay." He turned to the jury. "Now let's get to what this case, or I should say this mess, is really all about.

"The one witness who I predict will say just exactly what the prosecutor says he will say will be Pepe Rivera, the sixteen-year-old boy, now seventeen I guess, who admits he drove the car and assisted in the deliberate murder of Edgar Delgado and the tragic, unintended killing of Ginger O'Connor. He will say just exactly what the prosecution wants him to say, because if he doesn't he will spend the rest of his life, instead of just twenty years, locked up in prison. He's a kid who assisted in two murders, and he's here looking for the door marked 'Exit.' A way out.

"One thing that the prosecutor didn't tell you is that the story Pepe will spin for you on the witness stand a few days from now is not his first story. Oh no. When he first came up with Moon Hudson's name, he had a different, entirely screwball story about how Moon didn't tell him he was going to be shooting anyone, just going to wave the gun at the victim to scare him, and Moon was going to pay Pepe a hundred bucks to drive the car. It was a story that Pepe now admits was a bald-faced lie, a total crock. It was not until several weeks after Moon's arrest that he changed his story and came up with this fable, this new lie, about his uncle Carlos supposedly hiring Moon.

"Now you might ask yourselves why Pepe changed his story. The reason is another thing the prosecutor didn't tell you. A short time after the police arrested Moon, law enforcement officers down in San Juan found a body floating in the harbor that they're pretty sure was Carlos Arcera. And this guy didn't choke on a clam. He'd been shot in the face before somebody tossed him into the harbor. When he heard this, Pepe realized he didn't have to cover for Carlos anymore, and he decided, or maybe somebody told him, to make his story a little bit more plausible by cooking up this crazy new fairy tale that Carlos Arcera hired Moon Hudson.

"But the evidence will show that it is far, far more likely that Carlos Arcera himself committed these crimes, that Rivera was instructed to shove the blame onto Moon Hudson if he got caught, and that after Delgado's drug-dealer friends caught up with Carlos and settled the score, somebody got Rivera to change his story. This teenager's fake decision to come clean will be quite understandable when you hear about the stampede of government investigators and lawyers, including a Holyoke police captain who is Ginger O'Connor's uncle, who were pounding on Rivera's door day after day, hammering on him with the fact that his first story wasn't going to do the trick. The revenge murder of Carlos Arcera freed Pepe, with a little help from his government friends, to come up with this new concoction of nonsense.

"But it's still a house of cards. If you touch it, ladies and gentlemen, it collapses immediately. When you get down to it, all the prosecution really has in this case is Pepe Rivera, a terrified child who admits he helped kill two people. That's it. I am confident that after you hear this boy's testimony you will have to conclude that no reasonable person, no one in this room, no one in the entire universe, would trust the word of Pepe Rivera in this situation, for one single solitary minute. And at the end of the trial, when I speak to you again, I will be asking you to return a verdict of not guilty, and end this nightmare for Moon Hudson and his family. Thank you."

39

Later that day, David was sitting with Marlene on the stone terrace behind his house, pondering the slow sunset. The tallow-colored light threw shadows of leaf patterns on the judge's sweet-smelling lawn. Marlene rested, alert on her haunches, scanning the edge of the trees for chipmunks and other interlopers. At a respectful distance, two robins hopped stiffly. Too much time had passed since David had seen Claire, and he was thinking about her again.

She had called the evening of the garage catastrophe, around bedtime, to ask how his hand was. Then she'd started to apologize about talking to Novotny with a quaver in her voice that he'd found close to unbearable. David remembered interrupting her, telling her how sorry he was about what he'd said—that it was stupid, unforgivable—but the conversation started jumping around at this point, and his memory of exactly who said what got murky. He did remember that after a long silence she'd asked what was going on, as if it weren't obvious, and that he'd lied and said that nothing was going on, and there had been another silence, followed by a sudden, intense burst of questions from Claire that jarred him so badly he just went blank. He couldn't recall what either of them said after that, except that whatever it was made him want to hang up, get in his Subaru, and drive to Alaska. In the end, they decided to take a break. He'd sat in his recliner that night, staring out the French doors into his backyard until three a.m. He hadn't been up so late since Faye died.

A few days later, Claire called again. He let the machine take her message. Her voice sounded thin and remote.

"Hi, it's me. Ummmm, I'm honestly not sure what happened last time, David. But I would like to give it another try. Are you there? Pick up the phone, please. Come on." There was a pause while she waited. "Okay. David, I don't want to be . . ." Another pause. The image of Claire rifling through her mental thesaurus looking for the right word made David start to smile. Was she trying to be diplomatic, or just clear?

"Testy," she said finally. "But I also have to say that I don't think either of us deserves whatever's going on here." Another, shorter pause. "So call me, okay? Please. This is . . ." She sighed. "This is the pits."

Of course, she hadn't phoned since then. She wouldn't. But she was the first thing on David's mind before he opened his eyes in the morning, and she was the final pang as he turned off the light each night. In the darkness behind his closed eyes, he would relive the totally unforgivable spectacle he'd made of himself the last time he'd seen her.

David scratched Marlene's neck as she watched the robins closely. Right now would be a perfect time to call Claire. The jury had finally been chosen, and the openings were behind him, with no IEDs exploding in the courtroom so far. Plus, with any luck, Claire would be out with friends, and he'd only have to speak to her machine.

But the air was so consoling, the high western sky was such a perfection of iridescent teal and peach, and the spring aroma of the lawn was so rich that David kept procrastinating, kneading the back of Marlene's thick neck. In a minute he'd go in, microwave his dinner, and spend the evening working up a summary judgment motion in an age discrimination case his clerk had squeezed onto tomorrow's docket. For now, he'd sit. The bolder of the two robins bounced in their direction, and the dog shifted restlessly.

The phone rang, startling the birds, which flew off with indignant cries. David could barely allow himself to hope it might be Claire, but as he hurried into the house he went through an absurd pantomime of making himself presentable, tucking in his shirt and running his hands back over his hair.

It was Liz Coffman, Raymond Norcross's long-time secretary, a pretty, highly competent woman David had grown fond of over the years, calling from Washington, DC. They exchanged greetings and inquired about each other's dogs. She had two rescue greyhounds, Tammy and Pete. She asked him to hold for Ray. The delay while he waited for his brother to come on the line was shorter than usual.

"Hello, Your Honor!" Ray sounded happy, or at least hearty.

"Hello, Ray," David said, a little more cautiously.

"Listen, I'm sorry Lindsay complicated your life with her death penalty essay. Somebody at Deerfield Academy is going to wish he or she had never been born."

"It's not a problem. The girl's a chip off the old block." After a pause, David added limply, "How's the weather down there?"

"Damned if I know," Ray said with renewed gusto. "Just got back from Korea, Taiwan, Singapore, and I forget where else. It's been frustrating, because I've been dying to get in touch with you about the WFSC, and I've been too tied up to call."

The acronym went over David's head, but he avoided letting his brother know. Ray did this sort of thing. Maybe it would come to him in a minute.

"Well, you're a very busy guy," David said. "They tell me you had cherry blossoms down there. Too bad you missed them."

"You know what the WFSC is, don't you?"

David shifted from one foot to the other and pulled on the end of his nose, hoping something might click. Nothing did.

"Not really, Ray."

"It's short for the World-Famous Springfield Cock-Up."

"Ah."

"You're a celebrity."

"Is that so?"

"It's very much so. You made the *International Herald Tribune*. What happened?"

David explained in general terms the Pratt dinner, Professor Novotny, and the disruption of the trial. When the topic of Claire arose, he could almost hear Ray's antennae whirring.

"We're back on track now," David said, dropping the words into his brother's pregnant silence. "We finished openings today. Tomorrow we'll get started with the government's first witness."

Raymond had obviously not been listening. "Will you forgive me if I say something, little brother?"

"I doubt it."

"You're a very, very decent fellow, you always have been, but as usual you're missing the forest for the pine needles. Allow me to summarize for you: One, you're on the young side; two, you're extremely smart; three, you work as though God were standing next to you holding a big fat stick; and four, you're an inoffensive moderate. Barring terrible luck, we'll have you up on the First Circuit Court of Appeals in two or three years. Faster, if someone would shove dear Judge Leaky in front of a bus. After that, who knows? We might just see you wandering among the cherry blossoms yourself. So, no distractions or dillydally, dear boy. This is no time to tiptoe through the cow pies."

"Dillydally?"

"Exactly. Let me tell you how this world wags. One mess, and you have an opportunity to prove your mettle. Two messes, and you're a theme for late-night TV. This Claire enchantress can wait until the trial is over. For now, keep the old eye screwed to the ball, and the zipper tightly zipped. It was a lot of work getting you in there. Don't mess us up."

The waxy sun had disappeared, and the air had turned chilly when David and Marlene returned to the back terrace. It was dark in the surrounding trees, and the sky high above the tallest branches was a deepening blue. Soon there would be stars. David let his eyes follow a pinkish-gray wisp of cloud for a while, then he turned and walked quickly into the house, heading for the phone. He needed to talk to Claire. His brother could go fish.

40

A few miles south of Amherst, the air was muggy over the Flats in Holyoke. Pepe Rivera's mom, Maria Maldonado, and her cousin Hannah had the windows open in Maria's one-bedroom apartment, trying to catch a little breeze as they rearranged the space to make room for Hannah. With Pepe sitting in a cell in Ludlow, Maria decided it didn't make sense to keep carrying the rent on her own. Tomorrow morning, her uncle, Hannah's father, would be coming by with his pickup bringing Hannah's things.

Maria was in the kitchen, unpacking a box of dishes, washing them and carefully placing them on the shelves. The radio was tuned to a Spanish-language station, playing softly so as not to disturb the neighbors. Maria moved deliberately, like someone convalescing from an illness. It had been a rough time for her—first, her son was arrested, then the news of her half brother Carlos, killed and thrown into the harbor in San Juan.

She could hear Hannah busy in the bedroom, crooning to the radio and cleaning out what was left of Pepe's things from his bureau and closet. It was kind of her to do this. Maria had tried going through her son's stuff, but it disheartened her to find a stack of old *Penthouse* magazines in his underwear drawer. When did he stop being a little boy and start with this kind of trash? She would let Hannah have the bedroom while she continued to sleep on the couch in the living room. Maria had no boyfriend and was in no hurry to get one, whereas Hannah was talking about some new guy she'd been seeing and dropping hints about needing her privacy.

Suddenly, Maria heard Hannah cry *"Jesús Maria!"* This was followed by a quick thumping of knees and feet from the adjoining room. Maria set down a plate and hurried to see what the problem was. Hannah rarely moved fast, and Maria was almost sick with dread at whatever this new thing might be. Her main fear was that Hannah had found baggies of marijuana or, God forbid, a taped-together bundle of clear plastic envelopes with white powder.

Hannah was struggling to her feet as Maria entered the room. She was a heavy woman, and she grunted as she pulled herself upright. No question she was upset. She was brushing back her henna-streaked hair and avoiding eye contact.

The two women spoke in Spanish.

"What is it?" Maria asked.

"It's nothing. Nothing."

"It's not nothing, Hannah! I can see by your face. In the name of God, tell me what it is."

Hannah did not reply but tipped her head toward the closet.

Maria stooped, putting her hands on her knees as she peered into the shadows. A broken floorboard was lying next to a dark space with something inside it that she could not make out. Crawling into the closet on her hands and knees, she saw a piece of green canvas and, protruding from the top of the cloth, the barrel of a gun. She pulled back the canvas and felt the cold metal. There was a big space under the boards; the gun was large, not just a pistol. An oily smell rose from the hole.

At the back of Maria's mind, a dormant memory shifted and pressed itself against her consciousness: Carlos, back in October, on the morning of the shooting, coming by the apartment as she was cleaning up from breakfast, and disappearing for a few minutes into her son's room. She recalled it had been a beautiful fall day, cool and sunny. She'd asked no questions—not even how he'd gotten in without knocking. The dark look on her brother's face told her that he would take no questions. One peep and she'd get the back of his hand.

In the dimness, Maria became aware that Hannah was working her way into the closet next to her. She pulled Maria's hand away from the cloth and slid the broken board so that it fit snugly back in the hole.

"Leave it," Hannah said. She struck the board with her fist to seal it in tightly. "We never saw this. We know nothing. Nothing! Come." When Maria hesitated, Hannah tugged on her cousin's arm and spoke more urgently. "Come on, Maria!"

They moved back into the bedroom and stood up, whispering fiercely although no one was within earshot.

"It's terrible. Carlos must have put it there," Maria said, pointing at the closet.

"Carlos is dead. No one will know."

"But Pepe told them the black man Hudson threw the gun into the river. I was there, Hannah! They wrote it down."

Hannah placed her hands on her hips. "Do you want your son

to spend the rest of his life in prison? I tell you, Maria, we know nothing about this."

Maria, breathing hard, looked into her cousin's eyes and saw something she didn't like. Hannah's new boyfriend came from a bad group, and Maria sensed a kind of desperation in Hannah's desire to please this man. Could her cousin be trusted?

"You're right, Hannah," Maria said, dropping her eyes. "We'll forget this."

The shadow in Hannah's eye faded, and she wrapped her arms around Maria, murmuring, "It's okay. It's okay."

Maria allowed herself to be held. Standing in her son's old room, with the aromas of his childhood still gathered around her, she stared over Hannah's shoulder through the cloudy window and out into the darkness. A pale light fanned across the ceiling as the sound of a car drifted by and disappeared into the night.

41

Bill Redpath arrived in the courtroom early. As he unloaded his briefcase, the door from the lock-up swayed open, and the two marshals entered, escorting his client. Moon Hudson stepped gingerly into the room, looking up at the ceiling and rubbing his wrists where the cuffs had been. His face had clouded up again, and he nodded to his wife and then his lawyer without changing expression.

Neither Hudson nor Redpath felt good about the new jury. They were especially uncomfortable with the foreperson, a white kid in his late twenties who sold time-shares. The guy's knee jigged constantly, and he'd responded to questioning during voir dire by saying, among other things, that he thought being on a jury in a death penalty case would be awesome. Like TV. The long process of sifting the jurors had produced only two minorities on the panel: a Latina who was married to a correctional officer, and

an African-American alternate—just enough "diversity" to insu-
late the process from any legal challenge, but not enough to make
a real difference in the jury's basic sympathy.

"What's up?" Moon asked dully as he slid into his seat. "Still
the cop?"

Redpath looked over at Gomez-Larsen, eight feet away at the
government table. "Captain Torricelli still your first witness?"

"Uh-huh." The prosecutor was facing away, talking inaudibly
but with some urgency to her lead-off man. She seemed to be
ignoring the "captain" dig. Might not be a bad idea to twiddle her
dials, since it seemed like she had something important to say to
her guy. See if he couldn't fuzz up her reception.

"Think you'll be all morning with your direct?" he asked.

"Hope so." She didn't bother to look Redpath's way, but kept
talking to Torricelli, now holding her hand out to him. Redpath
caught the phrase, "Don't do this to me, Al."

He leaned toward her. "You folks enjoying this nice spring
weather?"

"Fuck off, Bill." She was gesturing at Torricelli with both hands.

"All rise!"

Norcross hurried in. He was leaning forward, as usual, looking
as though he were trying not to crack his head on something.

Everyone got up while Dickinson droned through the call
to order. Norcross's two law clerks slipped in behind the judge,
each clutching a yellow pad, and took seats at a table off to one
side. Redpath had been speculating during the pretrial proceedings about whether he might have an ally in the female clerk.
She looked Jewish, which could sometimes be a good sign, and
her facial expressions, so far as he could read them, conveyed a
mighty discomfort with something. He'd have to find a pretext
to exchange a friendly word with her. Nothing directly about the

trial, of course, but some chummy comment if he could dream one up. The fat male co-clerk looked like a dud.

Once everyone sat, Judge Norcross leaned forward and spoke. "We'll be bringing the jurors in here in just a moment, but I wanted to warn you that we'll be breaking early today, at noon. I've got a massive motion for a temporary restraining order this afternoon, unfortunately." He paused, looking weary. "They're about to bulldoze another wetland. It's maddening, but I doubt the jury will mind taking off early before the weekend."

Dammit. This was bad. Gomez-Larsen would have no trouble dragging her direct out for the entire morning, and the early break meant that the jurors would have all weekend to think about Torricelli's testimony, with no chance for Redpath to smudge it up on cross.

When the jurors filed in, Norcross informed them of the shortened day; the foreperson rewarded him with a grin of delight, and the other jurors, the lazy bastards, seemed either pleased or indifferent.

Then Norcross nodded at the prosecutor. "Government's first witness, please."

Gomez-Larsen rose, pausing before she spoke to ensure that she had all thirty-two of the jurors' eyes on her. "Your Honor, if it please the court, ladies and gentlemen of the jury, the government calls, as its first witness, Officer Alex Torricelli."

Redpath noticed with pleasure that Torricelli's shirt collar was too tight, and this had forced him to leave the top button undone and push his tie up as high as possible to look tidy. But the knot had slid down, revealing the subterfuge and leaving the cop with a slightly unkempt appearance, as though he were already at the end of an exhausting day.

"Raise your right hand, please." Ruby Johnson stood behind

her desk with her hand up. "Do you solemnly swear that the testimony you give at this trial will be the truth, the whole truth, and nothing but the truth, so help you God?"

"I do." It did Redpath's heart good to see Torricelli so uncomfortable. The man was keeping his face unnaturally staunch, trying to imitate some tacky movie-star hero or something.

Torricelli squeezed into the box, bumped against and quickly rescued the water jug, and finally settled down with a heavy plop. His eyes flickered around the courtroom. No easy escape.

A noisy shuffling and throat clearing arose from the front row of the gallery. Were they about to be interrupted again? This time, Redpath wouldn't mind.

A tall, overly handsome, dark-haired man in a gray silk shirt was shoving into the front row. He clearly had some special connection to the trial. His expression was proprietary, and his presence was having some kind of effect on Torricelli, who was so studiously *not* paying any attention to this pushy guy that something had to be going on.

Gomez-Larsen took her time getting to the podium, letting the disturbance fade, and smiled briefly at her witness.

"All set in there?"

Torricelli nodded back. "Ready to go, I guess."

"Would you please introduce yourself to the jury, and spell your last name for the record."

"My name is Alex Torricelli. T-O-R-R-I-C-E-L-L-I."

"Mr. Torricelli, are you married or single?"

"Married."

"How long?"

Torricelli hesitated, working back the math.

Gomez-Larsen smiled and glanced at the jury. "Take your time." Two of the jurors chuckled.

"Seven, no eight, years."

"Sure?"

"Pretty sure." More chuckles.

"And children."

"One. A girl, Angie."

"How old?"

"Fourteen months."

"No problem with that one?"

"No, ma'am." More little smiles and toasty glances passed among the jurors. A pair of older women side-by-side in the back row were fluttering maternally.

Redpath tossed his pencil down with a carefully measured half teaspoon of impatience and leaned back, folding his arms. The eyes of several jurors wavered over to him, and things settled down.

"Are you employed?" Gomez-Larsen continued.

"I'm a police officer for the City of Holyoke."

"How long?"

"Ten and a half years."

"Please describe the course of your employment since you first became an officer and tell the jury generally what your duties have been."

An unremarkable summary of the officer's shifts and assignments followed. Redpath jotted "No Promotions" on his pad and leaned back again.

"Now, Officer," Gomez-Larsen went on, "I want to take you back to the Tuesday after the Columbus Day holiday, just this past fall. Do you recall that morning?"

"Yes."

"Where were you?"

Torricelli described his route from home toward the center

of Holyoke. Redpath jotted another note for cross: "Late for shift? Why?"

"Did you notice anything unusual at that time."

"Yes."

"Would you please describe to the jury what you observed and what you did?"

Torricelli cleared his throat. "I saw a vehicle, a gray Nissan sedan, coming out a side street, the wrong way on a one-way. Part of the back window was blown out and the rear tag was covered with mud."

"Tag?"

"License plate."

A pivotal moment in the testimony was approaching. Redpath casually reached forward and drew a folder toward him, setting it so that more than half of it protruded over the side of the table. He placed his left hand on the folder to prevent it from falling and continued jotting notes with his right hand. Moon Hudson leaned forward and gave his attorney a curious glance.

"What happened next?"

"Can I have some water?"

"Of course."

Torricelli pulled a paper cup from the stack. His hands shook slightly as he filled it carefully and took a sip. "I noticed the Nissan slow down, and a guy jumped out, very quick. He had a hand up against his chest, like this." Torricelli put the cup down and demonstrated. "Then he, like, trotted down the alley alongside the Elm Street projects."

Redpath drummed his fingers on the file folder.

"Can you tell us what this person was wearing, and his approximate height and weight?"

"Dark pants and a black or navy blue hoodie with the hood

up. Between five ten and six feet, maybe two hundred pounds, give or take."

"A hoodie?"

"One of those hooded sweatshirts, with the hood up."

"Were you able to see this man's face?"

Redpath lifted his left hand to scratch his ear, and the file slithered onto the carpet. He emitted a stage whisper, "Oh dear!" and bent hastily to retrieve the scattered papers. He forced himself to stay down, pulling the loose sheets together, but Torricelli's answer was taking a long time coming.

"Did you hear the question?" Norcross's voice broke in.

"Yes. And the answer is . . ." The witness paused, and Redpath heard a slurp of water. "No. I was looking from the side, and he had the hood up. I couldn't see his face."

"I'm sorry," Redpath said, finally sitting up and slapping the messy file on his table. "I didn't catch that answer." He patted the papers back into the folder.

Gomez-Larsen turned. With her back to the bench and jury box, she tossed defense counsel a glare.

"Your Honor," she said, turning again, "may the stenographer read back that last series of questions and answers, so we can be sure that Attorney Redpath will know exactly what Officer Torricelli said?"

Redpath reckoned that Judge Norcross knew what was going on, but he also knew that the fact of his knowledge, like the true reality of what was happening, would never make it into the cold transcript. The judge would have to protect the record by having the passage read back. As defense counsel looked up at the bench with an expression of innocence, however, he could see in Norcross's eyes that he'd played this particular trick for the last time. Once more, and His Honor would find a way to skewer him in front of the jury.

Judge Norcross nodded coldly at the court reporter, and she drew out a band of white recording tape.

"Question: 'Were you able to see this man's face?'

"Question from His Honor: 'Did you hear the question?'

"Answer: 'Yes. And the answer is no. I was looking from the side, and he had the hood up. I couldn't see his face.'"

A shuffle broke out behind Redpath, and as he turned he caught the retreating form of the handsome spectator in the gray silk shirt banging out through the courtroom doors. He was about to face forward again when he noticed something else. The two goons who'd been attending the trial all along, one bald and one with a stubby ponytail, also rose and made their way more slowly out of the courtroom. The bald one was chewing gum, and he did not look happy.

42

The plan for David's next outing with Claire took some negotiating. During the first two phone calls, they just talked, mostly showering each other with apologies, and he didn't even suggest getting together. Finally, during a third call, he proposed a lunch at his house that weekend so they could talk more comfortably. After an awkward pause, Claire offered a counterproposal: that he take her for a tour of his courthouse that Sunday, when nobody would be around. David instinctively resisted the idea. Claire and his job did not mix well.

"Come on. We need an outing, David. If I come over there, we know what will happen."

"Well," David began, "that wasn't what I . . ." A wave of something skittered over him that woke up every cell in his body.

"Uh-huh. We were doing just fine in that department before the crash, dearie. Time to branch out." As she was speaking, David found himself visualizing how Claire's navel made a perfect zero. They'd gotten tomato sauce in it once, eating pizza in bed.

"Time to view you in your natural habitat, David. See what all your protective coloration is about."

In the end, he couldn't deny her. As they headed south on the interstate toward Springfield, the view opened up, displaying a broad vista of the Holyoke Range, pale green lower down in the Connecticut River flood plain, turning to dark blue-green on the upper slopes where the conifers took over. The profile of the hills was like a giant sleeping under a lumpy green bedspread.

"So pretty," she murmured.

David turned, took in Claire's profile against the greenery. "Beautiful."

In a few minutes, they were passing the exit for Holyoke, and Claire asked suddenly, "Do you think Hudson didn't do it?"

"What?"

"Are you worried he didn't do it? Is that what's so hard?"

"I don't know. Maybe." David craned over his shoulder to check the traffic as he accelerated into the passing lane, taking care not to look at Claire. "Okay, yes, a little, among a lot of other things. But we'd probably better not talk about it." He got around a long semi and back over, concentrating on his driving.

"I get it. The biggest thing in your life, and we're not allowed to touch it." Several seconds passed, and David could feel Claire gathering herself. Finally, she said, "Is that because you can't discuss it generally? Or because you opened up to me once, and I dropped the ball?"

"That was my mistake, not yours."

"Because you talked to me."

"I put you in an unfair position."

"Would it matter if I were your wife?"

The car lurched, and David accidentally flipped on the turn signal. Claire gave a snort and laughed.

"Don't worry, Igor, I'm not proposing. Just trying to get the rules down."

There was a silence before the conversation resumed on other topics. By the time they arrived at the courthouse and parked in the judge's private spot in the basement, some of the awkwardness between them had dissipated. They rode the elevator to the fifth floor, made their way along the wide hallway that led to the courtrooms, and stepped at last through the ten-foot oak door that formed the public entrance to Courtroom One.

"Well," David said, spreading his arms up toward the vaulted ceiling. "Here it is, my little piece of heaven." The courtroom felt to him like the interior of a church: well ordered, portentous, watchful—as though it had a life of its own, separate from the people standing inside it. He pointed at the witness box. "We'll be picking up with the cross-examination of Officer Torricelli in about"—he consulted his watch—"eighteen hours and twenty-four minutes."

"Torricelli?"

"Holyoke cop who arrested the driver. Chunky, squirmy guy."

They strolled down the carpeted aisle through the public gallery, six rows of polished benches on either side, until they reached the waist-high wooden partition separating them from the well of the court. Three walls of the courtroom were paneled in oak. A high row of windows on the fourth wall admitted a blue-gray glow, with the outline of a tree limb dancing in one corner. At the foot of the room the bench towered; behind it, above the judge's enormous black chair, a bronze art deco eagle spread its fifteen-foot wings.

"That's your pulpit, huh?" Claire pointed over the swinging doors that led into the well.

"Yes, and that's where the jury sits." David gave a nod to the closed-off box that contained two sedate rows of blond wood and burgundy velour seats, screwed into the floor.

"They bring the defendant in through there from the lockup." The small door at the side, made of the same wood as the paneling, was almost invisible. "He and his attorney sit at the defense table there." He pointed to a long table at his right, and went on wearily. "No cuffs or leg irons of course. The assistant U.S. attorney sits there with the case agent. They always grab the table closest to the jury."

David listened to himself rambling. The trial lay heavily on his stomach; he felt his body tensing around it.

"Come on." He pushed open the swinging gate and strode down between the counsel tables, around the podium and toward the bench.

Claire held back.

"Am I allowed in there?" She peeped through the gateway at the freshly vacuumed carpet. "I'm not a lawyer, you know."

David turned and looked back at her. Her outfit was simple: khakis, a green silk blouse, and a black corduroy jacket, unzipped. Her hands were in her pockets, and she was looking at the area in front of the swinging doors as though it were a swamp where an unsanctified person might sink and disappear. Sucking on her lower lip and widening her eyes, she flashed her loopy goose expression at him inquiringly.

This, David thought, *is the Claire Lindemann trapeze.* One moment everything was tumbling and chaotic, and he couldn't make anything out. Then her face would come into focus, and there they would be, gently swinging, hand in hand over the serene world. How many times now had she worked this magic?

"I think you'd better lead me," she said quietly. "I'd feel safer that way, passing into the underworld." She held out her hand, palm up.

The judge hesitated. Standing there beneath his own heavy bench, looking at this woman in green, he felt himself beginning to crack open. Love? It was not what had lifted him up so long with Faye, the certainty that they had been born to be with each other forever. But something new was wrestling out of the egg-shell within him. This woman might drive him crazy, but he did not want, very much did not want, to be without her.

She was still waiting for him.

"You're safe with me," he said, taking her hand and drawing her through the gate. "See? You just passed the Bar."

The feeling of astonishment at how exactly their two hands meshed, and how deliciously, struck him hard, and a prickle of lust began its familiar crawl up his spine and along the back of his neck. Nice to know they'd have the whole rest of the day.

"That's the witness box." He gestured to the right of the bench. "My stenographer, Maureen, sits there, and my court-room deputy, Ruby Johnson, swears in each witness from her desk right here."

"Where do you come in?" Claire dropped his hand and drew her arm around his waist companionably.

"Right over there." Another paneled door stood at the side of the bench. The judge and the professor looked at each other, smiled, and kissed. Claire put her hand on the back of David's head and hungrily pressed his mouth down onto hers.

Of course, David thought delightedly. *She's as ready to bust as I am.*

After they'd been kissing for some time, David began to feel self-conscious about where they were. Claire, he knew, had few inhibitions about anything, beyond avoiding conduct that might actually get them arrested.

"All rise?" Claire asked when they finally broke, sweeping her hand up his lower belly.

"You bet."

"Can I check out what it's like up there?" Claire pointed at the bench.

"Go, please. I'll take a seat here at defense table. Try to restore my heart rate."

Claire circled around to the back of the bench and climbed the stairs.

"Wow," she said. "It's high up here. How do you avoid nose-bleeds?"

David gazed at his girlfriend. The massive chair made her look as though she belonged in junior high.

"I have no idea."

Claire leaned forward and blew into the microphone, which crackled. Her voice suddenly boomed out over the courtroom. "You're a little freaked— Whoa!"

"It's voice-activated," David laughed. "There's a switch on the base."

Claire turned off the microphone and continued. "You're a little freaked out about this trial, hmm?"

David slumped forward, setting his elbows on the door-size oak defense table, and scrubbed his hands over the back of his head.

"Claire," he said. "I have never been so, so . . . I can't think of the word. It's not nervous, exactly. Nervous is when I'm on a plane, and it starts bouncing around." He paused and looked up at her. "Nervous is when I think you're about to start winging croquet balls at me."

"So I noticed."

"Yes, well, this is not that. I'm just so pumped, I guess. I feel like I could burst into flame any second."

He stood up, walked behind the chair, and gripped the leather back with two hands, tipping it backward slightly.

"Right here is where Clarence Hudson will be sitting tomorrow at nine a.m. I'll be up there." He sniffed and pulled on the end of his nose. "This probably sounds awful, but to tell the truth, I try not to worry too much about whether he did it. I think about it, naturally, but the main thing is I want Hudson to get a fair trial. A *truly* fair trial. And the simple fact is this." He'd been speaking louder than he needed, almost at his workday courtroom volume. Now he noticed and dropped his voice.

"The simple fact, which I can tell you but no one else, is this: In my whole life, I've never done anything this hard. I'm pretty sure I'm up to it, but unpredictable things happen in trials, and we definitely can't afford another *ka-boom*." He waved at the witness box. "If I exclude testimony incorrectly, the government may be unfairly pinched, and a killer could go free." He gestured down at Hudson's chair. "But if I mistakenly admit evidence or instruct the jury incorrectly, this human being here could die of a botched trial—like those poor guys they hanged over in Northampton way back in eighteen-whatever."

He walked around to the front of the table and sat on it, swinging his legs.

"There are so many ways to make mistakes. You can do it just with a tone of voice, or a sarcastic comment. I was a very good trial lawyer, if I do say so, but I mostly did employment, personal injury, and civil rights cases, for crying out loud. Now here I am, with a man's life at stake, and tomorrow I'll be the guy in charge."

Claire got up from the big black chair, daintily shifted her behind onto the bench, and then swung her legs up after her. She pushed the water jug and blotter to one side and sat hugging her knees, looking down at the judge.

"I have a suggestion, Your Honor," she said.

There was a light behind her eyes, her naughty-girl look. Seeing it, David felt his mouth twist into a tired smile. He was expecting too much of her, going on like this.

"Well, I'm open to anything, believe me."

Claire looked up at the ceiling and took a deep breath. "Thirty-some years ago there was a pitcher named Mark 'The Bird' Fidrych, who played for Detroit," she began in her professorial voice.

"Oh, cripes, not baseball again."

"Hey!" She held up a finger. "Baseball players deal with a lot of pressure. And you said you were open to anything."

David flapped a hand at her. "Fine. Go on."

Claire swung her legs down over the edge of the bench and crossed her ankles, tapping her heels against the oak veneer.

"As I was saying . . . The Bird pitched for the Tigers. He was a starter. He used to talk to himself the way you do."

"I don't talk to myself."

"You do, dear, incessantly. But getting back to Fidrych, he was famous for talking to himself when he pitched, and especially famous for talking to the ball. The most pertinent fact, however, for our purposes today, is that he had a really hard time for a while in the minors. He struggled like crazy with the pressure, being up there on the mound all by himself, having to hit the corners, kind of like you."

"I see."

"So his girlfriend came up with this idea to help him. The two of them climbed over the fence to the ballpark in the middle of the night. Whew, it's hot in here."

She took off her jacket and smoothed it out beside her.

"And they crept out onto the pitcher's mound and made love,

right there under the stars." She looked down at him and tapped her heels against the side of the bench again. "Right where he'd be working the next day."

David's mouth dropped open. Claire tilted her head, made her goose face, and lifted her eyebrows.

"So"—she ran her tongue over her upper lip—"somehow, after that, he just felt a lot more comfortable up there. He won nineteen games as a rookie and started for the American League in the 1976 All-Star Game. Lord, don't they ventilate this place on the weekends?" She unbuttoned the top button of her blouse. "It's stifling."

"Claire," David said. "We could damage something."

"Oh, I don't know, this seems like a pretty well-constructed piece of furniture." She slapped the heavy wooden surface a couple times. "Seems pretty solid to me."

"I'm not talking about the bench."

She looked at him. "Don't you keep a blanket or something in your office?"

He paused. "I have an afghan."

"Why don't you go get it?"

43

That same weekend, Captain Sean Daley was putting in some overtime on the Hudson case. He was accompanying a Massachusetts Department of Social Services case worker, Irma Wallace, a close friend of one of his nieces, on a home visit to the residence of Zinnia "Spanky" Sanderson. The temporary custody the DSS had awarded Spanky over the child of her deceased daughter had been called into question by the discovery of drugs and the arrest of a drug dealer and accused murderer in the two-family house where she lived. A foster-care placement for the child, Tyler, was under consideration. Captain Daley was joining the caseworker strictly on an informal basis, to see if Spanky might cooperate in answering a few questions about her old downstairs neighbors, Clarence and Sandra Hudson.

"Will, you know, will this make a difference for Tyler?" Spanky asked, searching them with eyes like those of an enormous, frightened bird. The social worker, arriving without prior warning, had backed her into her untidy living room, and Spanky's huge body, tipping backward onto her overused sofa, was threatening to sink into the cushions. With her behind sagging so low, Spanky's knees were almost level with her chin. Wallace, the social worker, had taken a seat on the edge of Spanky's green lounge chair.

Daley was leaning against the entryway's doorframe. The police captain had declined Spanky's offer to sit down, with thanks, telling her that a back problem made it more comfortable for him to stand. This was not true, but it gave him a better vantage on the situation.

"Well," Wallace began, patting the clipboard on her knees, "your willingness to help might . . ."

Daley quickly broke in. "Not at all, ma'am. Not one bit. And I want you to remember that."

Gomez-Larsen had given Captain Daley clear instructions about this visit: They needed Spanky to play ball, but they did not want her testifying in court that they'd pressured her. It would be the easiest way for Redpath to attack the woman's credibility.

Daley took a step into the room and gestured down at Spanky. "Your hanging on to your grandson does not have anything to do with whether you help me out with some questions. Will you remember that for me? Please? In case anyone ever happens to ask you?"

"Okay," Spanky said uncertainly. She flapped the ends of her housedress down to mid-calf. From her sunken position, Daley seemed gigantic, standing above her in his uniform, with his gun in his holster. Spanky's lips quivered as she spoke, and her big eyes darted from the lounge chair to Daley.

"Thing is, I don't think Tyler would do that good in a stranger's house, that's all." She tried to make eye contact with Wallace, but the caseworker was looking down as she wrote on her clipboard. Daley, on the other hand, smiled at Spanky encouragingly and nodded sympathetically as she spoke.

"He's a lot better off with me. With . . ." She hesitated, not sure whether she was speaking to the point. "With somebody who loves him." Wallace continued to write without changing expression.

"I bet you're absolutely right," Daley said. "And there's nothing I'd like more than to be able to put in a good word for you." He held his hands out. "Can you spare me just five minutes?"

44

Sandra Hudson was finishing her Monday morning visit with Moon. She had come, as directed, to the marshal's lockup to drop off her husband's courtroom clothes, so he could change before the trial resumed. The marshal's suite included no formal visitors' area, so she spoke to Moon standing outside his cell. Redpath, who was finishing up with his client as she arrived, had already hurried off to grab a cigarette before court.

Sandra pointed at Moon. "I want one more thing from you before I go."

He was facing her through the chipped gray bars. The expression on his dark face was grave; the pleasure he took at seeing his pretty wife had softened his brooding eyes only a little. He shook his head.

"What do I have left to give you, babe?" he asked in a low voice. He lifted his hands up and looked around the empty cell. "You think I've got a bunch of roses or something hid in here?"

"Oh, you've got what I want," Sandra said. "I know you have it, sugar."

Moon rocked his head back and folded his arms. The posture accentuated his broad shoulders and his muscular arms and hands.

"Okay. You tell me what I have. Tell me what I can give you, in this place, and I'll give it to you. Anything you want."

Two deputy marshals, one white and one black, were seated on metal chairs on the far side of the small, windowless room. The men had enough experience to know when to be strict and when they could slacken a little. They were comfortable allowing this defendant and his wife a few moments together. The distance of eight feet between their desks and the cell provided the couple an illusion of privacy, but Sandra knew the men couldn't help hearing. It was part of her plan.

As she hesitated, Moon paced off the corners of the cramped lockup.

"Let's see now. I'm looking around, and I don't notice any flower garden in here. I don't see any four-leaf clovers, or any rabbits' feet." He turned back to Sandra. "So you tell me what you want."

"Well, here it is," Sandra paused. "I want you to give me one of your smiles."

Moon put his head to one side and touched the tip of his tongue to the middle of his upper lip. Sandra knew he tended to do this when he was trying to figure something out. After a moment looking at her this way, Moon retracted his tongue and shook his head solemnly.

"Girl, you're tough. You know I don't have a whole lot of smiles in me right now."

"But, I can't recognize you without your smile, baby. How do I know this is you?" She lifted her chin. "It's been so long. Just give me a little one."

Moon was looking down at the floor. The two deputies had abandoned any pretense of ignoring the drama.

"Well, you know," Moon said. "I don't . . ."

"Moon Hudson," Sandra broke in, "if you don't give me a smile, I'm going to take all my clothes off right here."

"What?"

"And I'm going to sing 'The Star Spangled Banner' while I do it."

"What?"

"Here I go." She started pulling her arm out of her jacket. " 'Oh say, can you see . . .'"

The two deputies looked at each other nervously. Nothing in the regs covered this.

She had the top button of her blouse open and was working on the second.

"Here I go now! 'By the dawn's early light . . .' Don't fool with me."

Moon's transforming smile, brilliant and shining, burst onto his face.

"Girl, you are something else. Damn! You are crazy, just crazy." His amazed grin was crinkling the corners of his eyes. "What in the damn world am I supposed to do with you?"

"Aw," Sandra said, dropping her hands and nodding at the marshals, "you see what you've gone and done now? You just cheated these boys out of the best free show they're going to see all year."

"Got that right," the white marshal drawled.

Moon took hold of the bars and looked over at the deputies. "And this woman's a librarian, man. A librarian! Shit!"

"Okay," Sandra said with a sigh. She buttoned up and readjusted her collar. "Now I know it's you, I can go. Stick that smile in your pocket, lover, and I'll see you upstairs. You don't have to look for me; I'll be right over your shoulder."

She blew him a kiss, picked up her purse, and left the room.

On the ground floor of the courthouse, Jack O'Connor and his three sons were making their way onto a crowded elevator. The older boys had gotten into one of their screaming matches before they'd left the house, and the two were avoiding looking at each other. Jack still didn't know what the fight was about. Then, Michael had vomited over the porch rail just as Jack was trying to corral everyone into the van. A hint of rotten egg smell still clung to the boy, and his father was keeping a watchful eye on him. Mike's mouth twisted as the rising elevator pressed his stomach down.

"You a juror, too?" a dark-haired woman in her early thirties asked Jack. She was pretty, but her eyes had a worried look.

"No," Jack said, with a glance at his sons. "Just spectators."

"Huh!" she said. "Lucky you!"

45

Monday had always been Judge Norcross's favorite day, especially the morning, when the workweek still had the dew on it. Through the tall windows by his desk, a generous orange light poured down onto the chambers' burgundy carpeting and splashed against the tan and crimson volumes of federal appellate decisions that lined the opposite wall.

The memory of Claire, and of the previous day's adventure, hung in this rinse of brightness like warmth inside a sun porch. Never in his life had Norcross laughed so hard with anyone. With some difficulty, he'd gotten Claire to agree to a change of venue from the top of the uncomfortable bench to the large sofa in his office. Afterward, they'd fallen asleep in each other's arms for more than an hour, then taken turns using the shower in chambers. When he'd emerged from the bathroom—dried, deodorized, and reassembled as a respectable adult—Claire, who'd gone first, had been right where he was sitting now, in this very chair, fiddling with his computer, as artless and composed as one of those girls in the J.Crew catalog. Nothing in the past five years, not even the call from the White House, had so thoroughly filled him with joy.

Now he knew he would manage. Now he knew he was loved, and no matter what happened he could not fall out of the universe. Even the latest offering from crazy Mrs. Abercrombie, a wrinkled heap of single-spaced pleadings on the corner of his desk, could not darken his mood. It was okay; he'd get to it. He tapped in the code to access his computer and buzzed Frank and Eva. Time to confabulate.

Frank had been down the corridor to check with Tom Dickinson and confirm the arrival of the jurors and attorneys. He reported a long stream of reporters and spectators inching through the metal detectors, setting purses and wallets on the conveyor belt, and standing with arms outstretched to be sniffed by the wand.

"One box cutter, two canisters of pepper spray, four knives," Frank said as he sat down opposite Norcross.

"Any trouble starting on time today?" Norcross asked.

"I doubt it. Ruby's checking the courtroom. Everything looks good."

"Are you still thinking you'll let the government put in Hudson's priors if he testifies?" Eva asked. "You know what I think."

Her fervent brown eyes reminded Norcross of Marlene praying for a cashew. He knew Eva was having a hard time with the trial, and he wanted her good opinion, but the problem she raised was not simple. The basic rule was that if the defendant testified, then the government could attack his credibility by pointing out his prior convictions; if he didn't testify, the jury would remain ignorant of his criminal record. But it was tricky; there could be exceptions.

"We'll see," Norcross said. "We don't know yet whether he wants to testify." He tapped his blotter with the eraser of his pencil and looked out the window. "I have an idea about how to tackle the problem that might be reasonably fair to both sides. Let me just think out loud with you for a minute here, and . . . what?"

Norcross, puzzled, turned back from the windows. Frank and Eva were alternately glancing over his shoulder and peeping sideways at each other with tightly controlled smirks, scarcely even pretending to follow what he was saying. Eva clapped her hand over her mouth, her eyes glistening with merriment. Frank began pulling on his ear, looking down, and biting his lip.

"What?" Norcross could feel himself getting irritated; this was a serious topic. Their stifled amusement was turning infectious, though, and his own temptation to burst into a grin was making him even more annoyed. He started looking down and patting himself to see if he'd forgotten to button his shirt or left his fly open or something. Finally, following his clerks' eyes, he looked back at his computer.

While they'd been talking, the computer's screen saver had kicked on, set as usual on the scrolling marquee. Today, however, the inspirational quote was different. It was a message from Claire, tapped into the machine's software the day before while he'd been showering, as a surprise memento of their afternoon.

The words made their way across the screen in big red letters: "Here's to dear Judge Norcross—Best lover in the Land!" Norcross sensed himself starting to color as a bubble of confused happiness took shape in his chest. This was, in a way, wonderfully sweet, but he was shy, too, and the ice here felt thin.

It got thinner. A second line continued: "I crave his playful Frankfurter—Adore his Learned Hand!!!!"

Norcross quickly tapped the mouse to get out of the screen

saver and turned to face his two clerks, trying to compose himself. But there must have been something in his expression that burst the balloon of mirth they had both been struggling to hold in.

Eva exploded first, bending forward and holding her stomach with one hand while the other was clapped over her mouth. She rocked, emitting faint yips, like a dog having a dream. Frank, more restrained, had thrown his head back and was making huffing noises at the ceiling, trying to catch his breath.

"Right," Norcross said. Then, after a pause, "Okay, okay."

Eva, at last, reeled herself in and looked at him with an attempt at sobriety, but the corners of her mouth were twitching and another squeak burbled out of her. Frank had both hands over his face and was taking deep breaths.

"You realize that message was not from Lucille," Norcross said.

"Yes," Eva managed. But her voice was more high-pitched than usual, and she wiped a tear out of the corner of her eye.

"Rule Seventeen," Frank said.

Another explosion from both of them instantly followed.

Norcross shook his head. They'd never get back on track. He let it go on for another minute, trying to maintain his dignity, but feeling like a man caught stepping out of the bathtub.

"Okay," he said, "in the words made immortal by Dave Brubeck, let's take five."

46

The spring deepened. The forsythia and the daffodils bloomed and faded, then the tulips, azaleas, and lilacs. The days lengthened out. To Lydia Gomez-Larsen's intense disappointment, they lost the no-nonsense-looking Latina juror, who went down with appendicitis. She was replaced by an older, white mail carrier from Stockbridge with a face that was far too empathic for Gomez-Larsen's taste.

The witnesses flowed through the box. The jury heard the medical and ballistics experts and the testimony about the inner workings of street gangs with reasonable patience. Moon Hudson's employer appeared, with his newly discovered records confirming that Moon left work at six thirty a.m. on the day of the murders. Since she knew from Bill Redpath's opening that Sandra Hudson would be testifying that Moon was home with her, Gomez-Larsen made sure the jury realized that the records left Moon ample time to kill Delgado and O'Connor after he clocked out. She looked on with studied indifference as Redpath tore into the floundering, inconsistent testimony provided by Nono and Spider, and the junkie Fournier's disjointed description of buying the assault rifle for Carlos Arcera in exchange for heroin. Finally, the trial reached a crucial moment: the appearance of the government's star witness, Ernesto "Pepe" Rivera.

As she worked through the preliminary portion of her direct examination, Gomez-Larsen noted, with relief, that the kid was doing much better than she had dreamed possible. He looked perfect, for one thing. The khaki Dockers, new white sneakers, and the dark-blue button-down shirt Pepe's mom had picked out for him struck the perfect balance between casual and formal. He seemed a pleasant-looking, nervous kid, fresh from the barber—ironed, but not starched, just the way Gomez-Larsen wanted him.

As she went through her deliberately easy, initial questions detailing his age, schooling, command of English, and so forth, Pepe was even calling her ma'am occasionally, the classic boy-next-door.

The mistrial had saved Gomez-Larsen's life. In their first prep sessions, Rivera had been sourly unimpressed by her reminders that the quality of his effort would likely determine how much time he spent in prison. Of course, Gomez-Larsen told Pepe that she expected him to tell the truth, and only the truth, but it was critical that he testify believably as well as honestly, and he seemed incapable of caring. Only a few weeks ago, if the little guttersnipe had sworn, using a chalkboard to demonstrate, that two times two was four, no juror would have believed him. He'd been worse than useless.

But following the dismissal of the first jury, Gomez-Larsen had had the inspiration to bring Maria Maldonado, Pepe's mom, back in for one of their proffer sessions with her son. Afterward, she had spent nearly an hour alone with Maria, describing to her, gently but clearly, exactly what her son would be facing if he didn't come through. The fact that she could do this in Spanish made a huge difference. Then, she made sure that Maria had plenty of time to talk to her son in private.

After that, the boy was more pliable. Once they'd gotten him loosened up, Captain Daley, who'd testified hundreds of times over his career, swallowed down his revulsion and took to spending his afternoons with the youngster, calling him Ernesto, rather than Pepe, and passing on courtroom war stories to help the witness understand what he would be facing from Redpath. Before long, the new Ernesto Rivera, who'd never known his father, was eating up Coach Daley's praise and viewing the trial as the homecoming game he was determined to win.

Sitting in the box today, the witness's transformation from Pepe the Snitch to Ernesto, the reformed young man who any father would be proud to have dating his daughter, seemed miraculous to Gomez-Larsen.

"Now, Mr. Rivera, do you know the defendant, Clarence Hudson?"

Rivera sat with a straight spine, leaning slightly forward, hands in his lap.

"I know *Moon* Hudson."

"Would you point him out for the jurors please?"

Rivera nodded in the proper direction and pointed.

"The guy in the gray turtleneck and blue jacket."

Gomez-Larsen looked up at Norcross.

"Your Honor, may the record reflect that the witness has identified the defendant, Clarence, aka Moon, Hudson?"

"It may so reflect," Norcross replied, not looking up from his notes.

Redpath sighed loudly through his nose and looked at the ceiling, conveying his boredom with the choreographed, totally meaningless identification.

"How do you know the defendant?"

"I've seen him, you know, in Holyoke. Springfield sometimes. With my uncle Carlos."

"I'll get back to that in a moment. First, let me ask you this. Are you familiar with a western Massachusetts street gang called La Bandera?"

"Yeah." He looked to his left, to where Sean Daley and Ginger's family were seated, and he corrected himself. "Yes, I am."

"You were a member of that gang, weren't you?"

"Objection!" Redpath rose to his feet. "Ms. Gomez-Larsen has several times during this direct examination led the witness, and I have not objected. I do object now. The testimony should come from the witness, not from the prosecutor."

"Please, no speeches, Mr. Redpath," Norcross said. "Just state your objection and indicate your ground."

Norcross nodded to the jury. "Please note, I'm sustaining Attorney Redpath's objection to that question. The jury will disregard it. Ms. Gomez-Larsen, please rephrase."

"Mr. Rivera, would you kindly inform the jury," she resumed with the barest trace of impatience, letting the jury know how completely their time was being wasted by these foolish technicalities. "Would you kindly inform all of us, whether you have ever been a member of the La Bandera street gang?"

"No, I've never been a member."

"You haven't?" Gomez-Larsen, despite all their preparation, was caught off-guard.

"Objection!" Redpath was on his feet again, speaking more emphatically, and with his own note of impatience.

But before Norcross could rule, Rivera broke in, "I was an initiate, not a member."

"Objection!" Redpath repeated, even louder.

"Wait now," Norcross said.

"Of course," Gomez-Larsen said. "Well, let me . . ."

"Wait, wait, wait," Norcross said. "We're getting all tangled up here."

He looked down at Rivera.

"Look, I know you're new to this, Mr. Rivera." Norcross smiled kindly. "And our procedures may seem strange to you, but keep in mind, when there is an objection, you must not answer the question until I have a chance to rule. Do you understand me? Wait. Okay?"

"Yes, your Honor. I'm sorry. I forgot." The boy ducked his head and scratched the back of his neck sheepishly.

So perfect, Gomez-Larsen thought. *God bless him.*

Norcross nodded in satisfaction—"I'm sure you did"—and turned to counsel.

"That goes for you two, as well. Remember, Rule Number One in this courtroom: 'Judge Norcross wears the robe, and when he talks, nobody else gets to talk.'"

Norcross cast a wry look at the jury box as he delivered this mild bit of jocularity, and some of its inhabitants smiled appreciatively.

"Now," he continued, "the objection to the question—which I believe was 'You haven't?'—is sustained. It was leading. The jury will disregard that question and everything that was said by the witness or counsel following it. Ms. Gomez-Larsen, please put your next question."

But Gomez-Larsen could see that Redpath was steaming. He was still on his feet from his last objection, his jaw muscles were working, and he was tapping on the table with his large hands. Something was clearly eating at him, and she had a pretty good idea what it was—just the kind of mistake a judge without many criminal trials might make. She watched out of the corner of her eye, giving defense counsel time to speak.

"Your Honor, may we approach sidebar?" Redpath asked.

"I don't see the necessity for a sidebar at this time."

"I would be happy, if Your Honor prefers, to state my reasons in front of the jury, but I think a conference at sidebar would be preferable." Redpath's tone was not rude, but something steely lay behind his words, and the hint of peril got the judge's attention.

"Very well. You may approach."

It was tight alongside the bench with the bearlike defense counsel, the AUSA, and the stenographer squeezed in with her steno-machine. Gomez-Larsen was not surprised when her adversary took off on what had just occurred.

"Your Honor, I move for a mistrial. This is outrageous!"

"What do you mean?" Norcross asked. "What's outrageous?"

"In front of this jury, you just said that this witness—I think your words were that he was 'new to this' or something like that. He's not new to this! He not new to this at all."

"Please keep your voice down, Bill," Gomez-Larsen interrupted.

Redpath continued in an intense whisper. "He's got a lengthy juvenile record, he's been arrested three other times that I know of, even though the cases were ultimately dismissed. He's been in court numerous times as a juvenile offender, a witness, or a spectator. His uncle was a La Bandera warlord. None of what's going on here is new to him at all."

"Oh applesauce, I was only making a point about his manner of testifying."

"This is the government's key witness!"

"Bill ..."

Redpath paused to control himself before continuing. "This is the government's key witness. She wants to present him like some cherub. Judge, if the jury believes this kid, my client goes down. A key part of our defense is that Pepe Rivera is *not* some innocent child, and there are mounds of evidence to back that up. By commenting in front of the jury about how this key witness is 'new to all this'—which is just plain false—you have bolstered the government's case on a point that will be central to this trial. Your Honor, I don't want to appear disrespectful—I'm sure you did not do this intentionally—but you have just vouched for this witness. This jury has heard Your Honor refer to this critical witness in a manner that makes him look pure as the driven snow. He isn't. Under the circumstances, the only fair thing to do is dismiss this jury and select a new one."

"Oh for heaven's sake," Norcross began. "A comment like that ..."

The three of them began speaking over one another.

"Wait a minute," Gomez-Larsen interrupted. "Hold on a minute. I'd like to be heard."

"There's no other way!" Redpath said.

"Wait a minute! I'm entitled to an ..."

"It couldn't have the slightest ..." Norcross leaned back and shook his head.

"One at a time, one at a time, please!" the stenographer broke in. The young woman's fingers had been flying over her machine, trying to keep up with Redpath's ferocity, but it was clear that she was at her limit.

"Okay, take it easy. That's enough," Norcross said, tapping on the bench with the butt of his pen. Clearly, Redpath's diatribe had gotten His Honor's attention. From Gomez-Larsen's point of view something needed to be done, quick.

Norcross nodded to her. "I'll hear you."

Gomez-Larsen spoke in a deliberately measured way. It was crucial to slow things down.

"First, defense counsel is blowing this one remark, made in passing, way, way out of proportion. How am I doing?" She looked at the stenographer, who returned a grateful smile. "This situation does not come anywhere near justifying a mistrial. That's flat-out ridiculous."

"Your Honor," Redpath began.

"You're taking turns, okay?" Norcross said. "Right now, it's the government's turn."

"Just ridiculous," Gomez-Larsen continued. "The jury, if it gives any weight to the remark at all, will consider it in exactly the light Your Honor described—simply a clarification of a courtroom technicality, nothing more. The court's comment certainly does not establish Mr. Rivera as 'pure as the driven snow,' as defense counsel suggests. As for this supposed mound of evidence, counsel will have a full opportunity to cross-examine."

"Your Honor," Redpath began again, "I can't cross-examine on the kind of . . ."

"I'll hear you in a moment," Norcross said.

"I thought she was done."

"No, I'm not done," Gomez-Larsen said. She continued at her careful pace, as though her words were cards she was setting down one at a time.

"Second, if the court is really concerned about some possible mis-impression the jury might have somehow obtained—and that's really stretching a point—then Your Honor can give a brief, corrective instruction. That's the most that's needed."

Norcross nodded to Redpath. "Now it's your turn."

"Judge, you can't un-ring this bell. No cautionary remarks by you can stuff the words back in your mouth, or yank them out of the jurors' ears. And there's simply no way to effectively cross-examine on something like this. Mr. Rivera, or Pepe, or Ernesto, or whatever he's calling himself these days, is the heart and soul of the government's case. If the jury likes him, my guy dies. There's no alternative. I press my motion for a mistrial."

Gomez-Larsen was pleased to notice that His Honor's momentary look of distraction had disappeared.

"Well, here's what I'm going to do," Norcross said, jotting on his pad as he spoke. "First, for the record, the motion for a mistrial is denied."

"Please note my very strenuous objection."

Gomez-Larsen could practically hear Redpath's teeth grinding. Terrific.

"Duly noted," Norcross continued. "Second, we were coming up on our morning break anyway. We'll take ten minutes now to let everyone stretch their legs. I'll put together a few words to address your concern, Mr. Redpath, and we'll keep things moving. Thank you. That'll be all."

47

Norcross hurried into his chambers and threw his robe on the sofa. The highest priority during any recess, no matter how grave the crisis in the courtroom, was always to get to the bathroom. Everything else could wait.

But Frank, blast him, was standing at the far side of the room holding a sheaf of papers and looking fraught.

"Judge, can I grab you for a quick second?"

"No," Norcross said, surprised at his own rudeness.

The phone buzzed, and he held up two fingers.

"I need two minutes of privacy," he told Frank, softening his tone. "Then you can have me for at least thirty full seconds. I promise." The phone buzzed again.

"For heaven's sake," Norcross said, "tell Lucille to take a message." The bathroom door closed and he was alone, finally, with his thoughts.

Had he really managed to gum up the trial? Norcross respected Redpath, and the man's huffing and puffing bothered him. Could his offhand boost to Rivera be as indelible as Redpath suggested? He had to admit the kid was coming across well.

He brushed the thought away, finished up, and began rinsing his hands. A fifteen-second comment in the middle of a six-week trial? Please.

As he stepped out of the bathroom, Norcross found Frank still standing doggedly next to his desk. He looked like Horatio-at-the-bridge, holding his wad of papers against his chest like a shield. Norcross knew that sometimes it was a clerk's job to block a judge's path until he looked at something. Still, the interruption was making him cross.

"Okay, what's up? Let's be quick."

"It's Mrs. Abercrombie," Frank began. "It seems . . ."

"Oh, for heaven's sake. Tell Mrs. Abercrombie to go jump in a lake."

He took a seat behind his desk and began writing "Rivera Instruction" on a yellow pad. But Frank, curse him, would not leave.

"The sheriff's going to evict her tomorrow at noon, Judge. She's filed a motion for a temporary restraining order, and she's requesting an immediate hearing. It has to be today."

"What possible jurisdictional basis is there to challenge a routine eviction in federal court? I'm very sorry for whatever pickle she's gotten herself into, but frankly I've had it with Mrs. Abercrombie." He turned his attention to the wording of the cautionary instruction.

Frank was nodding as Norcross spoke, rocking on his heels and scratching with his free hand at the end of his mustache.

"I know. I know, Judge. She's dreamed up some nutty theory under the Truth in Lending Act. The finance company says she hasn't paid her mortgage for a year and a half now."

"Give me the papers."

Mrs. Abercrombie's documents were immediately recognizable—hand-pecked on an old-fashioned typewriter with copious Wite-Outs and impenetrable paragraphs that rambled on, single-spaced, for eight or ten pages without the relief of an indentation or subheading. As usual, her pleadings also featured many exclamation marks, often double or triple, and whole pages capitalized and underlined in red ballpoint.

"Lord help us," Norcross said. "Is there anything here?"

"I'm almost positive there isn't. The Truth in Lending Act won't help her, that's for sure. But I feel bad. She's lived in the same house for forty-two years. She says she mortgaged the property because she needed the money for her lawsuits. It's horrible."

There was a knock on the door, and Ruby stuck her head in.

"Jury's ready anytime."

"Thanks." Norcross took his fountain pen out of the drawer.

Frank cleared his throat and added, "And the First Circuit affirmed your dismissal of her utility suit this morning."

"Big surprise." He bent over the papers. "The only mercy I can give her today is a quick decision. Maybe she can get some help in state court. That's where the case belongs, if anywhere."

He turned Mrs. Abercrombie's motion for a temporary restraining order sideways and wrote in the margin, in large black letters: "DENIED, for failure to demonstrate a likelihood of success on the merits. David S. Norcross, U.S.D.J."

"I feel terrible for her," Frank said.

"Well, you're still new to this world." Norcross looked up at his child-obsessed clerk, and his mind wound back to when, during his wife's pregnancy, he and Faye used to watch *Sesame Street*, getting warmed up for Jessica. Wasn't there a frog?

Norcross handed Frank the papers. "It isn't easy being green."

48

As the weeks of trial continued to unfold, Alex Torricelli got more used to the courtroom. He picked up a new, lightweight suit and, for the first time in his life, spent twenty bucks on a haircut. Lydia Gomez-Larsen gave him a yellow pad and a felt-tip pen so he could jot notes during the testimony. His scribbles were mostly useless, but note taking gave him something to do with his hands, and Lydia said it would impress the jury.

The hours passed more quickly. Alex's picture appeared in the newspaper, and when the reporters came up to him after a day in court, he had the pleasure of telling them that, unfortunately, he could not comment. None of this was doing him much good with Janice—he was mighty tired of the guest bedroom—but at least the workday was more bearable.

The best thing was that they had Redpath and his man Hudson on the ropes. Pepe Rivera came through with stars, and even the kid from UMass, a true punk, told his story about buying drugs from Hudson—full of details about location, time, weight, packaging, even the clothes Hudson was wearing—in a way that felt convincing. You could see the foreman eating it up like cheese popcorn.

This particular afternoon's testimony from Alex's pal, the tailor Marco Deluviani, was turning out to be another high point. When Deluviani described the scar on the arm of the man running down the alley, and Lydia got Norcross to make Hudson show his gouged forearm to the jury, the dead silence that followed the defendant back to his seat might as well have been the final bell.

"May I have a moment, Your Honor?" Lydia was wrapping up with Deluviani, but, as with all her witnesses, she made a display of checking one last time with Alex. She leaned forward to keep her whisper private: "Okay, *amigo*, did I miss anything?"

Alex frowned down at his notes. They contained two short phrases from the tailor's testimony, the words *WAR HERO!!* with a 3-D box around them, a doodled lightning bolt, and the rough draft of a limerick whose first line was "Nymphomaniacal Jill . . ."

Alex made a show of reviewing the page carefully, then nodded. "Looks like you've covered everything."

"You know," Lydia dropped her voice to a barely audible murmur, "you're good. You're very good."

Alex spoke without moving his lips.

"Kiss my butt, Lydia."

The prosecutor's stride was brisk as she returned to the podium and retrieved her binder.

"No further questions at this time, Your Honor."

Norcross nodded at defense counsel. "Mr. Redpath, you may cross-examine."

Throughout this pause, Deluviani sat in the witness box looking straight ahead, a perfect image of barely contained irritation. His curly toupee and twisted face made him look as though he'd dropped into the trial out of a fairy tale by the Brothers Grimm. Who could ever believe a Rumplestiltskin like him would lie?

One more tap and down the son of a bitch goes, Alex thought. He drew a double line on the page and wrote "MARCO CROSS" in large black letters above it. Even the slow, tough-guy way Hudson had walked over to the jury rail to show his arm made him look guilty. Who'd want to meet a character like that in a dark alley?

"Just a few questions," Redpath said. He locked his eyes on the witness as he approached the podium. Deluviani stared back with a sour face.

"Your injury in Vietnam, Mr. Deluviani, resulted in burns to your face, correct?"

"Other places got it worse, but they don't show."

"And there was some injury to your eyes?"

Deluviani scratched one of his front teeth. "Not really."

Redpath stepped to the side of the podium, resting his hand on it. "You received severe burn injuries to your face, among other areas? Can we agree on that?"

"Yep."

"And your injuries affected your eyesight, didn't they?"

Again, the witness paused. He cocked his head and nodded.

"My eyesight, yes, not my eyes. I was bandaged up a long time."

"You need glasses for distance now?"

"Right. For anything close-up, I'm fine."

"When you're working, for example, you don't need glasses?"

"Right."

"I notice you're not wearing glasses now."

"I have them here." Deluviani slipped a pair of black frames partway out of his shirt pocket and dropped them back in.

"You don't wear them normally?"

"What do you mean 'normally'?"

"As a matter of routine, or habit. For example, you don't have them on now."

"Correct. I'm not wearing my glasses right now."

Alex had the pleasure of hearing a couple of the jurors snigger.

"Mmm-hmm. Would you put your glasses on please?"

Deluviani cast an impatient look up at Norcross. The judge nodded down at him.

"Oh-kay." The witness drawled the word out. He slid the glasses onto his face. They were off-kilter, with a safety pin securing the right earpiece to the frame—all of which made him look even more like a kook.

"Now," Redpath raised his voice and turned to the jury. "Isn't it true, Mr. Deluviani, that you can see me at least somewhat better now, with your glasses on, than you could a minute ago, when you weren't wearing your glasses?"

"Okay. Somewhat."

"And, for the record, what would you estimate is the distance between the two of us?"

Deluviani peered over the witness box.

"Maybe twelve, fifteen feet."

"All right. Please feel free to remove your glasses now, if you'd prefer."

Deluviani took the glasses off and put them back in his pocket.

"Now on the morning you say you saw the man with the scar, before you say you saw him, you'd been doing work, am I right?"

"Yep."

"Tailoring work."

"That's the only kind I do."

"And you don't need your glasses to see close-up?"

"Nope."

"So you were not wearing your glasses."

"Probably had them in my pocket, same as I do now."

Alex felt a tap on his arm and looked over to see Lydia shifting her pad toward him. In three neat lines, she'd written: "Stop looking so sweaty!! You'll spook the jury. This is only the usual B.S."

Alex, keeping a straight face, scribbled "Sorry!" on her pad. Redpath's questions had, in fact, been making him uncomfortable. The lawyer's pushy tone felt, somehow, like cheating.

The questioning moved into another area.

"Before you say you saw this gentleman with the scar," Redpath continued, "you were working, as you said, correct?"

"Yep."

"No question you were working."

"No question."

"You were at your machine toward the rear of your shop."

"No."

"You weren't? Didn't you just say that you were working, just ten seconds ago?"

Deluviani shifted in his seat and, for the first time, looked off-balance. "Well, I was at work, but I'd stopped working at the machine."

"Wait now. Let's be sure I understand you, sir. Were you working, or weren't you?"

"I was at work, okay? I wasn't home having a beer. I wasn't on the can. I was working, but I wasn't, like, at my machine working. I was in the front of the store, paying bills or taking a break or something. Answering the phone. I forget what."

"So your testimony now is you weren't working."

"I wasn't in the back at the machine. I know that." He hesitated and added in a lower voice, "I couldn't have seen anything from back there."

"Exactly!" Redpath said. "If you'd actually been working, as you said you were a minute ago, there was absolutely no way, from where you would have been sitting, that you could have seen something like a scar on the arm of a man running past, especially since you would not have been wearing your glasses. Isn't that right?"

"Objection." Lydia stood, unruffled, speaking more in sadness than in anger.

"I never said I was in the back," Deluviani broke in.

"I don't mind if counsel wants to . . ." Lydia continued.

"I'd like an answer to my question!" Redpath said.

"Objection is sustained," Norcross said, raising his voice slightly and tapping his pen on his microphone. "That's a multiple. Break the question up, please."

Redpath gave the judge a long look and then nodded. He took a while to consult his notes, letting the silence grow in the courtroom. Deluviani shifted and cleared his throat.

Lydia shoved her pad over to Alex again.

"I like this," she'd written. "Nod at me a little."

Alex looked over at Lydia and nodded, projecting a very good impression of a man who had just been reminded of something highly significant. His peripheral vision picked up the eyes of several of the jurors wandering over to him. Everything was going fine.

At that moment, the door at the side of the bench opened, and a woman entered the courtroom. She glanced nervously out into the gallery, approached Norcross, and handed him up a note. The judge looked at the note; a frown flickered, and then he leaned toward the jury rearranging his face into an easy smile.

"Good news," he said. "I'm going to give you a short unsched-uled break. Something has come up that I have to deal with." He put down his pen and rubbed his hands together. "Please don't speculate about what this may be. Just relax, stretch yourselves, and we'll see you again in about fifteen minutes. I admonish you, as I have already so many times, not to discuss the case or any-thing about it with one another. Keep an open mind. We'll pick up with the continued cross of this witness in just a few minutes, then roll right on to the end of the day. You're excused for fifteen minutes."

49

The note Lucille handed up to the bench read: "Tom D. needs to see you ASAP. Bomb in the building."

Judge Norcross still had the slip of paper in his hand when he got back to his chambers and found the court security officer, Tom Dickinson, waiting in the chair facing his desk, looking agitated. Dickinson, portly and silver-haired, was a retired Amherst police officer and, Norcross had learned, a distant relative of the town's famous poet Emily Dickinson. He'd been a CSO for several years before Norcross took the bench.

"So, what's up?" Norcross asked as he slipped off his robe.

"Clerk's office got an anonymous call ten minutes ago, Judge, reporting a bomb in the building. Sounded like a female, they said, possibly elderly."

"So it's a bomb threat, not an actual bomb so far."

"Right."

Norcross laid his robe over the back of his sofa. "Anybody notice anything funny this morning when you were screening people?"

"No, sir."

The window next to Norcross's desk had a good view down to the plaza in front of the courthouse. It was a pretty spring day, with bright flowers dancing in the planters along the Jersey barriers. Norcross dropped into his chair, pulled a yellow pad in front of him, and wrote "Bomb" at the top with the date and time. Silly, but it helped him think.

"Did Sheba alert to anything?" Norcross was very fond of Sheba, a bomb-sniffing dog assigned to the court for the trial. She was totally no-nonsense. Whenever the judge patted her, she would wag her tail exactly three times and then sit.

"No, sir. We swept the building as usual during lunch. Not a whimper."

Norcross peered up at the sky through the window. A few high horsetails, fair weather clouds. He turned back to Dickinson. "It's a hoax."

"Probably."

Suspending the trial was one way to go, to give the security staff time to search the building, but given how badly Deluviani had mauled the defense on direct, Norcross preferred not to interrupt cross if he could help it. Redpath's questions seemed to be building up to something.

"Did this person say when the bomb was supposed to go off?"

"Three thirty." Dickinson looked at his watch. "In about thirty-five minutes."

"How often do these calls come in?"

"Now and then," Dickinson said. "More in the high-profile cases."

"And how often does it turn out to be an actual bomb?"

"For us, so far, never. Course we haven't had a trial like this monster before. They weren't so lucky in Oklahoma City."

"Got a recommendation?"

Dickinson leaned forward, putting his elbows on his knees. "Safest thing would be to knock off for the day, Judge. To be honest, that's what I'd recommend to cover my own tail. I hate these whackos. But it's your call."

It was an easy decision, really, which didn't necessarily make it right.

"We're not stopping," Norcross said after a pause.

Dickinson breathed deeply and nodded. "Want to stretch out the break? Let Sheba have another good sniff around?"

"We'd end up burning most of the time we have left today, and the reporters would notice. We'll go back in."

"Yes, sir," Dickinson said slowly. "How about, once you get started again, if we just take Sheba for a trot around the halls where the jury can't see? This call gives me a bad feeling. We'll make it look routine."

"Fine."

"Want me to evacuate nonessential staff?"

Norcross shook his head. "That would get us in the papers, too, and we'd have a new nut calling every day. Thanks. I appreciate this."

"Yes, sir." Dickinson stood and turned to go.

"Think Emily would have any words of wisdom for us?"

Dickinson turned in the doorway. "How about 'To die takes just a little while, they say it doesn't hurt'? It's a comforting thought, sort of."

"It's also untrue," Norcross said, remembering Faye. "Dying can take quite a while sometimes, and it can hurt a lot."

As he resumed his seat back up on the bench a few minutes later, Norcross caught himself looking with special attentiveness at the courtroom clock. Five after three. He let his eyes drift over the crowded gallery, wondering if any of the spectators had managed to sneak a package in. When the big hand dropped down to the six, he'd know. This time he wouldn't have to wait for the Court of Appeals to tell him if he'd made the wrong call.

"Mr. Deluviani," he said to the witness. "We're going to pick back up on Mr. Redpath's questioning now. It is not necessary to readminister the oath. You are still sworn to tell the truth." He nodded to defense counsel. "Mr. Redpath. Your witness."

Redpath quickly returned to the podium. *Wants to keep his momentum,* Norcross thought. *Can't blame him for that.*

"Mr. Deluviani, let me ask you this. How many times did you meet with Ms. Gomez-Larsen before today?"

"Two, three times."

"How many times with law enforcement officers?"

"The cops? A lot of times."

"And was one of the officers Captain Sean Daley, the uncle of Ginger Daley O'Connor?" Redpath turned to point into the gallery. "That gentleman there."

Deluviani stretched his neck, but didn't seem to see who Redpath had pointed to.

Probably a ploy to make the jurors wonder about the witness's eyesight, Norcross thought. *Clever.*

"There was one named Daley," Deluviani said, squinting into the gallery. "He didn't mention any relatives."

Redpath placed his elbows on the podium, slowing things down a bit now. Norcross looked up at the clock again and found himself musing about Claire. If something happened, would Lucille think to call her, or would Claire just learn about it on the news? How much did people know about the two of them?

"And how many times did you meet with Captain Daley?"

"Oh, boy. He came by maybe six, eight times."

"Looking for evidence against Mr. Hudson?"

"Looking for evidence against anybody."

"And Ms. Gomez-Larsen asked you, and the officers asked you, and Captain Daley asked you, every time they talked to you, about the man you say you saw running by?"

"Every single time."

Redpath scratched the back of his neck meditatively, letting the questioning slow even more now, down to a crawl.

Fifteen minutes after three, Norcross noticed. *My, how time flies.*

"But in all those conversations, you never mentioned any scar to any of them, did you, Mr. Deluviani?"

"Never asked me."

Redpath raised his voice. "Never mentioned any scar in all those conversations?"

"Never asked me."

"I see."

Redpath searched through his notes for a count of five, then looked up, and resumed.

"But you did tell Officer Torricelli, this gentleman here, right? Months after the incident, isn't that right?"

"Right." Deluviani looked over at Torricelli.

Norcross noticed with displeasure that Torricelli, his mouth open, was nodding faintly in Deluviani's direction. Was Torricelli signaling the witness? He'd have to call Gomez-Larsen up to sidebar and tell her to have Torricelli cut it out if he caught any more gawping or twiddling. Torricelli, perhaps noticing the judge's stare, dropped his head and began writing on his yellow pad. He made a couple of emphatic underlines, whatever that meant.

"And, in fact," Redpath continued, "your testimony is that

Mr. Torricelli never asked you about any scar, either, did he? You brought the topic up yourself."

"Just happened to think of it when we were talking."

"Just happened to think of it. For the first time in all those months, after Moon Hudson was arrested, and after everyone knew about his scar, you finally just happened to think of it?"

"I had thought of it. I just didn't tell anybody about it."

"Didn't you just say, twenty seconds ago, that you 'just happened to think of it when we were talking'? Isn't that what you said?"

"I guess so."

"But now you're saying you *had* thought about it before. You just didn't think to tell anybody about it until you happened to be talking to Officer Torricelli months after the police first contacted you and months after everyone had seen my client's scar. Is that your testimony?"

Deluviani turned to the side and looked annoyed. "I guess so."

"Isn't it true, Mr. Deluviani, that it was, in fact, Officer Torricelli"—Redpath pointed back at the prosecutor's table without looking around—"or perhaps Captain Daley, who first told you about my client's scar, and then, and only then, you miraculously remembered seeing it on the arm of the man you supposedly saw running past your shop? Isn't that what really happened?"

"No."

"I see."

Not suspending the trial was turning out to be a good thing, Norcross thought. It was important for the jury to have this testimony under their thinking caps—a good thing, that is, assuming they all weren't blown to kingdom come in a few short minutes. No problem about any death penalty for Hudson then. They'd all go together, including quite a few innocent spectators and court staff, and the catastrophe would be his fault.

Redpath was flipping pages. "Now, a few minutes ago, you said the distance between you and the gentleman running past was about fifteen to twenty feet, correct?"

"About."

"Roughly the distance between you and me right now, correct?"

"Just about."

"And you weren't wearing your glasses then, just the way you aren't wearing your glasses now, correct?"

"Like I told the police, I'm not sure one way or the other."

"Okay. But you might not have been wearing your glasses, isn't that fair?"

"Might've been, too."

"And you never saw the gentleman's face? I mean, you don't recognize my client's face here, correct?"

"He had his hood up."

"You mean, whoever ran past your store that morning had his hood up, am I right?"

"The hood was up. Couldn't see a face."

"Whoever it was?"

"Whoever it was."

Redpath checked his watch and looked up at the bench. "Your Honor, I'm just about done. Could I have a moment to review my notes?"

"You may." Norcross glanced from Redpath to the clock. Three twenty-five. Nothing was going to happen, of course, but it was interesting to notice how precious and distinct each morsel of time felt. The judge looked over at the jury and drummed with his pencil eraser on his blotter. They were looking, on the whole, blissfully relaxed and attentive. If he'd known Redpath was going to be this quick, he might have let Sheba have a trot through the courtroom.

Redpath resumed, musingly, flipping pages again.

"The hooded gentleman ran past from your right to your left, you say?"

Deluviani sagged a little. He'd obviously been hoping his ordeal was over.

"Yeah." He waved with his finger, right to left. "Like that."

"So this gentleman's left side was toward you as he ran past?"

Deluviani looked into the distance and nodded. "I guess. Yes."

"And the sleeve of the sweatshirt, on the arm toward you, was pulled up?"

"The sweatshirt was way too small for the guy's shoulders, that's for sure."

"And it would have been the left arm that was toward you as the gentleman ran past from your right to your left, right?"

"I'm sorry? Left, right?"

The jury foreman wriggled with amusement.

Redpath continued patiently. "Am I correct, Mr. Deluviani, that it was the left arm that you saw that morning when you observed the scar?"

"I'm not exactly sure."

"Well, you certainly could not have seen the gentleman's right side as he ran past, correct?"

"I guess."

"You saw the scar on his left arm, the arm toward you, isn't that true, sir?"

"I'm not sure."

"Well, the left arm was toward you, correct?"

Gomez-Larsen rose, shaking her head. "Objection, asked and answered."

"Sustained," Norcross said. "The witness's testimony is that the gentleman's left side was toward him as he ran past."

"Thank you, Your Honor," Redpath said, keeping his eyes on Deluviani.

Unless Redpath had a rabbit to pull out of a hat, Norcross thought, this didn't seem to be going anywhere. Three twenty-nine.

"Your Honor," Redpath said. "I would request that the defendant be permitted, once more, to display his arm to the jury."

"Go ahead, if you think it would be helpful."

"Moon, please just stand where you are. But this time, show the jury your left arm. They can see it from there."

Moon rose slowly and slipped off his jacket. He rolled up his shirtsleeve and displayed his unscarred left arm, rotating it side to side.

"Now your right."

Moon showed the jury his right arm again, with the pink scar.

"Thank you. Thank you very much." As Moon resumed his seat, Redpath nodded up to Norcross. "No further questions, Your Honor."

The clock's minute hand had crept past three thirty. Everything was going to be all right, as Norcross had known it would be—assuming the courtroom clock or the bomb's timer wasn't off.

In almost every trial he'd ever done, as a lawyer or as a judge, there came a moment in the testimony when the effort to re-create the past entered the Twilight Zone, when all the possible realities were implausible. Was Deluviani deliberately lying about seeing the scar? Maybe, but that seemed unlikely. Had he convinced himself that he'd seen something that wasn't there? Had Torricelli, who was not exactly Mr. Smooth, done such a great job of manipulating the little guy? Or had someone else, with the defendant's same build and height, and with an identical scar on his other forearm, happened to run past Deluviani's shop?

Norcross would never know. It was unlikely anyone would know for sure. A year from now, even Deluviani—if he were being honest—wouldn't be able to say for certain what he saw. But these mysteries arose in every trial, and it was up to the jury and not the judge, thank heaven, to decide what to make of them.

Gomez-Larsen's redirect repaired Deluviani's credibility somewhat; then Redpath had another short whack at him on recross. They wrapped up by four o'clock, and the judge sent everyone home for the day, all in one piece.

Two days later, the government rested. The defense, Redpath told the judge, would be short. They'd be calling no more than two witnesses: Sandra Hudson and possibly the defendant.

50

"It's your decision," Redpath said. "But I'm telling you, Moon . . ." A peppery sneeze surged up into his nose, interrupting him for the third or fourth time. "I'm telling you, uh, ah . . ."

The final syllable of the sneeze was so loud, so like a shout for help, that the rankled face of a guard appeared in the mesh window of the conference room door.

"It's a bad idea. Jesus Christ, where'd I get this cold?" Redpath drew a very rumpled gray handkerchief out of his jacket pocket and blew his nose. The correctional officer shook his head and vanished.

Tomorrow, Judge Norcross would expect the defense to begin presenting its case, and Redpath felt like he was drowning in mucus. His eyes itched, his throat was sore, his nose was blocked up, and at night when he put his head on the pillow to sleep, his sinuses drained down the back of his throat and had him up half the night coughing. On top of this, he and Moon were facing the biggest decision of the trial. It would have to be made in the next few minutes, before Redpath returned to his room at the Marriott to finish preparing the direct examination of Sandra Hudson, his first witness, due to take the stand in less than eighteen hours.

Redpath thought yearningly of the hot bath he planned to take before he got down to work. A quiet smoke in a steaming tub, maybe a quick call to his son, Tom, in California. That always cheered him up. Then, later, three Extra Strength Tylenol PMs and a dive under the sheets. Heaven.

Moon was on the opposite side of the table, leaning back in his wooden chair and staring up at the ceiling. His eyes were half closed, and his nostrils dilated as he inhaled methodically— as though he were making himself wait to let a current of pain, or anger, move through him and drift far enough away to give him space to think. After several breaths, a sigh of disgust hissed through his lips, and he shook his head. Through the long trial, Redpath and Moon had grown closer, but now Moon spoke as if he were alone.

"So I keep still. And I let those twelve nice ladies and gentlemen go off and decide whether I'm guilty, without saying one single word to them." He rocked forward and held out his hands. "That's what you're telling me I should do?"

"That's my advice. That's your best shot, in my opinion." Redpath sighed and rubbed his fingers over his eyes, scrubbing so hard the deeply lined skin of his forehead was pulled taut. "Norcross denied my motion, so if you testify the jury will learn about your prior drug convictions. It's unfair, but that's where we are. We can't risk it."

"After Pepe, after Nono and Spider, after all their bullshit, after that scrunched-up little tailor man, I don't say anything?" Moon shook his head. "That's messed up! You know they're bound to think I'm ducking. You know they're bound to think I did it—or else why don't I get up and say I didn't do it?"

"Norcross will instruct them that they cannot consider the fact that you didn't testify."

"So, you're saying I should trust these twelve people to do what he says. How much chance is there of that? Really."

"I don't know."

"You're telling me I'm better off not saying whether I did it than saying I didn't do it. That does not make one damned bit of sense to me."

"Wait a minute. Wait a minute." Redpath took his time unwrapping another cough lozenge. He was remembering a conversation just like this one, in March 2004, with a young man named Stevenson James, a low-IQ nineteen-year-old charged with murdering a convenience store clerk. Trusting Redpath, and relieved to avoid the humiliation of getting up in court, Stevie had exercised his Fifth Amendment right to remain silent. A year ago, Redpath had flown down to Texas to be present at his execution. If his client had taken the stand, perhaps the jury would not have believed the older co-defendant when he said that the cold-blooded and entirely unnecessary murder of the young woman was Stevie's doing. Now, no one would ever know, and Redpath had one more dead man he was responsible for.

"Listen to me, Moon," he said finally. The cold was making his voice even deeper than usual. "I don't have a crystal ball." He worked the lozenge into the corner of his mouth. "And we only get to play this hand one time. If we don't like what happens, we don't get to go back and try again. I don't know if the jury will think you're God or Godzilla. But my best guess is you shouldn't give Gomez-Larsen the chance to tear into you on cross-examination. She's good, and I doubt the jurors will like what they hear."

While his attorney spoke, Moon shifted in his chair as though he were writhing against tight, invisible chains. Redpath waited in the silence, sucking on his cough drop, until Moon burst out.

"What do these twelve people know about me anyway?" He pressed his splayed fingers against his chest so powerfully that, when he dropped his hands, they left dents in the heavy cloth of his jumpsuit. "They never, not a single one of them, in their whole lives, ever talked even five minutes with somebody like me, somebody who grew up like I did, lived like I did! If we had twelve black jurors, or even three or four . . ."

"But we don't," Redpath interrupted. "We have one very middle-class black RN, who's still an alternate." He coughed. "Look, I could be dead wrong . . ."

Moon gave a short laugh and looked up at the ceiling. "Right, except I'll be the one who's dead."

"You think I've forgotten that?" Redpath asked, raising his voice, then dropping it. "Thanks very much." He pulled out the soggy handkerchief and blew his nose again. His words were heavy with clog and exhaustion. "You've got my advice, Moon. I've been saying the same thing for two weeks now. Once and for all, tell me what you want to do. I feel like hell, and I've got a ton of work to do before tomorrow. Make your choice."

Moon slumped back and stared up at the ceiling again. He opened his mouth, breathed deeply, and let his heavy arms drop. In the silence, Redpath heard footsteps receding down the hall outside, the distant sound of a sliding security gate, the hum of the light overhead. Moon smiled faintly at something, then squeezed his eyes shut and dug in his ear with his pinkie finger.

"You know what's really messed up about this whole thing?"

"What's that, Moon?"

Moon rocked forward, rolled his shoulders nervously, and rubbed his temples. A flickering, almost childlike smile was playing the corners of his mouth.

"I really hate shots, man."

"You hate shots. Great."

"I hate the motherfuckers. . . ." A wheezing laugh escaped him.

"You hate shots," Redpath sniffed. "Well . . ."

"I always have. They scare me to death!" He looked at his hands and laughed in short, breathy spasms. "When I was a little kid, my momma had to practically tie my ass up just to get me to go to the doctor." He wiped the corner of his eye. "Shit."

Redpath scratched his head. "Maybe I could . . ."

"I keep having these dreams, you know? About this big motherfucker of a needle, about three feet long, right? Some white guy, with his evil blond mustache, in one of those long white coats. That cold shit they wipe on your arm, so you know they're just about to stick you."

"How about if I . . ." Redpath began again.

"If they find me guilty, maybe you could get them to rope me to a pallet of tuna fish or something. Tip me off the Memorial Bridge."

"How about if I just hit you over the head with that chair there?"

"That's good. I'd appreciate that, Bill. I really would."

"All part of the service."

Moon held up his fists. "And I could take a couple pops at you first, bruise up your ugly face a little, so it would look like self-defense, right? I could get with that right now."

He feinted with two quick jabs toward his lawyer's head.

"Great idea," Redpath said, not moving. "We'd need to make it look good." Another thunderclap of a sneeze broke through his face. Out came the overused handkerchief.

"Otherwise," Redpath blew his nose. "Otherwise, hell, they might give me a lethal injection."

"Don't talk like that, man!" Moon sat back and slapped the table. "I don't want to snuff it in some damn doctor's office, strapped to a cart like a side of beef. I'd rather give it up on the sidewalk, in the old neighborhood. Let some hoodlum shoot my ass."

As he replaced his wad of handkerchief, Redpath groaned again. "Lethal injection doesn't sound so bad to me at the moment."

Moon gave his lawyer an appraising look, drumming with his fingers on the scarred wooden table. Finally, he sighed and shook his head.

"Shit," he said softly. "Okay, time to do this. Time for Clarence to play the big boy. Tell me again why I shouldn't just get up and tell these twelve nice people, who think I come from Mars, the truth, the whole damn truth, and nothing but the truth."

"Once more, Moon: Your drug record will come in if you testify. Most of the jury will want to hang you just for that."

"I thought you said Norcross would tell them not to think about my priors."

Redpath cleared his throat. "If you testify, he'll tell them they *can* consider them in weighing your credibility as a witness, but *not* in deciding your guilt or innocence."

"Another one of your rules that makes no damn sense." Moon folded his arms and gazed at Redpath intently.

"Right. It makes no sense," Redpath said. "Fact is, I doubt half the jurors will even understand what Norcross is saying. But that's why you can't take the stand."

Moon continued looking at Redpath. Finally, he shook his head. "And you spend your life doing this shit?" He dropped his voice. "I'd rather sell dope. Live an honest life."

Redpath dabbed at his nose and looked at the table, avoiding Moon's stare. The silence grew, scored lightly by the sound of Redpath's breathing.

"Okay," Moon said finally.

"Okay what?"

"You're my man," Moon said, "and this is your game. We'll play it your way."

51

Redpath ran a nicotine-stained forefinger down the notes he'd prepared for the direct examination of Sandra Hudson, trying to be sure he'd hit everything. When he began to feel Norcross's eyes on him, he glanced up.

"Excuse me, Your Honor. If I might just have a moment?"

The questioning had not gone badly; in fact, it had gone damn well. Moon's wife had revealed herself as a loving but honest woman—well spoken, attractive, and, like most of the jurors, utterly middle-class—a bridge of sympathy, perhaps, between them and the defendant, a causeway over which a reasonable doubt might tiptoe.

"Thank you very much, Sandra," Redpath said, trying to make it sound as if he had just finished a prayer. "I have no further questions."

This was, for Redpath, the most dangerous passage in any

trial: the hour of hope. *How in the hell,* he wondered as he shuffled back to his seat, *could any juror fail to have a reasonable doubt now, after hearing this intelligent, loving woman tell them the accused was definitely with her when the shootings occurred?*

As he lowered himself into his chair, Redpath remembered to turn and put his hand on Moon's shoulder. His client's face was unreadable, but Redpath felt his muscles stiffen, repressing a flinch.

He hates this crap, Redpath thought. *Tough.*

Redpath looked up at the bench, hoping His Honor would call a recess, to let the jurors' minds marinate in Sandra's testimony a little longer.

But Norcross was down in his notes, scribbling away in his own world. He addressed Gomez-Larsen without looking up.

"You may cross-examine."

Gomez-Larsen took her time. She sighed regretfully, smoothed down her dark gray skirt, stood, and moved to the podium, holding her yellow pad at her side.

"Just a few questions, Your Honor. I'll be brief." For several seconds, she stared at the wall above the judge's head. When all the jurors had shifted to look at her, she licked her lips and began in a low voice.

"How long did you know the defendant before you two were married, Ms. Hudson?" The question was delivered with no eye contact. Gomez-Larsen had dropped her gaze to the surface of the podium and was examining her fingertips.

"Let's see," Sandra said. "We were both at UMass. It was my second year. Hmmm."

Redpath smiled inwardly. If Gomez-Larsen thought this no-eye-contact trick was going to buffalo Sandra Hudson, she was wrong.

She was taking her own sweet time with her response, and Redpath noticed the faces of most of the jurors swiveling back to her.

"I would say nine—no, let me think—more like ten months, nearly a year."

Redpath leaned forward and slid his behind further into the chair, willed his shoulders to relax, and drummed on his knee in a deliberately bored way. When anxious, he had a tendency to tilt back stiffly, like a man trying to avoid a punch in the forehead. His task now was to look as unconcerned as possible. There was little he could do to rescue Sandra if she started to go off the rails. From this moment, she was pretty much on her own.

"So you had no idea what your husband's life was like in the more than thirty years before you met him, apart from what he chose to tell you, correct?"

Sandra's expression contracted, and she started to answer quickly, then paused to bring herself under control.

Just answer the question, Redpath entreated her silently. *No speeches.*

"No. Not correct." She opened her mouth to say more, to explain, but again hesitated and merely shook her head, repeating. "Not correct."

"So your testimony to this jury is that you were somehow familiar with your husband's life before you even met him?"

"Somewhat," Sandra nodded. "After Moon and I got engaged, before his mother passed away, she and I talked. I got to know some of his old friends, that kind of thing. I'd ask them about what he was like when he was little. The way you do when you . . ."

"But you obviously had no firsthand . . ." Gomez-Larsen continued.

"Well, wait a second," Redpath said, pulling himself up awkwardly. He'd made such an effort to appear bored, it was difficult to get himself untangled.

"You have an objection?" Norcross looked up from his notes. "If you have an objection, say 'objection.'"

"Well, Your Honor," Redpath replied in an injured tone, "I'd ask that the witness at least receive the courtesy of being allowed to finish her answer."

"I thought she had finished." Norcross looked down at the witness box. "Ms. Hudson, were you done with your answer?"

"I was just going to say, 'The way you do when you love someone.'"

"Ah, yes," Norcross said. He rubbed the end of his nose and returned to his notes.

Gomez-Larsen folded her hands on the podium. "But you do admit that, even after you were married, you and your husband were not together every single minute of every day, correct?"

"That's true."

Gomez-Larsen left the podium and returned to counsel table. Was this going to be all she had? Redpath wondered. A rising pressure of optimism began pushing at his lungs. It couldn't be.

It wasn't. Gomez-Larsen looked down at her notes and flipped a page, reading something. The trip from the podium to counsel table had the jury's attention. After a pause, she spoke without looking up.

"Are you acquainted with a woman by the name of Zinnia Sanderson?" Gomez-Larsen turned her face to the witness. "Goes by the name Spanky?"

"Yes." Sandra hesitated. "I know her."

"Right. In fact, she lives upstairs from you, correct?"

"Yes."

"Mm-hm." Gomez-Larsen pulled a smaller piece of paper on

counsel table over to her and examined it. "And this Zinnia, or Spanky, Sanderson has a son, Tyler, correct?"

"I don't know."

Gomez-Larsen straightened up and lifted her voice in disbelief. "You do not know whether Ms. Sanderson has a young boy living with her directly upstairs from you whose name is Tyler? Is that your testimony?"

Now it was Sandra's turn to lean forward; she spoke with an edge to her voice. "I know Tyler lives upstairs with Spanky, of course; I just don't know if he's her son or not."

"Well, did you . . . ?"

"I don't think he is, but I don't know. I thought he was her grandson."

"Uh-huh. But you don't disagree that you and your daughter, Grace, and Ms. Sanderson and Tyler would sometimes spend time together, right? You knew each other fairly intimately."

"Intimately? I'm not sure . . ."

"Well, let me ask you this. On the day the defendant was arrested by officers of the Holyoke Police Department at approximately twelve thirty a.m., you knew Ms. Sanderson well enough that you went upstairs to her apartment with your daughter and stayed with her?"

Redpath felt a wave of unease, remembering how he had instructed Sandra to stay away from the details of the search, the destruction of the apartment, the hours the officers had spent on the premises. Given that the fruits of the search had been suppressed, letting the jury know about this nightmare might do more harm than good. Now he wondered if his advice had been correct.

In any event, Sandra's quick glance told Redpath that she had remembered his words. No details.

"Yes."

"You didn't call any other friend or relative?"

"It was late, and she was up."

"But that wasn't my question." Gomez-Larsen returned to the podium; once more, the jurors' eyes followed her. "You chose not to call any other friend or family member at this time of crisis. You went upstairs to take shelter at your friend Zinnia Sanderson's. Isn't that right?"

"For that one night. Yes."

"Thank you." Gomez-Larsen sighed wearily as she prepared herself to continue.

"Now, to return to the point we were discussing a minute ago, it is true there were times, nearly every day, when your husband was on his own and you had no firsthand knowledge of what he was up to?"

"Up to?"

"Right. What he was doing."

"Well, I knew enough about what he was doing to know he wasn't out breaking the law."

"Well, once again, that wasn't my question, was it, Ms. Hudson? I asked whether there were times during the day when . . ."

"If you're trying to say that Moon might have been out committing crimes and I wouldn't know about it, that's, you know, that's nuts. I knew what he was up to, and he knew what I was up to, if you want to put it that way. We didn't keep secrets."

"Really?" Gomez-Larsen took a few seconds to stare up at the wall behind the judge again, propping her chin on her hand and reflecting about something. "We may get back to your remark about 'secrets' in a minute. Right now, let me ask you this: It is true, is it not, that sometimes in the mornings you and Ms. Sanderson and your children would take off for as long as two or three hours on your own?"

"Excuse me?"

"I'm just asking whether it's true that you and your neighbor Ms. Sanderson would go for walks in the mornings sometimes."

"I suppose. Yes."

"Stop and buy yourselves doughnuts?"

"I'm sorry?"

"You'd sometimes stop with the kids at the Dunkin' Donuts, right? Wouldn't be back for two, three hours?"

Redpath felt Moon's foot tap his. Moon was leaning forward on his elbows, using his arms to form a triangle with his hands at the top, so the jury's view of his mouth would be blocked.

"Bill," he whispered. "Not good."

Sandra was answering the question. "I don't know if it was that long. You're saying, three hours?"

"Okay," Gomez-Larsen said, "why don't we make it two hours then."

"Maybe two hours."

"Okay, now a minute ago, Ms. Hudson, you stated that you and the defendant had no secrets from each other?"

"Objection." Redpath wasn't sure where Gomez-Larsen was going, but he didn't like it.

"None," Sandra broke in. "No secrets."

"Objection," Redpath repeated more emphatically.

"Your Honor," Gomez-Larsen said. "May we approach sidebar?"

"Not necessary." Norcross nodded up at the clock. "We'll take the normal recess instead. I've been intending to give our jurors a chance to stretch their legs." He tossed a benevolent look toward the jury box. "Mr. Foreperson, ladies and gentlemen, we're going to take fifteen minutes now. Please remember not to discuss the case. Keep an open mind."

Norcross looked down at Gomez-Larsen. "You did say, I believe, that you would be brief."

"Almost done, Judge. Ten more minutes, max."

"Good. Ms. Johnson, please escort the jury to their room. If counsel will stand by, we'll clear up the sidebar issue. Ms. Hudson, you may step down from the stand."

Redpath watched the jury leaving with a sinking heart. He'd been praying that the judge would let counsel go for a few minutes, too, which would give him time to think up some basis for his objection. Unfortunately, as soon as the jury was out of the courtroom, Norcross nodded down.

"All right, I'll hear you. But let's jump right to the point."

"Obviously, Your Honor . . ." Redpath paused and leaped. "Ms. Gomez-Larsen is trying to move into the area of the drugs seized at my client's residence, which you have excluded."

"Really?" Norcross turned to Gomez-Larsen. "Is that where you're going?"

Redpath was gratified and surprised to hear her reply, "Mr. Redpath is absolutely right, Your Honor. They've opened the door. The defense is entitled to a fair trial, but not to a license to lie."

"Nice phrase," Norcross said. "But who's lying?"

Gomez-Larsen turned to look around the courtroom until her eye fell on Sandra Hudson.

"Before I continue," she said, staring at where Sandra and her family sat together. "I'd ask that Ms. Hudson be excused from the courtroom, pursuant to your sequestration order."

"My order bars witnesses from the courtroom during the testimony of other witnesses. We're not hearing any testimony right now."

"Nevertheless, I'd ask that Ms. Hudson be excused before I continue my remarks."

"Very well. Ma'am?" Norcross nodded to the Cummings group. Sandra rose slowly and gave her mother a hug. As she did this, Moon, freed perhaps by the absence of the jury, allowed himself to twist around and watch her. Emerging from the embrace with her mother, Sandra saw her husband and gave him a smile, which Moon shyly returned. Redpath felt a spasm of frustration; he would, literally, have given one or possibly two of his fingers for the jury to catch that moment. Then, Sandra strode out of the courtroom, and Moon turned to face forward—his expression, as always, reverting to blank.

"Okay," Norcross said. "Proceed. But let's be quick. Time's a-wasting."

"Ms. Hudson just testified that she and the defendant had 'no secrets' from each other. I submit to you that that statement was a conscious and intentional lie. By that I mean the witness actually knew what she was saying was not true, and she was deliberately attempting to mislead this jury with her falsehood."

A rustle arose from the Cummings group, and Gomez-Larsen turned again to glance back at them. Mr. Cummings had put an arm around his wife and was patting her shoulder. Mrs. Cummings was glaring at Gomez-Larsen with eyes of fire.

Gomez-Larsen turned back to the judge. "Believe me, I take no pleasure in having to say this. As you'll recall, during the course of the search of the Hudson apartment, law enforcement officers uncovered a large quantity of marijuana, packaged for distribution, and a smaller quantity of ninety-two percent pure, so called 'fish-scale' cocaine, the very type being distributed by La Bandera at the time of the murders. Based on the court's suppression order, the government has been prohibited from offering or even mentioning this highly probative evidence."

"Right," Norcross broke in. Redpath was pleased to see that Gomez-Larsen had stepped on His Honor's toe. Her aggressive tone was going to make him defend his ruling. Norcross leaned forward and tapped his pen on the bench. "And, as you no doubt recall, the officers had no valid search warrant. The search was a flat violation of the Fourth Amendment."

"They had an unsigned warrant ..."

"Look, are we going to rehash all this again?" Norcross fell back in his chair and raised his hands. "A warrant not properly executed has no force. The officers didn't even bother to bring this unsigned document along with them because, I imagine, they knew the darn thing was worthless. Come on. We have a jury waiting. Let's get a move on."

"I apologize, Your Honor," Gomez-Larsen responded in a gentler tone. "I got off on a tangent. If you'll bear with me for another two minutes, something very important is at stake here."

"Two minutes. And I'm watching the clock."

"During the search, Judge, Sandra Hudson was in the bedroom when they pulled the marijuana out of the back of the closet. I have four officers, four, who will testify that when the officer who found the contraband, an officer ..."

Torricelli leaned forward and murmured behind her.

"Thank you. Officer Torricelli has just reminded me it was Officer Candelaria. When Officer Candelaria opened the shoe box and found the cash and the marijuana, Judge, Sandra Hudson expressed complete surprise and immediately stated to the defendant, who was standing on the other side of the bed, no more than six feet away from her, 'Moon, where did that come from?' or 'How did that get there?' or words to that effect—words expressing the simple reality that she, in fact, had absolutely no idea there were any controlled substances in the house."

Gomez-Larsen stepped closer to the bench. She jabbed at the witness box.

"Sandra Hudson knew from that moment, Your Honor, that, in fact, Moon was keeping secrets from her. Big secrets. She knew then, and she knew five minutes ago when she sat on that witness stand, that Moon Hudson was selling drugs throughout their marriage and was concealing that fact from her. The door on the marijuana issue is now open. The lid to the shoe box is off. I'm entitled to question Sandra Hudson about her lack of knowledge of the presence of illegal narcotics in her house, in her own bedroom, and to put witnesses on the stand who will rebut her claim that she and the defendant had no secrets from each other. I'm sorry, but without that evidence this trial will be a travesty, plain and simple."

Gomez-Larsen swiveled to check the clock at the far end of the courtroom.

"That's my two minutes, Your Honor. Did I make it?"

"Twenty seconds to spare. Mr. Redpath, what do you say?"

Redpath was on his feet immediately. "I say, 'baloney!' This is just an attempt . . . Judge, may I request that counsel resume her seat while I address the court?"

Gomez-Larsen had remained standing by the podium, occupying the foreground from the judge's perspective. She now nodded and returned to her seat. Redpath moved quickly to reclaim the podium and waved his hand back at opposing counsel, as though he might flick her away with his fingertips.

"This is just an attempt on the part of the government to slide in through the back door what they could not get through the front. They botched the search, and they've been trying to get this evidence in by hook or by crook ever since. Sandra's comment was nothing more than an innocuous remark, something any husband or wife might say . . ."

"Oh, please," Gomez-Larsen said, getting to her feet.

"Your Honor, where's my two minutes?"

"Proceed. Ms. Gomez-Larsen, I'll hear you in a moment."

"I say, again, it was innocuous. A remark made in passing. It didn't prejudice the government at all. Beyond that, the statement was not responsive to the question before her. If it's any problem, the remark may be stricken, and the jury ordered to disregard it on that basis."

"Your Honor, may I be heard?" Gomez-Larsen broke in again.

"I've still got ninety seconds!"

"Wait, wait," Norcross interposed.

After an indignant glance back at the prosecutor, Redpath continued. It was important that he take as much time as she did, and that he look angry.

"The whole point of this exercise, Judge, is not to put the alleged statement Sandra Hudson made during the search into evidence in order to show that the witness was supposedly lying when she said she and her husband had no secrets. The point is to get suppressed evidence, the fruits of an illegal search, before this jury. That's not proper. It's an out-and-out attempt to make Your Honor's well-considered ruling meaningless, and you shouldn't let the government get away with it."

Redpath barely had time to step away from the podium before Gomez-Larsen was speaking.

"Your Honor, that's not fair. We accepted your suppression decision. Frankly, I did think our argument that the agents were in good faith was more than colorable. Other judges might have bought it."

"I doubt it," Norcross interjected. "Anyway, you're stuck with me."

"I wouldn't say 'stuck' exactly, Your Honor." She paused for a beat to toss Norcross the smallest of smiles. "Anyway, whatever our disappointment, we're living with the court's interpretation of the law. Remember, though, that the price exacted by the Fourth Amendment in this instance was very high. Powerful, relevant evidence was kept from the jury. But to add to that a license to Ms. Hudson to testify falsely, to give the defense carte blanche to distort the truth. That's going too ..."

"Okay, pardon me, but I've heard enough," Norcross interrupted. "Here's what I'm going to do. We have to get going, or this recess will outlast a night in Russia. Mr. Redpath is right. The witness's comment was not responsive to your question. I'm going to strike her answer and order the jury to disregard it, put it out of their minds."

"Judge, they've heard it. No curative instruction is going to ..."

"Nope, nope, nope. There's no perfect way to deal with this situation, but as usual, I like my solution best. I'm going to strike the answer and instruct you not to question the witness either about the contraband found in the apartment, or her remarks in regard to it. That's off limits." Norcross turned to defense counsel. "Mr. Redpath, will the defense have any further witnesses after this one?"

"No, Your Honor."

"Your client has chosen not to take the stand?"

"That's correct. The defense will be resting at the completion of Ms. Hudson's testimony."

Norcross's eyes shifted to Moon, who was staring at his folded hands.

"Mr. Hudson, do you realize that you have a right to take the stand and testify in your own behalf?"

Moon glanced at Redpath. Some judges did this—confirmed directly that the defendant had made a knowing decision not to offer testimony—but Redpath hadn't mentioned this possibility of questioning to his client. Redpath felt a wave of concern. What would Moon say? Redpath twitched his chin up, signaling his client to stand.

Moon got to his feet. "Yes, Your Honor, I understand."

"And you've made a knowing and voluntary decision after discussion with your attorney not to testify?"

"Yes, Your Honor."

"Very well." Norcross looked satisfied. "So, we'll be moving on to arguments and charge tomorrow morning?"

"Well, Your Honor, may I be heard?" Gomez-Larsen's tone was clipped, and her eyes still glistened with indignation.

"Of course," Norcross said.

"The government will be calling a rebuttal witness . . ."

"I rarely allow rebuttal," Norcross began.

"A very short witness, Your Honor, no more than twenty minutes on direct." Gomez-Larsen paused. "I believe in the circumstances we have the right to do that, Your Honor."

Redpath stood. "May I ask who this witness will be?"

Gomez-Larsen did not turn and look at Redpath but addressed the court, as though Norcross had asked the question.

"Zinnia Sanderson, Judge. The neighbor, Spanky, you just heard Ms. Hudson refer to."

"Why didn't you call this witness during the government's case-in-chief?" Norcross asked. "You can't drag a trial out by reserving ammunition for rebuttal just to get the last word. Give me a proffer of what you expect this Sanderson person to say."

"We could not possibly have called her during our case-in-chief, Judge, because her testimony only became relevant after the defendant's wife took the stand. As an officer of the court, I represent to you that Zinnia Sanderson will testify that, at the time of the murders, Sandra Hudson was *not* at home with her husband as she has just testified. She was, in fact, walking with Ms. Sanderson several miles away, as Sandra Hudson just testified they regularly did during the mornings, eating doughnuts and strolling with their infants in Naismith Park."

52

Tom Dickinson sat on a metal chair outside the jury room, legs crossed, reading from a volume of his great-great-aunt Emily's selected poems. He always brought the book with him when he was babysitting jury deliberations. The words soothed him.

Dickinson needed soothing on this occasion. It had been a long, frustrating vigil for the court security officer—six days since the jurors had heard final arguments and received their instructions on the law. Every day, Dickinson carried notes from the jury to Judge Norcross with some problem or other. The deliberation room was too hot. Could they have a chalkboard? Would the judge say more about what a racketeering enterprise was? Through the mornings and afternoons, a current of mostly indistinguishable voices hummed through the walls, people talking over one another, angry sounds sometimes, and occasionally loud laughter and hoots. Once he heard a male shout and slap the table, and in the frozen silence he thought he caught a high squeak, like someone crying. This morning so far, only low murmurs. Nothing he could catch.

The door clicked open, and Dickinson quickly stepped to the threshold. His position gave him a view of one corner of the table, where the Asian accountant had her hand on the shoulder of the bank teller with the spiky blonde hair, saying something he couldn't hear. The girl's face was pink, and she was blinking.

The kid who was the foreperson, who'd started out so perky, looked as though he'd aged a few years. A folded slip of paper hung in one hand against his side. He started to lift the note to Dickinson, then hesitated, and turned to the room.

"Is everybody okay to do this?"

There was a mumble of agreement.

"Janie? You all set?"

The pink-faced girl looked at her friend, then turned to the foreperson, and nodded.

"Okay," the kid said. He handed Dickinson the slip of paper. "Tell him we're ready."

Dickinson found the judge sitting with Frank and Eva over sandwiches in his inner office. He mostly liked Norcross, a decent man who worked hard and wasn't snooty. Lately, though, over the long trial, and especially during the endless days of deliberations, a dangerous silence had gathered around the judge, and Dickinson kept his contact to a minimum. The guy might be okay, but he still carried a lightning bolt. No point in standing within range.

"Another note from the jury," Dickinson said, holding out the piece of paper.

Norcross sighed, took it, and unfolded it on his desk. His face changed as he read it.

"Well, well." He pursed his lips. "We have a verdict."

Eva went pale and stood up to look out the window at the plaza below.

Norcross pushed some papers aside. "Let's get everyone collected, Tom. Tell the marshals. Do we know where Redpath is?"

"I can see him from here," Eva said. "Same as always. Sitting on a planter, smoking a cigarette. Flicking his butts at the pigeons."

The defendant's wife, her mother, and her brother were at their usual post on the bench at the end of the hall near the elevators. The mother's hand was resting on her daughter's forearm, but they weren't speaking.

"Excuse me, ma'am," Dickinson said, bending down. "The judge has asked me to let you know we have a verdict."

"A verdict?" Sandra Hudson said. She seemed to be coming out of a dream.

"Yes, ma'am." Dickinson pointed down the hallway. "Thought you'd want to beat the crowd." A reporter hovering nearby overheard and strode quickly off toward the courtroom.

Mrs. Cummings squeezed her daughter's hand. Sandra began looking around in confusion. "Where's my pocketbook? Oh my God!"

The brother closed his cell phone, stood up, and touched the CSO on the shoulder briefly. "Very nice of you, Tom. We appreciate it." He nodded in the direction of the courtroom. "We can find our way in now."

Guy wants to get rid of me, Dickinson thought as he shoved off. *Don't blame him. Smart of him to get my name, though.*

At the other end of the hallway, outside the courtroom, Jack O'Connor was waiting with his two older boys. The youngest either hadn't come today or was in the john again. The little guy had been spending a lot of time on the disabled list.

Peach Delgado's girlfriend, Carmella Díaz, was a few feet away, in the small marble foyer in front of the courtroom door, bending down to reread the plaque with the Bill of Rights. No one accompanied her.

"Folks," Dickinson announced, "the judge wanted you to know the jury has reached a verdict. They'll be coming in now."

"About time!" the younger of the two O'Connor boys said with disgust. "Finally."

O'Connor nodded to him. "Go get Mikey, Ed." The boy stalked off, shaking his head.

Inside the courtroom, Ruby was already in position at her desk in front of the bench, organizing papers. Two deputy marshals were escorting the empty-faced defendant to his seat at the defense table; the other security staff were filtering in to their positions. Redpath entered and remained standing at the defense table. Gomez-Larsen and Torricelli took their places without speaking. The room filled quickly. There was very little noise for such a large group, maybe sixty people, including spectators, reporters, and security.

They barely had time to get settled before the judge's door opened, and they had to stand up again. Dickinson called out, good and loud, "All rise!"

Norcross, looking around, hurried up into his chair. He told everyone to be seated and got right to it.

"As I believe most of you know, we have been informed that the jury has reached its verdict. As of this moment, no one other than the jurors knows what that verdict is."

Dickinson let his eyes move around the room, watching the reactions.

Gomez-Larsen looked vaguely annoyed. Alex yawned nervously. Redpath was flushed and leaning back in his chair, watching Norcross. He seemed to be readying himself to jump up if something needed to be done. Beside him, Moon Hudson sat with his hands clasped, elbows on the table, motionless except for the rise and fall of his chest. It occurred to Dickinson that if Hudson's life had been different, he might have made a good cop. He certainly knew how to keep his cool.

When Sandra Hudson, her mother, and her brother arrived in the courtroom, the defendant did not turn his head to look at them, and Sandra did not try to speak to her husband. Now, while Norcross went on, she sat looking into her lap, her mouth slightly open. Her expression made Dickinson think of a small child caught red-handed in some horrible misbehavior. The whipping hadn't started yet, but the real torture was having to sit and wait for something she might not be able to endure.

The mother had placed a hand over her forehead, obscuring her face; the brother stared out the courtroom windows, as though miles away.

The O'Connors held the front row on the right. Jack and the oldest boy sat side by side, leaning back like matching statues, with their arms folded across their chests and their eyes fixed on the bench. Eddie shifted in his seat, scowling as though he thought the entire show was a pathetic joke. The face of the youngest kid, Mikey, had the same expression as Sandra's. He'd done something bad, and he was going to get a whipping. The similarity was so startling, Dickinson looked quickly back and forth to compare.

Carmella sat by herself. She shook her head quickly and wiped her eye.

"I don't want to drag this out," Norcross was saying. "I know this moment must be very hard for some of you. But I have to say a couple things before we bring the jury in.

"First, I am ordering that there be no outward expressions or demonstrations of emotion, either positive or negative, in this courtroom when the verdict is returned, whatever it may be.

"Second, a final point for the lawyers." Norcross dropped his eyes to counsel table. "As I see it, once the jury returns the verdict, we will proceed in one of three directions. First, if the defendant is acquitted on all counts, he will be discharged. Second, if he is convicted on one or both of the drug counts, but acquitted on the capital counts, I will be fixing a sentencing date. Third, if the defendant is found guilty on one or both of the murder counts, I'll let the jury go until Monday, when we will begin the penalty phase of the trial. Ms. Johnson, please bring the jury in."

After two long minutes of silence while Ruby retrieved them, the jurors filed in. Not one looked at the defendant.

Norcross asked, "Mr. Foreperson, has the jury reached a verdict?"

The kid stood, swallowed, and answered, louder than necessary, "Yes, we have." He raised a rolled sheaf of papers the size of a relay baton toward the judge.

"Kindly hand the verdict slips to the courtroom deputy."

Ruby took the papers; Norcross directed the jurors to be seated. He received the papers, checked them over quickly, and handed them back to Ruby. Dickinson noticed that, as usual, the judge's face gave nothing away. Now there were thirteen people who knew the jury's decision.

"Please listen carefully as the clerk reads the verdicts. I will be polling each of you afterward to confirm that you agree with them."

"Will the defendant please rise and hear the jury's verdict." Ruby's West Indian accent was curved at the edges, but, as usual, firm and clear.

Redpath stood first, and Hudson obediently followed, resting the tips of his fingers on the edge of the table. His face was gloomy and distant.

"We, the jury, unanimously find the defendant, Clarence Hudson, not guilty of possession with intent to distribute, and distribution of, marijuana.

"We, the jury, unanimously find the defendant, Clarence Hudson, not guilty of possession with intent to distribute, and distribution of, cocaine.

"We, the jury, find the defendant, Clarence Hudson, guilty of the first-degree murder of Edgar, aka Peach, Delgado during and in the course of a RICO conspiracy."

A gasp rose from the gallery. Carmella's head flopped back. Her eyes were squeezed tight, and she was breathing hard, trying to control herself.

"We, the jury, find the defendant, Clarence Hudson, guilty of the first-degree murder of Ginger Daley O'Connor during and in the course of a RICO conspiracy."

A loud, hoarse voice burst through the silence. Eddie O'Connor stood, raised both fists, and shouted, "Yes!" Jack O'Connor reached over to snatch at his son's shoulder, but Eddie shrugged him off and ran out of the courtroom. His cries of, "Yes! Yes! Yes!" echoed down the corridor.

53

It was hell. A familiar spot for Redpath, but one whose suffocating heat he always managed to forget until he found himself seared by it once more. Moon was to his right, motionless. Nothing Redpath could say, nothing he could do, but sit and feel himself being roasted alive.

His Honor went on for some time—God damn him for being a complacent son of a bitch!—instructing the jury to disregard the outburst from the O'Connor boy and polling the members individually to confirm their agreement with the verdict. While the judge rattled on, Redpath was blessedly unable to speak to Moon. Then Norcross turned to a summary of the next phase of the case, death or life, and Redpath's mind began to wake to the terrible challenge that still lay ahead, the complicated path that could lead Moon to the execution chamber.

When Norcross finally paused before giving his last comments to the jury and letting them go until Monday, Redpath started to lean toward Moon, having no idea what quick words might come out of his mouth, but with the sense that to say nothing would be inhuman. The sound of Sandra's crying behind them, however, cut off whatever he might have come up with. Moon's dangerous look told Redpath not to lay a hand on him. He would bear no insult of comfort.

As soon as the jury made its way out—one or two members glancing nervously toward the defense table—and Norcross did his ostrich walk through his private door, the two deputies came quickly over to cuff up the defendant and get him out of the courtroom. They would want him back in Ludlow ASAP, to avoid any possible problems. The ante had just been seriously upped.

Redpath noticed that both deputies' faces were glazed over. Had the convictions caught them by surprise? Their expressions had turned mercenary. They would do their job.

"Can I talk to him before he goes?" Redpath asked. "Can his wife have a word with him?"

"I don't want Sandy," Moon muttered.

"Five minutes. Then we're hitting the road," the black marshal said, taking his handcuffs out. "I'd come straight down." They took their man out of the courtroom through the side door, each taking an elbow and walking fast. Moon did not look at anyone.

Sandra, her cheeks wet with tears, insisted on coming—she had to see Moon, she said—and Redpath was too overcome to push her away. He'd have to pretend he hadn't heard what Moon said. During the elevator ride, Sandra held herself together, pressing a hand over her eyes and working to catch her breath, but when they got downstairs to the lockup, she ran up to the bars immediately, took hold of them in both hands, and burst into sobs again.

"Oh baby, how could they do this? Are you okay?"

The white deputy stepped toward her. "Going to have to ask you to step back, ma'am, behind the yellow line."

Moon moved to the far corner of the cell. He spoke to the grimy wall, slow and careful.

"Babe, go away, please. I love you, but I can't do this right now. You understand what I'm saying?" He glanced over his shoulder at his attorney and spoke in a harder voice, as though Sandy couldn't hear. "Bill, get her out of here. I mean it."

"There are things we can do, baby. Lot of things. We'll . . ."

"I mean it, Bill."

The deputy repeated, "Going to have to ask you to step back, ma'am."

"I love you. I'm never, never . . ."

Moon turned around. He crossed his arms over his chest, as though he were trying to hold his heart in. His eyes were shut; his lips were pressed together. After a terrible two seconds, he opened his eyes, kicked a small plastic stool against the wall, and shouted, "No!"

"What?" Sandra's eyes were wide, shocked.

"No, no, no!" Moon opened his arms and held his clenched fists up in front of his eyes.

"What is it? What is it?" Sandra slapped the marshal's hand off her shoulder.

"Just step back, please, ma'am. We're going to have to . . ."

"Don't you see?" Moon said, his eyes wide and his mouth gaping. "Can't you see, after all this damn time? They got me right! They got me dead right! Now please, Bill, please. Just get her the fuck out of here!"

54

*W*hen Daley and Halligan were brought before him the day after the guilty verdicts, Justice Sedgwick wasted no time.

"I have the painful task to inform you," he told the two, "that for the murder of Marcus Lyon, according to the laws of our land, you must die. You are to return to prison, there to remain until the time appointed, thence to be conducted to the place of execution. There to be hung by the neck until you are dead, and your bodies be dissected and anatomized. May God Almighty have mercy on your souls!" The date of execution was set for six weeks following this final appearance before the court: June 5, 1806.

A contemporary report of Justice Sedgwick's last eight words described them as being delivered "in a very solemn and impressive manner."

The Hampshire Federalist of April 29, 1806 offered the extraordinary understatement that, upon hearing the sentence, Dominic Daley *"seemed to be in some degree agitated," observing that he "fell upon his knees, apparently in prayer." Daley's behavior, according to the paper, contrasted sharply with the reaction of his co-defendant James Halligan, "who previous to the trial was by many supposed much the least criminal." Upon hearing his sentence, however, he "exhibited stronger marks of total insensibility or obstinate and hardened wickedness than is often witnessed."*

Whether Daley and Halligan were "obstinate," contrite, or simply petrified at the nightmare that had ensnared them, their actions after the sentencing make it clear that they needed no reminder that they were soon to stand before the seat of eternal judgment. The two of them immediately contrived to write and post a letter to Father de Cheverus in Boston, the nearest Catholic clergyman, begging him to come to Northampton and minister to their spiritual needs. De Cheverus, after his appointment years later as the archbishop of Bordeaux, France, retained the message of these two unlettered, condemned men among his private papers, where it was found after his own death.

"We adore," they wrote, "the decrees of Providence. Although we are not guilty of the crime imputed to us, we have committed other sins, and to expiate them, we accept death with resignation. Please do not refuse us this favor, we are solicitous only about our salvation: It is in your hands. Come to our assistance."

In the last week of May, Father de Cheverus, having walked the entire distance, arrived in Northampton, where Sheriff Matoon appointed Pomeroy's Tavern on lower Main Street as his residence. The innkeeper, Asahel Pomeroy, however, refused de Cheverus accommodation when his wife declared that she would never be able to sleep with a "Popish priest" under her roof. As a result, for several nights Father de Cheverus found himself billeted with his parishioners in the county jail. Finally, Joseph Clarke, a non-Catholic living on the south end of Pleasant Street, offered the priest a room in his house. A history of Northampton notes that the inhabitants of the city felt vindicated when, a few years later, Mrs. Clarke died and the residence was struck by lightning, events that were viewed by the locals as divine chastisement for the Clarke family's kindness to a Catholic.

Meanwhile, Dominic's wife, Ann Daley, back in Boston and in desperation at these events, drafted and submitted a petition for clemency to Governor Caleb Strong. The document pointed out that "the evidence offered in the trial was not positive; but merely circumstantial; that a child not fourteen years old was the principal witness." Mrs. Daley's petition also reminded the governor that "neither can Your Excellency be unconscious of the strong prejudice prevailing among the Inhabitants of the interior against the common Irish people who have emigrated to the United States; and in the present case the public mind has been influenced in a great degree by conversations and newspaper publications which precluded the possibility of that impartiality of trial which the law contemplates." In entreating the governor to be merciful, Ann Daley concluded by pointing out that Dominic Daley "has ever been a good son, father, and husband; and ever sustained the reputation of an honest man and a good subject."

With one eye no doubt on his upcoming election campaign against Attorney General Sullivan, Governor Strong declined to respond to the petition. The public hanging of Dominic Daley and James Halligan would proceed as ordered by Judges Sedgwick and Sewall, on June 5, 1806.

At this time, the inhabitants of Northampton numbered roughly twenty-five hundred, counting thirteen foreigners and three slaves. The entire population of Hampshire County, which in those days extended south all the way to Connecticut and included the town of Springfield, was no more than twenty-five thousand. Out of this number, the Hampshire Federalist *estimated the crowd that streamed into Northampton on the morning of June 5, 1806 at fifteen thousand. The most distant outreaches of the region—its farms, mills, and shops—on this late spring day must have been virtually drained of their inhabitants, with people of all ages traveling the muddy roads for hours by wagon, on horseback, or on foot to enjoy what was, however sober its purpose, a rare holiday.*

The first public segment of the ceremony began at ten a.m. at Northampton's Jonathan Edwards Church, a town landmark dating from 1737 and known as "the old church." Custom in 1806 decreed that a condemned man be afforded the dubious privilege of attending his own funeral service, and Daley and Halligan were transported under guard from the jailhouse to the Protestant church, crowded with onlookers, at the appointed time.

The two convicts had received some comforts. They had been up before dawn and met in private with Father de Cheverus, who had heard their last confessions and gave them the Holy Communion— thus marking the Hampshire County Jail as the site of the first Catholic Mass ever performed in western Massachusetts. Moreover, that morning, both men were granted their wish to die clean-shaven. Their jailers had lent them the necessary razors, after the priest gave his word that neither prisoner would try to cheat the crowd of its spectacle by using these implements to attempt suicide.

The original plan had been that the funeral sermon would be offered by the town's resident pastor, Reverend Solomon Williams, but Father de Cheverus protested. Daley and Halligan, in a second letter to him urging the priest to make haste, had written: "Do not reduce us to the necessity of listening, just before we die, to the voice of one who is not a Catholic." Now, Father de Cheverus insisted to Reverend Williams: "The will of the dying is sacred. They have desired to have no one but myself, and I alone will speak." Whatever adjustments may have been required to smooth over this hitch, the priest's sermon was received with approval and described by the Hampshire Federalist *as "an appropriate and eloquent discourse." The text was based on 1 John 3:15, "Whosoever hateth his brother is a murderer."*

Father de Cheverus began his remarks by taking indignant note of the throng, especially the large number of women, that had crammed the church to witness the event.

"Orators," he declaimed, "are usually flattered by having a numerous audience, but I am ashamed of the one now before me. Are there men to whom death of their fellow beings is a spectacle of pleasure, an object of curiosity? But especially you women, what has induced you to come to this place? Is it to wipe away the cold damps of death? Is it to experience the painful emotions which this scene ought to inspire in every feeling heart? No, it is to behold the prisoners' anguish, to look upon it with tearless, eager, and longing eyes. I blush for you. Your eyes are full of murder! You boast of sensibility, and you say it is the highest virtue of women; but if suffering of others affords you pleasure, and the death of a man is entertainment for your curiosity, then I can no longer believe in your virtue." A contemporary report stated that upon hearing these words, all the women in the church rose and departed.

At three p.m. in the afternoon, the main event began: the procession to the place of execution. Major General Ebenezer Mattoon, the sheriff of Hampshire County, led the way, magnificent in his full uniform, including saber and gleaming brass helmet. According to a biography of the Mattoon family, the major general had been up pacing the floors of his home on East Street in Amherst all night, dreading his responsibility to officiate at the execution, and particularly his duty to release the mechanism that would break the necks of the two prisoners. An Amherst neighbor, observing his distress, had offered to perform the job for a payment of five dollars, whereupon Mattoon exploded: "Would you take a man's life for five dollars?" and insisted that he would not surrender his duty, no matter how repellant. He rode from Amherst that morning with his aides trotting along beside him, all armed with pistols hanging from their saddles and presenting what one witness described as "a very imposing appearance."

Behind Major General Mattoon in the parade that afternoon, the Northampton militia marched in formation, followed by a band playing the Death March. The site of the hanging was an area west of the town known as Pancake Plain, traditionally an Indian burial ground and adjacent to what would later be the entrance to Northampton State Hospital, a public mental institution. At a modest pace, the distance from the church to this location would have required no more than half an hour.

When everyone had arrived, and the prisoners and officers had mounted the scaffolding, Dominic Daley faced the crowd and drew out a small piece of paper. In a voice that carried clearly over the murmuring assembly, he read the following statement on behalf of himself and James Halligan:

"At this awful moment of appearing before the tribunal of the Almighty, and knowing that telling a falsehood would be eternal perdition to our poor souls, we solemnly declare we are perfectly innocent of the crime for which we suffer or of any other murder or robbery; we never saw, to our knowledge, Marcus Lyon in our lives; and, as unaccountable as it may appear, the boy never saw one of us looking at him at or near a fence, or any of us either leading, driving, or riding a horse, and we never went off the high road.

"We blame no one, we forgive everyone! We submit to our fate as being the will of the Almighty and beg of Him to be merciful to us through the merits of his Divine Son, our blessed Saviour, Jesus Christ. Our sincere thanks to Father de Cheverus for his long and kind attention to us."

At that point, according to the Hampshire Gazette, *Dominic Daley handed the scrap of paper to Major General Mattoon, and he and James Halligan lowered their heads to allow the officers to place* the nooses around their necks. *An eight-year-old boy, Theodore Rust, was watching from the branches of a nearby tree. He recalled eighty years later how Major General Mattoon rode up to the gallows "and with a knife or hatchet cut the rope" dropping the two prisoners to their deaths.*

The corpses of Daley and Halligan were removed to a barn to be "dissected and anatomized" in obedience to Justice Sedgwick's order. Their work done, Major General Mattoon and the party of guards retired to the home of one Captain Cook for a banquet that cost the county more than \$25; other expenses included \$8 for the dinner served to the clergy, \$7 to Hezekiah Russell, who built the gallows, and \$2.17 for ropes and cords.

PART FOUR

55

"What are you eating?"

Eva stood in the doorway of Frank's office, writhing and reaching behind her as she tried to scratch an itch the middle of her back.

Frank waved a brown rectangle at her before taking a bite.

"Diet bar. Trish says I'm getting alderman's jowls," he said. "They're not bad. This is my third one this morning. You okay there, or what?"

Eva turned away from Frank and pointed.

"Scratch my back please."

A week had passed since the guilty verdicts, and the days spent watching the penalty-phase evidence had been brutal. Gomez-Larsen held nothing back, dominating the courtroom with the efficiency of a tennis pro humiliating an overmatched opponent. She led off with the testimony of the EMTs, who described Ginger Daley O'Connor's terrified face and their desperate efforts on the sidewalk to stop her bleeding. Then, one after another, Ginger's coworkers marched to the witness box, sketching for the jurors the impact of Ginger's violent death on the clinic and their children's nightmares, as well as their own. Ginger's seventy-nine-year-old mother followed, groping for words to convey to the jury the horror of learning what had happened, the black cloud over every holiday and birthday. The old woman's faltering passage back across the courtroom after she finished testifying brought her within six feet of Moon. When she paused before him for several seconds with her hand pawing the air, and it looked as though she was about to say something, Norcross quietly asked her to return to her seat in the gallery.

After that, Ginger's husband, Jack, offered his testimony, and then her son, Edward, came forward to offer his. As the boy lifted his hand to take the oath, before he'd uttered a single word, four of the jurors were already wiping tears away, and Norcross called a ten-minute recess that extended to nearly an hour while the exhausted panel regained its composure.

Carmella Díaz proved to be the government's secret weapon. In a lightly accented voice, she described her pregnancy, Peach Delgado's joy at the prospect of fatherhood, their shattered plans for the future, and her miscarriage, brought on by the sight of Delgado lying dead in a pool of blood in the crosswalk. When it was her turn to make her way back across the courtroom, the eyes of the jurors followed her and then shifted to where Moon sat—iron-faced, still staring at the backs of his hands, the perfect image of unrepentant viciousness.

The defense witnesses during this stage were only two so far: Sandra Hudson and a child psychiatrist who testified that the defendant's execution might eventually have a "deleterious effect" on his baby, Grace. Gomez-Larsen, in a bored tone, waived any questioning of Sandra. The guilty verdicts already confirmed the jury's opinion of her. Gomez-Larsen made cruel sport, however, of the defense psychiatrist's clinically phrased assumptions, brought out that he was being paid three hundred dollars per hour, and left him looking, as Eva put it, "like the hired gun who couldn't shoot straight."

Now as she reveled in Frank's vigorous scratching, Eva said, for the tenth time, "I still can't believe they found him guilty."

Frank moved his hands up to give his co-clerk a shoulder rub. "Like I said, Hudson was dog meat after Pepe testified. You could tell even the judge thought he was a Boy Scout."

"He was lying, lying, lying, Frank—lying to save his little round behind. Thanks, that's better." Eva put her hands in the small of her back and stretched. "Buddy Hogan is not going to cut Pepe any deals for saying his dead uncle Carlos did it, that's for sure."

Frank returned to his desk and sat down. He reached into a drawer for another diet bar.

"Maybe not. But if I've learned one thing here, it's that a trial is about believability, not necessarily truth. Whatever that is." He peeled back the wrapping and sniffed before taking a bite. "Speaking of which, how about the horrible jury instructions?"

"Well, it's anybody's guess what the word 'justified' means, but come listen to what we've got this time. And leave the crud bar please. It's making me nauseous."

The battle over the wording of the judge's final penalty-phase instructions to the jury had been hot, both in the courtroom and in chambers. Norcross had read, edited, and tossed back drafts of the final pages to Eva three times, trying to get the words perfect.

"He's crazy," Eva said. "It's impossible." She stepped around piles of paper on her office floor as she made her way to her cluttered desk. "Language won't slice so fine. It's like trying to perform brain surgery with a trowel."

"Let's hear."

Eva dropped into her chair and tapped her keyboard. "Okay, this comes after we tell them the aggravating factors have to outweigh the mitigating factors, blah, blah, blah." Sighing deeply, she read off her monitor: "The careful judgment that the law expects you to exercise in this regard is further reflected in the fact that, even if you are persuaded beyond a reasonable doubt that the aggravating factors outweigh the mitigating factors, you must still be unanimously convinced beyond a reasonable doubt that the aggravating factors are sufficiently serious to demand the penalty of death."

"I thought he wanted 'justify' there, not 'demand,'" Frank broke in.

"What the fuck does 'justify' mean? And what's the difference between asking the jury to find that death is 'justified' versus death is 'demanded'?"

"Come on. It's obvious."

"I'm going with 'demand.' Let him change it."

Standing in the doorway, Frank placed the heels of his hands together, tapped his fingers, and quoted Dr. Seuss. "'He meant what he said, and he said what he meant. An elephant's faithful one hundred percent.'"

Eva stared at the screen and swallowed twice before her fingers began to dance over the keys. A few taps, and it was done.

"... that the aggravating factors are sufficiently serious to justify a sentence of death. If even one juror thinks justice could be served by a sentence less than death, the jury is not permitted to return a decision in favor of capital punishment."

" 'May not return' was the phrase, I thought," Frank interrupted again.

"He wants it this way," Eva said, still staring at the screen bleakly.

" 'One fish, two fish—red fish, blue fish.' "

"You should get out more, Frank. Here's the grand finale: 'I also remind you, ladies and gentlemen, that you are never required to impose a death sentence. For example, there may be something about this case that you are not able to identify as a specific mitigating factor, but that nevertheless creates a reasonable doubt about the absolute necessity for the defendant's . . .' "

"You're fudging again. 'Absolute' wasn't in your earlier draft."

"He stuck that in during the last round. Shut up and let me finish." She continued: " 'Any one of you is free to decide that a death sentence should not be imposed for any reason you see fit. Indeed, I am specifically required to advise you that you have this broad discretion.' Blech!" Eva shook her head with disgust. "Really. What the fuck does 'justified' mean?"

"You're right. It stinks. But it's the best you're going to do, little buddy." Seeing the twisted look on her face, Frank took a step forward and added: "They're words on paper, Eva. They can only do so much."

"It's fucking horrible." She folded her arms on her desk and buried her head. "And don't call me 'little.' "

The orange light reflecting off the brick of the buildings across from the courthouse gave Frank's face a flush as he sucked on the end of his mustache.

"I have some good news," he said in a wheedling voice.

"You have good news," Eva parroted. "You would." She looked up. "Shit, you haven't written any more gay marriage letters, have you? The judge will have a . . ."

"Nah, one near-death experience was enough. This is better. I promised Trish I wouldn't tell, but . . ."

"Oh no," Eva said, starting to smile despite herself. "You're not . . ."

"We are," Frank said, bursting into a grin. "We're pregnant! Can you believe it? God, I'm praying for a girl this time!"

56

Judge Norcross's voice cut the air with a note of warning: "I take it the defense has no further witnesses?"

Redpath felt the weight of his exhaustion pressing down on his shoulders. He tapped with his large, square fingers on counsel table, counting the moments before he replied, still uncertain whether to plunge. Finally, he bowed slightly and took a breath.

"Judge, I'm going to offer one final witness." He paused, noticing Norcross tuck in his chin. "A very brief one." Gomez-Larsen leaned back in her chair and folded her arms.

He could see the judge working to keep his cool. "I'll see you at sidebar." Norcross's expression did not crack, but several jurors did not trouble to conceal sour looks. One cleared her throat loudly and coughed. The whole front row shifted and rustled.

I've lost them, Redpath thought as he and Gomez-Larsen

walked, one more time, across the spongy courtroom carpet toward the far right corner of the bench.

As soon as the stenographer wormed her way into place, Norcross spoke. "I don't see any other witnesses on your list, Mr. Redpath."

"I didn't list him," Redpath said.

"If the witness was not disclosed, then how can I allow you to put him on? Or her on. It wouldn't be fair to the government."

"Judge, the witness is a minor. I only learned last night that his father would permit him to testify."

"Well, at a minimum, you could have listed him as a potential witness, to put Ms. Gomez-Larsen on some kind of notice." Norcross dropped his voice to be extra sure the jurors wouldn't hear, and Redpath caught, with respect and some gratitude, the note of sympathy in the judge's voice. "Think about what you're doing here. I told the jury: final arguments and charge today. They're not going to be happy if we don't get to it."

Redpath hesitated, then plowed forward. "It's the son of one of the victims, Your Honor. I had no idea until last night at eight thirty."

"Whose son?"

"It's Michael O'Connor, Ginger O'Connor's youngest."

Norcross rocked back, looking surprised. "Criminy Christmas! You're calling him?" He seemed to consider, then shook his head. "He's only, what, eight or nine years old? I'd need to examine him outside the presence of the jury to see if he's competent to testify. Are you sure you want me to let you do this?"

"He's eleven, Judge. I'm told he's mature for his age."

"You haven't even spoken to him?"

"Not directly."

"Wow." Norcross began scratching the back of his neck and

shaking his head. Redpath placed both hands on the edge of the bench. If he was going to do this, there was no point in antsing around.

"Your Honor, Jack O'Connor, the boy's father, called me." He placed a hand on his chest with deliberate melodrama. "*He* called *me*, Judge. Last night, at eight thirty at my hotel. I about had another heart attack, frankly. He said the boy wants to testify, *needs* to testify. That's the first I heard of it."

"And you don't even know what he's going to say?"

"Only a vague idea. I'm probably committing malpractice here."

"Good gravy." Norcross had his chin on his hand, thinking hard.

While the interchange between defense counsel and the court twisted its way downstream, Gomez-Larsen had remained to the side of Redpath a step or two back from the bench. She was looking down at the carpet, nudging a piece of lint back and forth with the toe of her black pump, as though she were concentrating on some private game and not paying too much attention to the boys at the bench. Her serenity was giving Redpath the willies—what was she up to?—and now Norcross turned to her.

"What's the government's position?"

This was fair enough, but Redpath hated the thought of sharing control with the prosecutor. Should he have asked for a recess?

Gomez-Larsen took her time answering, rolling the ball of lint under her toe to play out the final set of whatever match she'd been fixed on.

"We don't object," she said at last in a neutral voice. She turned to Redpath. "Mikey will be twelve this August, Bill. He's going into the seventh grade, and, you're right, he's pretty grown up for his age." She lifted her dark eyes toward the bench. "We'll stipulate to his competency. Fact is, Jack O'Connor called me last night, too. He said it's important to the boy, and we owe it to him. So I've made my peace with this. It's up to you, Judge. I don't have much idea what the boy's going to say, either. But if defense counsel wants to play Russian Roulette, we're happy to let him pull the trigger."

Norcross shook his head slowly.

"Well, I can feel the Court of Appeals breathing down our necks right now, all the way from Boston. The phrase 'reversible error' keeps running through my mind."

"How about 'ineffective assistance of counsel'?" Redpath broke in.

"It's been, you know, an honor and a privilege," Norcross continued. He smiled briefly and cleared his throat. "Spending all these weeks with you two, a true barrel of laughs, but . . ."

Redpath and Gomez-Larsen looked at each other wearily.

"Feeling's entirely mutual," Gomez-Larsen said.

"I'll second that," Redpath said.

"But it sure would be nice not to have my pals on the First Circuit remand this gorilla for another go-round."

Redpath watched as Norcross lifted his eyes to the ceiling, thinking. The silence deepened, and the judge stroked the bridge of his nose. One of the jurors muttered something; another, a female, coughed.

"Okay, Mr. Redpath," Norcross looked down. "Call your witness."

Redpath returned slowly to counsel table, feeling as though a trapdoor could open up beneath him at any second. He nodded up at the bench and said in a lowered voice, "If Your Honor please, the defense calls Michael O'Connor."

The jury, which had been carrying on with its unhappy fluttering, died into a stillness at the lawyer's words. Every eye turned to the undersized, dark-haired boy who now rose from the first row of the gallery, glanced back at his brothers and father, and then walked, quite alone, toward the swinging oak door that marked the entry to the well of the court.

"Please take care as you cross the courtroom, Mr. O'Connor," Norcross said. "There are some wires taped down for our electronics."

The boy peeked apprehensively over the barrier at the crisscrossing duct tape.

"It's all right," Norcross said reassuringly, and a couple of the jurors smiled and nodded at the child as if to help him out. "Come on in. The water's fine."

In silence, the boy nudged the wooden door the minimum necessary to squeeze through, then walked, with an oddly bobbing step—as though the carpet were made of marshmallows—across the well and around behind the witness box.

"That's the ticket."

He was a small, elflike child. His face was thin and pale, with a pointed chin, and his eyes were strikingly large and dark. From Redpath's perspective, they seemed the color of shiny tar. Michael wore parent-approved, special-occasion attire: pressed khakis, bunched at the sides from being a little large in the waist, a blue blazer, and yellow shirt with a blue and yellow tie whose knot was so large compared to the boy's face that it seemed the size of a baseball. His hair was deep black and a little disordered; a strand of it danced over his forehead as he moved.

He looked, Redpath thought, like a fragile version of his mother, the pert, dark-haired woman who smiled out of the eight-by-eleven photos offered into evidence by the government.

"Raise your right hand, please," Ruby said. Michael was so

short that only his head and the tops of his shoulders were visible over the witness box. He lifted his hand to the level of his lower lip. His pale fingers curled.

"Do you solemnly swear that the testimony you are about to give to this court and jury will be the truth, the whole truth, and nothing but the truth, so help you God?"

Michael nodded and said, "Yes."

"Please be seated."

The silence in the courtroom by this time was so stark it was almost a species of sound. For the first time in the trial, the faint squeak of the hinge on the door to the witness box was audible, as well as the scrunch as Michael settled himself onto the corduroy upholstery of the witness chair. The seat, which was designed to allow the witness to rotate, swiveled unsteadily.

Redpath took no notes to the podium to assist him in his questioning, merely folded his large hands on top of the wooden frame and looked up at Norcross.

"May I proceed?"

Norcross nodded, and defense counsel began his examination.

"Michael, we haven't met before, have we?"

"No."

"Then I'll tell you my name is Bill Redpath, and I'm here representing the defendant Clarence Hudson, who most people call Moon. You understand that, don't you?"

"Yes." Michael's gaze drifted uncertainly toward his father and back to the lawyer. "Yes, sir."

"And you understand that Mr. Hudson has been found guilty of two murders, including the murder of your mother, and that this jury will very shortly be deciding whether he should be put to death?"

Michael nodded. "I understand." He tried putting his elbows up on the chair arms, but they were too high. He gave up and dropped his wrists to his sides.

"How are you feeling right now, Michael?" Redpath's voice changed, and he sounded concerned.

"Scared." The boy breathed deeply. His glance floated up to the judge's perch, ten miles above him, as if he were afraid he'd admitted something that might get him into trouble, then his eyes dropped again.

"But you asked to be here, right, Michael? You called me, or you asked your dad to call me"—Redpath turned to where Jack O'Connor sat in the gallery, bolt upright with his mouth open, then back toward the jury and continued, slightly louder—"because you wanted to come here, and sit where you're sitting now." He faced Michael and concluded quietly. "Isn't that true?"

"That's true."

"Why?"

Redpath's question broke a cardinal rule of trial advocacy: Never ask a "why" question when you don't know what the answer will be. *Here we go,* he thought.

"Because Mom wouldn't want . . ."

"I'm sorry. Just a little louder, please, Mr. O'Connor," Norcross broke in.

Michael cleared his throat and shot a look at his dad. "Because Mom wouldn't want him . . ." He nodded at Hudson. The defendant, like the jurors, was as still as wood, his eyes fixed on the floor in front of the defense table.

"Wouldn't want him to be, you know. To die. I know she . . . wouldn't want that."

Redpath waited until he assumed the witness had finished his answer. But Michael had only been looking down, gathering himself, and so both voices resumed simultaneously.

"How do you . . ." Redpath began.

"She's not . . ." Michael said, looking at his lap.

"Hang on, hang on," Norcross broke in quietly, holding up one hand. "Let's be sure the witness has finished his answer. Nice and loud now, Michael, okay?"

The boy was still looking down, taking careful breaths. He opened his mouth to speak but his chin trembled, and he closed it again. He lifted his elbows high up onto the chair arms, inhaled deeply, and looked at Redpath.

"She's not. She can't, like, be here to talk for herself. Somebody has to talk for her, so I have to. I have to say what she would say if she could be here."

"And what would she say if she were here?"

Michael looked searchingly over at Hudson, who still stared at the carpet in front of counsel table. The boy shook his head.

"She wouldn't want him to die." His chin dropped, and the hair tipped over his eyes. "She never wanted anything . . ."

"Just a bit louder please," Norcross said gently.

The twelve jurors and three remaining alternates were leaning forward in their seats. Two had their hands over their mouths. Redpath noticed Norcross take off his glasses and begin cleaning them with a tissue.

"Mom never wanted anything to die." He looked at his feet and then up. "Not even bugs. Even baby birds, we'd keep them in a shoe box and try to, like, help them fly. It never worked. She wouldn't want anybody to die on purpose, no matter what."

"What kind of effect would Moon's execution have on you, Michael? How would it make you feel?"

"Bad."

"Why?"

"Because I know it would be making Mom sad, and that would make me even sadder. It would make everything worse."

"Thank you, Michael. No further questions."

As Redpath turned, Michael's shoulders dropped with relief, and he began to slide out of his chair.

"Hold on a minute, please, Michael," Norcross said. "We may not be quite done with you yet, I'm afraid." He looked at the prosecution table. "Will there be any cross?"

Gomez-Larsen was examining the eagle behind the bench, scratching her chin absentmindedly. After a beat of three, she rose to her feet.

"Yes, Your Honor, very brief."

"Proceed."

Gomez-Larsen walked to the side of the podium closest to the jury and put one hand on the heavy frame. She carried herself with an air of delicacy, as though she were determined to preserve something in the mood of the courtroom that might dissolve. She stood for a moment, apparently in some inner debate, then shook her head sadly, answering herself, and began.

"Michael," she said. "I have just two questions for you."

"Okay."

"What's the first thing you think of when you wake up in the morning?"

It was terrible to watch. At first, Michael sat back and looked at the ceiling with an air of relief, to give this simple question his honest attention. His chin lifted slightly, and his head tipped to one side as he pursued the trail of recollection. But, when he reached the end of his search, his face darkened, and his fingers bunched on the chair arms.

Gomez-Larsen had been reading his expression as the seconds passed. When she saw the click, she said in a low voice, "I'm sorry, Michael. I'm so sorry. What's the first thing?"

Michael's face was paler than ever, and he leaned forward, speaking with a quaver. "Mom's gone."

"Yes. And what's the last thing you think of when you go to sleep at night?"

This time, no search was necessary.

"Same."

"No further questions, Your Honor."

57

Maria Maldonado stood at the bottom of the dark stairway leading up to her apartment. Another ten-hour day at the nursing home, and she was so tired that she could feel gravity pulling her shoulders down, as though she were carrying buckets of sand.

It really made no sense to keep this place. Hannah was off with her new boyfriend most nights and had stopped contributing to the rent; her parents, both ill, wanted her home. Tomorrow was Saturday, which meant she had to be up by six for her job at the Sheraton. With no rent or utilities to pay, she could at least drop the hotel job, maybe help out more at church.

Upstairs, in the darkness on the landing it took some fiddling to get the lock to turn. When Maria finally managed to get inside the apartment, she paused to stuff her key back into her purse before flipping on the light. Suddenly, she caught sight of a tall figure in the shadows by the sofa, gliding in her direction and reaching its arms out. A bolt of terror shot through her, and with it came the sickening certainty that she was about to be raped again. Her knees went weak, and she started to scream. But someone behind her clapped a hand over her mouth and twisted her head back. The man's other arm snaked across her, grabbing her breast and squeezing her painfully against him. She couldn't breathe; her heartbeat was slamming in her ears.

The dark figure came closer, his hands ready to tear at her blouse. He flashed a penlight across his face so she could see him.

"Quiet," he said in Spanish. "Quiet. It's only me."

The grip relaxed a bit, but the hand stayed over her mouth.

"It's me, it's Carlito. It's okay." He waved at the person behind her, and the hands dropped and smoothed her shoulders.

"Sorry," a soft voice behind her said in English. "Did I hurt you?"

Maria stared, astonished, at her older brother, come back from the dead.

"Carlos, is that you?" She spoke to him in Spanish, as they always had. "How can this be? The paper said you were killed. Your body was floating in the ocean."

Carlos sniffed and moved back over to the sofa. "You need to work harder on your English, Maria. The newspaper only said the body was 'thought to be' me."

"We were sure you were dead."

"Not yet, little sister. Not yet." Carlos snapped his fingers and pointed. "Mannie!" He gestured down the hall, switching to English. "In the bedroom, like I said, in the back of the closet. Close the door and stay in there until I call."

"Are you all right?" the voice behind her asked.

Maria looked over her shoulder but saw only the shadow of a very large man. She said nothing.

"Mannie!" Carlos repeated, gesturing furiously toward the bedroom. Maria watched the man's shadow as it disappeared, and she heard the sound of the door closing.

"Come sit here," Carlos said, pointing next to him on the sofa. "I need to talk to you." He nodded in the direction of the bedroom. "He speaks very little Spanish. He won't understand us even if he tries."

Maria didn't move. Her voice trembled. "Carlos, my God. I can't believe it's you. I thought . . ." She began to cry. "It's too much. You know what happened to me."

"It's all right, Maria. I'm very sorry we scared you. Now please come sit here. We need to talk." He patted the cushion next to him.

As Maria drew closer, her heart still banging against her ribs, the familiar features of her brother's handsome face drew together. He had regrown his beard, and now it was silver up toward his sideburns and halfway down his cheeks. A pair of tinted, black-framed glasses concealed his eyes. Without looking closely and hearing his voice, she might not have realized who he was.

She sat down on the sofa, still shaky, pulling her skirt over her knees.

"Who is Pepe talking to?" Carlos touched his sister's hand. "I need to know. The papers say he's blaming me now. Why is he saying these things?"

"The police captain told him you were dead. Truly dead. I was there."

"That old trick? The little fool!" Carlos took the glasses off and put them in his shirt pocket. He wiped his eyes with the heels of both hands. After a few seconds, Maria saw that he was focusing back on her, realizing she might be offended. He waved his hand. "It's not his fault. I should have prepared him better. Damn it, though! He's fucked up my life." He took a deep breath and frowned, sucking through his upper teeth like a man steeling himself for a sting, a habit Maria had seen many times. He continued. "Is it true, do you think? Do they really suppose I'm dead?"

"That's what they told us. I believed them."

Maria watched her brother, rubbing his hands over his knees and shaking his head, and she began to recall the depth of her anger at him. The terror of being grabbed like that had driven the rage out of her head. Now her bitterness was like blood seeping back into numb flesh.

"Carlos, I have to ask you something."

"No questions," he snapped. He stood up abruptly. "I may be going away." He pointed with his thumb over his shoulder. "South. You may never see me again, or you may see me tomorrow." He turned toward the bedroom, his voice a sharp whisper. "Mannie!"

Maria remained on the sofa. "Was it really you who put Pepe, your own nephew, in that car? Could you, his uncle, do such a thing to him?"

Carlos looked down. His mind had obviously moved far away again, fixing on the next problem. Maria saw her brother's face grow cloudy as he turned to her, heard him sucking through his upper teeth again. If he started to hit her, she would not even try to duck.

"Maria, I swear I did not do this. It was the nigger Hudson. I don't know why Pepe is saying these things."

"Pepe says the judge keeps doing things to help Hudson. The jury found him guilty, but Pepe says the judge could change that if he decides that Hudson didn't do it. What would happen to Pepe if the judge thinks he is being a false witness? I don't understand these things."

But Carlos was staring out the small living-room window, his attention, apparently, turning once more to other problems. The silence brought him back, and he gave a quick, wolflike smile.

"Then perhaps I'll have to get you a new judge."

The shadowy man, Mannie, floated into the room, holding a long, dark object. He took a position by the door. Carlos looked at him and nodded.

"Good." Then he leaned over so his face was very close to Maria's. "I was never here. Do you understand? You know I would never hurt you, but I cannot always control others. It would be very bad for you, and very, very dangerous for Pepe, and maybe even for our parents, if anyone ever knew I was here. Do you understand me, Maria? I was never here. You never saw me. I am dead."

"I understand."

Carlos pulled the glasses out of his pocket and set them on his face. Mannie opened the door, and Carlos stepped out ahead of him. The bodyguard hesitated in the doorway. "I am very sorry if I hurt you," he said, and then he was gone, too.

Maria sat on the edge of the sofa for nearly an hour, hugging her elbows and staring into the darkness. Eventually, one fact in the swirl of confusion became clear; its force pinned her where she sat. She had been watching her brother carefully for more than twenty-five years, gauging Carlos's moods—ready to dodge a slap, a fist, a thrown stone. Now she knew one thing absolutely, knew it with solid intuition even before the truth took shape in words. Carlos was lying. He'd put Pepe in that car. That much, at least, was the truth.

58

The Friday-night crowd in Springfield's Entertainment District—a few square blocks of upscale bars, restaurants, and gentlemen's clubs not far from the courthouse—had pretty much evaporated by three a.m., when Tony Torricelli nosed his Firebird up to a dumpster behind a hot spot called the Fish Eye. A stocky man positioned by the back doorway wiped his hands on his apron, nodded, and went back inside, leaving Tony in the spidery darkness. The Firebird's engine idled softly, echoing off the trash bins. Scraps of paper clawed over the blacktop in puffs of warm breeze that smelled of cooking grease.

Tony checked his watch—he was on the button—and lit a cigarette, doing his best to look unconcerned. News of Alex's unhelpful testimony at the Hudson trial had reached the South End, and it wasn't long before Tony received a call from one of the runners he'd placed bets with, a mid-echelon wise guy named Perez. Seemed Perez's boss wanted to talk to Tony.

"What's he want to talk about?" Tony had asked Perez.

"Chill out, Tone."

"I'm just asking . . ."

"He's not upset with you, man," Perez had said. "He's just, you know, disappointed. Now he's got another idea to get you out from under."

"What kind of idea?"

"You think he'd tell me? Come talk."

Tony had met Perez's boss once, briefly, at a wedding. He remembered the man's deadly stare as they shook hands. No way you refused a meeting with this guy. So now here he was, and God help him.

The rear door of the Fish Eye reopened, and three shadows drifted out. The first two split off, one moving to his left toward the driver's side and the other toward the passenger door. The interior light popped on as the guy on the passenger side slid in next to him.

"How you doing?" Tony asked. He'd never seen the man, a big, bald-headed bruiser.

"Fuck you." The man reached over, turned off the Firebird, and took the keys. He nodded toward the third man, who'd trailed up and was standing opposite the front left fender with his hands in the pockets of his gray sport coat.

This was Perez's boss. His crisp white shirt was open at the collar, and he was looking down at Tony with a sad, almost fatherly smile.

The man in the passenger seat spoke again, "Out." Tony's keys gave a plaintive clink as the guy stuffed them into his jeans pocket. The man on the driver's side opened the door, and Tony stepped onto the blacktop.

"Mr. Calabrese, how you doing?" Tony transferred the cigarette to his left hand and held out his right. Calabrese kept his hands in his pockets, looking even sadder. A crunch on the gravel told Tony that the guy on the passenger side had exited, walked around the rear of the car, and was coming up behind him.

"Not too good," Calabrese said. "I want my fucking money."

"I'm trying, really. I just, I need some more time." Tony could feel Baldie breathing into the hair on the back of his neck; the driver's-side guy, shorter, with a stubby ponytail and a thin mustache, was half an arm's length to his left, crowding his space. No place to run.

"Well, congratulations. You just made a down payment." Calabrese poked his chin toward the Firebird. "We like your car."

Tony took a puff on his cigarette and gave a hollow laugh. "Piece of crap's not worth the loan I got on it."

"We drive the car, pal. You pay the loan."

Calabrese nodded to the guy behind Tony, and two iron-hard hands shoved up under his armpits and locked behind his neck, levering his face toward the ground. The cigarette dropped from his hand and bounced, scattering the orange ember. The man with the mustache hit Tony hard in the gut and followed with a jab that cracked Tony's nose and sent salty blood flowing into his mouth. As Tony staggered sideways, he could see the guy was grinning.

"Goddamit," Tony said. "Where the fuck are you guys?"

The arms jammed his head down more fiercely, and he felt as though his neck would break. The guy throwing the punches had to be at least semi-pro. He planted a foot and hit Tony fast, three times—*bam-bam-bam!*—in the ribs, and a jolt of pain shot up his left side.

"Hey!" Tony gasped. "Come on! For Christ's sake."

The bald muscleman swung Tony around and slammed him into the car. Tony felt another hard punch in the kidney, then another, and then, at last, all hell broke loose.

A black SUV tore into the parking lot and skidded up so close it tapped the nose of the Firebird and knocked Tony backward. The window was down and the driver was holding a gun that looked as big as a horse's leg, pointing it at Calabrese.

"Up, up!" the driver shouted. "Up with the fucking hands!"

Several other cars roared in, and there was a sound of shouts and running feet.

The arms vanished, and Tony sat down on the pavement so hard his teeth snapped together. Bright searchlights on two marked cruisers abruptly lit the scene, giving Tony the pleasure of seeing his friend from the passenger seat getting tripped and kicked in the nuts as he tried to scramble away. The welterweight was already on the ground, and Calabrese, with a disgusted look on his face, had his arms pinned behind him. Tony heard the satisfying click of the cuffs.

The case agent, Simonelli, leaned over him.

"Great job! You okay?" He reached out a hand to help Tony up.

Tony ignored the hand and began pushing himself to his feet. "Does it look like I'm fucking okay? They broke my fucking nose."

"Let me turn you off." Simonelli reached inside Tony's shirt and deactivated the recording device.

"Where the fuck were you guys? Fuck!"

"Oh, stop being such a whiner!" Another agent trotted up, smiling broadly. "We got the whole thing on video, clear as a bell. Damn! Just wish they'd popped you a couple more times."

"Fuck!" Tony sputtered. "Fuck all of you! Give me a towel or something. Look at my fucking shirt!"

Simonelli put his hand on Tony's shoulder. "Why didn't you use the distress signal? It took us a couple seconds to tell you were in trouble."

"Distress signal?" Tony was patting blood off his face with someone's handkerchief. His nose stung horribly. "What fucking signal?"

" 'Help' was the signal, Tony. You were supposed to yell 'Help' the minute they touched you. We went over it three times."

" 'Help'—that was it? Just 'Help'?"

"Three times, Tony."

"Huh," Tony said. He dabbed his nose and winced. "Fuck a duck."

59

Even with Michael O'Connor's testimony, Judge Norcross might have squeezed in the arguments and charge that Friday, except that, of course, this being *Hudson*, something had to go haywire. After the boy left the witness stand and the defense rested—right as he was drawing breath to describe the next portion of the trial—Juror Six, a young woman with spiky blonde hair on the far end of the front row, stood up suddenly. To Norcross's astonishment, she began floundering over the feet of the other jurors, muttering, "sorry" and "excuse me" like a movie patron clambering out for a pit stop.

Predictably, she didn't make it. With one hand on the jury rail and one on her diaphragm, she retched volcanically into the lap of the foreperson, paused, shuddered, and then vomited again, off to the side, so a few stray chunks ran down the front of the jury box's beech paneling.

What else could he expect? He'd had to put everything over to Monday. It was disappointing but, as Eva reminded him, picking up with the final arguments at the beginning of the week might work better anyway. They'd have the weekend to repolish the penalty phase instructions and air out the courtroom.

Claire returned very late that Friday after four days at a conference in Hawaii, and Saturday morning Norcross was hurrying into town to meet up with her. As he drove, he embroidered details of the vomit performance to improve the comedy, chuckling to himself at the points where he hoped his lady would laugh. They were meeting for breakfast at The Lord Jeffery Inn, an upscale establishment popular with visiting alumni on the edge of the Amherst Common.

As Norcross was easing into a parking place, he got an unwelcome surprise. Florence Abercrombie was emerging from Hastings News, a stationery store across the street. He ducked down over the passenger seat, pretending to fuss with something in the glove compartment, hoping she wouldn't notice him.

No such luck. She bustled into the crosswalk, more stooped than he remembered, and began waving her arms. "Yoo-hoo! Over here!" she called, as though she were shipwrecked and he were a sail on the horizon. The old woman's long white hair danced behind her in the breeze. By the time she drew up, Norcross was out of his car attending to the parking meter.

"They're taking my house!" Mrs. Abercrombie said, with a lopsided grin and large, unnaturally bright eyes.

"I'm sorry, Mrs. Abercrombie." The meter buzzed as it digested his quarter.

Her off-center smile did not change.

"You denied my motion." A strand of hair flapped across her face. "Without a hearing."

"I know. I'm very sorry." She seemed to have gotten shorter, and Norcross had to put his hands on his thighs as he bent down to her. "Can I tell you something? I'm about to meet somebody—you remember Professor Lindemann?—and, to tell the truth, I'm pretty excited to see her. She's waiting. So this is not a very . . ."

"I know, it's not a good time." Mrs. Abercrombie looked down at the pavement before squinting up at him. "It's never a good time." The wretchedness in her eyes made her unchanging smile seem daubed on.

"Sorry. It's just . . . I'm just, kind of . . ."

"It's all right, Your Honor." Mrs. Abercrombie waved her hands, fanning the air. "But, don't worry, you'll be seeing me again. I'm not giving up, you know!" Her fingers tapped his chest as she stepped closer and dropped her voice. "A good time is just around the corner."

"That's the spirit," Norcross said, stepping back. Then he added, wincing inwardly at his hypocrisy, "Always good to see you, Mrs. Abercrombie."

Claire was waiting for him in the lobby when he arrived, wearing a dark green blouse, black slacks, a pair of earrings he'd given her, and perhaps a little more makeup than usual. She didn't need it, but it was a pleasure to know she'd taken the trouble. They had just gotten to their table, and David had not even had time to start in about Juror Six, when Claire reached down and handed him a Lord & Taylor bag containing a package in lavender wrapping paper.

"Hey," she said. "I brought you a present."

"Oh no," David said, smacking his hand over his eyes. He should have brought something, flowers at least. No, flowers would have been wrong, but he should have brought something.

"You didn't get anything for me, right?" Claire asked. And

when David nodded, she smiled and said, "Such an asshole! Come on, open it up."

While the waiter poured their coffee, David slowly removed the paper, being careful not to tear it and thinking furiously. He could try getting her something on the way home, but what? A flowering plant?

The ceramic object inside the box seemed to be some sort of doll. Placed on the table, it revealed itself as the grinning bust of a round, pink-faced woman, eight inches high, who waggled back and forth and gaped at him.

Claire chuckled and poked his arm.

"Know what it is?"

"It's some kind of . . ."

"It's a Wife of Bath bobblehead!" Claire leaned back in her chair and clapped her hands with delight. David noticed her moist tongue on the tip of her teeth. "It's one of only two Canterbury Tales bobbleheads in the entire universe, as far as I know. I ran into an old student of mine at the conference, an amateur sculptor who once had a crush on me, and he gave them to me." Claire's quick tap sent the doll's head rocking. "Isn't she wonderful?"

"Fabulous." David peered closer. "She's got a big space between her front teeth."

"That's how Chaucer describes her! Isn't that a riot? In the Middle Ages, gap-toothed women were supposed to be extra lusty." She nudged the doll again and quoted. " 'Boold was hir face, and fair, and red of hewe.'"

"He's got that detail." David paused. "In love with you, huh? Meeting you at conferences in steamy places and bringing you nifty gifts."

"I said he had a crush on me, once."

"Hmm. Who's the other bobblehead?"

"The knight, of course." Claire tapped out the pentameter on the tablecloth. " 'A knight there was, and that a worthy man.' Him, I'm keeping."

"Maybe he'll miss her." David nodded at the Wife of Bath. "All alone on his shelf."

He watched the doll ogling him impertinently; her jiggle had a coquettish quality. "She makes me think of something, but I can't quite put my finger on it."

"Would you like me to?"

"To what?"

"Put my finger on it." When David leaned back and raised his eyebrows, Claire threw him her goose face, then said, "Why don't we go back to my place for breakfast? I have ripe mangos."

"You have ripe mangos." David felt his pulse quicken and something press against the back of his throat. He swallowed.

"Yep," Claire said. "I brought them back for you from Maui." Her voice was carefully innocent, but her eyes were alight. "They're very juicy."

When the waiter returned to take their order, David said, "I think we'll stick with coffee. We're in more of a hurry than we thought."

Smirking ridiculously, they gulped down their coffee and agreed to reconvene at Claire's house in fifteen minutes.

As he made his way down the stone walk leading from the inn, David paused to gaze across the Common, brought to a stop by the happiness ballooning inside him, beyond hope or dream. The morning air was sweet, with the nip of early spring entirely gone. The grass of the Common, a deep crayon green, sloped down toward him from Pleasant Street onto a broad shelf the length of a football field. Sugar maples on the perimeter and on the higher ground up by the parking area were tossing great pompoms of vivid leaf against the blue sky. Everything was soundlessly cheering, especially him.

Two students, a girl and a boy, were flinging a red Frisbee nearly the entire length of the Common. Their exuberance, the power and accuracy of their throws, seemed to David almost magical. As he resumed his walk in their direction, the girl dashed toward him, thumping the earth so hard he could feel the vibrations through the sidewalk. Ten feet away, she leaped with a grunt and stretched full-length, straight up, to snatch the Frisbee out of the air, then twirled as she landed and fired her return like a bullet, four feet off the ground a good sixty yards down the grass, where the boy caught it, galloping like a colt. The girl cast David the briefest of looks, wiped her nose on the sleeve of her purple sweatshirt, and trotted off again as the Frisbee floated back toward her, an easy toss.

David lifted his eyes once more to the tops of the scrubbing maples, the boundless sky over the town's low brick buildings, and the distant hills. The Wife of Bath swung by his side in her bag, matching her fantasies to his, and the whole weekend spread out before him, as spacious as the heavens, with nothing to do until Monday.

The last phase of *Hudson* was still there, of course, nagging at him. He kept imagining the moment, if the jury opted for death, when he would be sitting at his desk, pen poised, preparing to put his name on the execution order. He pushed down the thought. Who really knew what would happen? At least now the end was in sight. Soon Hudson would be off to Texas to begin his life sentence, or to Indiana for the long wait before his appointment with the Bureau of Prisons' medical team. In a few days, a week at the most, a new parcel of baffled jurors and a new cast of attorneys and witnesses would be assembling before him.

United States v. Hudson, whatever its outcome, would begin its slide into oblivion.

David didn't notice Mrs. Abercrombie until she bustled into view around the rear of his Outback, five or six car-lengths away. A small wicker basket covered with a red-and-white checked napkin was dangling from her left hand.

Heaven help me, David thought. *More ginger snaps.*

He kept walking; somehow, he was not surprised. This was exactly the sort of thing the dear old crackpot would do. But it had to stop. It was way past time to get Mrs. Abercrombie out of his in-box. If she kept stalking him like this, he'd end up having to send the marshals to pay her a visit, maybe have to stick her gnarled old bottom in a jail cell.

She was waiting for him next to the driver's side door where he could not avoid her. Her body seemed to be teetering, so rickety it looked as though it might fly off on the next puff of wind.

"Hello!" She waved.

When David drew up, the old woman dropped her voice and nodded at the basket. Something about her appearance was worse, even odder than when he'd seen her earlier. Her eyes narrowed in a kind of squint.

"I've got something for you," Mrs. Abercrombie said. "I made it up myself."

"Ma'am, we really do have to talk." He shifted the bag to his left hand. "You have to stop doing this. Really."

"You want to talk now? This is a good time?"

"It may be the best time we're going to get, Mrs. Abercrombie."

She shook her head, looking down at the pavement, then back up at him. "No." Her eyes were searching up, as though she didn't quite have him in focus. "I don't think so."

"I'm sorry?"

"Everyone's always sorry." She glanced down at the basket. How small she'd gotten!

Her face broke into a frowning grimace as she reached under the red-and-white napkin and drew out a tiny silver pistol. David, focusing on the hole at end of the barrel, drew in his chin. Was it real? The contraption was pointed directly at his heart, less than a two feet away.

Mrs. Abercrombie bit her lower lip, glared down at her hand, and pulled the trigger. The force of her tugs made the barrel jiggle, but the pistol merely emitted three dry clicks. David shook his head, speechless. A trickle of hot sweat was working down the inside of his arm, and his heart was racing.

"Lord, Mrs. Abercrombie," he said finally. "You almost scared me to death with that thing. Why don't I ..." He grasped the end of the barrel and tipped it up to pry it out of her hand, working with care, not wanting to twist the old lady's fingers. She set her lips and tightened her grip against him.

David had time to think, *This is probably not smart*, when the pistol discharged with a loud snap. He flew backward as though he'd been speared in the face by the butt of a rake handle. When he tried to gather his feet under him, his grasp fumbled against a parking meter, and he fell onto his side. The Lord & Taylor bag hit the pavement, bounced, and spat out its cardboard box. Propping himself on an elbow, David tried to force back the searing pain by pressing with his free hand against his eye and forehead. But the world was quickly growing dark, and the warm blood was pulsing through his fingers. It was difficult to get air. A smell of dirt, a wondering thought of Claire, of Marlene waiting, a thin strand of regret, and that was all.

The athletic girl stopped in her tracks to take in what had happened, allowing the red Frisbee to sail past her into the parking area and run scraping along the asphalt. When she saw the blood, she clapped her hand over her mouth, but for only for a moment. Then she began to shout fiercely, summoning the boy from far down the Common to help. The air carried the sweet smell of gunpowder.

Mrs. Abercrombie replaced the pistol back under the napkin and walked unnoticed toward her leprous old Volvo—grinning and nodding, rather in the manner of Claire's Wife of Bath bob-blehead.

60

Later that morning, Lydia Gomez-Larsen, her husband, and their two children were sitting down to their regular Saturday brunch. The dining room had French doors looking onto an elegant brick terrace with two rows of day lilies along one side. Just as Lydia picked up her fork, the phone rang, and she jumped up with an irritated expression to hurry into the family room.

"Go ahead and start," she called over her shoulder in Spanish, but her husband, son, and daughter were already gobbling. Greg was not even on call this weekend; it was not fair.

"So! How's my favorite prosecutor?" It was the too-familiar voice of Buddy Hogan.

"Uh-huh," Gomez-Larsen said, sighing. "I bet you say that to all the girls."

She flopped onto the couch, cradling the phone against her head. Her feet were bare, and she was wearing a pair of bright white slacks and an orange rugby shirt, untucked. She stretched out her legs and propped them on the coffee table.

"Listen," Hogan hurried on. "Sorry to harass you at home. Everybody's saying you were brilliant yesterday, absolutely brilliant, with the O'Connor kid and everything. You're the talk of Beacon Hill. When I get to be president, you're going to be the best-looking broad on the Supreme Court."

"Well," Gomez-Larsen said, pulling a TV remote out from under her, "we'll see what the jury does. Now that it's almost over, I can tell you I haven't been Señora Popularity in my extended family the past few weeks."

"Really? Why?" Hogan asked.

"Castro shot two of my uncles. The Gomez clan is not real big on capital punishment."

"I thought you were Puerto Rican."

Gomez-Larsen sighed. "Have someone buy you an atlas, Buddy. You'll be amazed how many islands there are down there."

"Shit." Hogan laughed uncomfortably. "If I'd known about your relatives, I might have thought twice about giving you the case."

"So what's up? I don't want to be rude, but my breakfast is getting cold."

A pause on the other end made Gomez-Larsen lift her feet from the coffee table and sit up. Something funny was coming.

"A couple of us happened to be in here on a Saturday, kicking your case around." Hogan's voice had lost some of its breeze. "And we realized there's, ah, one loose end we need to tie up."

Gomez-Larsen drew open the middle drawer of the coffee table, took out a pen, and turned over a torn envelope for scratch paper.

"And that is?" She doodled a five-pointed star.

"The wife. Was it Susan?"

"Sandra."

"Right. We can't let the perjury slide, Lydia. People can't pull that crap."

Gomez-Larsen didn't say anything, and Hogan added, a little lamely, "So, we've had an intern bang up the research, but you're obviously the best one to put the case to the grand jury."

Gomez-Larsen set the pen down. "That's not a good idea."

"Why's that?"

"First of all," Gomez-Larsen said, "I'm not a hundred percent sure she committed perjury."

"What about Spanky Sanderson, the neighbor? She said she and Sandra were walking their kids in the park, and ..."

"Spanky was so scared we'd snatch her grandson, she'd have stood on her head in the witness box if we'd asked her. I'm fairly sure she was telling the truth, or at least thought she was, but ..."

"That's close enough for me."

A silence followed. Lydia heard the sound of the forks clicking on the plates in the other room. She bit her lip and took a deep breath through her nose. Finally, she said, "Buddy, it's time to fold the tent on this one. It's over."

"It's not over until I say it's over."

"Then say it's over."

"It's not over," Hogan said. "Hey, if you don't want it, I'll understand. You've been a trooper. I'll put another assistant on it."

"No way, Bud."

"What the hell's that supposed to mean?"

"I mean, it's time to end this."

"Lydia, are you listening? I just said ..."

"Buddy, you know my husband is a surgeon, right?"

"Congratulations. What does that have to do with the price of bananas?"

"I don't do this job for the money. I could step aside any time. And, um, if something happened to make me take a hike, I might have a few things to say, you know?" She paused. "I really think it would be better all around if you and I stayed friends."

The receiver had gotten sweaty, and she switched it to her other ear. She could hear her boss open and close a desk drawer on the other end.

"Well, fuck you, Lydia," Hogan said finally, using his most amiable voice.

"Fuck you, too, Bud," she replied, carefully mimicking his tone.

There was a sound of muttering from Hogan's end of the line. Was someone else in the room? No sound of breathing. If there was somebody hiding on the line, he was keeping his hand over the mouthpiece.

"You still there?" Gomez-Larsen asked.

"Not really."

"Buddy, listen to me . . ."

"No, no, no, no," he said, briskly. "It's okay. Maybe I'll give this one some more thought. We'll kick it around here a couple more times. But I wouldn't count on that Supreme Court thing, sweetheart."

"The humidity in DC is bad for my hair, anyway."

"Good-bye, Lydia. I'll be in touch."

"Good-bye, Buddy."

Though she hadn't raised her voice, the electricity in her words had attracted the attention of her children, Alejandro and Lucía, who had been listening closely from the next room. Eight-year-old Lucía leaned forward and solemnly whispered to her father, "Daddy, Mommy just said 'fuck you' to someone on the phone." Except for the words *fuck you*, she spoke in Spanish. Alejandro, eleven, was grinning gleefully.

Greg responded, also in Spanish, "Don't worry, sweetheart. If she said that to somebody, I'm sure he deserved it."

Gomez-Larsen was halfway back to the dining room when the phone rang again. "Oh, mother of God!"

"Let the machine take it," Greg called. "You're missing out here."

"Buddy's thought of something else. He always does this." But when she picked up, she heard a female voice speaking Spanish very quickly.

"This is Maria Maldonado, Pepe's mom? I need to speak to you right away, ma'am. I know who killed the judge. I hid the gun."

"Who is this? Maria?"

"Carlos is alive. He came to my apartment last night with another man. He took the gun with him when he left. Now he's killed the judge."

"The judge? What are you talking about?"

"You don't know? It's on the radio. They haven't caught him, but I know it was him. It's all my fault. I should have spoken."

Lydia dropped onto the edge of the sofa, glancing up at the clock to jot down the time.

"Where are you? Can you come to my office at the courthouse in one hour?"

"I'm at the Sheraton. It was just on the radio. They say whoever did it is unknown. Yes, yes, I can borrow my cousin Hannah's car."

"Don't speak to anyone about this."

"My cousin knows everything. I told her."

"Okay, no one but your cousin."

"Ma'am?"

"Yes?"

"If I say something that makes you think that Pepe has not been telling the truth, what will happen to him? My cousin says he will go to jail for the rest of his life. Is that true?"

"No." Gomez-Larsen spoke quickly, the way she usually did when she wasn't sure about something. "Twenty years. He'll get the same deal."

Pepe's plea agreement said that the boy would get life without the possibility of parole if he was not completely truthful. The U.S. attorney might still decide to recommend a lower sentence, but that decision would belong to Buddy, and Gomez-Larsen wouldn't put any money on his mercy. Still, Pepe theoretically could get the twenty years, and this was no time to quibble.

After hanging up, Gomez-Larsen punched in the cell number for Sean Daley. She'd want him at the courthouse for the conference with Maria. As she waited for Captain Daley to pick up, she was aware of her husband standing in the doorway of the family room, looking concerned. For the moment, she ignored him. What in the name of God was going on?

61

Eva could not shake her worries about Monday's penalty-phase jury instructions. The final draft that emerged from the Friday afternoon conference with Judge Norcross still needed a lot of cutting and pasting, and Friday night she'd barely slept, positive that the most recent version had two long revisions switched around. She waited until a respectable hour Saturday morning before calling Frank and begging him to come to the courthouse to run over a final clean copy with her. It wouldn't take long, she promised, and they could meet Trish and Brady for strudel at The Fort afterward. Her treat.

Two hours later, Eva was pacing up and down a side street next to the courthouse's private security entrance, pulling at her hair and trying to remember the file name for the latest edits. She caught sight of Frank, noodling down the block, walking with his toes stuck out. She could not help smiling at what a total loser he was.

"You're frigging weird, Meyers!" Frank called out. Then, more quietly as he drew closer, "This trial is giving you OCD."

"Humor me, okay? Jesus, have you bathed?"

Frank had on a pair of baggy blue jean shorts, a Red Sox T-shirt, and dirty sneakers.

"I'm clean enough for present company. Everything else was in the wash."

Outside the normal workweek, the area around the courthouse was deserted. The Massachusetts Department of Social Services office across the street, the bar down on the corner, and the Korean clothing store were all closed. The two or three cars parked illegally looked as though they'd been abandoned for the weekend, except for a dark blue Lexus that was idling with two men inside, apparently waiting for someone. The sun had not quite reached its zenith, and a diagonal splash of light hit the side of the courthouse, sliced by the shadows of the NO PARKING signs.

Frank took his pass card out and was just slipping it into the electronic slot to open the side door when Eva heard someone yell, first in surprise and then louder, frightened. She turned and saw a small brown woman, whom she instantly recognized as Pepe's mother from the trial. Maria something, Tom Dickinson had told her. The woman was halfway down the block struggling with a very large, dark-skinned man, who was coming out of the Lexus. The front passenger door stood open, and the man was pulling the woman by her elbow. She was punching and scratching at him and yelling in Spanish. Eva felt a surge of nausea; she hated this kind of stuff.

Frank didn't look too happy, either. After a few seconds of hesitation, he took two steps in the direction of the fracas, calling out in a pleading tone, "Hey! Come on!"

There was no way to ignore what was happening. Maria had wrapped her arms around one of the signs, hanging on desperately, screaming and crying, and the large man was trying to pry her hands loose. The big guy's eyes shifted toward Frank with a clear message: Mind your own business.

Frank glanced back at Eva and reluctantly shifted into motion. "Hey! Leave her alone!" he said, trotting most of the way to the struggling woman. "Come on. Really!"

He looked over his shoulder at Eva again and rolled his eyes up to heaven. He held up his palm in the shape of a phone and poked at it with his finger.

"Help me!" Maria cried out, switching to English. "He wants to . . ." But a sharp yank from the larger man detached her from the sign, and she fell hard onto the sidewalk.

Frank stepped nearer, still fighting himself. "Whoa! Hey, really, come on!"

The guy was huge. He made Frank look like Danny DeVito. Eva reached into her purse, dug her phone up from under her two small barbells, and quickly tapped in 911. Her phone took its time connecting, and as she waited, she saw the big dude's angry eyes move over to her, noticing that she was making a call. Did he have a gun? People got killed in situations like this. Scraps of old newspaper headlines flashed through her mind.

Meanwhile, Frank had drawn up to the pair and was reaching down to help the woman up, looking at her attacker and trying to sound reasonable. "Come on, look what's happened. Leave her alone, okay?"

The man shifted his eyes to Frank, shook his head, and punched Frank in the face, very hard. The sight of her friend being hit and Frank staggering back with blood streaming down his face, horrified Eva. Frank fell backward against the courthouse wall, and slid down onto the pavement. Eva felt herself starting to get sick to her stomach and, at the same time, enraged.

The big man thrust his arms out and looked down at Maria on the ground. "See what you made me do?"

Eva flipped the cell phone closed just as a voice answered. The police would never get here in time anyway. She had to do something herself.

She could see Frank, pushing at the pavement and shaking his head, blood running all down his chin and onto his T-shirt. The big man was leaning over, slipping his hand under the woman's back to lift or throw her into the front seat, and she was still wriggling and kicking at him. She was screaming apparently—her mouth was wide open, anyway—but Eva didn't seem to be hearing anything.

Eva forced herself into a run toward the Lexus, holding her heavy purse by its handle with both hands and yelling, "Hey! No hitting!" It was all she could think of to say.

The big man looked up at her and sighed, like a busy guy who'd been asked to deal with too many annoyances in one day.

"I don't hit women," he said dismissively. He bent over, heaved the small lady upright, and shoved her toward the car.

"Goodie for you!" Eva said, swinging her purse with all her strength. It struck the man a heavy blow in the lower part of his skull and upper neck.

Her small barbells did their work amazingly well. The big guy grunted, lost his grip on the small woman, and grabbed the side of the car to keep from falling. Shaken free, Maria staggered backward across the sidewalk toward where Frank was slowly pushing himself to his feet.

"Okay, enough!" The driver's-side door of the car swung open, and a bearded man with tinted glasses jumped out. He pointed a rifle with a curved banana clip over the top of the car at Eva.

"Have you ever been shot, honey?" he asked. "I have. I guarantee you won't like it." He nodded toward Frank, who was on his feet but wobbly, bracing himself against the courthouse wall and wiping his face with the bottom of his shirt. "Go help your friend." Then he directed something angry at Maria in Spanish, pointing furiously over the roof down toward the front passenger seat. When Eva didn't move, the bearded man looked back at her and pointed the gun at Frank. "You want me to put one in his belly? Go!" Eva moved back from the car. Maria walked past her with a look of despair and slid into the front passenger seat. "Mannie," the bearded man said. "Get in the back."

The big man, still leaning on the side of the car for support, looked reproachfully over at Eva and began opening the rear passenger door.

"Good," the bearded man said. He put one foot back into the car and began lowering himself to enter.

A police cruiser turned the corner at the end of the block and flipped on its siren and flashers. The bearded man wheeled around and fired a clatter of shots into the cruiser's windshield, then jumped into the Lexus. But even before he'd entirely disappeared into the driver's seat, the car's idling engine stopped abruptly, and the keys flew out the passenger window. They fell with a chink at Eva's feet.

The bearded man shouted in Spanish, there was the sound of a blow and a cry from Maria, and the man was out of the car, loping down the street away from the police cruiser, holding the assault rifle across his chest. He had just reached the far sidewalk when another shot cracked, so loud it made Eva jump, and she heard a voice shouting, "Police! Drop the gun!" She saw a cop with short gray hair standing behind the open door of his cruiser, bracing his revolver in two hands over the doorframe. The windshield was riddled with bullet holes.

The bearded man twisted back and lifted the automatic to his shoulder. He got off a wild burst before the cop fired again. The first shot hit the man in the midsection, and he doubled over. The dark gun clattered onto the concrete. At the second shot, he flew backward, and Eva's view of him was blocked by the car. A glob of something red spattered against a NO PARKING sign.

Eva was cursing her size and trying to get up on tiptoes to see what happened when she felt a hand on her arm. It was Frank. The side of his face was already turning purple and beginning to swell. His right eye was bloodshot and ghastly looking, but Eva could see that his sick expression was not just from getting punched.

"You really don't want to look," he said.

"He's dead?"

"As a doornail. Total, and messy." Frank squeezed his eye shut, wincing as he tried to work his jaw.

Eva started to speak, intending to tease Frank in their old way. "You look like . . ." But before she could get the word *crap* out, her voice broke, the boundaries of her vision started to darken, and a wave of dizziness came over her.

Frank, wobbling, grabbed her, and the two of them sank slowly down to the pavement. They sat there for quite a while, holding each other and saying nothing, as more police cruisers pulled up and, eventually, an ambulance.

62

Death took the form of an oversize doll, like a ventriloquist's dummy. The way he sat there, tilting his head with a happily expectant smile, reminded Norcross of Howdy Doody, except that this puppet was bigger, older and wore a light gray suit.

Norcross's mouth opened to ask, "Have you come for me?" But the only sound that flushed itself from his throat was a croak that rattled his head horribly. The painted face tipped toward him, swirled, and began to dissolve into blackness. *Perhaps*, Norcross thought as his mind dove down, *this grinning thing and I are going on a journey somewhere.* He didn't really care.

A long while later, he was sitting up; the room was drifting in and out of focus. Voices spoke to him and hands were touching him, rousing up the pain again, worse than ever. Howdy Doody had vanished, but the ghost of Faye was nearby, at the edge of his wavering field of vision. Or was it someone else? Claire? Did he catch the edge of tears in her low voice? Years ago, during those last hours in the ICU when his dear, frightened wife was moving beyond his reach, was this the atmosphere of blur and bobbing shadows she had melted into?

They were putting a needle into him, a distant pinch, and he was startled by a new thought so crisp it was almost an object, a bright yellow birch leaf disappearing down a blood-dark stream: Hudson. Was it over? What happened?

After a long while, he found himself in the present again, in a way, but at a great distance from his physical surroundings and in unbelievable pain. Something was pressing down on his head so intensely he was afraid his skull might crack. The burning behind his eyes forced the room into a kind of wobbling, violet-edged focus, and he could perceive that, far across the room, the doll had returned, collapsed backward with its eyes closed. The creature seemed to be sleeping while it waited to start their journey. Beyond the window, the day was dark, and the light on the far side of the room was faint. Everything was quiet. It bugged him that this little guy should sleep like that.

"Hey!" Norcross cried, awakening a roar of pain. With a forward twitch, the dummy's eyes rolled open; its limbs started to float up but then drooped back onto the sofa, lifeless. Norcross lost interest; the pain from his cry was blinding him. Half his world was black, the other half fading.

After another gap, Norcross found himself in conversation with the little man, whispering, "Are you death?" Among the perceptions that had failed him was time; the window was now a glowing butter color. The pain, too, had receded, though he sensed it might lunge at him again at any moment. His cranium had cooled to a steady throb. He must not move; he must speak very, very softly.

"No," the little man replied. "Just a judge like you, Dave. Just a very tired colleague."

"Skip?"

"Got it in one."

"Cripes." The pain squirmed menacingly, and Norcross sipped a tiny breath. "Where?" He steadied himself. "Where the heck am I?"

"Massachusetts General Hospital. Boston. We got you a lift in a helicopter."

"Sorry I missed it. I always wanted a ride in one of those things."

"I know. It's a great pity." Skip's voice seemed far away.

Norcross formed his words slowly, planning them out first with care; the pain was like a pillar of China plates, swaying precariously. Any extra movement, and the tower would crash down and kill him.

"I thought . . ." He waited to let the crockery settle. "I thought I was done for."

"Oh heavens, no," Chief Judge Broadwater said. "They tell us you survived by a good three-sixteenths of an inch."

"That much?"

"Sleep. Just sleep now, Dave."

"What did they do?"

"What did who do, Dave?"

"What did they . . ." He paused to let a rumbling tremor pass. "What did they do with my guy? With Hudson?"

"Oh, there have been some developments. I thought I might lend a hand with the case. Would you mind?"

But Norcross was slipping away, back down into the darkness, and barely heard the question.

When he awoke, he was alone, and his world had taken

another step toward coherency, though the level of rank unpleas-
antness was the worst he'd ever known. A chrome pole next to his
bed held a bottle and a dangling intestine of tube leading into his
arm. A similar strand of entrail, he noticed glumly, was leading
out from between his legs. Wires attached to itchy things on his
chest led off in another direction. The place smelled like petro-
leum jelly and Band-Aids.

Well, here I am, he thought. *God's little science project.*

Some time later, he noticed that the angle of the light had
shifted again. Feeling bolder, he decided to see if he could change
position. An extremely cautious turn of his head—it seemed to
take him fifteen minutes—brought two objects into view on an
aluminum stand next to him.

The first was his Wife of Bath bobblehead, displayed in profile with her expression of manic indomitability. And, just beyond
her, the solemn face of a second bobblehead gazed directly at him,
a sad Quixote-like visage, with a long mustache and the visor of
his battered helmet pushed up onto his forehead: Chaucer's "ver-
ray, parfit gentil knyght."

63

It was only the second time in his twenty-eight years on the bench that an emergency had required Skip Broadwater to take over another judge's case. And it was the first time he'd done it on almost no sleep, with borrowed help. A deputy marshal picked up the chief judge and Judge Norcross's two law clerks at the Boston federal courthouse at six thirty Monday morning. The face of the male clerk, Frank Baldwin, was swollen on one side, and he spoke through gritted teeth. The female clerk, sitting in front, twisted around to pass him a thick packet of paper, the penalty phase instructions.

"Are these in final?" Broadwater asked. "I'm sorry. I've forgotten your name."

"Eva Meyers. Yes, they're ready."

"Lord," Broadwater said flipping the pages. "Did Dave proof them?"

"The judge read them over Friday after court and made a couple changes," Frank said.

"We were coming in on Saturday to give them one last look," Eva added, but her voice cracked, and she shifted around to face forward.

From his discussions with the marshals, Broadwater had some notion of what the two clerks had been through. Frank's trip to the E.R. and their debriefing with the FBI ran late into Saturday; around midnight, one of the agents drove them to Boston to join the vigil at Massachusetts General. They spent what was left of that night sitting in the waiting room, hoping for news. Eva burst into tears when Broadwater told them Sunday morning that their judge was probably going to pull through, and Frank walked down the long hallway with his hands in his pockets, looking up at the ceiling and breathing hard. Sunday afternoon, Broadwater lent them an office in his chambers at the Boston courthouse to finish their review of the instructions and reassure themselves that everything was in good order. Whatever their legal ability, they were certainly hard workers.

"Where did you two sleep last night?" Broadwater asked.

"Found a couple sofas in the courthouse," Frank said. The young man had an unattractive habit of sucking on the end of his mustache.

Eva took off her glasses and ground the heel of her hand into her eye. "He snores."

Broadwater turned his attention to the intricately organized penalty-phase instructions.

"Whew! The words are swimming a bit," he said after a few minutes. He looked out the window, blinking to clear his eyes. "Have any motions come in?"

"The government filed one to postpone the trial for twenty-four hours," Frank said. "It hit the electronic docket at three o'clock this morning."

"The reason?"

"Unforeseen developments."

"I should say."

Two hours later, Chief Judge Broadwater was climbing up onto Judge Norcross's bench. Presiding in this ill-fitting courtroom was like wearing someone else's overalls. The chair was too low—Dave was a good ten inches taller than he was—and the court officer was louder than he preferred. The jury box was on the right instead of the left, and the windows provided a view of trees, which he found distracting. Boston's elegant courtrooms had no natural light.

The shooting of Judge Norcross had been front-page news in all the Sunday papers, so of course the courtroom was packed. The Latina woman representing the government was looking up at him with unusual expectancy. Defense counsel was bending sideways whispering to his client.

Broadwater pushed off into the current.

"As you know, Judge Norcross is in the hospital in Boston. He is out of danger, but in view of his temporary incapacity the Circuit Council has authorized me to take responsibility for the final stage of this trial. I see that the government has filed a motion, with no details, for a one-day continuance. What's up?"

Broadwater checked his notes to remind himself of the names of the attorneys. Lydia Gomez-Larsen, the assistant U.S. attorney, exchanged glances with William Redpath, the defense attorney. They nodded to each other, and Redpath stood. The man was enormous, and his voice seemed to come up out of a subway tunnel.

"Your Honor, may I be heard first? The defense has a motion

to present orally that might render the government's motion to postpone moot."

"I'll hear you."

Redpath moved to the podium, coughed into his hand, and looked up at Broadwater.

"I'm moving to vacate the two guilty verdicts and for a new trial."

"Really! On what ground?"

Gomez-Larsen got up to join Redpath at the podium; the defense attorney shuffled his large frame to one side to make room for her. The unusual move puzzled Broadwater.

"Judge," Gomez-Larsen said, "you should know that the government does not intend to object. It's an agreed motion."

The words prompted a dozen reporters to drop their heads simultaneously and begin scribbling in their notebooks. The non-journalists leaned toward one another and whispered.

"An agreed motion for a new trial?" Broadwater asked. "You can't be serious. How long has this thing been going on for?"

Redpath and Gomez-Larsen looked at each other. The AUSA gave a half smile, and the defense attorney shook his head.

"It's been going on forever," he said.

As it turned out, the facts made Broadwater's ruling easy. According to counsel, that morning the government had provided the defense with a lengthy revised FBI-302, a new statement from the government's star witness, Ernesto "Pepe" Rivera. During an interview on Sunday, the boy had substantially recanted his earlier testimony implicating Hudson in the murders. His new version now identified the shooter on that October morning as Pepe's uncle Carlos, the La Bandera warlord shot dead by a Holyoke police captain on Saturday. Preliminary tests confirmed that a Norinco SKS assault rifle found in Carlos's possession was almost certainly the weapon that killed Delgado and O'Connor. A statement from Pepe's mother, Maria Maldonado, also implicated Carlos.

"So," Broadwater said, "you're telling me you got the wrong guy?"

"No," Gomez-Larsen said. "At least not yet. What we are saying is that, the way things stand, we agree that Mr. Hudson is entitled to a new trial."

"Only on the RICO murder charges? Or on the drug charges, too?"

Redpath looked over at Gomez-Larsen, and she nodded.

"Your Honor," Redpath said, "it's our position that the acquittals on the drug charges mean that any retrial on them would violate the Constitution's double-jeopardy clause."

Gomez-Larsen frowned. "Counsel is correct, unfortunately. Retrial, if it occurs, will be on the murder charges only."

"In light of what I've just heard," Broadwater said, "the joint motion for new trial is allowed."

Two reporters strode quickly out, bumping the door loudly.

"Judge," Redpath said, "there is one other matter, and on this one the prosecution and I disagree. If I might be heard?"

"Yes?" Broadwater said, a little sharply. "What else is there?"

Redpath braced his arms on the podium and looked back at his client. "I'm moving for reconsideration of the pretrial order detaining Mr. Hudson. He's been in custody now for more than nine months. With these new developments, there is no justification to detain him any further. The government can't admit that they have the wrong guy yet, but I'm pretty sure they will, soon. I am requesting that you set conditions that will allow Mr. Hudson to return to his wife and daughter pending the government's decision about a retrial."

As defense counsel was making his pitch, Broadwater became

aware of the intense focus of the eyes of a young African American woman in the front row. She was leaning forward slightly, as though she might stand up and take a leap over the bar. An older woman beside her took the young woman's hand, and a well-dressed man on her other side touched her shoulder. The energy coming off the group was so intense, Broadwater could feel it pushing against his face like heat from a sun lamp.

He looked over at Gomez-Larsen. "Counsel?"

She stood and spoke stiffly, without inflection.

"Your Honor, after consultation with my superiors in Boston, I am obliged to note the government's objection."

She was obviously not one of the better assistant U.S. attorneys, Broadwater thought. She sounded so stilted. Why on earth did Hogan pick her for a trial of this importance?

"Okay," he said, "the government objects. On what ground?"

"It is the position of the government . . ."

Broadwater could feel his displeasure deepening. The position was absurd, and Gomez-Larsen's deadpan tone was irritating.

". . . the position of the government, following consultation, that this is still a capital case. I am therefore obliged to note that the risk of flight remains too great to justify the defendant's release on any conditions."

"Seems to me based on what I've just heard that this has become a highly triable case from the defense viewpoint." Broadwater nodded at the defendant. "Fellow would be out of his mind to head for the hills now."

At this point, Gomez-Larsen's dark eyes locked on Broadwater's for the first time, and her intention became clear.

Oh, Broadwater thought, *shame on me for misjudging her.* He could feel the woman receiving the connection. The two of them understood each other.

"Nevertheless, it remains the government's position …" Gomez-Larsen continued mechanically.

"I see. I understand. Thank you, Counsel," Broadwater broke in. He'd faced this situation before. The transcript would reflect that Gomez-Larsen had followed her boss Hogan's orders, but her tone made sure he knew what she really thought. If he weren't so exhausted, he would have grasped the situation more quickly.

It was time to unscrew the top of the jar, and let Moon Hudson out.

64

The creak of the screen door hung in the silence as Moon and Sandra stepped into their front room. Grace was still on her way from Rochester, being fetched by her uncle Lucas.

Sandra watched as Moon hesitated by the coat stand, his eyes passing over the furniture, the sagging gray sofa, the oval hook rug, the yellow curtains she'd washed and ironed yesterday. Shyly, she saw his glance fall on the foolish vase of purple tulips she'd placed in the middle of their scuffed coffee table that morning. Moon looked at her, closed his eyes, and shook his head. He had not spoken a word the whole way home. The fridge clicked and started to rattle. A car horn tooted, and at the end of their block some child called out, and another answered, laughing.

Suddenly, it all hit Sandra at once. They were, really and truly, back home together, at last. She reached out abruptly and clasped Moon's face in her hands, then put her arms around his waist pulling him to her as hard as she could. She felt his arms encircling her, and a sob burst up through her throat.

"I thought you'd never hold me again," she cried. "I thought I'd never feel this again."

"It's okay now, baby," Moon said, speaking for the first time. "It's okay." He held her tighter.

"I thought you'd never hold me again," she repeated. Her breath was coming hard, she was sobbing uncontrollably now, and her face was wet with tears. Once more, she said, "I thought you'd never hold me again."

"It's okay now," Moon said. "I'm here now."

He began kissing her, first on her forehead and cheeks, pausing to press her against him. Then he started kissing her on the mouth, first softly and then with increasing urgency. After a while, he tugged the back of her blouse out of her slacks and slipped his hands up inside, slowly over her shoulder blades. As Sandra touched Moon's face again, she found she could not stop her fingers from trembling. He was unhooking her bra, sliding his hands over her breasts. Her shuddering stopped, and her breathing got steadier and deeper, but still the tears continued to stream down her cheeks.

"I thought I'd never feel this again," she said, more quietly, tipping her head back to look into his eyes. "I thought my life was over."

Joining hands, they moved to the bedroom. When Moon saw the corner of the dark brown bedspread and green sheet turned back invitingly, he looked at Sandra and raised his eyebrows. "No chocolate on the pillow?"

Sandra wiped her cheeks with both hands and sniffed. "I got your candy right here, babe," she said a little hoarsely.

The mechanics of their lovemaking unfolded easily, as though they had never been away from each other. Sandra was soon lost in the fireworks. When they lay together afterward, though, she found herself a little worried about whether Moon's passion might have had a deliberate quality. Was this something he thought he owed her? Something he needed to get out of the way? She clung to his back and breathed in the warm bread smell. It was still early. Whatever it was, they'd get past it.

As she let herself drift into a doze, she heard Moon say, "I didn't kill Peach . . ."

"Course you didn't, baby," she murmured. "You couldn't. You're . . ."

"Wait up," Moon interrupted. Though he spoke softly, something in his voice lifted Sandra into wakefulness. After a pause he said, in a dead tone, "Time I finally told you what kind of man you got yourself married to."

He turned over and searched her face. After a long while, he rolled around onto his back, drawing her with him so that her head rested on his chest just below his chin. Moon's strong, fluid motion thrilled Sandra, even in his ominous mood.

He spoke to the ceiling. "Like I said, I didn't kill Peach. And I never did hurt that poor boy's mother."

"Course you . . ."

"Listen to me now. I have taken a life, though. Somebody I didn't hardly know, back when I was on the street. You hear what I'm saying? What I did wasn't any different from what Carlos did, except they never did catch me. *Shhh*. Listen now. The exact same thing, babe. That's who I am, no different from Carlos. The jury got me right. That's who you've gone and married."

"Moon . . ."

"Wait now. Let me do this." He paused and breathed. "And the stuff they found. That was all me, too, just like they said.

The shit I sold got us the bed we're lying on, the table we eat off, the TV we watch. All of it. And I can see now I can't never stop. Who do I think I'm fooling? Even some fat white college boy with no more brains than a monkey can see just exactly what I am."

Sandra waited. Moon's left hand stirred on her shoulder, stroking her. His right arm lay palm up at his side, revealing the long scar. His voice was tired.

"Seems like I been in the blood and the dirt so long there's no way now for me to ever get clean again. The street can see it, the street can smell it, and the street can give me a tug anytime, and I'll just come. Just like my poor mama, belting up in the bedroom to get high one more time. All her promises, nothing but dead words. You see what I'm saying?"

"Not really." Sandra could feel something building in her.

"You see what I did to you? And Grace? Where I went and put you? If that crazy old lady didn't shoot the judge, I'd be on my way to Indiana—that's where they take you—waiting for them to bring in their big damn needle and stick me. And if some clerk or somebody hadn't messed up, I'd be looking at twenty years for the stuff I was selling, bottom. And in Ludlow all this time? I had to lie the tongue practically right out of my head, just to stay alive. Fact is, it was a plain miracle put me back here in this bed with you. And there's no telling when the street will call again, and you and Grace be right back there with me, only there won't be any miracle next time."

"Can I talk?"

"Even if I can stay away, babe—and I know I won't—even if I could drop that string back to the old life, and even if Carlos's friends decide to leave me alone, which I doubt they will, I'm maybe twenty dollars an hour, tops. That's it. That's what I am. And every time we're up short, I'll be hearing the old call. Even if I stay clean for you and Grace, we're just bad streets, and beat-up cars, and ugly old school buildings with spray paint and hoodlums and crackheads on the street corners. That's the best I got for you. You'll fly a lot higher without me, a lot higher. And Grace will, too."

"Can I talk now?"

"You don't have to."

Sandra rolled off Moon onto her side and rested her chin on his shoulder so she could speak directly into his ear.

"Just how dumb do you think I am, Moon Hudson? You think I didn't know what I was doing when I married you? You think I couldn't have had ten guys just like Lucas if I wanted? Okay, five. And not bad guys, either. Some of the ones Mom made him bring around were sweeter than you and almost as good looking. But I fell in love with you, Moon, and you are the one I want. And now you want me to go all strategic."

"Strategic."

"Plan it all out on a piece of paper. Say to myself, 'Now Moon is probably not going to be a partner in any Boston law firm. So I better step off this streetcar and give Lucas a call.' Give up the man I love, and go find somebody else who's less trouble and has a bigger gravy boat. That's the strategy. As though love never happens."

She stopped for a moment, then rushed on before Moon could interrupt.

"Have a smart plan and follow it even if I could search through that plan from the top to the bottom and never find even one ounce of real love in the whole thing."

Moon rolled over onto his side toward her, ready to start arguing, but she wouldn't let him.

"I didn't marry you because it was the smart thing to do. How stupid do you think I am?" Sandra shifted up onto her elbow and looked down at Moon. "And don't tell me you're going to go back to your old life, like you're some kind of pitiful robot or something. I don't care if we have to eat Corn Flakes for dinner, sitting on boxes. And if you ever lie to me again, I'll . . ."

The sound of a car door slamming and voices outside jerked both of them upright. Sandra hastily pulled the sheet up over her breasts, and Moon swung out of bed, lithe and silent. He grabbed a fistful of clothes and then peered around the doorframe into the living room with its big window that looked out onto their front walk.

When he got a good look, he leaped back into the room and began hopping on one foot, working furiously to pull on his pants.

"Shit! It's your folks." He hesitated and, for the first time since they left the courthouse, broke into one of his smiles. "Girl, what is so damn funny?"

65

Bill Redpath sat at his desk behind a crenellated bulwark of case files and volumes of appellate reports, smoking a cigarette and reading a draft memorandum in support of a motion to suppress. Perched precariously on the extreme corner of his desk, occupying the only three inches of bare surface, a lime green ashtray was overflowing onto the floor.

Redpath became aware of Judy's presence in the doorway, and he lifted his rumpled face. He was still recovering from *Hudson*, and he didn't feel good.

"What's up?" He blew out a lungful of smoke. His tie was loosened down to the second button on his shirt, and his sleeves were rolled up over his elbows. The Suffolk County Superior Court was expecting this memorandum from him this afternoon; it would have to be walked over and, even then, it was going to be tight.

A long drag on his Lucky allowed Redpath time to absorb the ominousness of his secretary's face and posture. Her arms were folded, and she was looking around the room, always a bad sign.

"What?" he asked, knowing very well what the problem was. While he'd been working in Springfield, Judy had undertaken the massive task of tidying up his office. For nearly a week after his return, he couldn't find a thing. Now the place was finally getting comfortable again.

As if in reply to his not very innocent question, a three-foot stack of papers abruptly toppled off the radiator and shot its contents across the carpet toward Judy. She poked a folder away with her toe and looked at Redpath darkly.

"Oh dear," he said, craning his neck over the mess on his desk to get a better look. "Don't worry about that. I'll take care of it in a minute."

Judy shook her head. "It's okay, Bill. I can pick everything up in a year or two."

"I'll give you this draft in half an hour, tops," he said. "We're kind of up against it, I'm afraid."

"*We're* up against it. That's rich," she snorted. "Anyway, you got a message over lunch from Tom, wishing you happy Father's Day."

"Father's Day? That was—what?—ten days ago?"

"He's been on trial."

A sad look darkened Redpath's face. "Story of our lives."

Judy waved a message slip. "You also got a call from Gomez-Larsen, and it sounds like good news."

"Oh God!" Redpath started to get up, then fell back, wincing. "God, that's fantastic!" He grimaced and massaged his upper arm.

"Any place special you'd like me to stick it?" Judy gestured with the slip, then stopped and leaned forward. "Are you okay?"

"I think so," Redpath said, standing up and plopping down again. "Could you bring it here? I'll call her right now." He pressed his hand over his stomach and groaned. "No more KFC for lunch."

As Judy left the room, she looked over her shoulder. "Good luck finding your phone."

66

Bedtime, and newly promoted Sergeant Alex Torricelli had hopes. He stood in the bathroom, looking into the mirror and trying to imagine what his wife could possibly see in his large, square, hairy body. His frame was decked out in a pair of fresh pajamas, green ones with white stripes. Before he met Janice, he'd been a T-shirt-and-boxers guy. The pajama outfit was still warm from the dryer and smelled of Tide. After a close exam, Alex decided he looked like a bulldozer with a tarp thrown over it.

It had been a long, long, really long, time. He watched his misshapen lips as he brushed his teeth, his mouth bulging and rotating as though it had laundry inside. Janice was the only girl who'd ever told him he was cute, and that only once. Maybe she'd changed her mind. The scarred right ear still gave him a loony kangaroo look. He wouldn't blame her. Things happened; people changed.

He spat. The aroma of the aftershave he'd purchased at CVS was making his eyelashes tingle. *She'll catch the smell and realize I'm fishing,* he thought anxiously. That would ruin everything.

The last time he'd done the deed had been months ago at the Motel 6 in Deerfield with Dina the Vagina, and the memory of this crime all but smothered any sense of possibility. If he was remembering that, she probably was, too. How long would it last? He splashed cold water on his face to dilute the Old Spice and toweled himself off, then tried to dab away the wet blotches on his pajama top. No matter how hard he tried, he always came out the same.

No gurgles from the baby drifted toward him as he made his way down the hall. The coast was clear.

Janice was in bed already, sitting with the daffodil-colored sheets pulled over her knees, reading one of her John Grishams in a pool of light from the nightstand. It was a relief that his wife's mood seemed okay, meaning she wasn't giving off that arctic wind he'd been turning blue in for so long. On the other hand, she didn't have her pink chiffon nightie on, either. It was the regular cotton, with the kittens, the one they'd taken to the hospital when their daughter was born. As Alex hesitated by the bed, Janice patted his side encouragingly, but without looking up from the page. Her brown hair against the yellow pillowcase was more beautiful than anything Alex could remember.

He lowered himself carefully, as though Janice were asleep and he did not want to wake her, pulled up the covers, interlaced his fingers on his stomach, looked at the ceiling, and waited. There was a papery flap as a page turned. Under his hands, Alex felt the thump of his heart, not fast but hard. Janice breathed. Another page turned. The bed creaked as she leaned over and took a sip of water.

"I talked to Cindy today," Janice said, distantly. She was still looking at the book. "She called after lunch."

"How's she doing?"

"Great. She's enjoying having the house to herself."

The mattress creaked again as Janice put her book on the nightstand and turned out the light. A series of bounces rocked Alex for a few seconds, while his wife pulled her pillow down and got settled. They lay in the darkness, not touching.

"Tone's living at his office, sleeping on the couch." Alex spoke to the ceiling.

"Serves him right."

Janice shifted onto her right side, away from him, and one of her feet brushed his ankle. It was her old sleeping position. Maybe tomorrow, or next week. The touch of her foot was so thrilling it made Alex's Adam's apple swell. He had trouble speaking.

"Tony's got medical problems," he said, and cleared his throat.

"Does he now."

A pause. A breeze of early summer swished and blew a puff of sweet-smelling air in through the window. A car crackled by on the street outside, fanning a fluffy gray light over the ceiling. Janice turned toward him. He felt her knee against his upper thigh and her voice close to his ear.

"What kind of problems?" She sounded concerned, or at least interested, despite herself.

"Don't tell him I told you, but he's . . . He's got genital warts, I guess."

"Oh, that's perfect! More than one?" Janice was wriggling happily, and parts of her body were brushing against him. It was close to driving him nuts. Her movements released the scent of her hair; the aroma of her cotton nightgown was flooding up from the sheets and over his face. Outside, the breeze got stronger. It was time to take his chance, but he felt ill with dread that he would screw it up. He wasn't smooth at jokes.

"I think so. I'm not sure." Then he added, in as serious a voice as he could contrive, "But it's bad, Jan. It's real bad, I guess."

Her movements stopped, and her body broke contact. Alex maintained the same position, face to the ceiling, hands on his stomach.

"How bad is it? Is it . . ." She hesitated. "You mean, they think it might be cancer or something?" Janice Torricelli was vengeful, but only up to a point.

"No, but it's bad enough they may have to try and operate."

"Well," Janice said with a sigh, "that sure won't be pleasant for him."

"Yeah. But the real problem is, cause it's gotten so bad, the doctors can't tell anymore."

"Can't tell what?"

"Can't tell which is the genital and which is the wart."

A pause followed and, since it was very dark in the room, Alex was not sure how he'd made out. A gust of muffled laughter finally burst out from the other side of the bed, and out of nowhere he was being playfully thumped over the head and chest with a pillow. Janice's body was partly on top of him and he felt her breasts against his ribs. Then, as he reached up to put his arms around her, he felt a sob shudder through her shoulders, and tears of jubilation springing into his eyes.

67

Despite the hospital's confounded plastic chairs, which always made his low back hurt, Skip Broadwater had come to enjoy his visits with Dave Norcross. The man was almost young enough to be his son, and the chief judge felt a certain pride as he witnessed, over the weeks, Norcross's determination to recover, the return of his sense of humor, and, most of all, his disinclination to complain. One afternoon when he was dropping by, he brought a newspaper with him that included a profile of Mrs. Abercrombie and the details of her indictment. The article mentioned that a judge from Connecticut would be coming up to handle the case; all the Massachusetts federal judges had recused themselves.

"Do you think," Norcross asked, "if she had been a better shot, the attorney general's death committee would have approved a capital prosecution for her?"

"Oh, Dave, please!" Broadwater peered over his half glasses in mock astonishment. "How can you say such a thing? A nice old Caucasian lady like that?"

"I can see why she did it," Norcross said. He squirmed uncomfortably. "But I sure wish she hadn't."

Broadwater shifted and crossed his legs. Given his colleague's condition, he couldn't bring himself to whine about the chair, so he directed his impatience at the legal system.

"Who had the inhuman idea that we could rationally select people for execution anyway? It's lunacy." Broadwater's voice turned peevish. "Then they say to us trial judges, 'Here, you manage it!'" He shook his head disgustedly and shuffled the pages of the newspaper. "And did you notice this article about the O'Connor boy?"

"Which one?"

"Edward, the middle kid. Says here he's still positive Moon Hudson killed his mom, and he always will be." Broadwater eyed the photograph of the boy and quoted. " 'Justice in America a joke, says victim's son.'"

"Can't please everybody."

A nurse with short blonde hair hurried in to adjust her patient's IV and check his vitals. She smiled briefly, but said nothing before disappearing. After she was gone, Norcross lifted his head slightly.

"Buzz me up a little, will you?"

Broadwater walked over and pushed the button to raise the top of the bed six inches. Despite his improvement, Norcross was, after three trips to the operating theater, still semi-mummified in bandages and warned to keep his movements to a minimum.

"After my last procedure, when I was still kind of a mess," Norcross said after he resettled, "Claire got a little worked up. Said she wanted to see Mrs. Abercrombie boiled in oil, or worse. She got pretty upset. I was afraid the nurse was going to have to ask her to leave."

"Well, that's it, isn't it? Human beings aren't designed to handle this sort of situation as though it's some form of arithmetic. It's like asking a chimpanzee to make gingerbread. People don't work that way."

"Same as love, I guess," Norcross said, drifting a bit and closing his one unbandaged eye. "Doesn't follow instructions very well."

"Drawing tidy boundaries around the irrational," Broadwater muttered. "Might as well try putting pantyhose on a gust of wind."

Claire entered the room with a leather satchel on one shoulder and let out a happy cry at seeing Broadwater. After a quick hug, she walked over and gave Norcross a kiss. "Hey, tiger."

At this point, the blonde nurse rejoined them, carrying a food tray. Claire pulled up a chair next to Broadwater while the young woman organized her patient for his meal.

"I wanted to ask you a question," Claire said, touching Broadwater's arm. "I have a friend, or at least an acquaintance, at UMass. One of his students is threatening to sue him for sexual harassment."

"Oh God, not one of those horrors."

"He's saying that what he did couldn't be harassment, since the two of them did not actually, um . . ." To Broadwater's amusement, Claire hesitated. " 'Hook up,' as my students say, until after he'd submitted her final grade. Does that make sense?"

"Not to me," Broadwater said, shifting uncomfortably in his chair. "But I doubt I'll be on the jury. There might be some group of twelve men and women that would swallow that argument, though. You never know. Who are the parties?"

"Forty-seven-year-old legal studies professor and a blonde undergrad with an inconsistent lisp."

"Ouch," Broadwater said. "I'd get out my checkbook."

"Salt and pepper," Norcross said, chewing. He wiggled his eyebrows at Claire.

As the nurse departed, Broadwater tried to work through what this exchange might mean. His friend and his lady had their own little jokes. Then he noticed the time and jumped up. "I'd better run, or I'll be late for the memorial."

"Oh dear. Who died?" Claire asked.

Norcross swallowed and shook his head. "One of the lawyers who tried the *Hudson* case, Bill Redpath. It was very sudden, very sad."

"A phenomenal trial lawyer, and a good man," Broadwater said. "His secretary found him sitting at his desk with a draft motion to suppress and a cigarette still burning in the ashtray. He'd just gotten the news about the *Hudson* dismissal. Half of Boston will be at the church."

The three of them fell into a moment of silence for William P. Redpath Jr., defense attorney. While they paused, a car moved by outside the window, playing hip-hop. The insistent rhythm rose, hit a crescendo, and faded into an addictive refrain that stuck in the mind, like the arc of a particularly effective cross-examination.

As Broadwater said his good-byes, Claire had to resist the temptation to kiss the man on the top of his shiny bald head. Time and again, his kindness had kept them afloat. After he left, Claire pulled her chair closer to David's bed. She sighed and took his hand.

"I have to do this right away or I won't manage it," she said. "We've been talking to your doctors, and there's some lousy news. I'd like to get through this without another one of my famous meltdowns." She took a deep breath, gripped David's hand, and let it all out at once. "You've lost most of the vision in your left eye for good. There's nothing more the surgeons can do. They're at an end point."

"Huh."

"The bullet was small, .22 caliber, and it hit at an angle, so it mostly just sort of dug a furrow in your skull. In a few days, they'll have the bandages off. But your eye . . ." She steadied herself. "With the powder flash. There was too much damage."

"Is it going to keep giving me . . ." David tugged at the sheet. "Will it keep hurting like this?"

"No. They don't think so. You'll just . . . in that one eye . . ."

"I'll be sporting a patch, like Jack Sparrow."

"If you like." Claire lifted his hand and kissed it. "I'm sorry, but I'm just glad the eye is the worst. It's been so scary."

The machine beside David's bed whirred. A dolly rumbled down the hallway outside the room. Claire heard a mingling of voices calling back and forth unintelligibly.

"Guess I won't be making the bigs now," David said finally.

"Probably not. Be hard to catch up with the high heater."

They sat together without speaking. Claire looked around and noticed that more flowers had arrived since her last visit. The room was beginning to smell like a florist's shop.

"May I touch your nose?" she asked.

David let go of Claire's hand and interlaced his fingers on his stomach. He breathed deeply, getting ready.

"All right," he said, "go ahead, but control yourself."

Claire ran the tip of her finger down the bridge of David's nose and drew a slow circle around his mouth.

"A patch," she murmured, "might give you just that touch of continental panache that is the hallmark of tall, awkward guys from Wisconsin." She sat back. "The girls of Green Bay will go apeshit."

In the long silence that followed, Claire could not tell whether David was taking the time to absorb the bad news or drifting off to sleep again. His unbandaged eye remained closed for a long minute. Finally, he spoke without opening it, and Claire realized he had been awake the whole time.

"You know Lady Justice?"

"The long-waisted babe with the great tomatoes and the scales?"

"That's the one." The edges of his mouth turned down as something struck him. "I wonder whether I'd have gone into law if Justice had been a short fat guy with hair on his shoulders."

"I bet not."

David turned his head slowly and rolled his eye toward Claire, crinkling it into a smile. "Those were the very first words you spoke to me. Remember?" He cleared his throat. "Anyway, maybe the blindfold hides the fact that Lady Justice has only got one good eye. She has to do her best with just the one." He sighed drowsily. "Considering everything, she does okay." There was another pause, and then he added, softly, as he faded, "The point is to try . . . as hard as you can. Come here for a sec."

Claire stood and leaned over him, putting her face close.

"I love you," David said. "I can see that plenty clearly." His face relaxed; sleep was overtaking him.

"That's nice," Claire said and kissed him lightly on the lips. "Tell me again some time when you're not on so much Demerol. Rest now. I have papers to grade."

She moved her chair back to the far wall so as not to disturb David, settled herself, and pulled a sheaf of papers out of her bag. The grading occupied her for about thirty seconds. Then, she put the papers on the floor, pulled out a Kleenex, and dabbed her eyes.

In a few minutes, David was asleep, breathing regularly,

and Claire leaned back in the chair, letting her eyes drift over the vases of flowers from David's various friends, judicial colleagues, and old law partners. The summer sunlight, filtered by the mini-blinds, made the room seem to glow, and the current of air-conditioning caused a few curling flower petals to flutter. One stray band of gold made its way across the wall and touched a chrome table in the far corner, where the Knight and the Wife of Bath sat side by side, and a cluster of red, white, and blue balloons tied to one of the metal legs bounced gently against the ceiling.

68

On March 18, 1984, Governor Michael S. Dukakis issued a proclamation exonerating Dominic Daley and James Halligan. Their
prosecution, the document read, "was infected by such religious and
ethnic prejudice" that they had been denied a fair trial.

Photograph by George Peet

ACKNOWLEDGMENTS

I want to thank my earliest readers and supporters, Ted and Esther Scott; Julie Perkins; Nancy Winkelman; Carolyn Mitchell; Jeni and Scott Kaplan; Sheila Graham-Smith; Dr. Peter F. Shaw; and Dr. Randall H. Paulsen. My gratitude extends particularly to my author friends, whose guidance has been so important and reassuring: the poet Ellen Bass, Tracy Kidder, Richard Todd, Jonathan Harr, Elinor Lipman, Anita Shreve, Joe McGinniss, Joseph Kanon, John Katzenbach, Madeleine Blais, and Suzanne Strempek Shea. Others whose advice was particularly helpful include the literary agent William Reiss, David Starr of Springfield's *Republican* newspaper, and David's friend Loring Mandel. Boston's Grub Street provided invaluable help through its annual Muse & the Marketplace seminars.

I also thank judicial colleagues who have read the draft,

including my former boss and now dear friend, US District Judge Joseph L. Tauro, as well as Chief Judge Patti B. Saris, Judge Nathaniel M. Gorton, Judge Rya W. Zobel, Judge Denise Jefferson Casper, and Judge William G. Young. My thanks also go to my former colleague Judge Nancy Gertner, currently a professor at Harvard Law School.

Several of my law clerks and coworkers at the US District Court in Springfield read drafts of the book—during their time, I must emphasize, *outside* working hours. These include Luke Ryan; Emma Quinn-Judge; Ruth Anne French-Hodson; Beth Cohen (now of Western New England University School of Law); my judicial assistant of nearly thirty years, Elizabeth Collins; and the court's supervising pretrial services officer, Irma Garcia-Zingarelli. Stephanie Barry of the *Republican* newspaper helped by reading the draft in light of her unique knowledge of the Springfield community. My wonderful friend Bill Redpath, who does not smoke and is not an attorney (though he'd be outstanding if he were), kindly lent me his name.

The early support of Massachusetts Continuing Legal Education was crucial in getting the book into the light of day. I am especially grateful to Jack Reilly, Maryanne G. Jensen, Annette Turcotte, and Richard Millstein, and particularly to Ben Monopoli for his sharp-eyed editing and helpful suggestions.

All the people at my publisher, Open Road Integrated Media, have been smart, warm, fun, and full of good ideas. The opportunity to work with someone like Jane Friedman, with her intelligence, vision, and experience, has been awesome in every sense. I also offer my thanks to Tina Pohlman, Nina Lassam, and Luke Parker Bowles, consummate professionals who have steered the book through its production and promotion. I am most especially thankful to Maggie Crawford, my editor, whose tactful, persistent, and good-humored support has done so much to improve the manuscript and make her dear to me.

My literary agent, Robin Straus, deserves her own paragraph, and more. She has been, at every step, a supremely competent advocate, a knowledgeable adviser, and the best of friends. I am so grateful to her.

My parents, Ward and Yvonne Ponsor, and my sister, Valerie Pritchard, were kind enough to trudge through the manuscript when it was barely embryonic. Their loving support has kept me working. My gratitude to them, for everything, is beyond words.

The tragic story of Dominic Daley and James Halligan has been told and retold over the years. My best resource about the incident has been the Honorable W. Michael Ryan, retired first justice of the Northampton Division of the District Court Department of the Commonwealth of Massachusetts. Judge Ryan not only provided detailed comments on the draft, but he put his extensive collection of materials on the events of 1805–06 into my hands. This is not intended to be a scholarly work, so I will not canvass all the references I have dipped into. Three articles were most helpful: Massachusetts Superior Court Associate Justice Robert Sullivan's "The Murder Trial of Halligan and Daley—Northampton, Massachusetts 1806" in the *Massachusetts Law Quarterly* (1964) at 211–224; James M. Camposeo's "Anti-Catholic Prejudice in Early New England: The Daley-Halligan Murder Trial" in the *Historical Journal of Western Massachusetts*, Vol. VI, No. 2 (Spring 1978) at 5–17; and James C. Rehnquist's "The Murder Trial of James Halligan and Dominic Daley" in *Legal Chowder: Lawyering and Judging in Massachusetts*, edited by Hon. Rudolph Kass (retired) (Massachusetts Continuing Legal Education, Inc., Boston, 2002), at 232–235. Particularly helpful was a detailed document, lent to me by Judge Ryan, "Report of the Trial of Dominic Daley and James Halligan," compiled anonymously by "a Member of the Bar" and published by S. & E. Butler in Northampton. I also enjoyed and found helpful Michael C. White's fictional treatment of the story in *The Garden of Martyrs* (St. Martin's Press, New York, 2005).

Central to my efforts was the late Yale Law School professor Charles L. Black Jr.'s book *Capital Punishment: The Inevitability of Caprice and Mistake* (W. W. Norton & Company, New York, 1974). This small volume still offers the most pointed analysis of capital punishment I know of. My novel may be viewed, in part, as an attempt at a fictional version of his excellent book.

Last and most important is my beloved wife, Nancy. We live together; mornings, we write together. Then, we have lunch together, and we talk about our writing together. Her eyes, her voice, and her smile are the most beautiful things I have ever known. Without her, there would, of course, be no book, but that would be small beans, since without her, there would be nothing at all. With her, there is everything.

ABOUT THE AUTHOR

Michael Ponsor graduated from Harvard, received a Rhodes Scholarship, and studied for two years at Pembroke College, Oxford. After taking his law degree from Yale and clerking in federal court in Boston, he began his legal career, specializing in criminal defense. He moved to Amherst, Massachusetts, in 1978, where he practiced as a trial attorney in his own firm until his appointment in 1984 as a US magistrate judge in Springfield, Massachusetts. In 1994, President Bill Clinton appointed him a life-tenured US district judge. From 2000 to 2001, he presided over a five-month death penalty trial, the first in Massachusetts in over fifty years. Judge Ponsor continues to serve as a senior US district judge in the United States District Court for the District of Massachusetts, Western Division, with responsibility for federal criminal and civil cases in the four counties of western Massachusetts. *The Hanging Judge* is his first novel.

OPEN ROAD
INTEGRATED MEDIA

Open Road Integrated Media is a digital publisher and multimedia content company. Open Road creates connections between authors and their audiences by marketing its ebooks through a new proprietary online platform, which uses premium video content and social media.